Please feel free
filters these em:

Molly Stegall – molly_stegall@awesomeauthors.org

Sign up for my blog for updates and freebies!
molly-stegall.awesomeauthors.org

Copyright © 2018 by Molly Stegall
All Rights reserved under International and Pan-American Copyright Conventions. By payment of required fees you have been granted the non-exclusive, non-transferable right to access and read the text of this book. No part of this text may be reproduced, transmitted, downloaded, decompiled, reverse-engineered or stored in or introduced into any information storage and retrieval system, in any form or by any means, whether electronic or mechanical, now known, hereinafter invented, without express written permission of BLVNP Inc. For more information contact BLVNP Inc.The publisher does not have any control over and does not assume any responsibility for author or third-party websites or their content. This book is a work of fiction. The characters, incidents and dialogue are drawn from the author's imagination and are not to be construed as real.While reference might be made to actual historical events or existing locations, the names, characters, places and incidents are either products of the author's imagination or are used fictitiously, and any resemblance to actual persons living or dead, business establishments, events or locales is entirely coincidental.

About the Publisher
BLVNP Incorporated, A Nevada Corporation, 340 S. Lemon #6200, Walnut CA 91789, info@blvnp.com / legal@blvnp.com

DISCLAIMER
This book is a work of FICTION. It is fiction and not to be confused with reality. Neither the author nor the publisher or its associates assume any responsibility for any loss, injury, death or legal consequences resulting from acting on the contents in this book.The author's opinions are not to be construed as the opinions of the publisher.The material in this book is for entertainment purposes ONLY. Enjoy.

Praise for The Vampire's Pet

Honestly, this book is great. The plot is enticing, drew me in quickly. Not your average intriguing Vampire love story. This is a refresher on all demonic romances with different twists then what is expected. It's sweet, daring, and has a great bite of action.
-Kaylee M., *Goodreads*

The book hooked my interest from the very start due its different setting. I love the story line, its different and fresh.
-P.Eva, *Goodreads*

I liked this book since the very beginning! It has love, trust, family issues… what can you want more?!
-Cristina Sosu, *Goodreads*

This book is a do-not-miss story of love, family, loss, control and coping. Stegall is a master at creating memorable characters and at interesting us to keep turning the pages.
-Ashley DeCourteney

The fantasy genre books were always my favourite but this tops it. The characters were full of life and amazing. This book is a masterpiece and I look forward to her new books and the adventure coming with it.
-Hew Yar Qin

The Vampire's Pet

By: Molly Stegall

ISBN: 978-1-68030-965-2
© **Molly Stegall 2018**

Table of Contents

Chapter 1 1
Chapter 2 9
Chapter 3 19
Chapter 4 29
Chapter 5 35
Chapter 6 40
Chapter 7 46
Chapter 8 52
Chapter 9 58
Chapter 10 63
Chapter 11 68
Chapter 12 74
Chapter 13 79
Chapter 14 84
Chapter 15 88
Chapter 16 95
Chapter 17 103
Chapter 18 109
Chapter 19 113
Chapter 20 118
Chapter 21 124
Chapter 22 130
Chapter 23 135
Chapter 24 140
Chapter 25 146
Chapter 26 155

Chapter 27 162
Chapter 28 169
Chapter 29 176
Chapter 30 184
Chapter 31 190
Chapter 32 196
Chapter 33 205
Chapter 34 217
Chapter 35 224
Chapter 36 231
Chapter 37 236
Chapter 38 242
Chapter 39 248
Chapter 40 254
Chapter 41 261
Chapter 42 266
Chapter 43 272
Chapter 44 283
Chapter 45 290
Chapter 46 296
Chapter 47 303
Chapter 48 308
Chapter 49 318
Chapter 50 327
Chapter 51 335
Chapter 52 343
Chapter 53 348
Chapter 54 352

Chapter 55...360
Chapter 56...367
Chapter 57...376
Chapter 58...386
Chapter 59...395
Chapter 60...404
Chapter 61...410
Chapter 62...419

This is dedicated to my best friend, Bri, who taught me how to use Facebook.

FREE DOWNLOAD

Get these freebies and MORE when you sign up for the author's mailing list!

molly-stegall.awesomeauthors.org

Chapter 1

The bell that hung above the door of the Pet Shop rang as it opened, shaking back and forth before it closed. A tall man wearing a suit entered. He immediately smelled the grunginess of the shop and cringed his nose at the unpleasant smell. The Shopkeeper lifted his head from his paperwork, as he lowered the pen to the desk and turned to look at who had entered. His mouth stretched into a thin smile. He ran his fingers through his thinning, curly red hair.

"Ah, Lord Henry. What a pleasant surprise," he said nicely, showing that he had done this several times. He went over to shake his hand. A few of the pets rolled their eyes in disgust. The vampire was a lord because he, or one of his relatives, was one of the vampires that started the uprising. This meant that they took millions of dollars from people.

"I'm looking for a new pet," Henry said as he looked around the room, not really paying attention to what the Shopkeeper was saying. The color of the shop was a faded yellow from the dim lights. A window wasn't in sight. In the middle, where the vampires would walk, was a concrete walkway, while the floor of the cages was dirt. The pets knew better than to throw filth on the concrete.

Many eyes peered through the cage bars, staring at Henry. Some averted their eyes quickly. Others stared right at Henry, almost challenging him.

"Of course. Do you want a boy or a girl?" The Shopkeeper asked as he started to walk.

"I was thinking of a girl," Henry said as he scanned a few cages. One had a girl with blonde hair and blue eyes. She was sitting against the wall, staring at the opposite direction, and she seemed very young. Another had a girl with light brown hair and hazel eyes. She was drawing on the dirt, trying to pass the time. It looked like a pyramid surrounded by other shapes. The cages were so small that a child's head would barely touch the top of it. Each had three cement brick walls and had a metal bar door.

"Do you have anything in mind?" the Shopkeeper asked as he continued to walk, not bothering to look in the cages.

"No," Henry said as he looked in a few more cages. The ages that he saw varied; some as young as six, others as old as fifty. Henry stopped suddenly as something caught his eye. "What about this one?" he asked as he looked in a cage.

The Shopkeeper stopped and knew which human was in there. "Oh, her name is Rose," he said in disgust. His eyes burned into the cage, showing how much he despised her.

"Rose," Henry said to himself, almost in a whisper. He stared at the sleeping girl on the dirty floor, but he couldn't see her face. She was sleeping away from the door of the cage. Her body was slowly falling and rising with each breath. She was curled up in a small ball, as if it would protect her. Her shirt, though big, showed off her ribs as it pressed against her.

"If you wish my Lord, I could wake her?" the Shopkeeper asked as he peered into the cage.

"Yes, please," Henry said as he moved to the left a little, giving the Shopkeeper more room. He kept his eyes on Rose.

"As you wish," he said as he laid his hands on a chain that was connected to the door. It was also attached to the metal collar that Rose had around her neck. The chain was there to remind the pets that they were nothing but pets.

He yanked the chain, and it tugged Rose along from the force that she had received. She rolled over on her side coughing and gasping for air. Her hands grasped the collar trying to relieve the pressure. She took deep, unsteady breaths.

"This-" the Shopkeeper pulled the chain again, this time even harder. Rose slid to the ground and into the cage bars. She put up her arms to block her face from the hard metal which hurt her as her body collided with it. She winced in pain. A cloud of dirt rose around her before it settled on her skin and clothes. "-is Rose," the Shopkeeper finished as he moved to the side so Henry could get a better look. He started to kick some of the dirt that had come onto the concrete back into her cage.

She looked down to avoid eye contact with him, but Henry put his finger under her chin and tilted her head up. Her lip quivered as he touched her. His hand, however, wasn't hard and harsh but smooth and gentle. She had matted brown hair that hadn't been brushed, by an actual brush, in years. She had emerald green eyes that seemed to be the only color in the pet shop. Her clothes were ripped, old, and covered in dirt, showing that she hadn't been given new clothes in a while. She was one of the smaller girls, height wise. They were about all the same skinniness. She slowly lifted her eyes to meet his.

He had brown hair as well that was cut shorter on the sides and longer in the middle; it was styled upwards. It didn't look like it had taken hours, but more like it was natural. He had red eyes, but his eyes were different. They weren't a dark, violent red like her old master, but a soft, kind red that she had never seen before on a vampire. They seemed to sparkle in the dull light. He was wearing a black suit with a red tie and a black belt. He was an entire foot taller than Rose, making him more intimidating.

"There are bruises on her. What from?" Henry asked as he tilted her head to the side. He looked at her arms too, examining her. A variety of blues and purples rested on top of her once tan skin.

"Ah, those are from her old master," he said with a hint of satisfaction in his voice that was only noticeable to him and Rose.

"You mean she was owned before?" Henry asked as he raised an eyebrow, glancing back at the Shopkeeper.

"Yes sir, she actually got back about two weeks ago," the Shopkeeper said, dropping the hint of satisfaction, scared that Henry could sense it.

"Why?" Henry asked as he turned his head back to Rose. She had dropped her head downwards, avoiding eye contact again.

"Her master didn't say. He just didn't want her anymore," the Shopkeeper said, going back to his professional voice.

"How old is she?" Henry asked. The pet shop lighting, dirt, and bruises had made Rose's age hard to tell.

"Eighteen," the Shopkeeper responded. Henry's eyebrows rose.

"Has she been drunk from yet?" Henry asked looking at her neck, trying to find any bite marks.

"No sir," he said, still a little surprised that she hadn't been drunken from, especially because of her blood type.

"What is her blood type?" Henry asked. Not that he cared. It was just the questions everyone asked. It almost came like second nature.

"AB Negative," Henry's eyebrows rose. AB Negative blood was a very rare blood type.

Henry sat there for a few seconds thinking. He blankly stared at Rose. Rose stared at the ground, her bottom lip started to quiver again. *Please don't pick me. I can't handle another master. Please don't pick me.* Rose pleaded to herself. Tears formed in the corners of her eyes.

"Does she have any family?" Henry asked.

"Ah, no sir," the Shopkeeper replied, his lips forming a straight line.

"I think I'll take her," Henry said as he stood up and fixed his suit and tie.

"Are you sure? She is very shy," he said trying to change his mind.

"Yes, I am sure," Henry said. His tone indicated that he was getting a little annoyed. He firmly stared at the Shopkeeper, showing that he doesn't want to be questioned.

The Shopkeeper sensed it. "Ok," he said as he opened the squeaking rusty door to the cage. He unchained Rose and attached a leash to her collar. Rose got out of her cage and stood up too fast. She got dizzy and stumbled, nearly falling toward Henry. The Shopkeeper yanked her toward him. "Behave," he said through gritted teeth. He pushed her away from him. She nearly ran into Henry again. "Will you please follow me, sir," the Shopkeeper said as he started to walk toward the back room with Rose behind him and Henry at her side.

As they were walking, they heard a torturous scream behind them. They all turned around. Henry's and the Shopkeeper's faces showed no emotion as the scene unfolded. A girl was being dragged by a fairly big man across the floor by her hair. Her hands were wrapped around the man's arm, using all her strength to release the pressure. "I'm sorry, I'm sorry. I didn't mean it!" She begged as she struggled. The man had no trouble dragging her across the smooth concrete.

"You need to learn not to talk back!" The man yelled as he harshly stomped his foot down on the girl's stomach. She started to gasp for air but did not fight back. He took the opportunity to drag her with more ease and brought her into the disciplining room. A lock sounded after he shut the door. The bloodcurdling screams echoed again from within the door.

Henry's and the Shopkeeper's face remained the same. Henry glanced down at Rose.

Her face was filled with sorrow and pain; her eyes were shut tightly. The Shopkeeper leaned down into Rose's ear. "It only happened to you once." he beamed. She turned her head away, not wanting to be around him.

"Can we please continue," Henry said in more of a command than a question. He sounded annoyed. The Shopkeeper snapped out of his daze. He quickly nodded. He turned around and tugged the leash on Rose's collar. She was too caught up thinking about the disciplining room, and she nearly stumbled as the Shopkeeper pulled harder on it. They all walked.

They entered the back room. "Would you like any other accessories?" The Shopkeeper motioned his hands at a wall that had leashes, collars, and muzzles. There were other nicknacks too.

Henry put his finger under her chin, tilting her head up. "These won't be necessary, correct?" She quickly shook her head. He nodded and went to the wall, picking out a lapis lazuli colored collar that had gold swirls on it making the blue pop. "Just these," Henry said as he handed them to the Shopkeeper.

"Ok, I will need you to sign these papers, and I'll exchange the collars and leashes," the Shopkeeper said while Henry nodded his head. Henry walked to a table to sign the papers as the Shopkeeper made his way to Rose.

He unlocked the collar to reveal raw skin on her neck where the collar had been. Scratches were on top of it, the cold air stung her.

"If you come back here, I will kill you; just like I did with your family," he whispered into her ear, as he fastened the collar as tight as it would go before he put the leash on the collar. He wiggled the part of the leash that connected to the collar, making sure it was hooked on. "Here you go, my Lord," he handed Henry the leash after he had finished signing the paperwork. "That will be 60,050 dollars, my Lord," The price of Rose and the collar didn't even seem to faze him. He pulled out a check from his checkbook. He signed and gave it to the Shopkeeper.

"Thank you," Henry said as he nodded his head a little. He grabbed the leash and started to walk out of the building with Rose behind him.

Rose drudgingly walked behind her new master knowing that she was going to have to start a new life.

Chapter 2

They walked out of the Pet Shop, the sunlight blinding Rose. It was her first time in two weeks that she had seen actual light. She held up her hands, blocking the sun from her eyes. She breathed in deeply, not only because the collar was tight on her throat, but also because she had been smelling in the grunginess of the Pet Shop. She inhaled the clean, fresh air. She quickly glanced around, taking in the outside. It had been awhile since she had been in an open air or stepped foot outside of her cage.

Henry put his sunglasses on to block his eyes from the sun. He moved his suit closer to his body, wrapping the left side of the suit under the right side, protecting as much as he could. He turned his head away from the sun. The sun didn't seem to faze him as badly as other vampires. The older the vampire, the less the sun affects them because their skin gets used to it.

Rose's collar was making it hard for her to breathe; with each passing breath, she felt the collar tightening around her neck, like a snake choking its prey.

Henry walked toward a black limo. The driver was there waiting, his hands clasped together and his head bowed. Once he saw Henry, he opened the door. Henry motioned with his hand for Rose to go in first. She went in and scooted to the far side of the car as Henry sat down and closed the door behind him. They were on opposite ends of the car; she was on the far left while he was on the far right. There were long seats on either side of the car, facing each other. A blue light illuminated the cup holders, the seats were spotless as well as the floor. Showing just how rich he was, if the suit didn't prove that.

Henry had let go of the leash, and the handle had fallen to the floor of the car. Rose dared not touch the leash, even if it was to move it on the seat. If she were to touch it, she feared she would be beaten.

The driver quickly got in the car and started the engine. "Take me home," Henry said to the driver in a dull yet demanding voice. The driver nodded, understanding his orders. He fixed his eyes on the road and started to drive. Henry pressed a button that closed the black tinted window that allowed the driver to see and hear them. The window slid up and locked once it was in place.

Henry removed his sunglasses, folded its hinges, and tucked them into his pocket. He looked at Rose and noticed that the collar around her neck was tight. A surface of her neck was turning red. He listened to her hard breathing that she was trying to sustain. She was slowly breathing in and out through her nose.

He reached for her collar; she flinched and closed her eyes, expecting him to hit her. Her hands started to tremble at the thought of being beat. "It's ok, I'm not going to hurt you," his voice was calm and soothing. He slowly reached his hands toward the collar. She opened her eyes as he loosened the strap, allowing her to breathe properly.

He pulled his hands away and sat back while looking at her. Rose slowly lifted her eyes to meet his. She looked at him questionably. *Why didn't he hit me?* She thought as she glanced back down, not wanting to stare at him for too long.

"I didn't hit you because you didn't do anything wrong. And even if you did, I still wouldn't hit you," he said simply, as if reading minds was normal.

Did he just- she lifted her eyes to him again, shocked.

"Yes, I did. The power I have is to be able to read minds, look at memories, and use telepathy," Henry said as he looked at her, she looked back down as they made eye contact.

Silence fell between the two, a strange almost awkward silence.

"Do you even speak?" He asked as he looked at her, realizing that she hadn't said anything at all.

Yes, she thought as she glanced at him again, this time she didn't avert her eyes when they made eye contact.

"Then why don't you?" He asked.

"Because up until now you haven't given me permission to," her voice was timid, and a little shaky.

"Is that a rule that your old master had?" Henry asked.

"And the Shopkeeper," she added and looked down, avoiding eye contact again. She twiddled her fingers together, rubbing her thumb over a blue bruise on her hand.

"Mmhh," he said staring off into space, thinking. Silence fell over them again. He glanced at Rose and saw that she had started to look out the window. He did the same.

***

The car finally arrived at the house. They drove over a gravel driveway that went straight, then formed a circle at the end. It was circling a fountain. Once the car stopped, the driver got out and opened Henry's door. Henry stepped out and motioned his hand for Rose to follow. Rose slid out of the car and stood to the side as the driver closed the door. Henry grabbed her leash.

"Is there anything else you need, sir?" The driver asked.

"No, you can go home," Henry said. The driver nodded his head.

The driver got back in and drove off. Rose looked up, her eyes immediately widened in awe at the house; it was beautiful. This even exceeded her last master's house. She blinked a few times, thinking that this must be a dream.

It was a huge mansion that had dark grey walls and dark brown beams; other things like windows were outlined in dark brown. Huge windows were parallel to each other, with two on the top and two on the bottom. The windows and windowpanes were polished, the sun was reflecting off of them, and the light contrasted well with the darker shades of the house. The house was two stories but looked as tall as three. A garage with dark brown doors was on the very left of the house. Behind it was a glass dome. The roof was dark grey too. Part of the roof, where the doorway was, came out providing shade and protection from the weather.

Rose snapped out of her daze as Henry started to walk toward the front doors. They sauntered up to the main doors that were a dark brown oak. He laid his hand on the iron handle and opened them to reveal the interior. It was even prettier than the exterior of the house. Where the outside was more on the dark, mysterious side, the inside was more on the light, relaxing, kind side.

The floors and stairs were a light marble. Black couches, a chair, a small cocktail table, as well as a giant flat screen TV were to the left, creating a spacious living room. To the right was a half curved marble staircase. The railing was black, and the balusters went straight down into the stairs. The stairs led up to the six bedrooms. The floor that the bedrooms were on was more of a giant loft. It was a hallway with a railing on the outside; from there you could see the main floor. Past the large living room was the kitchen. It was quite open, except for a wall that blocked the left side, dividing it from a hallway. The hallway stretched down a long corridor. Straight ahead, in between the kitchen and the stairwell, was a dark brown door.

Rose stared in awe at the house. She tried to memorize every detail, just in case her new master sends her back to the Pet Shop. At least, she would have the beautiful image in her head. He started to walk upstairs; the leash was tugged very slightly from her collar, snapping Rose out of her wonder. Rose walked a few feet behind him, her head slightly bowed, hoping that she wasn't in trouble for not paying attention.

"So, this is your room," Henry said as he opened the dark brown door. He walked in a few feet with Rose following behind him. Rose froze from her spot and widened her eyes at the sight – she hadn't expected a beautiful room with windows, furniture, and a bed.

The room was painted light grey. There was a queen size bed against the wall next to the bathroom. The sheets were dark blue with white swirls mixed on it. The frame of the bed was painted dark brown, as well as the wardrobe, nightstand, and dresser. She had only seen these things in her old master's house. The thought that it was all hers was overwhelming.

Rose's eyes teared up from happiness. She had never had a room of her own. She had always had to sleep on the floor of her master's room and was consistently kicked awake in the mornings, creating bruises on her stomach and ribs. She had never known the comfort of a bed; only a hard floor. The only thing she could call hers was her collar and leash, even then she had no control over that.

"Th-this is all mine?" She asked still in disbelief, forgetting that she hadn't been given permission to speak. He didn't seem to mind. He didn't even notice.

"Yes. If there's something you don't like, tell me, and I'll change it, ok?" Henry asked her. She nodded her head. Henry started to walk around, showing Rose where everything was. After the small tour, they stepped out and proceeded to the room next to hers. "This is my room," Henry said as he knocked on the door with his knuckle. "Then all these other rooms are guest bedrooms." She looked at all the dark brown doors down the hallway.

They walked down the stairs and entered the kitchen. "This is the kitchen," Henry said. She looked at the offset white colored counters. The island was in between the table and the counter which went from the back of the room. In the back of the counter was the refrigerator while on the right side was a stove, an oven, and a grill.

They walked out of the kitchen and went down the hallway next to it. "This is the indoor garden," Henry said as he opened a set of glass doors to reveal a beautiful garden. It had trees, bushes, and flowers, including roses. All of the flowers were full of life, probably watered daily to keep them like this. In the middle of the room was a small waterfall that fell out from a giant rock and into a small pond that was about ten feet wide and twelve feet long. It had large stones encircling the water. There was a glass dome that surrounded the entire room, dimming but not blocking out the light. Rays of the sun fell on the water, making it sparkle. The ground was gravel and made paths around the garden.

They made their way back to the main room. Henry let go of Rose's leash. He took off his jacket, folded it down the center and threw it on the couch. He grabbed his tie and wiggled it back and forth, loosening it. He pulled it over his head and took it off. He unbuttoned the first two buttons on his shirt, giving his neck room. He untucked his shirt from his pants, letting it fall naturally around him. He took off his shoes, he moved them next to each other. He no longer looked strict and proper, but relaxed and like an average person.

Rose looked around, realizing that she hadn't seen another pet. Usually, the master always had one or two other pets. It was rare to not have more, since that meant the master would have to clean and cook. Rose's best guess as to where he got his money was from being a Lord. Rose snapped out of her daze as Henry moved.

He took a step closer to her; her heartbeat increased. She was waiting for him to hit her, beat her. He reached out his hands and laid them on her neck. She flinched, not only because his hands touched her bruised skin, but also at the thought of being hit. He undid the strap and took off her collar along with the leash. He laid them down on the couch, next to his jacket and tie. She looked at him questioningly as he removed his hands. She didn't understand why he had taken off her collar. With her old master, if her collar was loose, she would be beaten.

"We need to go over the rules. Well, I guess they're not really rules," Henry said looking at her as she subtly nodded in understanding. "You don't have to wear your collar unless we go out; you may speak whenever you want to; you can also call me Henry when we aren't in public; and if you want, you can go into the garden or read books." He pointed to a closed door that Rose guessed was the library. He paused shortly, staring off into space, thinking. "I don't believe I have left anything out. If I have, then I will remind you later, ok?" he said kindly as he looked at Rose. She nodded her head in agreement. "Well, I'm hungry," he said as he walked to the kitchen with Rose trailing a few feet behind him. "Do you want anything?" he asked as he looked in the fridge and cereal cabinets.

"No, master," Rose said as she looked down. He was shocked to hear her voice again. It was only the third time she had spoken.

"I don't believe you, you are basically skin and bones," Henry said as he moved to another cabinet. She looked down at herself and felt her ribs. He was right.

"What is there to eat?" Rose asked as she peered into the cabinet that Henry was looking in.

"Whatever you want," Henry said as he shrugged.

"Which is...," she trailed off.

"Well, we have pasta, chicken, steak, salmon, rice, basically anything you want." She was completely lost. Her eyes moved from cabinet to cabinet, confused. "What did your old master feed you?"

"Bread," Henry looked up at her from behind a cabinet, his eyebrow raised.

"Pasta and chicken it is," he mumbled as he grabbed a pot and filled it with water. He turned on the grill and stove, and he jumped up and sat on the counter, waiting for the grill to heat up and water to boil.

Once the food was made, he laid it down on the table in front of Rose along with a glass of water, the same was for him. He had made the sauce and grabbed parmesan cheese. He asked if she wanted any, she, of course, said yes. Her portion of chicken and pasta was very small. He didn't want to overfeed Rose and have her throw up.

Rose looked at the food; she knew that vampires ate some human food, but most of them just fed off their pets. Human food was only for a different taste for the vampires. While it's common for vampires have some human food, Henry, however, have lots of it.

Rose picked up her fork, looking at Henry, imitating how to hold it and pick up the food. Henry put a fork full of pasta in his mouth. He glanced up at Rose. She quickly looked down at her food. She put her fork on the dish and twirled it, wrapping the pasta around it. She took a bite of it and instantly fell in love with the taste; it was mouthwatering.

She ate all of it in a matter of minutes. It was her first full meal in years. She waited about ten minutes for Henry to finish too. It was late at night by the time they were done, and Rose was tired, barely had any sleep from her previous master's house and the Pet Shop. They walked up to their rooms.

"Ok. No offense, but you can't sleep in those clothes," Henry remarked. Rose looked down at her clothes; they were disgusting, covered in holes and dirt. "So a..." he disappeared into his room and came back holding basketball shorts and a huge t-shirt. "You will have to sleep in these. Tomorrow, we will buy you some new clothes." He didn't care about the bed getting dirty. He could tell that she needed sleep badly.

He walked with Rose to her room. Once she was inside, he laid the collar and leash on the nightstand and started to walk away.

"Master?" Rose called timidly.

"Yes?" Henry replied as he turned to look at Rose.

"M-may I open the window?" Rose stuttered.

"Yeah," Henry said as he nodded. Rose slightly bowed her head, thanking him. "Do you need anything else?" Henry asked.

"No, master." Rose shook her head. Henry went out of her room, closing her door behind him. Rose walked to the window and slid back the light grey curtains. She laid her hands on the bottom of the window and grunted as she used all of her strength, struggling to lift it up. She raised the window up all the way and breathed out a sigh of relief. There was a screen, keeping bugs and other things from coming in. She faintly smiled as she felt the fresh, cool air on her face.

She changed into the baggy clothes. The basketball shorts went to her knees, and the shirt went to her thighs. She walked into the restroom, splashing some water on to get the dirt off her face. She climbed into her bed and brought the comforter up to her shoulders.

It has to be made out of clouds, she thought to herself as she laid there. She clutched the comforter tightly, as if this were a dream and holding it was the only thing that would keep her here. She closed her eyes and slowly fell asleep, letting the darkness consume her.

Chapter 3

It was morning, around nine a.m. Henry got dressed in a black shirt with a pair of blue jeans. Last night after Rose had entered her room he went back downstairs and grabbed all of the things he had laid on the couch.

He knew that Rose was still asleep, and judging from how she was awoken at the Pet Shop, he guessed that she didn't get a proper slumber. He rummaged through his drawers, grabbing some clothes. He walked into her room, he saw the curtains wildly flapping and swaying in the wind. Her back was facing away from the door, huddled in the covers and blankets, almost like a cocoon. He sat down on the bed.

"Time to get up," he said in a gentle voice, like a mother waking her daughter.

"Five more minutes, dad," she said in a little bit of an annoyed tone, she was in a daze. She snuggled closer to the blankets.

"We are going to the mall, and I'm not your dad," Henry said. Rose sat up quickly, startled.

"Master, I-I'm sorry I thought…," she stuttered scared that she had just talked back to him.

"It's ok. Here, put these on," he said gently, showing that he wasn't mad. He handed her the smallest pair of sweatpants he could find and a small t-shirt as well. She hesitantly took the clothes, still scared. "I'll be downstairs making breakfast. After you shower and get changed, come on down, ok?" he claimed.

"Master, I... I don't know how to use a shower," she admitted. Rose was born a long time after the vampires took over; she never had a home. She was always moving around in remote places. The closest thing she had to a shower was a river or creek.

"Follow me," Henry said as he got up from the bed and walked to the bathroom. Rose followed. He opened the glass door to the shower. "This knob turns on the water, and the more you slide it down, the hotter its temperature will get," he said as he pointed to the handle. "This is the shampoo, the conditioner, and the body wash," he said as he pointed to three bottles. "You put the shampoo in your hair first, rinse it, and then apply the conditioner, ok?" He asked as he looked at her. She nodded her head in understanding.

He left the room, shutting the door behind him. She took off her clothes, threw them on the floor, and hopped in the shower. The hot water felt good on her bruised skin. She watched as the dirt from the Pet Shop went down the drain with the water. She grabbed the shampoo bottle; once she figured out how to open it, she poured some into her hands and rubbed it through her hair. She moved on to the conditioner after rinsing out the shampoo. The dirt and tangles from her hair were removed. The shampoo and conditioner made her hair smooth, and the body wash made her skin feel soft. She didn't have to worry about shaving. One thing the Pet Shop did to improve the pets was to have them waxed. Once she was done, she hopped out of the shower, grabbing a towel and wrapping it around herself.

She took the towel off her and looked at herself in the mirror. Her ribs were covered with blue and purple bruises, and looked like they were about to rip through her skin. She turned around and looked at her spine. Her spine looked like it was about to cut through her skin too. She was covered in bruises and scars, especially on her stomach, ribs, back, arms, and one on her cheek. She tried to remember what she looked like without the bruises, but couldn't. She sighed deeply. She reached down and grabbed the clothes.

She put on the new shirt; pain spread through her ribs and stomach as she moved the wrong way. She grabbed the counter with one hand while the other was over her rib. She winced in pain, she didn't think that she would still be sore from the bruises. Once the pain ceased, she carefully put on the sweatpants.

She brushed her hair, which was easy to brush now because of the shampoo and conditioner. She rolled up the sweatpants at least three times before it reached the bottom of her ankle. The shirt went down to her mid-thigh. She grabbed her collar and leash from the nightstand and headed downstairs.

Henry was in the kitchen, cooking pancakes and eggs. The spatula was in his hand as he took the last pancake off the stove and laid it on a plate. Rose walked in, she sniffed the air trying to figure out what the delicious aroma was. He put a small plate of pancakes and eggs in front of her as she sat on the stool at the island.

She grabbed the fork, trying to remember how to hold it. Once she recalled how she held it last night, she started to eat.

"So your old master used to feed you bread?" Henry asked in full curiosity, leaning against the counter as he took a bite of his pancake. She nodded her head, her mouth full of food. "Seriously, he didn't feed you anything else?" he asked in shock.

She swallowed her food. "No. He told me that he wasn't going to waste that much money and time on something that was as pathetic as a human," she said as she took another bite of the pancake. Henry looked at Rose's posture. She was slumped over, not sitting up straight. Her free hand was across the front of her waist. She looked as though the bruises hurt her too much to sit up straight. Or if she were curled up, like at the Pet Shop, it would protect her.

There was a short pause before Henry spoke again.

"What about the bruises?" he asked as he looked at the bruises on her arms.

"He would find it... amusing to beat me," she still spoke timidly. She ran her finger over the bruise on her hand again.

He gave her a sympathetic look. "That won't happen here," Henry said in a reassuring, compassionate voice. He looked at her and she glanced up at him.

I don't believe that, she thought, forgetting he could read minds. He heard it but decided to not let it bug him. She had been abused for so long; it would take time for her to adjust. He had more questions.

"I thought the Shopkeeper said you didn't have a family, but in your sleep, you muttered dad," he asked. This time, instead of just a glance, Rose fully looked at him. Her face had pain and sorrow written on it.

"Well, I had a family. They... d-died when I was taken," she stuttered. She picked up her fork and started to eat the rest of the eggs. He had more questions about that, but he saw the pain in her eyes and decided to leave that for a later subject.

His phone vibrated on the counter. He picked up the phone and read the text. "Our driver is waiting outside," he said as he took the empty plate from Rose and put it in the dishwasher. He grabbed the collar that Rose had laid on the counter next to her.

"Sorry, but I have to put this on," he said as he walked over to her. He put the collar on her and set it to the loosest hole, allowing her to breathe.

She fixed her hair, and most of it covered up the scratches on her neck. He grabbed the leash, and they walked outside to the car where the driver was waiting. Henry opened the door and hopped in with Rose. The driver also went inside the car and started to drive.

They arrived at the mall. The driver got out and opened Henry's door. He bowed his head slightly as Henry got out. Henry motioned with his hand for Rose to get out too. She slid down the seats and got out of the car. The driver shut the door and asked, "Should I stay here, sir?"

"You can do whatever you want. I'll text you when we are leaving," Henry said. The driver nodded his head, got back in the car, and drove off. Henry grabbed Rose's leash as they started to walk toward the entrance of the mall.

"I might act a little different in public, but nothing bad, ok?" Henry asked as he glanced down at her. Rose nodded her head.

They entered the mall, and Rose's eyes grew a little. The mall was the biggest thing she had ever seen. It was also beautiful. The floor was a white tile, and there were diamond patterns in the middle. There were more people than Rose could've imagined being packed into one place. Most of the people had pets at their sides; some crawled, and others walked. Some were carrying their master's shopping bags, others were just sitting while their masters talked. Rose spotted a master hitting a pet several times. She quickly averted her eyes, not wanting to watch as the pet cried out and pleaded for her master to stop. No one seemed to care that the pet was being mistreated. They viewed it as something normal that happened everyday.

They strolled for a while until they reached a store called Rue 21 and went inside. They walked up to the cashier. "Is Britney here?" Henry asked. The cashier looked up from the register; her eyes widened, startled.

"Yes, L-Lord Henry. She is here. I'll buzz her right now," she said nervously, her hands trembled as she called Britney on the intercom.

About ten seconds later, a girl with long, straight blonde hair came running towards them. It shocked Rose that she wasn't tripping on the wedges she was wearing. Her hair bounced up and down as she ran. Britney was wearing light blue jeans and a light blue top. She had bracelets on her arms, dangling earrings, and a necklace.

"Henry," she chirped.

"Britney," he said in the same amount of excitement, she threw her arms around him, and they hugged.

"Oh my gosh. Who is this pretty little thing?" Britney asked as they pulled away from each other.

Ok, I'm not a thing, Rose thought. Henry looked down at her, and she stared at the ground. *How could I forget that he can read minds?* She hoped he wouldn't beat her. *Master, I'm so sorry. I didn't mean it,* Rose said through her mind, hoping her pleas wouldn't get her beat as well.

"This is Rose, my pet," Henry said as though nothing had happened. She looked at him confused.

"What can I do for you today?" Britney asked as she looked at Henry again.

"My pet needs some clothes, and I was hoping you could help," Henry said as he glanced down at Rose. She was still looking at the ground.

"Will do. I'll just take her around the store and see what looks good on her and then try some stuff on," Britney said excitedly.

He handed Britney the leash, and Rose looked at him worriedly.

It's ok, I promise, Henry said as he held his hands up and slowly brought them down, trying to get her to see she was safe.

"Come on sweetie," Britney said to Rose, she turned around and nervously went with Britney.

Henry sat down on a sofa, already exhausted. He looked at the clock on his phone; they had only been there for fifteen minutes. He sighed and groaned. He rubbed his face with his hands. He pulled his sunglasses from his pocket and put them on. He closed his eyes, crossed his arms over his chest as he started to think and rest on the sofa.

In the other part of the store, Rose was busy with Britney. Britney grabbed a hand full of clothes of various colors off the shelves. She held a few outfits up to Rose.

"You know, you look good in dark colors," she said enthusiastically as she tossed the other outfits that weren't dark red, black, dark purple, or any shade of blue on the shelf. "Let's go and see what size you are, ok?" Britney asked, Rose only nodded.

They walked into the changing room, Britney sat down. Rose tried on a dark blue – almost royal blue – t-shirt and black denim shorts. All the while showing off the extensive bruises on her body.

"Just sit there sweetie, I'll be right back, ok?" Britney asked. "You know that you can talk to me, right?" Rose nodded. "You're a quiet thing, aren't you?" She nodded her head again. Britney walked out of the changing room and found Henry laying down on the couch with his sunglasses on, his mouth slightly open and his arms crossed on his chest. He looked peacefully asleep.

"Stop resting, Henry. We found some stuff," she said as she slapped his arm. Henry sat up quickly, startled. He looked at

Britney and took off his sunglasses as he rubbed his eyes with his hand.

"Why do you have to do that?" Henry asked.

"Because every time you come with your mom, you fall asleep. And besides, it's fun," she said simply. Henry stood up and started to walk towards the changing room. Britney put her hand on his chest to stop him. "She's a size zero in pants and an extra small in shirts. She also has extensive bruising on her stomach and ribs, and it hurts her when she moves the wrong way. I think that you should give her medicine when you get home," she said, changing her tone to a more serious one.

Henry pinched the bridge of his nose and sighed. "Ok, I'll talk to her," Henry said. He knew that she had bruises, but he didn't know the extent of it. They walked into the changing room. Rose was sitting on the bench, fidgeting with the handle of the leash. Once Henry came in, she stopped shuffling. Henry sat down next to her.

"Britney told me that you have bruises on your stomach and ribs and it hurts you," Rose looked at Britney and her eyes filled with tears. "Hey, hey. It's ok, what's wrong?"

"M-master, p-please don't send me back to the Pet Shop," she said as her lip started to quiver, thinking about going back to the Pet Shop. He wiped away a stray tear with his thumb.

"Don't worry. I'm not going to send you back, you live with me now," Henry said sympathetically. Rose looked at him wide-eyed.

"T-thank you, master," she said quietly. He nodded his head, his hand still cupping her face.

"Aaaaaaaawwwwwww, that's so sweet," they both looked at Britney who they forgot was there. Her hands were cupped together and her head slightly tilted to the left.

"Anything that looks good on her, I'll buy it," Henry said, Britney opened her mouth to say something. "I want to get out of here as quickly as possible. Grab what looks good and take it to the counter. Also, get the uhm... other necessities," Henry said sounding tired and irritated.

Britney nodded her head, sorted through the clothes that were in Rose's size, and held them up to Rose. If it looked good, she would use her super speed to go to the counter and lay it down, and the cashier would scan the clothes. Henry waited at the counter with his credit card in his hand, ready to scan it at any moment.

Britney walked out of the room with Rose beside her. Henry scanned his card when the cashier was done; they put the clothes in bags. Rose was wearing the first outfit that she had tried on. Britney said that she could not have Rose walking out of her store wearing sweatpants that hung off of her and a guy's t-shirt that went down to her thighs.

Rose and Henry walked to the car, and the driver opened the trunk for them. They threw the bags inside, hopped in the car, and started to drive home.

Chapter 4

The ride to the house seemed faster than the trip to the mall. They were in complete silence, both caught in their own thoughts. Rose ran her finger over the bruise on her hand. Henry's head rested on his side; it was propped up against the window.

I wish that she would have just told me about the bruises. But then, she did seem highly upset that I found out. She even thought that I was going to return her. What am I going to do? Henry thought as he quickly glanced at Rose.

Why? Why didn't he want to give me up? It's a game, it has to be a game. No vampire has ever been this nice to me without it just being a cruel game to hurt me. I can't believe a word that he's saying, I can't, Rose thought. She pressed down a little on the bruise, reminding herself that a vampire had done this to her.

Just as they both wrapped up their thoughts, the car pulled into the driveway. The driver got out of the car and opened the door for Henry. They both hopped out of the car. "Do you need help with the bags, sir?" The driver asked.

"No, that will not be necessary," Henry said as they grabbed the bags from the trunk and headed inside. The driver hopped in and started to drive away.

They laid their bags down next to the couch.

"You just wait here, I'll be right back," Henry said as he dropped her leash and walked to the kitchen. Rose sat down on the ground in front of the couch, slightly leaning her back against it for support. Her old master didn't allow her to sit on the furniture and she thought Henry was the same. A minute later, Henry came back. In one hand was a glass of water and the other was balled up into a fist.

Rose didn't hear him approach. When he sat down, she jumped as she was startled by him. She saw his balled up fist and waited for him to hit her, but he never did. She continued to look at his hand, she subtly scooted back an inch or so.

He laid down the glass of water and unfolded his hand to reveal two tiny pills, and noticed her sitting on the floor, staring at him.

"You are allowed to sit on the furniture," he said as he reached down. He put his hands under Rose's armpits and lifted her off the ground and onto the couch. She sunk into the soft couch, savoring this act of kindness. "You are also allowed to speak when you want." His voice sounded a little annoyed and stressed. She nodded. He sighed as he pinched the bridge of his nose. "Here, take these." He picked up the pills from the table and handed her the pills and the water.

"W-what is it?" she asked, her voice full of fear as she stared at the pills.

"Nothing bad, it's medicine. It helps with the pain. You swallow it with the water," he said kindly. They only continued to make medicine because some masters would only buy it to get their pets to stop complaining.

She gave it a second glance, put one in her mouth and doused it down with the water. She did the same with the second pill.

"Let's just watch a show," Henry said as he grabbed the remote and turned the TV on. Rose stared at the screen in awe. Henry laughed to himself as he looked at Rose's reaction. Her mouth was slightly open, and her eyes were wide with amazement. It was like nothing she had ever seen. Her old master would not allow her to enjoy any sort of comforts such as TV, a bed, her own room, or anything like that.

He leaned back and sank on the couch. He stretched out his arms; one falling over the side, the other resting on Rose's shoulder. She tensed up and slightly flinched. "Sorry," Henry said as he removed his arm from her shoulder.

"It's ok, I'm just not used to not being hit. You can put your arm back on me, master," she said as she slightly glanced at him.

"Only if it's hundred percent ok with you. Is it?" Henry asked as he arched an eyebrow. She nodded her head, and he stretched out his arm again. Rose leaned back on the couch, allowing Henry's arm to wrap around her more. They both relaxed.

"Um..." Rose trailed off, remembering she hadn't been given permission to speak.

"You can speak," Henry said as he glanced down at her.

"Are those people human?" Rose asked as she looked at the vibrant blue eyes of the character.

"Yes, some shows only humans can do. Vampires either get stabbed in the heart and die, or we don't get stabbed, so they keep some of the old shows like that to give us a little bit more of a variety," Henry explained. He looked down at Rose who merely nodded. There was a pause.

"Master, what are we watching anyway?" she asked shyly. She didn't want to bug him with all these questions.

"It's a rerun of an old survival show. It's a little gory. If you want, I can change it." Henry offered, waiting for her response.

"No, it's ok. It's nothing that I haven't seen before." Henry glanced at the TV and saw one of the survivors gutting an animal for food.

"Are you sure?" he asked, his voice full of concern. He looked at the TV to Rose, then back to the TV.

"Yeah, I've done this couple of times to animals." He looked at her again, a little shocked. Rose continued. "My family and I had to eat. It's a rare occasion that we actually caught animals that's why we would quickly gut, cook, and eat it," she said simply, as if it were normal.

"If you rarely ate meat, what did you eat?"

"Some days, we would go without food. But if we could find anything that was edible, then we would eat it. Even so, we tried to stay away from meat so we wouldn't attract vampires with the scent of the blood," she said. A hint of sadness edged into her voice, remembering her family and old life. He nodded his head.

She had a tougher life than I thought, Henry thought to himself. Usually, the pets were born in the pet shop and not captured. It was rare for there to be a pet that was caught. He wasn't used to hearing about a pet's free life.

Henry turned his attention back to the show. They both watched the show intently, especially Rose who was more interested in the moving picture and the sound from the TV than the actual show itself. *How did those people fit on the screen?* She wondered. Henry laughed to himself as he heard her thought; it was adorable.

After about an hour and a half of watching TV, he could see Rose starting to close her eyes. He, himself, was a little tired of the show. Rose's head rolled onto Henry's shoulder from exhaustion. He let her head lay there a few seconds as he savored her not being timid to him, even if she was asleep.

"I think it's time to head to bed," Henry finally said. She looked at him a bit startled, she nodded.

They both stood up. Henry grabbed his jacket and tie. They took the bags and headed upstairs. They laid the bags down on the ground, next to her bed.

"I'll leave you to it," Henry said as he walked out of her room and closed the door.

Once he had shut the door, she rummaged through the bags until she found pajamas, which consisted of a black t-shirt and cotton shorts. She carefully changed into them but found that there was no need to be careful. The medicine had done wonders for the pain. She walked into the bathroom, closing the door behind her. She flushed and washed her hands, she looked up and froze. The image that she saw was sad and beautiful at the same time.

Her hair was brushed – she hadn't seen it brushed in a couple of years. Her green eyes sparkled a beautiful emerald green at the top, but at the bottom of her eyes was a faded, dull, lifeless green. Under her eyes were huge dark circles from lack of sleep. Anything that was visible, besides her face, was full of bruises. In the places where there weren't bruises, faded scars remained. She was skinny and her bones stuck out, making her look a bit older than she was.

She sighed, just looking at herself made her feel tired and exhausted. She left the bathroom, turned off the lights, and crawled into bed. She brought the covers up and around her, snuggling close to the blankets. She closed her eyes and slowly started to doze off as she allowed the darkness to slowly consume her.

Chapter 5

Henry laid in his bed, this night had gone by faster than usual. Most nights, he would just lay there, not being able to think of anything, or just watching the seconds tick by on his watch – feeling like the night would never be over and the day would never come.

This night had been different, his mind had been full of thoughts. He had already forgotten half of them – most were random. But the ones that he could remember were of Rose.

They were sad thoughts and peaceful ones. Sad, because of the way her old life had been; and partially now, the way she tenses up and spoke to him. Fear – there's nothing but fear in her voice as if that's all she knows; the bruises that covered her skin, and the emotional ones; thinking that he was like her old master or the Shopkeeper. *Fear.*

That's no way to live, Henry thought to himself. *She is a teenage girl who should have had a life ahead of her – not being abused and treated worse than an animal.*

But he didn't even know the half of it.

Peaceful, because of the way that her life will turn out; that hopefully she wouldn't look or speak to him as if he was going to beat her any second for no reason; that she would believe he was kind and not like any other vampire she had met. She was, however, starting to warm up to him and grasp the fact that he might not be like her old master or the Shopkeeper. He faintly smiled to himself at the thought that she might become happy.

He laid in his bed with his hands behind his head, staring up at the ceiling in complete silence. He watched the fan turn round and round, trying to only focus on one of the fan blades.

His silence was interrupted by a blood-curdling scream – Rose's scream. He quickly jumped out of his bed and rushed over to Rose's room. He threw the door open. She was still in bed, screaming. It was a nightmare. Her back arched as if she was struggling, making her stomach go in the air, along with the covers. She settled back down.

He ran over to the bed and grasped both of her shoulders. She screamed again, but this time she was saying something.

"NO, NO, NO. STOP IT, PLEASE!" she yelled and begged. She clutched the sheets tightly, making her knuckles turn white, and her hands started to shake from grasping them so hard.

"Wake up!" he exclaimed, trying to wake her up. Rose screamed again. "WAKE UP!" Henry shouted again. She opened her eyes and bawled as she sat up.

She was drenched in a coat of sweat, making it look like she had just splashed her face with water; some of her it rolled off her face and into the covers. She was breathing heavily as she looked around the room, realizing that it was just a dream. Her hands slowly unclasped the sheets, still shaking.

Her eyes froze when she saw her master sitting on her bed staring at her, worriedly.

"I-I'm sorry, master. It was just a bad dream," she said in a faint voice, scared that he would hit her for screaming. She looked down, pleading with herself. *He has to understand it's just a dream, I didn't mean to wake him up.*

"No, that wasn't just a bad dream," there was a pause. "Tell me about it." Henry's voice was calm and full of concern.

"It was noth-" she stopped, the memory too much for her. She quickly rushed out of bed and went into the bathroom. Henry trailed behind her

She ran to the toilet and threw up, grasping its sides with both hands. Henry held her hair out of her face, everything was emptying out of her stomach. There wasn't a lot of food. It turned to acid.

When she was finally done, she moved her trembling hand to the handle and flushed the toilet. She slumped back, breathing heavily. She sat there with no strength left to move, or let alone, stand up and walk back to her bed. Henry knew that, and he reached down to her. Rose slightly scooted back to the wall. He placed one arm behind her knees, the other wrapped around her back. With ease, he picked her up bridal style. She tensed as he touched her. He carried her to her bed; her head slumped over his arm, too weak to even support that.

He laid her down on the bed and walked into the restroom. He grabbed two washcloths and wetted them with water. As he walked back to the bed, he noticed that Rose was at least two shades paler and was slightly shaking, either because of the dream, the fact that she was sick, or the thought that he was going to beat her. She was leaning against the headboard, too weak to support her weight by herself. Her legs were curled up, she was in a small ball.

He took one washcloth and dabbed it over her lips. She slightly flinched as the cloth touched her lips, cleaning her mouth of the residue. He laid it on the nightstand. Then he took the other washcloth and gently placed it on her forehead. Rose lifted her trembling hand and touched the washcloth, stabilizing it. Their hands touched slightly.

Henry slowly took his hand away from the washcloth, waiting to see if her hand could support it.

"I'm sorry, master," she said, scared as she looked up at him.

"For what?" he asked as he sat down on the bed, next to her.

"You're taking care of me even if you're not supposed to. You're my master."

It was usually the pets that cleaned and gave blood. All the master had to do was feed them and give them something to drink. Sometimes, they don't even do that.

"I don't mind," he said affectionately. Rose looked him in the eyes, a little confused. Silence fell between the two before Henry remembered what he had previously asked. "Now do you want to tell me what the dream was about?"

"It was nothing, just a stupid dream," she said, hoping he would let it go. She knew that she technically denied something that her master had asked, but he hadn't commanded her to do anything.

"No, it's not. I'm commanding you, as your master, to tell me what it was about." She sighed, she was trapped. He had commanded her to do something. She couldn't disobey him. Henry felt bad for telling her what to do, but to get a better understanding of what she was going through, he needed to know.

"It was about my... family, but it's no big deal," she said, hoping he would drop the subject.

"Yes, it is. You called me dad in your sleep and I see the pain in your eyes when you talk about them. Just now, you had a nightmare that made you literally sick, there was a short pause. "I need to know what happened to your family to get a better understanding of what's going on with you." He pleaded.

She sighed again. "My... my parents and s-sister... where k-kil... killed." she stopped. "I-I'm sorry, m-master. I can't talk about it," she said, as she choked on her tears.

"Then show me." She looked up at him, puzzled. *Remember my powers?* She nodded her head. "All you have to do is think about the beginning of that day, then it will all just flow." He reached up and took the washcloth away from her forehead. He placed his hand on the side of her head. She flinched, but then relaxed, thinking about the day – the day her family died, and she was taken.

Chapter 6

~flashback~

Rose was asleep on the ground, in one of the only spots where the floor still remained intact. Her sister had just woken up and was stretching; her parents were already up and packing what little they had. They had only been living in the remains of the house for two days. The house had black marks where a fire had been, and the four walls were barely standing. Part of the roof had a hole in it, allowing light to come through in the corner of the house. Even though the house was destroyed, it was one of the only shelters they had found. They liked it and not having to sleep outside. However, they had to keep moving. They weren't going anywhere, just trying not to get caught by vampires.

"It's time to get up Rose, we have to go soon," her dad said as he continued to pack his bag, running his fingers through his long, dirty, and tangled hair.

"Five more minutes Dad," she said as she snuggled closer to the blanket. Her mother walked over to her and pulled the covers off of her. Rose moaned out of annoyance and sat up. She slowly woke up and started to gather her things. She picked up the only book she had and placed it carefully into the bag.

They were just about done packing when the door burst open. Vampires came in through the door. Rose's dad tried to reach the bag that had their weapons, but he was thrown against the wall, as well as everybody else. They knew they couldn't escape.

A vampire stared at them intensely – he was the Shopkeeper, trying to figure out which humans he wanted in his shop to sell. He tapped his finger against his lip as he thought.

"Her," he said as he pointed to Rose. A vampire picked Rose up and threw her into the Shopkeeper's arms before she could even react. He wrapped one arm around Rose, holding her arms in place.

"No!" Rose's dad screamed as he stood up, but he was pushed back against a wall. The vampire put his foot on her dad's chest. He pressed down, hard. Rose's dad groaned in pain.

"Shut up!" The vampire who had his foot on his chest practically yelled.

"Please, not my baby girl. Please," Rose's dad tried to plead with them. Even though Rose was the older sibling, her dad always called her his baby. Mostly because she looked more like him, while her sister looked like their mother, having dirty blonde hair and hazel eyes. The vampire grabbed Rose's dad by the collar of his shirt. He lifted him off the ground and slammed him against the wall. Rose's dad groaned in pain as he hit the floor. Rose's mom covered her mouth with both hands, shocked at the way her husband was being treated.

"Stay down, human," the Shopkeeper said as his teeth gritted together. He grabbed one of Rose's hands and brought it up to his mouth. She struggled as she saw his fangs descended. He pricked her finger as he tasted her blood.

"Mmmmm, AB Negative. Haven't had that in a few years." He laughed before he paused as he thought for a second. "I don't need any more of them. You boys can have a snack," he said as he smirked. The rest of the vampires leered, happy that they could get blood.

"NNOO!" Rose screamed as she struggled in his grasp. His arm didn't move. She kicked toward him and grabbed his arm, trying to pry or at least loosen his grip, but to no avail. A vampire picked up Rose's dad. He shoved him against the wall and held her father's hands together with one hand. His fangs descended and his head tilted toward his prey. Rose's dad moved his head away. The vampire took his free hand and grabbed his hair, holding his head in place. He leaned down and pierced his neck. Rose's dad held in a scream as he bit down on the side of his mouth. He wouldn't give these monsters the satisfaction that they wanted. He struggled, causing him more pain which made him wince.

Rose closed her eyes and turned her head away.

"Look," the Shopkeeper said as he grabbed her chin and turned it in the direction of her father. She wouldn't open her eyes. "Look, or I will literally rip your mom and sister apart while they are still alive."

She opened her eyes as her vision clouded from tears. She saw her dad right in front of her; His legs fell from beneath him while the vampire held him up.

Her dad looked at her and mouthed 'I love you' before he closed his eyes and breathed deeply. The hands that once struggled in the vampire's grip stopped. The vampire continued to drink before he dropped him on the ground.

"Well, I'm out," he said as he licked his lips, savoring the remaining blood on his mouth. Rose stared in horror at her dad's dead body. What was left of his blood came out of his neck, creating a small pool of blood. His once tan skin was now pale from blood loss, and his relatively muscular body was now smaller in size.

Another vampire walked up to Rose's mom and picked her up. Holding her wrist with one hand, he pinned her against the wall. He roughly grabbed her hair and slammed her head, creating cracks on the wall. Her vision became blurry, and her head swayed back and forth; she was nearly knocked out.

His fangs descended, and he leaned down to pierce her mother's neck.

"NO, NO, NO. PLEASE, STOP IT!" Rose yelled as she started to cry. Her pleas only gained laughter from the Shopkeeper.

Rose's mother finally screamed, not being able to contain it anymore. Her feet fell beneath her as she was held up. Before she closed her eyes, she was dropped to the ground. Her skin was pale and blood drained from the holes in her neck.

The last vampire in the group walked up to Rose's younger sister and pulled her up by the hair. She grabbed his arm with both her hands, trying to release the pressure. She struggled in his grasp and kicked him in the stomach and chest. He slightly laughed as his grip tightened.

"I like a little fight in my food," he said as he laughed again. His fangs descended, and he bit into her neck.

She braced her hands on his shoulders, trying to push away. It caused her pain, and she screamed. She screamed again, but this time, at Rose.

"Rose, help me. PLEASE HELP, ROSE!" Her voice got fainter and fainter. Her eyes pleaded with Rose to help her.

"PLEASE DON'T DO THIS, PLEASE LET HER GO!" Rose screamed, begging them to stop. It hurt Rose that she was the older sibling and couldn't protect her younger sister.

The Shopkeeper laughed. "No, my dear. We can't let anybody stay alive except you," he whispered into her ear. Rose's sister closed her eyes, her entire body went limp. The vampire let her go, and she hit the ground; her skin was pale, but not as pale as their parents'. The vampire licked his lips.

The Shopkeeper finally let Rose out of his grasp. She ran toward her mother and knelt down by her side.

"M-mom," Rose stuttered as she looked at her mom's almost lifeless body, and she started to cry. Her mom slowly opened her eyes and looked up at her.

"I-I love y-you," she said as a tear escaped her eyes. She reached up her hand and brushed Rose's cheek, wiping away a tear, before her eyes closed, and her hand went limp.

"M-mom, please... MOM, PLEASE! DON'T LEAVE ME ALONE, PLEASE!" Rose begged. An arm was placed under her stomach, and she was lifted off the ground. She watched her family lay in their own blood as she was being captured. She was going to be taken to a pet shop where she would eventually be bought by a vampire and become his pet.

~ end flashback ~

Henry removed his hand from the side of Rose's head, and she started to cry.

"M-my sister was only ten," she explained as she sobbed. She didn't expect Henry to understand; he was a vampire, and she was a human. *Vampires don't care about humans,* Rose thought as she looked down. Henry pulled her into his embrace and rubbed her back, telling her that he was sorry and it's ok. "Why?" Rose asked, her voice cracking as she spoke.

"Why what?" Henry asked as he continued to comfort her.

"Why are you nice to me? It makes no sense."

"Why doesn't it make any sense?"

"Because you're my master – a vampire – and I'm your... pet – a human," she said making the words sound like venom.

"When are you going to understand that I don't care that I'm a vampire and you're a human? I definitely don't care that I'm your master and you're my pet," he said kindly. Rose's eyes widened.

Rose hugged him back and cried even harder, but they were tears of joy. She had only known kindness from her family. That all changed when she was taken. From that point on, she only knew abuse. She had started to forget what sympathy felt like. Now, she was beginning to remember what it was. She cried on his shoulder, her arms wrapped around him, and her legs curled up on his lap.

They stayed like that until Rose eventually fell asleep in his arms, her head still resting on his shoulder.

Chapter 7

Rose had fallen asleep in Henry's arms. It was a rare and – he thought, rather – a precious moment. He stayed like that for about five more minutes, gently cradling her. Her face was nudged into his shoulder, and her arms had gone limp, but still held together around the back of his neck. Her body slowly rising and falling with each breath she took. Henry had started to rock back and forth to the rhythm of her breathing.

I think not only she is starting to warm up to me, but I to her, Henry thought as he continued to cradle her.

He remained in that position for a while longer. Henry slowly pushed her back a little so he could have room for his head to go under her arms. Once his head was free, he slowly leaned her back onto the bed, resting her head on the pillow. He gently unfolded her hands from one another, laying them at her sides.

He slowly reached down and moved her hair out of her face, tucking it behind her ear. He carefully and gently grabbed the covers and laid them on Rose. He smiled softly as he looked at her. Her face was calm, and for once, without worry or fear.

Rose snuggled closer to the covers, sleeping like a cocoon. Henry slowly walked toward the door, but looked back again at Rose. For once in his life, he didn't feel like a monster that has to drink blood to survive. He felt like a normal person. A faint smile appeared on his lips as he continued to stare at Rose.

He went back to his room to rest, leaving Rose peacefully asleep in her room, and happy that Henry was nice to her.

***

It was morning; Henry decided to not wake Rose up, since she barely got any sleep last night. He walked downstairs and started to prepare breakfast, which consisted of pancakes, eggs, and bacon. About twenty minutes later, Rose entered the kitchen. The dark circles under her eyes were almost gone, showing that she was getting much better sleep. She was still wearing her pajamas, as well as Henry.

"Hi," Henry greeted as he looked up from the stove, flipping another pancake.

"Hi." Rose sat down on the counter and smiled as she saw Henry cooking.

"Pancakes?" Henry offered as he put the last batch on a plate. Rose nodded her head. He placed a plate with two pancakes on it together with the syrup and a fork in front of Rose. He also put a medicine next to her.

Rose picked up her fork; it was becoming easier for her to use it. She then started to eat her breakfast together with Henry. When she was done, she took her medicine and swallowed it with the water.

"Master?" Rose asked as she looked at him.

"Please call me Henry," he begged. "And what is it?"

"Ok..." There was a short pause. "M-may I go into the garden?" She stuttered as her eyes were glued to the ground.

Henry stared up at her, a little shocked that she wanted to venture out a little. "Ah... yes, you may. Do you remember how to get there?" He asked, and Rose nodded her head.

***

Rose found the door leading to the garden and opened it. She was once again awed by the sight of the beautiful flowers, bushes, trees, and the mini waterfall. The walkway was made of gravel, dividing the plants from one another. The waterfall was sparkling because of the sunlight, making reflections of blue and white on the ground around it.

She walked along the gravel to a red rose bush and put her hand under the flower, careful not to prick her fingers. She leaned down and smelled it. She hadn't sniffed the fragrance of flowers in a couple of years. The scent brought her back to when she and her family were free, running around in the forest that smelled like flowers and sometimes, sleeping in flower beds when they could find them. She did a few laps in the garden looking at every bush, tree, and flower there was, memorizing everything.

She decided to make her way to the small waterfall that was surrounded by rocks and climbed up. She sat down on the rock and laid down. She relaxed as she let the heat of the sun fall on her body, even though it was dimmed because of the glass.

She had probably been laying there with her eyes closed, listening to the sound of water, for most of the day. It was the most peaceful moment that she had gotten since she was taken. The sound of the water had almost put her to sleep several times.

Henry walked in and saw Rose lying there. He walked up to her and tapped her lightly on the shoulder, startling her.

"Sorry, sorry." He held his hands up.

"It's ok, I just wasn't expecting that," she said as she relaxed.

"Can you come to the living room? I want to talk to you. Don't worry, it's nothing bad."

"Ok."

Henry grabbed Rose's waist, helping her go down from the rock. Even though she was warming up to him, Henry felt her tense at his touch.

When they arrived at the living room, they sat down on the couch, facing each other.

"I realized that I barely know anything about you, so I'm going to ask questions to get a better understanding of you, ok?" Henry explained while Rose just nodded her head.

"What's your favorite color? Mine's burgundy." He knew asking her favorite color sounded cliché, but he needed to start somewhere.

"Midnight blue," Rose said.

"Favorite flower?"

"This is going to sound kind of silly, but it's rose." Henry smiled a little at her answer.

"When's your birthday?"

"April thirteenth."

"That's... that's a month from today," he said.

"I guess it is." Rose was a bit confused at what Henry said.

"You will be turning...?"

"Nineteen."

"What did you like to do when you had spare time?"

"Read."

"Did you have books when you were free?"

"I had one book. The cover was too damaged for me to read the title, and the first few and last pages were torn, so I don't know what it's called." Henry nodded his head, but then got a little dizzy. He blinked a couple of times, trying to shake the lightheadedness. He needed to be alone.

"You tired?" He asked hoping that she would say "yes" even though she had been relaxing all day.

"A little." This was the longest rest she had gotten in years.

"Ok, let's get you to bed." Rose nodded happily.

They both stood up and walked upstairs. Rose walked into her room and closed the door behind her. Once it was closed, Henry immediately went to the kitchen. He frantically opened the fridge and cabinets as he searched for blood to drink. He grabbed his hair as he realized that he was out of blood supply. He thought he still had some blood for this month. He ran to the garage and hopped in his car. He looked ahead of him and saw that everything was spinning and blurry. He wouldn't be able to drive in that state. His brain seemed to pound against his head, and his chest seemed to be crushing itself. He felt his heartbeat throughout his entire body. It seemed that with each beat, his vision got more blurry.

He started to walk to his room but stopped as he felt a sharp pain in his chest and got lightheaded again. He leaned up against the wall to prop himself up. His free hand grasped his shirt, and he squeezed it in pain.

I need blood, but I'm out in my pantry, and I can't go out to get some. I can't drive like this, and I can't order blood. I can't let Rose see the monster that I truly am.

The pain became so unbearable that he couldn't think straight anymore. Anything rational left his brain as pain consumed him.

He fell to the ground, unable to support himself anymore. He crawled back to his room and climbed on his bed. His entire body was aching but numb at the same time. He felt like he was dying. He curled up in a ball as he clenched and unclenched his fists in pain.

He passed out – the pain and dizziness became too much for him to bear.

Chapter 8

Henry slowly opened his eyes, coming out of the darkness. The pain slowly subsided, so did the dizziness. He braced both his hands on the bed and lifted himself up. He placed his feet on the floor, but they started to shake as he tried to get up. He had to lean against the wall in order not to fall. Once he was sure he could stand on his own, he walked out of his room.

He went to Rose's room. The door was open, and he peeked in. He saw the curtains wildly swaying in the wind, but she wasn't in there. He looked at his watch – it was 12:30 in the afternoon the next day. He had overslept. He sighed, rubbing his face with his hands, and walked downstairs toward the kitchen.

He didn't see any sign of Rose in the kitchen nor the living room. He sat down on the couch as he got lightheaded again. He could barely stand more than ten minutes without getting dizzy, so driving was out of the question. His driver couldn't get the blood either because Henry needed to sign off on it.

He sat there as he thought about Rose and the garden. He stood up as he walked down to the garden. He opened the door and saw her on the same rock she was on yesterday.

Except that she was sitting on the rock and not resting like she did the other day. She looked at him when the door opened and gave a slight smile as did Henry. She looked carefully at Henry – something was different. Then she noticed that he was paler than usual and seemed almost sick and drained, but she didn't think anything of it.

"I knocked on your door, but you didn't answer. So I waited for a while and tried again, but you still didn't respond, that's why I came here. Is that ok?" There was a hint of nervousness in her voice as she spoke, clearly still in the mindset that Henry was like her old master.

"Yes, that's alright. You can come here anytime you want." She nodded. He looked around. "What do you do in here anyway?"

"I listen to the waterfall, walk around, and smell the flowers..." She trailed off.

"Boring here?" Rose didn't say anything, so he took that as a yes, but she did like being bored instead of being beaten. "You want something else to do?"

"Yes," she said with some excitement in her voice.

"Follow me." He helped her down, and she followed him out of the garden. They walked to a door that Rose had never been to before. Then Rose remembered that it was where Henry had said the books were. Though he had given her permission to go in there, she never did because she was scared he would beat her.

He opened the door, and they both walked in. Bookshelves lined the entire room, a small couch was in one corner, a plush chair in another, and in the middle of the room was Henry's desk. It had a computer, pens, pencils, paper, and an office chair. The desk was dark oak, as well as the bookshelves. The desk had small racks on it. Henry would occasionally have to manage money and make calls about it so he would come in here to do that.

"Sorry that this isn't the most exciting thing to do, but it's something," Henry said as he shrugged. He wanted to take her outside, but he knew the light would cause his headache to go into overdrive, and make him pass out again.

"This is amazing, thank you." Rose's eyes sparkled as she looked around the room in amazement. She didn't know this many books existed. She walked around and gazed at every single book in the library. *Where do I start?* Rose thought as she looked at more books.

Henry sat down at his desk. He picked up a book that he had already started and continued to read it. He removed the bookmark from the book and propped his feet on top of the desk.

After about twenty minutes of exploring the entire room, Rose had found a book that she liked. It was a romance book series about two star-crossed lovers that were doomed to fail from the start. She sat down on a circular chair that was plush and had huge fluffy pillows. She read a few pages to make sure that she liked it.

Henry had already read about a hundred pages of his book in the time that it took Rose to find a book. He was about two-thirds of the way done.

After Rose and Henry got bored of reading in his office, they decided to go into the living room and read. Henry was almost done with his book, so he grabbed another book to read once he had finished.

Rose was about one-third of the way done. Every now and then, she would ask Henry what a word meant, and he would tell her. Henry was, nevertheless, still impressed with Rose's intelligence. For someone who never had proper teaching, she was smart. Most pets didn't even know what books were.

They sat on the couch, both of them lost in the books they read but still listening to the TV in the background. Their shoulders were touching as Rose was leaning a little bit toward Henry, her head almost resting on his shoulder.

Rose turned the last page and closed the book. "Can I go into your office and pick another book?" Rose asked. Henry finished the sentence he was on and looked up.

"Yeah." She nodded and walked back into his office.

She walked around the room, trying to remember where she had gotten the book from. She couldn't remember where, so just she laid the book on Henry's desk. She walked around looking for the second book of the series.

She walked for about five minutes before she finally saw the book that she was looking for. She picked it up, and sure enough, it was by the same author.

She went back to the living room and sat down on the same spot that she had previously been sitting in. Henry had just finished his book and grabbed the other book that he had brought with him, and he began to read it.

After a while, Henry broke their silence.

"Are you hungry?" Henry asked as he finished the chapter.

"Yeah," she said, realizing how hungry she was. She hadn't had breakfast because Henry wasn't up. She laid down her book on the cocktail table as did Henry.

They walked into the kitchen. Rose sat in her usual spot as Henry started to cook dinner. It was rice with grilled vegetables. He hadn't had time to go to the store and get fresh food because of his headache. The thought of calling his driver to get the food didn't even cross his mind. They both sat down at the table with their plates, and they started to eat.

I wish that food would fill me up, but instead, it only maintains my hunger for blood for a certain amount of time. I need to do something before I can't control myself, but what?

"You ok?" Rose asked as she looked at him, a little bit concerned.

"Yeah, why?" Henry responded as if nothing was wrong.

"You were just zoning out."

"Sorry, I was just thinking."

"Ok," she said as she nodded.

They carried on a mild conversation as they continued to eat. Once they had finished, they sat in silence for a few seconds.

"You want to go read some more?" Henry asked.

"Yes," They both stood up and put their dishes in the dishwasher.

They walked back to the couch and picked up their books from the table and started to read. Henry felt a little sick and lightheaded, but he tried to concentrate on the book, hoping that it would go away and that he wouldn't pass out again. He blinked multiple times, trying to clear his head.

After about thirty minutes of him concentrating on his book, his symptoms had nearly gone away. He heard Rose gasp next to him and looked down at her.

"Sorry, there was a twist in the story," she said as she glanced up at him.

"It's fine." He lightly laughed at Rose's enthusiasm for the book. He looked back down at his book and began to read again.

After a short period of time, all of his symptoms had disappeared completely. He was utterly focused on his book now.

Rose put her bookmark in her book and laid it down on the table. She stood up and walked toward the kitchen.

"I'm thirsty. Do you want anything to drink?" Rose asked as she stopped in the middle of the room, turning to face Henry.

"No, I'm good. Thank you, though," Henry said as he glanced back at her. Rose nodded her head and walked a few steps before Henry said something else. "Actually, there is something that you can get me." He closed his book, slowly placing it on the table. His voice sounded a bit different, but she didn't think anything of it.

"Ok, what?" Rose looked at Henry.

"Your blood."

Chapter 9

Your blood. Those two words rang in Rose's ears, repeating over and over again.

I knew it, I knew that it was all just a game. They are all the same. How could I have been so stupid? Why did I ever start to trust him? He's no better than my last master. All vampires are monsters. A tear rolled down Rose's face as she thought about it even more. "W-why?" Rose stuttered as her voice came out cracked and timid. Henry was no longer sitting on the couch but in front of it standing, looking at Rose. His eyes were no longer the light, kind red but the dark, violent red like her last master.

He took a step forward, Rose took a step back. "Because," in a second, he was in front of Rose. "I'm the predator, and you are my prey." His voice wasn't smooth and kind, but rough and stern. He smirked at her as he brushed her cheek with his hand. She closed her eyes as she flinched a little. Rose knew that running from a vampire was pointless, so she stayed still. His touch no longer made her feel safe, but scared.

Another tear rolled down her face. "P-please don't do this, Henry," she said as she looked up at him. Henry took his hand and slapped her hard.

"Call me master, and besides, my little pet, you don't have a say in this." Rose cried even more. "Don't cry, I hate it when my food becomes emotional," he said with little to no emotion. She looked down and tried to stop crying but she couldn't. She watched as her tears rolled off her face. He quickly moved his hand and punched her in the face. He grabbed her hair and pulled her head upward, making her look at him. She gasped at the pure roughness that he used to yank her head back. "Stop crying!" Henry glared at her. He paused and breathed in a shaky breath, calming himself down. "Be a good little pet and don't disobey your *master* again, understand!?" he shouted. Rose nodded her head as best as she could, his hand still gripping her hair. "I don't believe I heard you!" His teeth clenched together and his grip on her hair tightened.

"Y-yes, master," Rose said in a shaky voice as she avoided eye contact with Henry.

"Good. Now, be a good little pet and don't move that much." He let go of her hair and quickly moved behind her, wrapping one arm around her body to hold her in place. He used his other hand to move her hair away from the side of her neck. He grabbed her chin, tilting her head to the side a little. His fangs descended, and he bit down on her neck.

Rose screamed as pain spread throughout her neck. It felt like a dagger was slowly being pushed into her arteries. A few seconds went by before it faded to a suctioned feeling. Rose started to cry again, knowing that she was going to die at the hands of one of the only vampires that was nice to her, even if it was just for a cruel game. Rose moved a little, trying to get out of his grasp but she whimpered in pain – it was pointless.

Her legs started to shake as she became weaker. She couldn't support her weight anymore. She felt her body go numb and saw black spots cloud her vision. "M-master, please." Rose pleaded; her voice barely audible. She felt blood trickle down her neck as he continued to gulp her blood, paying no attention to her pleas. *This is how I'm going to die, just like my family, but by a vampire that actually cared for me and I for him. Or so I thought.* A tear escaped her eye and rolled down her face. *I liked him, and I thought he liked me…* she closed her eyes and blacked out.

Her entire body went limp in his arms. Henry relentlessly drank her blood; he couldn't seem to stop. It had been a long time since he had drunken blood, especially AB Negative type. After a few more gulps, he finally felt full. He let go of Rose, her lifeless body hitting the ground. Blood continued to slip through the holes in her neck.

Henry licked his lips. *Why am I licking my lips and why does it taste AB Negative blood?* He thought for a second, then it hit him. *Rose.* He looked down and saw her lifeless body on the ground. *No, no, no, no, no,* he thought frantically. He quickly bent down and cradled Rose in his arms. Listening for a heartbeat, he found a *very* faint one.

He licked the wound, healing the two holes on her neck. A tear rolled down his face as he saw new bruises on her face. *What have I done?* He pulled Rose closer to him and lightly cried on her shoulder. His arms were wrapped around her waist. She laid limply on his lap, her head resting on his chest. He continued to cradle Rose in his arms, gently rocking himself and her back and forth. *How have I hurt her?* Henry thought. *I think I was beginning to feel something for her and now I've nearly killed her.* Another tear rolled down his face.

After sitting there for a period of time, he decided that he needed to get Rose somewhere more comfortable. He picked her up bridal style and carried her up to her room. One of her arms rested on top of her chest, and the other limp arm was dangling over her side, swaying with every step that Henry took. Her chest rose and fell with each heavy breath.

He laid her down on her bed as he did so her shirt came up a little showing some of her stomach and the very bottom of her rib cage. He saw a white line running from the back of her rib cage, and it seemed to go to her back. He gently turned Rose over on her side so he could see her back. His eyes widened as he saw about thirty of the white lines; then he realized that they were scars. The scars were long and relatively wide. They covered most of her back.

He decided to let it go for now as he had more pressing matters to deal with. He turned Rose on her back and put the covers over her. He took his hand and gently touched the now purple bruise that was forming on her cheek. He sighed deeply. "I'm so sorry," he whispered as he retracted his hand. He walked away from Rose and sat down against the wall next to the door, resting his head on his knees. *How could have I attacked one of the only people that I cared for? Not just that, but I abused her. She'll probably never trust me again. What have I done? How could have I done this to her?* He ran his fingers through his hair, frustrated with his terrible deed.

The hospitals didn't take good care of humans. They treated them worse than dogs. There was a limit of the amount of blood that they could give to the pets. The rest was for the vampires to drink. It would be suspicious if Henry told them he wanted his pet to live.

He sighed deeply. Now, all he had to do was wait for Rose to wake up... if she still can.

Chapter 10

Henry remained in the same spot as before. He had only gotten up to use the bathroom and grab Rose's book and put it on her nightstand, just in case she woke up, she would have something to do. Henry had left the window open, allowing the cool air to come in. Rose had been laying there for two days now; she hadn't moved so much as an inch. Henry was beginning to lose hope that Rose would ever wake up.

He listened to her heartbeat, it soothed him to know that she was still alive, barely. He sat on the ground with his head buried in his knees, still thinking about what he had done and how he had hurt her. Tears stained his eyes and cheeks, dark circles were visible under his eyes from stress and lack of rest. His hair wasn't as neat as it usually was.

All of a sudden, Rose's heartbeat increased rapidly. He quickly looked up to see Rose awake, staring at him – fear plastered all over her face. Her chest rose and fell as she breathed briskly.

Henry slowly stood up, trying his best not to scare her. "Is... is there anything that you need?" His voice came out cracked – it was full of sorrow and concern. Rose didn't answer.

She continued to look at him as if he was about to attack her again. "Rose, please. Is there anything that you need?" he asked again in the same tone.

"W-water, master." Her voice was hoarse and timid. As she spoke, she shrunk into the covers, as if to get away from him. He furrowed his eyebrows. He found it a little weird that she was calling him master again. He quickly ran down to the kitchen, grabbed a cup, and filled it with water. He carefully walked upstairs, back to Rose's room.

He walked in her room. "Can you move?"

"N-no, master," she said, afraid that he would not give her the water, or would come near her. He walked toward her and put his arm under her head. She seemed to tense as he touched her. He lifted up her head and brought the glass of water to her lips.

She drank it greedily. Once she had finished half the glass, Henry placed the glass on the nightstand and backed away.

"Thank you, master," she said in a small, timid voice.

"Please don't call me master, I'm not your master. I nearly killed you." Henry seemed so distressed. Rose stared at him in confusion.

Why is he upset that he almost killed me? Rose thought as her eyebrows furrowed.

"I'm upset because that wasn't me. That was a different side of me – a *monster*. I almost killed you, and I care for you, a lot. I never wanted to hurt you." His eyes seemed to tear up, showing that he meant every word that he said. Rose just stared at him with a loss of words, but also looked at him with a hint of uncertainty and fear. "I'll leave you alone. Call if you need me." With that, Henry left her room.

***

Henry walked into his bathroom and looked at himself in the mirror. He pinched the bridge of his nose and sighed. He had big bags under his eyes surrounded by dark circles. He leaned closer and looked at his red eyes and bared fangs – all he saw was a monster. He punched the mirror, in a fit of rage, shattering it. He kept his hand on the broken mirror for a while, breathing heavily. He slowly retracted his hand. He noticed that a shard of broken glass was stuck in his knuckle and he was bleeding.

He reached up his other hand and grabbed the glass tightly. He slowly pulled out the shard. It caused him a little pain, but not much. He watched as his cut slowly healed, but he let the blood stay on his hand. He sighed deeply and walked to his bed. He laid down and closed his eyes.

He didn't know how long he had been laying there. He looked at his watch. *10:40 pm*. He had been laying there the entire night. He sighed, closing his eyes and continued to rest. Until he thought that Rose might need some more water. He walked to her room. She was still laying in her bed. She hadn't moved an inch.

"Do you need more water?" She nodded her head. He grabbed the glass of water, lifted her head up, and let her drink. He laid the glass down on the nightstand again. "Can you feel anything?" He needed to know how well she was healing, if she even was.

"I can only feel my toes and fingertips." Henry nodded his head and started to leave. "Can you please stay with me? I need some company," Rose asked, her eyes pleading with him to not leave her alone. Even though he had attacked her, he showed her kindness, and she hadn't felt that kindness in years. She was willing to trust him to get some of that kindness, even if it was fake. He stayed and decided to give her some space, sitting down on the ground with his back against the nightstand.

"You want me to read to you?" Henry asked as he glanced at her. Rose nodded her head. He raised his hand and grabbed the book off the nightstand. He opened it where the bookmark was and began to read.

He had been reading for quite some time, a little over twenty chapters. "If you want, you can stop." Rose became a bit bored with the book.

"Ok." He slipped the bookmark in the book and set it back on the nightstand above him. There was an uncomfortable silence.

"I can feel both of my arms and feet," Rose said, trying to start a conversation and to relieve the awkwardness.

Henry looked up, happiness is written on his face, and his eyes glistened with hope. "That's good," there was a short pause. "I'm sorry, I never wanted you to get hurt."

"It's...fine." Rose glanced down at him.

"No, it's not. I almost killed you. Rose, I care for you a lot." Tears started to cloud Henry's vision.

Rose breathed in deeply. "I care for you too. That's why I forgive you because I believe you when you say that it wasn't you," she said sympathetically. She had never known a vampire who was kind to her.

Henry licked his lips nervously before he asked the question. "What did *I* do to you?" He looked down. He couldn't bring himself to look her in the face.

"You a... you hit me because I called you Henry instead of master, and also because I couldn't stop crying. You called me your little pet, and drank my blood." Henry ran his hand through his hair, nervously.

"I should go," Henry said as he started to stand up, but Rose stopped him.

"Please stay with me." Rose somehow moved her arm from underneath the covers to Henry.

He grabbed her hand and caressed it softly. "Why is there blood on your hand?" She asked as she stared at Henry's hand.

"I a... I punched a mirror, and a shard got stuck in my knuckle," he said as he stared at his hand too.

"Why?"

"I looked at myself and saw... a-a monster." Henry bowed his head, feeling ashamed about himself.

"You're not a monster," Rose said softly.

"Thank you," Henry said, his voice full of emotion.

They both continued to talk about different things until Rose fell asleep. What had happened was never mentioned that night again.

Chapter 11

Henry was still sitting against the nightstand, his hand still grasping and rubbing small circles onto Rose's hand. His head was leaning against the nightstand, his eyes closed. She stirred a little before opening her eyes and looking around. She looked down and saw Henry. Henry opened his eyes and looked up.

"Hey." His voice low, sounding tired.

"Hey." She responded in the same tone, she stretched, she froze in mid-stretch.

"What's wrong?" Henry looked at Rose, concerned.

"I can move already," she said while moving her arms to the side excitedly.

"That's great!" Henry said with the same amount of excitement. Her stomach growled. "Hungry?" Henry asked. He felt a little deflated from not eating. He couldn't imagine how she felt. She had just started to actually eat since moving in with him and now had not eaten in days.

"Very." She didn't deny it.

"Let's get you out of bed." He moved the covers off of her. She swung her legs over the side. Her legs popped from lack of movement. Her feet touched the floor as she weakly stood up. She was bracing herself on the nightstand. Her legs were wobbly, but she took a small step forward. Her legs gave up, not able to support her weight, and then she fell. She closed her eyes as she braced herself to hit the ground.

    Henry quickly caught her; his arms wrapping around her as she grabbed him for support, putting her weight on him. He stood her upright again, and he moved one of her arms across his shoulders for support. As she leaned against him, they started to walk slowly toward the kitchen, taking small steps. Henry doesn't want to overwork her. They reached the stairs and Henry could tell that she was too weak to go down the stairs even with his support. He wrapped his other arm under her legs, he picked her up. She tightly clung to his shirt and buried her face into his chest from exhaustion, even though she had help she was out of breath. He carried her down until they reached the kitchen. He sat her down on the stool around the island. She unclasped her hands from his shirt.

    "What do you want to eat?" he asked.

    "Pancakes," she said. It was one of the only food that she knew. Henry started to make the batter. In about fifteen minutes, they were done. He knew that she needed protein, so he made eggs for her as well. He set the plate down in front of her. She picked up the fork and started to eat them, slowly, letting her body get used to the food before she began to eat like there was no tomorrow.

    Henry looked at her. She had paler skin than before, from lack of blood. It made the blue bruise stand out on her cheek. The rest of it regained some of its colors, as if they were new. She had practically lost all the fat that she had – if you could even call it that – making her bones on her face, hands, and ribs stick out, once again.

She finished her breakfast and laid her fork on the plate. Henry put the plate in the sink. She shakily got off the stool, Henry rushed to her side just in case she fell again. She took a small step forward. "I need help." She said as she braced herself on the counter. Henry picked her up and walked toward the couch. He sat down with Rose still in his arms, and he moved her beside him. She leaned her head against his shoulder. "Can we watch TV?" She said weakly. He nodded his head and turned on the TV.

"What do you want to watch?" He scanned through Netflix.

"What's *The Walking Dead*?" She wondered. The name alone caught her attention.

"It's a show where zombies have overrun the world and humans try to survive by killing them." Henry read the description.

"Sounds interesting." Rose was looking at the man on the poster with the crossbow.

"This show is *very* graphic and a little depressing at times." He warned her.

"It's nothing that isn't already happening, just with vampires. Maybe I can relate." She said coldly but with a hint of sadness. She glanced down.

Ok, Henry thought as he went to the first episode. He turned it on.

"Sorry, that was out of turn." She said in an embarrassing tone, and she looked up at him.

"It's fine and completely understandable," he said with some sentiment in his voice. Rose snuggled closer to him for support, wrapping her arms around him and leaning her head on his shoulder. He wrapped his arm around her, bringing her closer to him. It felt nice. Henry was thankful that she wasn't scared or mad at him anymore.

They were in season three already. Somehow, despite Rose's weakness, she had stayed awake throughout the entire Netflix spree. They turned their attention to the TV to see T-Dog get bit by a walker. Rose groaned out of sadness. "Dang it, I liked that guy," she said, annoyed. A few scenes later T-Dog charged two walkers to save Carol. The zombies started to eat him. "That sucks." Rose was irritated. Henry couldn't help but smile at her enthusiasm for the show.

Later on, Daryl found Carol and carried her back to the main area. *They make a cute couple,* Rose thought. Henry laughed as he heard Rose's thought. "What?" Rose asked as she looked up at him.

"Nothing, it's nothing." Henry smirked as she raised an eyebrow.

"You read my thoughts, didn't you?" He nodded his head and laughed again. "Don't laugh at me." She slapped his arm.

"I'm sorry, I shouldn't laugh. It was a cute thought."

"Sure." Rose rolled her eyes.

"I'm serious. You're right, they do make a cute couple." She laughed a little too. She snuggled closer to Henry. "How are you feeling?" Henry asked as he looked down at her.

"A bit better, but I don't know if I'll be able to walk." Henry nodded his head, and they both went back to watching the show. Rose slowly closed her eyes and dozed off.

Rose tossed and turned uneasily. Henry looked down. He didn't know that she had even fallen asleep. She whimpered, Henry wondered what she was dreaming about. *Could she be having a nightmare about me?* After thinking he decided to take a look at her dream. He put his hand to the side of her head and entered her mind.

~Dream~

Rose was lying on the ground with multiple new bruises and cuts. They covered her body, like the old ones, almost as if they had never healed. Blood was scattered across her body from cuts, staining spots on her clothes. She was picked up by the hair and thrown against a wall. She whimpered as she hit the ground. Henry bent down on one knee, his eyes a crimson color and his fangs stained with blood as well as his mouth. Rose had three new sets of bite marks on her neck. Blood was flowing out of them.

He put his finger under her chin and made her look up at him. He laughed. "You honestly think that a vampire is capable of loving a human. His PET!" She didn't say anything. "Ok, I see how it is. The pathetic little human liked a vampire because he was nice to her. Am I correct?" He asked as he raised an eyebrow. She still refused to say anything. She just stared at him as tears formed in her eyes. "ANSWER ME!" He yelled as he punched her in the face, grabbed her hair and pinned her against the wall. Her toes were barely touching the ground. Her hands were around his arm, trying her best to relieve the pressure. "I'm going to ask you one more time. Is that what you thought?!" Henry glared at her.

"Y-yes," she said weakly. He laughed as he let go of her hair. She braced her hands on the wall, supporting herself.

He grabbed her chin, making her look at him. She looked into his red, violent eyes that were no longer the soft, kind red that she loved. "Well, in that case, killing you will just be all the more hysterical." In a blink of an eye, he grabbed her and sunk his teeth into her neck. She screamed from the pain, and unlike last time, it didn't turn to a suctioned feeling but remained an agonizing pain. She struggled in his grasp, worsening the pain.

She stopped moving as the pain became too much for her to bear. She slumped over into him as he continued to drink her blood.

~End of dream~

Breathing heavily, Henry couldn't watch anymore and got out of the dream. He needed to wake Rose up, but how? He didn't want Rose to know that he went inside of her dream. He saw a glass on the table. He sighed as he picked it up and slammed it down on the ground. Rose sat up, breathing heavily and looking around the room. Her eyes landed on Henry. "Sorry, I didn't mean to wake you up. I was stretching and accidentally knocked over the glass."

"It's ok." She stared at the shards of glass.

"Let's get you to bed." She nodded her head, and Henry picked her up. She seemed to tense then relax as he did so.

It's just a dream. It's just a dream, she repeated in her head.

"I'm going to go clean up the glass. I'll be right back." Henry went down the stairs to clean up the glass while thinking about what he had just seen. Rose began to fall asleep again.

Chapter 12

Henry picked up the pieces of glass and threw them away. He grabbed the remote, pausing the show then turned off the TV. He walked upstairs and stopped at Rose's door. His hand was inches away from the handle. *Should I go in there? She could be scared of me? But what if she needs something and I'm not there?* Henry thought as he looked at his hand. He leaned his head against the door.

He stayed outside Rose's room for a short while before he decided to walk inside. Rose was peacefully asleep, wrapped in her blanket like a cocoon. He laid down on the floor, next to her bed, and began started to rest.

***

It was morning. Rose slowly opened her eyes, looked around, and saw Henry laying on the ground. Henry also woke up and stretched his body. She stared at Henry, and he could tell that she was thinking about whether or not to say something. She stared at him for a few minutes and decided to speak. "Can I ask you something?"

"Yeah," Henry said. There was another long pause. He could tell it was about the dream.

"Last night, I had a dream and you-you hurt and then killed me because I'm a human and you're a vampire," she said as she averted her eyes, like she used to do.

"I would never hurt you." Henry sat up as he gently tilted her face in his direction, and stared into her emerald eyes.

"But isn't it illegal for a human to love a vampire?" She asked in a faint voice, and now, she finally looked at him straight in the eyes.

"Yes." The words tasted like poison. There was a short pause. "Why?" He thought he already knew the answer but still had to ask. She remained silent and looked down. "Rose, please. I want to know, and I won't tell anybody." He promised; his eyes burning into hers, pleading. She stayed quiet.

I think I like him. He was kind to me, brought me back to health, didn't send me to the pet shop, fed me, gave me my own room and bed, and treated me like no other vampire had. He had shown me kindness, something that was never given to me ever since I was taken, Rose thought to herself. She avoided eye contact again.

His eyes slightly widened. He had known that she was going to say that because of the dream, but the words still shocked him. She looked down. He gently slid his hand onto hers as he intertwined their fingers. Rose stared at their hands for a few seconds before she glanced up at Henry.

Henry slightly laughed and sat down on the bed next to her. He wrapped his arm around her, bringing her closer to him. She leaned her head against him, and they both leaned back. She wrapped her arms around his waist. He rested his head on hers. It all felt good and natural.

"But it's illegal," she said in a small faint voice, glancing up at him.

"No one has to know." They both smirked.

~2 weeks later~

They were both resting on her bed with their heads leaning on one another and their eyes closed. "I'm hungry," Rose said suddenly. She opened her eyes and looked at Henry.

"Let's get you something to eat." They moved out of the bed and made their way to the kitchen. He made lunch which consisted of grilled chicken. After she was done eating, they went to the living room to watch TV.

Then a thought hit Henry. "So your birthday is tomorrow."

"I guess it is. What's your point?" She looked up at him.

"My point is what do you want to do?"

"You do stuff for your birthday?" Her face was contorted with confusion. He stared at her blankly for a second.

"Yes, did you not celebrate it?" he asked in total disbelief.

"I wouldn't call it a celebration. My family just gave me extra food, and we didn't move around on that day."

"So I'm guessing you never had cake?" Henry raised an eyebrow, waiting for her answer.

"What's a cake?" Rose asked, completely dumbfounded.

"Come with me." He stood up and made their way to the garage. They hopped in the car and Henry drove to a bakery. When they arrived, Rose waited in the car. Henry came back with two cupcakes in a box. One was chocolate, and the other was vanilla.

He handed it to Rose. She looked at it suspiciously. "What is this?" She turned it around in her hand.

"It's a cupcake. You eat it," Henry said, still in disbelief that she didn't know what a cake was. She took a bite of it, and her eyes widened.

"This is really good," she said with part of the cupcake in her mouth. Henry chuckled.

"So which do you like better: the chocolate or the vanilla?"

"Which one is which?"

"The brown one is chocolate while the white one is vanilla." Rose thought for a second.

"I like the vanilla better."

"Ok."

"Why did you ask me that?" Rose's eyebrows furrowed in curiosity.

"Because I'm going to make you a cake and I wondered which one you liked better."

"That's going to be small," she said as she looked at the cupcake wrapper.

"No that's a cupcake. A cake is much bigger than that." Henry picked up the wrapper and threw it away.

"Oh." Henry laughed again at how utterly clueless she was. Rose laughed a little too.

Henry drove back to the house. When they arrived, they walked back to the couch. "Ssoooo...what are you thinking about doing for my birthday?" Rose batted her eyelashes.

"I have a plan, but you'll have to wait until tomorrow." Henry did not look at her. *I can't give anything away. I have to resist the adorableness.* Henry thought as he glued his eyes to the TV.

"Why would you do that? I'm going to die of waiting." Rose looked at him cutely. His eyes were still focused on the TV.

"Well, another thing that is done on a birthday is surprises, so you'll have to wait." She sighed heavily and leaned her head back.

Hours had passed, and one question still remained on her mind. *What is he going to do on my birthday, I mean I've never even had a party. I don't know what to expect,* Henry listened in on her thoughts and smiled at how much she wanted to know.

They continued to sit on the couch until Rose fell asleep, her head resting on his shoulder and her hand in his.

Chapter 13

Henry carried Rose upstairs and laid her down on her bed. She naturally snuggled closer to the covers. He looked at her face and smiled softly. He got out of his daze. He had a busy night ahead of him. He walked out of her room, shutting the door behind him.

In the morning Henry quietly snuck into Rose's room. He placed a rose next to her. He moved her hair out of her face and tucked it behind her ear. He smiled faintly and walked out of her room, closing the door. Then he knocked and placed his head on the door. He listened closely and heard her getting up. He ran downstairs.

Rose opened her eyes and looked around; something red caught her eye. It was a rose. She picked it up and smelled it. She brought it away from her face and twirled it in her fingers, looking at the fiery red that was the petals. She glanced up, she saw a rose next to the door. She swung the covers off of her, taking with her the rose that was on her bed and picked up the rose next to the door. She opened the door and saw a rose on the staircase and one at the bottom of the stairs.

The trail of roses led her to the kitchen. Henry was sitting casually down on a stool and smiled as he saw Rose. On the counter behind him, was a cake. It had white frosting and midnight blue roses on the sides of it. It had two tiers.

Rose looked at it in awe. "Is that a cake?" She pointed at it.

"Yep," Henry said as he proudly smiled at the awe and wonder on Rose's face.

"Wow." That was all she could say.

"Want a piece?" Henry asked as he picked up the cutting knife. Rose nodded her head fast. She placed the flowers in the vase on the counter, and sat down next to Henry, watching him cut the cake.

He cut a piece for each of them and put it on the plates. They both took a bite out of the cake. "Mmmmmmmmm," Rose took another bite, savoring its taste. "Did you make this all by yourself, last night?" He nodded his head, a piece of cake still in his mouth. "How did you learn to cook like this?"

"My mom taught me how to cook and bake." Rose nodded her head.

"Why is the cake so big?" She quickly added, "I'm not questioning it, just wondering."

"Well, since it's your first real birthday celebration, I thought I should make it one to remember."

"You also did all of this in one night?" He nodded his head proudly but yet jokingly. "Wow," she simply said.

Rose had eaten about three pieces of cake, and so had Henry. "I'm so full," She laid her fork on the plate.

"Same." He agreed. "Let's go watch TV and then we can do a few more things I have planned," he said as he stood up and walked to the couch.

She followed him to the couch. "What are the other things that you have planned?" She looked at him curiously.

"Can't say." He just looked down at her. She stared up at him; she gave him puppy eyes and placed her hands on his arm. There was a short pause. "Fine." He finally gave in. "You get to open presents."

She looked at him blankly. "Presents?"

"Yeah, things that you open on your birthday or on any other special occasion."

"Oh." There was a long pause. "Can we open the presents now?" She gave him the puppy face again.

"Fine."

"Yay!" She clapped her hands together excitedly.

They walked to the kitchen, and she sat down. "Wait here." No sooner had he said that he used his super speed and was gone. Three seconds later, he was back with a wrapped gift. He tossed the present from one hand to the other, nervously.

He laid the present on the counter. "You can open it." She tore the wrapper off to see a velvet, crimson-colored case. She opened the box to see a ring. It had a dark blue jewel that seemed to sparkle on its own and had diamonds surrounding it. The actual ring part went into a spiral. "It's a promise ring."

"It's beautiful," she said breathlessly as she placed it on her finger. She walked up to Henry and hugged him. He was in shock for a second before he hugged her back.

"There's one more present."

"What is it?"

"I'll show you." Henry started to walk to the front door, and Rose followed. Henry grabbed his hoodie and sunglasses and put them on. It was nearly sunset, but the light was still warm on their skin. "I know I should have let you go outside sooner, but I wanted it to be special," Henry said as Rose looked around in amazement. She hugged him again.

"Thank you."

"You're welcome." There was a short pause. "What do you want to do first?" She looked at him and smiled. She knew exactly what she wanted to do.

"I want to run." She bent down and grabbed her toes, stretching.

They had been running, racing, and playing games for two hours and Rose now laid on the ground on her side, exhausted. She was breathing heavily. Henry joined her. He wrapped his arm around her waist and brought her closer to him. Rose put her hand on Henry's, and he leaned his face in the back of her neck. He quickly moved his head away. "Sorry," Henry muttered faintly.

"It's fine." She assured him, giving his hand a gentle squeeze.

"Are you sure?" Rose nodded her head. Henry put back his face at the crook of her neck.

"If you ever want to drink my blood, you can," she said softly. She didn't want Henry to lose control again, so by allowing him to drink some of her blood, he wouldn't change and hurt her. She also didn't see the need for him to spend money on blood if he could just take hers.

"I can't do that. I don't want to hurt you." He shook his head, no.

"I don't want you to get hurt by not drinking my blood, like last time. I'm completely ok with it." She needed to prove to herself that not all vampires were the same.

Henry's phone rang. He sighed, took it out of his pocket, and answered it. "Hello...hey mom," his mom talked for a while from the other line. "Wait, when?" There was a short pause. "Ok, love you too. Bye."

He put his phone back into his pocket. "Why did your mom call?" Rose asked.

"She said that she'll be dropping by in a day or so. She doesn't know for sure what day, but she is coming."

"Should I...should I act like your pet?"

"No, she's like me. She likes humans and I know she'll love you."

Rose laughed. "How can you be so sure?"

"Because I know you, and you are a wonderful person, so I know she'll love you." Rose's cheeks turned hot and red.

They continued to lay on the grass, each one not ready to go inside. They were both too comfortable in each other's arms to move.

Chapter 14

They had stayed outside all night; Henry's arm still wrapped around Rose's waist and her hand still on his. The moon illuminated the grass, making it look like the grass was faintly glowing. "Henry?" Rose called.

"Yes." There was a short pause.

"If anything were to happen to me, I would want you to change me." Henry's eyes widened.

"I can't do that. I don't want you to live your life as a monster." He shook his head, disagreeing with Rose's sudden request.

"I don't want you to live your life alone. Promise me that you would change me." She pleaded. The thought made her sad.

Henry sighed. "I promise." Rose gave him a faint smile.

They went back to laying there in silence once more. Then all of a sudden, they heard thunder. A few moments later, it thundered again and started to rain. Rose stood up and let the rain fall on her. Henry took off his hoodie; a part of his shirt came up with it, showing his six-pack abs.

Lightning lit up the sky around them. "We should probably go in," Henry said as another lightning strike struck near them.

"Yeah, that's a smart idea," Rose said as they both ran inside.

They were both soaking wet. Water dripped onto the floor. "I'll get us some towels," Henry said as he used his super speed. He grabbed the towels and ran back.

He took one towel and wrapped it around Rose. She brought the towel closer to her, letting it slowly soak up the water. He wrapped a towel around himself too. They both walked to the couch and sat down, both careful to sit on the towel and not get the couch wet. Henry turned on the TV, and Rose leaned her head against his shoulder. He put his head on top of hers, and they both rested.

An hour had passed, and they were both almost completely dry. They both stared at the TV intensely. They had recently finished an older TV show. They kept looking for a new show to watch until they found a show about technology having a mind of its own and the vampires having to fight it.

Suddenly, Henry got a strange sensation. He tasted something in his mouth even though he hadn't eaten anything. As he tried to figure out what it was, the taste became more and more familiar; it tasted like iron. It was blood. It was sweeter than most blood, which meant it was AB Negative. Rose's blood.

Why am I tasting her blood? He thought. Then he remembered how good her blood was. He wanted more. *No, I have to resist this.* He tried to think of anything else. As if his body was screaming at him to drink from her, he started to hear her heartbeat. He started to smell her blood. He couldn't take it anymore; he needed blood. He didn't want to, but he couldn't take it.

He stood up and started to walk out of the door.

"Where are you going?" Rose asked.

"To the store... to get more blood bags." A hint of shame was evident in his voice.

"You... you c-can have my blood." Rose offered. She *needed* to convince herself that every time Henry got hungry, he wouldn't hurt her. She had to believe that not all vampires were the same, and this was the only way she could think of. She was willing to take that chance so she wouldn't be scared of him anymore.

"Are you sure?" Henry asked as he turned around.

"Yes," Rose said. Henry hesitantly walked back to the couch and sat down. "Is it going to hurt, like last time?" She breathed heavily.

"No, you'll just feel a small pinch," Henry reassured her as he looked her in the eyes.

"How come it won't feel like the last bite?"

"The pain is determined by how I feel. Last time, from what you told me, I was mad so it would have hurt more, but when I just want blood, it doesn't hurt." She nodded her head.

He slowly leaned his head down to her neck. About an inch away, he stopped. "Are you sure you are ok with me doing this?" He wanted Rose's confirmation.

"Yes."

Henry wrapped his arm around Rose's waist, holding her in place. His fangs pierced her neck. Her blood tasted better than he remembered. It was so sweet and rich.

Rose felt little to no pain. A few seconds later, she started to feel dizzy. She needed for him to stop. "Henry." She breathed out. He took his last gulp and brought his fangs out of her neck. He licked the wound and pulled his head away.

"How do you feel?" He placed his hand on her head and looked at the complexion of her skin, concerned.

"I feel a little lightheaded, but it'll go away in a few minutes," she said as Henry continued to examine her.

She laid her head on his shoulder, and he kissed the top of her head. They intertwined their hands, both of them smiling at each other while resting. Moments later, someone knocked on the door.

Henry sighed. "It's probably my mom. Stay here, I'll be right back." He got up and walked toward the door to open it. "Would it have killed you to give me a heads-" He stopped as he saw who was in front of him. It wasn't his mom, but two police officers. "Sorry about that, thought you were somebody else. What can I help you with?" A brutish officer stepped forward. He was about an inch taller than Henry. Every inch of him was covered in muscle.

"We are here to talk to you and your pet."

Chapter 15

"I'm sorry?" Henry was caught off guard.

The brute officer sighed. "We are here to talk to you and your pet," he said more slowly and sternly. Henry nodded his head.

"Pet, come here!" He changed his tone into a demanding one. He snapped his finger, pointing to the spot next to him.

Rose furrowed her eyebrows in confusion. She thought it was weird that he was calling her pet, but she stood up from the couch. She walked toward the door. "These are police officers. I need you to act like my pet," Henry whispered to her as soon as she reached him. She subtly nodded.

"Yes, master?" she asked as she bowed her head respectively and clasped her hands together. The police officers looked at each other, and they glanced at Rose, impressed.

"These gentlemen are here to talk to you and me. Oh, and would you fine gentlemen like to come in?" he asked, seeing how they both were dripping wet from the rain. The brute grabbed the collar of his jacket and flicked it up. Some of the water flew off his and landed on the ground.

"No, we are fine right here," the brute officer said as he released his jacket.

Rose looked up a little to get a good look at them. On the left was a small yet muscular man. He had blond, curly hair and red eyes; a few strands of his wet hair fell in front of his face. On the right was the brute; he had black hair that was gelled backward. The rain had made some of the gel stick out of his hair, making loose strands fall naturally around his head. He also had red eyes.

"So officers, what's this about?" Henry crossed his arms.

"We got a tip a few days ago that you were caught in a store comforting your pet. You and I both know that it's against the law to like or love a human." The brute stepped forward, almost warning Henry not to get an attitude, seeing as how Henry's arms were crossed.

I must have forgotten to close the door to the changing room. Henry thought angrily as he glanced down at Rose. She was still looking down. "I didn't do that. Besides, we went to the store about a month ago, and you're asking me questions now?!" Henry raised his voice – a bit upset – clearly not going to listen to the brute's warning on not giving an attitude.

"The man that reported it must have gathered up enough courage to tell on a *Lord*," the brute said mockingly. A small smirk spread across his face, as well as the blond officer.

"What do you need to ask or do or whatever?" Henry was getting annoyed. He readjusted his arms to where his muscles were more visible.

"We need to examine your pet to see if you've drunken out of her or beat her, anything normal like that." The brute took another step closer to Henry.

"Fine." Henry sighed. "You can examine her."

"Come here," the brute said to Rose. She did as she was told and walked to them, her head still bowed. The brute moved her hair away from her neck to reveal two sets of bite marks, one of which was more red and bulging than the other. He reached up and touched it. She whimpered and flinched, showing that she in pain. They both lightly laughed. "So I take it you just fed off of her?" He looked at the bite mark more.

"Actually, just a few minutes ago. She has AB Negative blood, so it's nice and sweet." Henry smirked, showing that he enjoyed her blood.

"What does she have to say about it?" The brute asked as he looked at her; he tilted her chin up towards him. She stared at Henry. He stood there silently as he looked at her. He very subtly shrugged. She could tell he was lost.

I'm asking if I can speak. Rose spoke to him through her mind.

"Yes, pet. You may speak," Henry said as he looked down at her. The brute turned her face towards him again.

"I'm happy to do whatever master wants." Her voice was so small; she avoided eye contact.

"Even if it brings you pain?" The brute raised an eyebrow.

"Seeing that it makes master happy is enough for me," Rose said as she glanced back at Henry, she quickly looked away as they made eye contact. The smaller brute wrote something down on his notepad, like he had been doing the entire time.

"Remind me to give you extra food tonight, pet," Henry commanded.

"Yes, master." Rose continued to look at the ground.

"What do you feed her anyway? She's skinny enough to be barely fed at all." The brute interrogated further as he looked at Rose. He could see some of her bones through her clothes.

"I feed her my leftovers, but sometimes, like today, I give her a little extra food." The brute nodded his head. The smaller officer continued to jot down every detail.

"What about the scars?" The brute moved Rose's head side to side, revealing scars and bruises on her neck. He grabbed Rose's arm and looked at the discolorations on her skin.

"It took me about a month to train her, but she got the hang of things after a few beatings," Henry told the officers, Rose visibly shook. Both the policemen chuckled and nodded.

"Well, it seems like you rule over her with an iron fist and that you don't like her." There was a short pause. "I believe we are done here." The brute said as the blond officer tucked his notepad into his pocket. They both went out into the rain, hopped in their car, and drove off.

Henry closed the door and wrapped his arm around Rose. "You are an excellent actress," Henry he smiled at her, clearly impressed.

"And you are a great actor." Rose complimented him too.

"Now let's go get you some of that food that I was talking about."

"Wait, you were serious?" Rose furrowed her eyebrows in disbelief.

"I'm always serious when it comes to food," he said, *seriously*. Rose laughed at Henry. They made it to the kitchen and made popcorn. The buttery aroma filled the air. Then they went to the living room, bringing the popcorn with them, to watch a show.

Just as they had just both gotten comfortable, there was another knock on the door. Henry sighed, annoyed. "I'll be right back." He got up, and Rose quickly ate all the remaining popcorn, leaving none for Henry. He opened the door. "What is it this-" he stopped as he was greeted by another person. "Hi, mom," he chirped, his lips stretched into a huge smile. He opened his arms for a hug.

"Well, that's one way to greet your mother," she said sarcastically as they hugged. She walked in. "Who is this?" She pointed to Rose who stood up when she arrived. Rose looked at Henry's mom's dirty blonde hair that went down past her shoulder by about an inch. Like Henry, she had kind red eyes.

"Mom, this is Rose. My... pet," Henry said hesistantly, not really knowing how to introduce her. His mom walked over and hugged Rose. Rose hugged her back and looked at Henry, her eyes wide as saucers, as if to say 'what's happening?' *It's ok, she's like me. Remember, she likes humans,* Henry thought to her. Rose exhaled as she relaxed more. Henry's mom stopped hugging her.

"My name is Lisa, and it's so nice to meet you. Henry doesn't go out much so I'm glad that he has you." They each smiled faintly at each other. Henry's cheeks lightly blushed out of embarrassment. "Has he treated you well?" Lisa asked.

"Yes," Rose said. Lisa stared at Rose

"I feel as though you're only telling half the truth." Rose raised her eyebrows.

"What-" Rose started to say.

"Oh, silly me. My power is to be able to tell when someone is telling the truth or lying." She looked closely at Rose's neck and saw the two sets of bite marks. "Henry, have you drunken out of her?!" Lisa snapped, almost yelling.

"The second time she allowed me to," he said nervously. He looked down and rocked back and forth on his feet, like a little boy being scolded.

"What about the first time?" Lisa inquired as she raised an eyebrow.

"I - I changed and bit her." He continued to bow his head in shame.

"Oh, Henry." She buried her face in her hand, looking so disappointed.

"It's ok, really. He helped me heal," Rose said. Lisa brought her face out of her hand, and her face softened as she looked at Rose.

"Are sure you're ok?" Lisa asked.

Rose nodded her head. Lisa looked at Rose more intensely, trying to remember something. She turned around to Henry, snapping her fingers as the thought hit her. "Oh, I almost forgot. Your brother said he's coming," she announced, sounding annoyed.

"What, no! He *hates* humans. Why would you invite him?" Henry crossed his arms, looking at his mother with an eyebrow raised.

"I didn't invite him. He just decided to show up." Lisa threw her hands up in the air in defense.

"If he lays one hand on her, he's dead!" Henry proclaimed as he pointed at Rose. Lisa nodded her head and then looked at Henry intensely, noticing something.

"Do you like Rose?" Lisa asked as she looked from Henry to Rose, then back to Henry.

"What, mom don't be ridiculous." Henry laughed nervously.

"Henry." Her eyes bore into him as she crossed her arms. "Don't even try lying to me. It never worked in the past, so it's not going to work now," Lisa vented as she tapped her foot, waiting for an answer.

Henry sighed. "Yes, I do." His cheeks turned bright red. He looked at Rose, and she smiled at him. All of a sudden, the door burst open. A man walked in and hugged Henry.

"It's good to see you, Henry." The man said as he pulled away.

"Good to see you too," Henry said, sounding a bit annoyed. Besides that, there was no other emotion in his voice. The man walked over to Lisa and hugged her.

There is something familiar about that man's voice, Rose thought to herself. The man stopped hugging his mom and let go of her. That was when Rose got a good look at his face – the light brown hair that was styled messily, and the dark red, violent eyes. Her eyes widened. *Henry's brother is my old master!*

Chapter 16

Henry's brother is my old master! Henry's brother is my old master! She kept repeating it in her head, like a mantra. By now, her heartbeat had increased, and she stepped backward. The man looked around and then stopped when he saw Rose. He walked toward her, she was frozen in place.

Rose breathed heavily as the man was just a few inches away. The man stared down at her with a small menacing smile on his face. "Rider, this is my pet, Rose." Henry's voice sounded so dangerous.

"I know. We've already met," Rider said as he stared at her more. She looked down, trying to hide her quivering lip.

"What? How did you know her?" Henry asked as he crossed his arms.

"I was her old master." He smirked. It sent chills down Rose's spine. He chuckled as he clearly saw that she was scared. Her hands started to tremble.

"What?!" Henry sounded like he was going to kill him. His voice echoed throughout the house. Rider didn't jump, but Rose did, slightly.

"You heard it right, Henry. I was her old master. I'm that I get to see her again. After all, she is so fragile." He raised his hand and gently brushed her cheek like he used to do. She slightly flinched at his touch and stared breathe heavier. Suddenly, Rider's hand was slapped away from Rose's face.

"Do not touch her!" Henry gritted his teeth and tightened his grip on Rider's wrist. His brother laughed as he tried to jerk his hand out of Henry's grasp but Henry's grip didn't budge.

"Why? She's just a huma-" he halted. He closed his eyes for a second, concentrating. "Wait, do you like her?" he asked as he opened his eyes.

"What makes you think that?!" Henry fired back. Rider's question had caught him off guard, and his brother took the opportunity to pull his arm out of his grip.

"Because my power is to tell people's real emotions, remember? That's how I found out about you and that other little pet when we were kids," he said in a knowing tone. He rubbed his wrist that was now a bit red. "Right now, I know that she is scared, but she is also glad that you are here. From you, I understand that you are outraged and protective of her. And not just because she's your pet, but because you don't want anything to happen to her. Why would a vampire be protective for his *pet's* wellbeing? More importantly, why would a *pet* be reliant on her *master*? You like her, don't you? And more than that other pet as well," he stated and smiled smugly.

"I don't like her," Henry said through his gritted teeth. His eyes burned into Rider's face.

"Then you won't mind if I... discipline her?" Rider asked as he looked at Rose. Her bottom lip started to quiver again. She looked down, almost like she couldn't bear to see his arms being raised and coming down on her.

"Why? She's done nothing wrong?" Henry furrowed his eyebrows.

"She always does something wrong." Rider lightly chuckled. Without warning, he used his super speed passing by Henry and ended a few inches in front of Rose. He quickly raised his hand to slap her. Rose flinched and closed her eyes, waiting for the familiar pain. Within a second, Rider was pinned up against the wall. Rider grabbed Henry's hand with his free hand and tried to pry it off his neck, but Henry's arm didn't budge.

Rider managed to laugh even though he was being choked and it came out gravelly. "I knew it, you do like her." He readjusted his grip on Henry's arm.

"I want you out of my house now!" Henry yelled. His arm tightened, and his muscles flexed through his t-shirt. Rider coughed as Henry's grip tightened.

"Why?" Rider managed to choke out before he coughed. Lisa walked over to Rose and wrapped her arm around her. Rose hugged her back as she tried to keep from crying. Lisa knew from experience that there was no way she could break up Henry and Rider from fighting. It was next to impossible.

"She's told me some of the things that you've done to her!" Henry said, not loosening his grip.

"She was over exaggerating." Rider looked at Rose, Lisa was still comforting her. *How pathetic*, Rider thought. He was disgusted that Rose was touching his mom.

"How can I believe you?" Henry asked even though he knew what Rose was telling him was true. He wanted to see what his brother thought.

"Easy. Look into her memories and see what I did. If it was nothing, then I get to stay. But if you don't like it, I'll leave," Rider said as he released his left hand from Henry's arm. He held it out for Henry to shake. Henry thought about it for a second.

"Fine." Henry let go of Rider's throat. Rider grabbed his throat rubbing it. Henry rejected Rider's outstretched hand. Henry, Lisa, and Rose made their way upstairs. They entered Rose's room and sat down on the bed. Henry put his hands on Lisa and Rose's head. "Ready?" Henry asked Rose, and she nodded her head. She closed her eyes and thought about the first day that she was bought and her suffering had begun.

~flashback~

Rose sat on the ground of her cage. She had been here for two months, but no one even gave her a second glance once they saw that they would have to train her. Her face was buried in her knees, and she was leaning against the wall, doing her best to try and stay in her imagination. But every time someone would scream or cry, she was pulled back to reality.

Rider walked in. The Shopkeeper looked up, laying the stack of papers to the side into a bigger pile. He stood from his chair, grunting as he did so. "Lord Rider, it's such an honor to have you here." The Shopkeeper walked towards Rider. Rider just nodded his head. "What kind of pet are you looking for?"

"One that is going to be a bit of a challenge," Rider spoke as he looked around. He couldn't help the small smile that spread across his face.

"I think we have just the thing." The Shopkeeper snapped his fingers, knowing exactly what Rider was looking for. He started to walk.

They walked over to Rose's cell where she still had her head buried in her knees. The Shopkeeper tugged on the chain that was around her neck, and she looked up. Rider looked at her, and she looked back at him with eyes that said 'leave me alone!' Rider smirked. "I'll take her."

"Don't you want to know anything about her?" The Shopkeeper asked, shocked.

"No, I just want the challenge." Rider grabbed Rose's chin, forcing her to look at him.

"Not even her blood type?" The Shopkeeper asked, still in utter shock.

"I don't care about her blood, I just want the challenge and fun." He said, sounding a bit annoyed at the Shopkeeper's persistence and the fact that he had to repeat what he said.

"As you wish." The Shopkeeper unlocked Rose's metal leash from the collar and grabbed her to stand up.

"Can you take off her collar as well?"

"Yes, my Lord." The Shopkeeper removed her collar, small drops of blood came out from the open wounds that were still on her neck.

Rider roughly grabbed Rose by the arm. They started to walk to the room where the collars, whips, muzzles, and leashes were. Rose struggled from his grasp as she tried to get away. Rider sighed, becoming annoyed. "Don't you have a disciplining room?" He asked as he looked back at the Shopkeeper.

"Actually, yes." The Shopkeeper said as he stared at Rose, knowing what was to come.

"I would like to start training her now, please," Rider said. His grip tightened around Rose's arm as she continued to struggle. She looked up into his eyes and saw them turn dark red.

"As you wish my Lord." The Shopkeeper said as he led them to the disciplining room. Rose inhaled a very strong smell. It smelled like iron – blood. She put her free hand over her mouth and nose, trying to block out the vile scent. They opened the door, and before Rose had a chance to look at her surroundings, she was thrown on the ground. A cloud of dust accumulated around her. It settled around and on her. Rose felt something sticky, holding the dirt together. She looked down, her eyes widened as she saw that the sticky substance was blood.

Rider grabbed a whip off the wall. "How many family members does she have or did have?" Rider asked as he rubbed his hand over the whip. His eyes were now so dark of a red that they almost looked black. Rose had never seen a vampire's eyes get that dark before.

"She had three, my Lord." The Shopkeeper said as he looked down at Rose. She clenched her fists tightly at the memory.

"Three. Then I'll be nice and only do... thirteen," Rider said. Before Rose had a chance to even process what he had said, he brought down the whip, hard. It tore through her shirt and skin. She screamed, he brought it down on her back and partly on her side again and again and again. The pain seemed to become greater each time. Tears had sprung from her eyes from the pain. She dug her fingers into the dirty ground.

What seemed like ages had passed, and he stopped. She breathed out a sigh of relief. No sooner had she done so, he brought the whip down on her again. This one seemed harder than all of them, and she screamed. Rider knelt down beside her. He had a little bit of blood on his face that had splattered off of her back and the whip.

"I'll be right back. I want to wait for your blood to dry, so you don't ruin my car. While I'm gone, I expect you to be a good pet and stay here. Do you understand, pet?" Rider asked and she nodded her head. He sighed. He put his finger into one of the lashes on her side. She whimpered and slightly squirmed. "See, when I ask my pet a question, I expect them to be polite and answer me and also call me master. I'll ask you again, do you understand, pet?!"

"Y-yes, ma-master." She whimpered in pain, his finger still in her gash.

"Good." He stood up and walked out of the room leaving Rose in a pool of her own blood. She laid her head down on the dirty ground as tears continued to escape her eyes.

What seemed like an eternity later, Rider walked back into the room. She hadn't moved an inch. Even if she did, it caused her pain. Even breathing caused her pain. Her fingers were still on the ground. The dirt had soaked up the water from her tears.

He knelt down beside her and put his finger on another one of the lashes. She groaned as pain spread throughout her back. He retracted his finger and brought it up to his face. Nothing was on his finger due to the dry blood. He threw a shirt next to her. "I want you to change your shirt," he simply said as he got up and walked out of the room.

She sat up, slowly and painfully changed into the new shirt. She looked at her old shirt with one or two strips of clothing still attached, holding them together. The rest of her shirt had been destroyed by the whip. It was completely covered in blood.

She went back to laying the way she had been before. A few minutes later, Rider walked in with the Shopkeeper. Rider knelt down and put the collar tightly around her neck, choking her. He turned her over on her back. She lightly cried out in pain. He fastened the collar as tight as it would go.

He grabbed her by the collar and roughly stood her up. She whimpered and winced in pain. "I've already signed the paperwork. Come on pet, we are going home," he said as he walked toward the exit. Rose was partly walking and partly being dragged, painfully following her new and cruel master to her new home.

~end flashback~

Chapter 17

Henry retracted his hands from the side of their heads, rage overfilled him. Now the thirteen scars on her back made sense; she had been whipped by Rider.

"He treated you like dirt, like fucking dirt!" He was shaking in anger. He stood up and used his super speed to rush downstairs. Lisa and Rose ran out of her room to see Rider on the ground and Henry on top of him. He punched him twice. "I want you out of my house now!" Henry said as he grabbed Rider's shirt collar. Henry was almost yelling. Rider looked at Henry's eyes and saw that they were darker than usual.

"I take that you didn't like it?" Rider said in a sarcastic tone. "But I did say that I would leave, so if you would be so kind as to get off of me, then I'll go." He leaned his head back, clearly annoyed. He closed his eyes for a second; when he opened them again, they became lighter in color. Rider looked around, slightly confused.

Henry got off of him and stood up. He grabbed Rider by the shirt and pushed him out of his house. Henry ran up the stairs and hugged Rose. She hugged him back and buried her face in his chest. He kissed the top of her head.

"I'm so sorry, Rose," he said softly. "I promise he won't be able to hurt you again." Henry tightened his grip on Rose, bringing her closer to him.

"Thank you." She sobbed as a tear rolled down her face. She felt safe in her arms. Henry pulled away from her and wiped away the stray tear with his thumb. She tilted her face as Henry cupped her face with his hand. They stared into each other's eyes and smiled. Lisa looked at the both of them.

"I'll go and make dinner," Lisa whispered, not wanting to disturb them.

She left Henry and Rose staring into each other's eyes. Henry leaned his head down and rested it on Rose's shoulder. She did the same. Henry gently rocked back and forth and wrapped his arms around Rose's waist.

What seemed like only seconds, Lisa yelled at them. "Dinner is ready!" They were both shocked that they had stayed like that for so long.

That felt like seconds, Rose thought as they pulled away from each other.

I was thinking the same thing, Henry thought to her as he looked down at her. He smirked.

You have to stop reading my-

"Let's go eat," Henry said, cutting Rose off. Rose walked downstairs with Henry beside her.

"We'll finish this later," Rose said to Henry as she squinted her eyes, he smiled.

"I made lasagna." Lisa laid the food on the table.

They had all finished dinner and placed their dishes in the dishwasher. Lisa had wrapped the leftover lasagna and put it in the fridge. They had walked upstairs, and Lisa was already in bed. Rose and Henry were in the hallway. "I'll see you in the morning," Henry said as he hugged Rose.

"See you in the morning," Rose said as she left his embrace. Henry leaned down and lightly kissed her on the cheek. Her face turned a very bright red. They both walked to their rooms and rested.

***

It had felt like hours had passed, but Rose couldn't sleep. She felt like she was being watched. She opened her eyes for the hundredth time and looked around, but no one was there. She sighed as she turned over on her back and she closed her eyes again.

A hand was placed over her mouth. "Remember me?" That too familiar voice whispered in her ear. Her eyes widened, and she started to breathe heavily. Her heart rate increased, and she reached up her hands and tried to pry his hand off of her mouth. It didn't budge. She looked at the window that she always kept open. Her eyes widened again as she saw that the screen was gone. She looked up at Rider and saw his dark, sadistic eyes.

Rider laughed, seeing that she was scared. "I miss this. I don't know why I ever gave you up. Actually, I do. But seeing you like this was always so funny." He used his thumb that was already over her mouth to gently rub her cheek. He knew that this gesture frightened Rose. He used to do this to her to scare her, she knew it meant that he was thinking about whether or not he was going to hit her. He looked like he was thinking. "You know, I want to see this face on Henry." He smirked.

He released his hand from her mouth, but no sooner had he done so, he grabbed her throat, choking her. He made her stand up and practically dragged her out of her room. Her hands were clasped tightly on his arm, trying to pry off his hand. He stood her next to the railing, his arm outstretched, she was standing behind him.

"Henry!" Rider yelled. Henry rushed out of his room, recognizing his voice. He stopped when he saw Rider's hand on her throat.

"You said you would leave!" Henry shouted. He couldn't believe Rider was this brainwashed that he would actually do this.

"Yes, I did. But I never said I wouldn't come back." Rider shook his head. "How can you love a human?" He looked at Rose in disgust. Her knees were bent and shaking.

Henry took a step forward as Rider tightened his grip on her throat. She gasped for air as her fingers dug into his arm. It, however, didn't break his skin. "Take another step, and I'll snap her pathetic neck." Rider warned. She whimpered at the thought of her neck being snapped.

"Please, don't hurt her." Henry was scared. He held his hands up in the air.

"Don't hurt *her*? *It's* a human. A pet that's *its* purpose is to be ruled over by a master, and we can do whatever we want to it because it's a pet." He laughed. "I mean look at this," he said as he squeezed her throat. She gasped for air, and she continued to hold her hands over his arm for dear life. "It can be broken! It is broken!" He was getting angrier.

"She's not broken," Henry said. He knew she wasn't broken. She was just hurt.

"Oh really. Tell me when you first got it: did it stutter when it was scared, thought you were going to hit it if you just looked at it, kept following my old rules, rarely talked, and so much more?" Rider asked, knowing that she still kept to his old rules.

"How? How did you know those things?" Henry asked. He heard his mother in the background calling the police. He was trying to stall for time.

"Because, you idiot, I'm the one that trained it, beat it, and set rules to it. I'm the one that broke it!" He beamed, clearly proud of his doing. Without knowing it, he tightened his grip again. Rose gasped for air and he sighed. "See what I mean?" He paused. Henry saw his eyes turn a dark red. "You know what, I'm going to end its suffering." He pushed her against the railing and leaned her head back.

Henry, please help me! Rose begged as her eyes filled with tears.

"Rider! Stop this, please," Henry said, scared. Rider pushed her back even further, and her feet were now off the ground; she was over the edge. She tightened her grip on his arm, even though she knew it wouldn't help. "Rider, she's my pet, stop!" Henry didn't like saying it, but if Rider was playing the pet card then maybe that could talk some sense into him. Rider only laughed. "Besides, I know that this isn't you. This is dad. You're not really like this."

"You don't really mean that. You're just trying to use my point of view and get on my good side. But since you seem to like it, then you can see that I'm going to end its suffering. I'm doing you and it a favor," Rider said as he pushed her back even further.

"Rider, please don't do this. Don't take her away from me. Please stop." Henry's eyes were clouded with tears.

"I don't believe it. Your eyes are tearing up OVER A HUMAN! Look at it, Henry. It's pathetic!" Rose had a tear spring from her eyes due to being choked and the fact that she was scared. "I'm doing you a favor by getting rid of such a pathetic and useless pet!"

Without saying anything else, he released his grip on her throat.

Chapter 18

He let go of her throat; she felt his cold, rough, harsh hand release her neck. Henry used his super speed and began to jump over the railing toward Rose. Rider quickly tackled him back.

Rose turned in the air and hit the ground. She felt and heard the snap of her hip breaking as it hit the hard marble floor. Her side followed, and she felt something move along her ribcage. Her head was the last thing to hit the floor. It was hit with just enough force to crack her head and cause it to bleed, but not to make her pass out.

She rolled over her back, pain spreading throughout her side and she winced in pain. Everything was blurry. She breathed in deeply, and she felt a sharp pain in her ribcage. She reached down her right hand and touched her side, there was an empty space. She slightly stroked along the broken rib and felt it go down.

It made sense why it hurt to breathe – her rib was slowly piercing her lung.

Henry and Rider continued to fight and wrestle. Rider threw Henry against the railing and ran toward him, meaning to knock him over. Henry quickly got out of his way, grabbed Rider, and threw him over the railing. Rider quickly grabbed Henry's arm and pulled Henry down with him.

Henry landed on top of Rider when they hit the ground. Henry turned around and punched Rider until he knocked him out. He breathed in deeply, exhausted. He quickly rushed to Rose. A small puddle of blood had formed on the side of her head. One of her hands rested on her ribs, the other was at her side, clenching and unclenching in pain.

Henry got on his knees and carefully propped her head on his lap. She winced. He put his hand on her head to try and stop or at least slow down the bleeding. "I'm so sorry, I should have made sure that he had left and wasn't coming back. This was all my fault," he said in great sorrow, tears rolling down his face.

"It's not your fault. You couldn't have known that this was going to happen," Roe whispered, afraid that if she were to speak too loud, it would cause her pain. She felt the rib push harder on her lung, she winced in agony. "I-I'm sc-scared." She managed to choke out. Henry wiped away a stray tear from her cheek with his thumb.

"Don't be. I'm right here," he said as another tear rolled down his face. He leaned down and collided his lips with hers; they seemed to fit perfectly together. The kiss was filled with passion, sorrow, and happiness. Somehow, all the emotions made the kiss even more special to both of them. She kissed him back. Rose's breath started to shorten as the rib pressed against her lung, Henry retracted his head, allowing her to breathe. "I'm right here." He reassured. Rose winced and felt her rib dig even deeper into her side. She knew that it was only a matter of time until the bone pierced her lung

"I-I love you." She confesses as a tear rolled down her face. She looked into Henry's kind, red eyes. His eyes soothed her, and she wanted to get lost in them forever.

"I love you, too." Henry reciprocated. They both knew that she was going to die. Rose felt a sharp pain in her side; this time, greater than all the other piercings. She couldn't breathe; she felt like she was drowning, but in her own blood. She rolled her head back onto his lap. Blood was coming out of her mouth and was streaming down the side of her face.

He grabbed her hand, knowing that she'll be gone soon. She leaned over and coughed up more blood. Rose stared into his kind, beautiful, red eyes again; it calmed her down. She moved her hand to his face and gently brushed it before her eyes closed. Her hand fell and hit the ground; her body went limp.

"Rose, ROSE! Please don't leave me, don't leave me!" He wailed. He rested his forehead on hers. After a few seconds, he remembered something and raised his head. *She said that if anything were to happen to her, I could change her. But should I really change her? I don't want her to live as a monster.*

He sat there for a second, thinking. He made the decision. He bit into his wrist, sucking his own blood. He leaned down his head to her side. He injected his blood into her neck.

Rider had come to consciousness and opened his eyes. He was somewhat confused, but he had seen Henry biting his wrist and her neck just before he blacked out again.

Henry felt a hand fall on his shoulder. He looked up – it was his mom. "Honey, I know that this is hard for you, but the police are coming. You need to stop crying so they won't suspect you." He simply nodded his head.

***

The police arrived, and Rider was still knocked out. They handcuffed his hands behind his back and carried him out of the house. The same police officers that had come to Henry's house earlier walked up to Henry.

"We are going to ask you a few questions," the brute stated as the small officer got out his notepad. "First off, how did he get in?"

"I don't know how he got in." Henry shrugged.

"Why is your pet on your lap?" Henry looked down to see Rose's pale body, bruised neck, and bloody head.

"She was a good pet and didn't disobey me. She didn't fight when I drank from her, and she had AB Negative blood. Those are hard things to have in a pet, so I tried to save her." Both the policemen nodded. After a few more questions, all the policemen left. A final tear fell out of his eye.

"Honey, I know that you loved her but... she's gone," Lisa said sadly. She had only known Rose for a concise time, but she had grown a liking to her, and the thought of her son being miserable again was saddening.

"No, there's still a chance that she can come back." Henry looked up at Lisa.

"What do you mean? Henry, did you give her your blood?" He simply nodded his head. "Henry, you know that it doesn't always work."

"I know, mom. But I *have* to try everything before I fully let her go." He was upset and sad.

Lisa left the room. Henry was still on the ground with Rose, waiting for her to wake up... if she can.

Chapter 19

~two days later~

Henry's head rested on Rose's forehead. His eyes and cheeks were stained with dry tears; he had run out of tears to shed. The blood on Rose's head and around her had dried, becoming sticky; his hand still grasped onto her pale, limp hand.

"Honey?" He heard his mom say. He slowly looked up. "It's been two days... I don't think that she's coming back."

"No, mom. If she wakes up, she's going to be in pain and scared. I don't want her to be alone." His mom simply nodded her head.

"At least eat something, you know."

"I'm not hungry." Henry shook his head.

I can't force him to eat, she thought to herself as she slowly walked away. It saddened her to see her son so sad and miserable. Henry laid his forehead back down on Rose's forehead.

Please come back to me Rose, come back. Please don't leave me.

Henry's back was starting to get sore. He raised his head and popped his back. Rose's hand seemed to shift just a bit. Henry looked down, but she wasn't moving. *I must be losing my mind,* Henry thought as he rubbed his eyes with his hand.

All of a sudden, Rose breathed in deeply and started to cough up all the blood that had been building up in her lungs. She fell off his lap and coughed more blood. Her rib and hipbone popped back into place. She screamed in agony and curled up on the ground, holding her side and hip. She looked at the floor and the walls. She sat up and looked around worriedly, and her eyes landed on Henry. He was in too much of a shock to do anything.

"Henry?!" Rose was shaking in fear. Henry nodded his head and hugged her gently.

"It's me, I'm here," he said breathlessly. Rose hugged him back tightly. They connected their lips for a moment and released from each other's arms.

"How...?" Rose asked.

"I changed you," Henry said.

"Is that why I healed when I woke up?" Henry nodded his head and a tear fell down her cheek. "I thought I wouldn't get to see you again."

"It's ok, I'm here. I'm here." Henry was on the verge of tears. She cried harder on his shoulder, from happiness.

Lisa walked down the stairs and froze as she saw Rose awake, hugging Henry. "Rose?" Lisa asked in disbelief. Rose looked up from Henry's shoulder and nodded. Lisa put her hands over her mouth and quickly rushed down to hug Rose and Henry.

After a very long time, Lisa released both of them. She wiped the tears from her face with the back of her hand. Both Henry's and Rose's stomachs growled. "You two must be starving." They both nodded. "I'll go and make dinner." She hugged them both one more time before she stood up and walked to the kitchen. Henry and Rose hadn't eaten in two days, and they realized how hungry they were.

"I'm going to change clothes," Rose said as she looked at her blood covered clothes. The smell of the blood gave her a weird satisfaction that made her somewhat sick. Henry looked down at his too. They were covered in blood as well. Both of them stood up as both of their legs popped from lack of movement. They both walked to their own rooms to shower.

Henry finished showering first and changed into a black muscle t-shirt and grey sweatpants. He walked out of his room and went to the kitchen. His hair was still wet, making his dark brown hair look almost black.

He leaned against the counter, placing his mid back on the edge. Lisa walked up to Henry and cupped his face with both her hands. "You look better already." She smiled, glad that her son was happy and up again.

***

Rose rubbed the towel over her face as she dried it off. She looked at herself in the mirror. She almost looked like a ghost, she was paler than usual and looked different altogether. She opened her mouth and stared at her small fangs. She took her finger and rubbed the tip of them – they were sharp. She wanted to see what her fangs looked like fully extended. She closed her eyes and thought only of blood. After a few moments, she felt them descend. When she opened her eyes, she was met with the creature that had tortured her for years, killed her family, and had shown her kindness – a vampire.

She closed her eyes and felt her fangs retract. When she opened her eyes again, she stroked the spot where her rib had been broken. This all felt weird to her. *I should be dead, and yet here I am, a vampire.* She smelled something amazing – dinner. She quickly put on her clothes and headed downstairs.

Rose walked into the kitchen as Lisa started to set the food, plates, cups, and silverware on the table. "Question: how come my hip and ribcage healed but the scars from the whip on my back didn't?" Rose asked as she walked into the kitchen,

"My best guess is that after a certain amount of time after you have been injured, you don't heal. I don't know, rarely anyone is changed," Henry said. Rose and Henry walked to the table and sat down, joining Lisa for dinner. The food made them both feel better and full.

After they finished eating, Lisa put the dishes in the dishwasher. Henry grabbed Rose and pulled her into his embrace. "You want to watch a movie?" Henry asked as he gave her puppy eyes. *I really want to watch a movie.*

"Sounds good," Rose agreed. Henry moved his right hand up in the air and brought it down, stopping as his arm was fully bent. Rose rolled her eyes. Henry picked Rose up bridal style. She was so startled that she squealed and clung to his t-shirt. Henry laughed. He sat down on the couch and moved Rose to the side and turned the TV on.

Henry wrapped his arm around Rose, and she snuggled closer to him. "I'm going to go to bed," Lisa said as she walked upstairs.

"Goodnight." Henry and Rose said at the same time.

~2 *hours later*~

Rose's eyes had been closed for some time now, but she couldn't sleep. "Henry?"

"Yeah?" Henry glanced down at her.

"How come I can't fall asleep?"

"Vampires don't sleep, but if you get into a deep thought, then you are in the state where you are awake, but you feel asleep. Does that make any sense?" Rose nodded her head, and they continued to rest on the couch.

Rose twitched a little and sat up. She looked around worriedly, breathing heavily. "What's wrong?" Henry asked, concerned.

"It's nothing. I just got *too* deep into my thoughts." She tried to calm down by relaxing her muscles.

"Rider?" Henry already knew the answer. Rose nodded her head in agreement. "Come here." Henry wrapped his arm around her. She snuggled closer to him and put her head in the crook of his neck. He laid his head on top of hers. "You're safe now, you're safe," Henry reassured. Rose curled her legs up on his lap, and she wrapped her arms around his neck.

She closed her eyes and started to rest, as did Henry.

Chapter 20

Rose slowly opened her eyes and looked around. "Good morning," Henry greeted.

"Morning," she said sleepily, and she stretched.

"My mom left already, so she told me to tell you goodbye."

"She left." She was upset. Henry laughed. "Don't laugh at me. Your mom was nice and an *amazing* cook."

"Hey, I'm a pretty good cook." Henry placed his hand over his chest, pretending to be hurt.

"Yeah, you are a good cook, but you can *never* beat your mother."

"I'm deeply hurt. You have hurt me." He picked Rose up and walked to the kitchen.

Wow, he's upset about that? She rolled her eyes.

I heard that! Henry thought, there was a pause. "What do want to eat? Or do you want me to call my mom to come back?"

"No, don't call your mom. If you're mad at me then why are you carrying me?"

"Because I couldn't bear to leave you again," He kissed her forehead. "But I sadly have to cook," he said as he placed her on the counter. He placed a kiss on her forehead again. It reminded him of when he laid his forehead on hers during her final moments. He turned around; the memory too much for him. He walked to a cabinet and started to look for stuff.

Rose could tell that something was bothering Henry, so she went to go stand beside him. Within a second, she was next to him. She ran into Henry and started to fall. He caught her before she fell, wrapping an arm around her waist and upper back. One of her legs was in the air. Her hands grasped onto the sleeves of his t-shirt. Henry, however, held her up with no problem. "What had just happened?" Rose asked.

"That was called super speed," Henry said as he helped Rose stand up.

"How do I control it?"

"You use the super speed whenever you want to get somewhere really fast. It's like regular running – just a lot faster." Rose nodded her head.

That was helpful, Rose thought sarcastically.

"What do you want to eat?" Henry asked as he opened the cabinets again.

Rose thought for a second. "I want... a sandwich."

"Ok." Henry grabbed some bread, turkey, ham, cheese, and various other toppings.

They finished eating. "So was the sandwich good?" Henry asked as he rose an eyebrow.

"You're still on this?" Rose looked at him and rose an eyebrow too.

"Yes, I am. Was it good?" Henry crossed his arms. Rose walked up to him.

"Yes, the food was good. I enjoyed it. Happy?" Rose threw her arms into the air.

"Yes, yes I am. Thank you. I feel better," Henry said as he nodded his head proudly while Rose laughed at him. There was a short moment of silence.

"Can you help me control my super speed?" Rose asked.

"Yeah." He agreed as he quickly ran to the other end of the room. "Run to me." He motioned with his hand for her to come to him. She thought hard about moving fast toward Henry.

Within a second, she ran into him. He caught her, wrapping his arms around her. "How do I stop?" Rose asked as Henry stood her up.

"You just... stop. It's like when you regularly run, and you stop. It's simple." Henry rushed to the other side of the room. "Try again." She nodded her head and tried again. She ran to Henry and was able to stop an inch in front of him. He rushed to the other side of the room. "Try it again to make sure it wasn't a mistake." She sighed and ran again, stopping in front of him.

"I don't think that that was a mistake," she said jokingly, but also with a hint of sass in her voice. Henry faintly smiled. It was one of the first times he had heard talk like that. He missed just the sound of her voice.

"Ok, ok, ok." He held his hands up in defense. She laughed. "No other powers you want to work on?"

"I want to see what the sun does to me."

"What? Why?" Henry was confused.

"I want to see how much damage the sun does to me." She simply shrugged.

"It will hurt you, and I don't want you to get hurt." He grabbed her arms, stopping her, and pulled her into his chest. "Please only your hand." He begged. He couldn't bear to watch her go through more pain.

"Ok," she said. Henry sighed in relief as he let go of her arms.

They walked outside, and Rose placed her hand into the sunlight. The sun turned her skin red at first, then started to make her skin boil. She watched as her skin blistered. She quickly pulled her hand out of the light. "That's enough for today." Henry put his arm around her.

"I told you that it was going to hurt." Henry said in 'I told you so' voice.

"How do I know what my special power is?" She glanced at Henry.

"It takes a while for your power to come, but eventually it will show up." She nodded her head.

They made their way to the couch and sat down. Rose noticed that the blister on her skin healed completely. Henry wrapped his arm around her, and she snuggled closer to him. "I'm glad you are ok," Henry said as he rubbed Rose's cheek with his thumb.

"Thanks." She smiled. She couldn't tell if he was talking about her hand or what had happened the other day.

They both continued to watch TV and rest.

~jail~

Rider sat in the interrogation room waiting for a cop. He tapped his fingers on the table impatiently. He sighed and a cop finally walked in. The cop sat down across him and began recording the interrogation with a video camera. "Why did you break in and kill Lord Henry's pet?"

"I snuck in and I killed her because my brother loved her." Rider answered his question blandly, giving no specific details.

"Lord Rider, tell us the truth," the cop demanded, a small hint of annoyance in his voice.

"I am!" He slammed his hand on the table. He breathed in deeply, calming himself down.

"Lord Rider, we already talked to your brother after the accident. The pet had bruises and had been drunken from by him. It was clear that he didn't like her."

"The bruises are from *me*. I was its old master. I abused it. He probably drunk from it because he needed blood and I guarantee that it was ok with that. I'm telling you that he loves it. After I killed it, I saw that he bit it, changing it, before I blacked out again!" Rider practically yelled. His eyes changed to a deeper red.

The cop slightly raised an eyebrow at the sudden change in Rider's tone. He went from relatively calm and collective to irrational and angry with little to no warning. He was like a different person.

The cop sighed. "Would you be willing to take a polygraph test?"

"Yes, I would," Rider said, calming down a bit. He shook his head slightly, and his eyes went back to its normal color.

After the test, the cops examined the results. "He's telling the truth." The cop said as he looked at the paper.

"Finally. Now, will you go check it out?" Rider asked. He was now back to his calm and collective state.

"Yes, we will, but this doesn't help your sentence. You still have three weeks to serve." Rider sighed out of annoyance as he leaned back in his chair. He looked at the cop and got even more annoyed as he read his emotion. The cop was annoyed and somewhat envious of Rider at the fact that he was a Lord and was practically bossing him around.

The cops walked out of the room and called the Special Units Force – they deal with humans that have been turned, vampires that like humans or the other way around. The Special Units Force hopped in their cars and started to head over to Henry's house.

Chapter 21

Henry and Rose cuddled on the couch, Henry's arm was around her. Her head was resting on his shoulder, and they were holding hands. They were watching a medical show on how vampires perform heart surgery. Though neither of them was really paying close attention to it; they were more interested in the presence of each other.

The Special Units Force had been outside their house, watching them for a while. They first gathered enough information before taking action. They had found her Pet Shop records and had made sure the description matched her perfectly. They decided to make their move. They could hardly remember the last time they got a call.

The door opened; Rose and Henry both sat up, startled. The Special Units Force rushed in, there were only about six of them. Henry pushed Rose behind him.

In a split second, three men ran toward Henry: two grabbed his arms, and the other one forced him on his knees. It happened so fast that Henry didn't have time to react. Another man grabbed Rose, holding her arms in place. He lifted her off the ground. He walked over with Rose in his arms a few feet in front of Henry. She struggled in his grasp, but to no avail.

A man walked up to Rose and grabbed her face. He had thinning black hair, few wrinkles on his face, and violent red eyes that looked like they held many secrets and pain. Rose couldn't tell if the pain was his own or from other people. He looked at her dull red eyes, a thin smile spread across his face.

"So it's true you turned a human into a vampire." He said to himself. He was somewhat mystified and disgusted at the fact that something as pathetic as a human turned vampire could even look similar to him. He hated humans. He thought they were just ruthless creatures that were willing to hurt anything or anyones to get what they wanted. Without realizing it, his hand that was on her face seemed to heat up. Smoke rose from her face before he broke through the skin. She winced in pain before she slightly screamed.

"Don't touch her!" Henry yelled. He struggled from the men's grasp, managing to get one foot on the ground. The men that were holding him forced him down, pulling his arms back and pushing his shoulders downward. The man let go of Rose's face, and her skin slowly started to heal. The man walked over to Henry and crouched down on one knee. He was now at Henry's level, their faces were only inches apart.

"You must be the one that changed her," the man said calmly. Henry didn't say anything but only stared in the man's eyes. "Well, I'm thanking you for that."

"What?" Henry's eyebrows furrowed in confusion.

"It's very rare to have a human being turned into a vampire, so we don't know if they heal like us, have the mental capability that we have, or anything like that. We are simply going to... test and experiment on her." His voice sounded a bit remorseful, but at the same time almost vengeful.

"You can't do this. You're the police," Henry said as he struggled in the men's grasp. They didn't budge. The man slightly laughed.

"You see, we aren't the police. We are the Special Units Force. We are our own organization; we don't take orders from the police, so we can do whatever we want. We can also tell the police what to do."

The man made his way back to Rose, whose face had completely healed. He grabbed her chin, looking at her face. "So you do heal," he said more to himself than to her. "I think it's time that we go. The sooner we get to testing, the better."

He went back to face Henry but remained standing. He pulled out his baton. "I am sorry, but you should've known that something like this would happen." His voice was filled with sorrow. However, within a second, he started hitting Henry with the baton repeatedly.

"HENRY!" Rose screamed as tears streamed down her face. She struggled in the man's grasp, kicking him frantically. The man, however, didn't budge. She cried harder as images of the Shopkeeper holding her and making her watch her family being murdered appeared in her mind. Now, the same thing was happening.

The man pulled his arm back and hit Henry in the head again. Henry went limp in the men's grips. His body leaned forward, only being held up by the men. They let go of his arms, dropping him on the ground. A pool of blood encircled his head. Rose looked at his battered face. He had cuts all over his face, and his nose looked broken. The area around his eyes was swollen. He had bruises all over his face.

Tears streamed down her face, as he looked at Henry. The man closed his baton and put it back in his holster. He closed his eyes and slightly paused, almost like he didn't want to hurt him. He walked back over to Rose. "I can see that both of you liked each other... that was a big mistake." He motioned his finger and wrist in a circular motion and walked out of the door.

They dragged her out of the house like the way she was dragged after her parents were killed. But this time, she was being taken away from Henry who rested in a pool of his own blood. She was screaming and struggling, trying to get out of their grasp.

They all put on their sunglasses and pulled their clothes closer to them, except for Rose. The sun burned her skin. She winced in pain as she moved her head away from the sun. By the time they reached the van, her skin was red, burned, and blistered.

They threw her in the van, and she slid across the metal floor, wincing. Two men quickly grabbed her arms and held her in place on the floor of the van. Their touch hurt her blistered skin. The man who seemed to be the Leader reached into a drawer and grabbed a needle and a liquid that was in a glass container. He stuck the needle through the lid and filled the syringe halfway.

Rose struggled in the men's grasp, but it didn't do any good. The Leader leaned down, and she furiously kicked in his direction. He grabbed her legs in one motion with one arm. He leaned down and stuck the needle in her arm. She winced in pain. Her vision got blurry, and a black haze surrounded the edge of her eyesight. The last thing she saw was the Leader looking at her, his eyes fillied with sorrow, before she passed out.

***

Rose's eyes opened slowly. Everything was blurry. She closed her eyes and opened them again, the blurry haze was slowly gone. The rest of her body felt heavy, like lead.

"Good, you're finally awake." She heard the Leader say in a somewhat bored voice. She turned her head to the right and saw him sitting in a chair. He had a transparent plastic apron on him and he seemed to be playing a game on his phone.

She tried to move away from him, but something was holding her in place. She looked at her hands and feet and saw that they were shackled to a metal table. She glanced to her left and saw a small metal tray next to her.

Her eyes widened as she saw knives, needles, and other devices on the tray. She looked to her right and saw the exact same thing on a different tray. She struggled even harder. The Leader sighed as he placed his phone in his pocket, under his apron.

"You can try all you want, but you'll never break those restraints," he said as he stood up and walked to the metal tray on the right. "I would know best," he mumbled to himself. Rose stared up at the ceiling and started to think about Henry and wondered if he was ok. Somehow, the Leader could tell what she was thinking about. "He won't be awake anytime soon. Even though he can heal fast, the number of hits he received will take a while to treat. He's still laying on the floor in a pool of his own blood."

He picked up a knife that was about four inches long. He put his other hand on the blade and started to it heat up. Once the metal began to turn bright orange, he pulled his hand away.

He laid it on her arm. She winced in pain as the knife pierced through her skin. She clenched her fists. He walked to the left side of the table. There was a window that had a thick, black curtain over it. He put on his sunglasses and moved to the side of the window. His hand clasped around the curtain.

Without saying anything, he opened the curtains. The sunlight fell on Rose, burning her skin. She closed her eyes and turned her face away. The Leader watched as the sun burned her skin. He closed the curtain back as he picked up a pen and a paper, writing down notes and details about the experiment. He sighed, knowing he would have to repeat this process multiple times.

Chapter 22

The Leader threw down the knife on the small metal tray as its sound hitting the surface resonated throughout the room.

"I think it's time that we take a break," he said as he took off his plastic apron that was now covered in blood. He raised it over his head and hung it on a coat hook. He walked toward a wall with a small key hook and grabbed the keys. He unlocked Rose's cuffs before he placed the keys back on the small hook again. He walked through the clear shredded plastic that separated her from the door and walked out of the room, leaving Rose by herself.

She breathed heavily and relaxed once she saw that he had left. Her hands unclenched, revealing scratches where her fingernails had dug into her palm. She had cuts and stab wounds all over her body. A huge cut was on her stomach. It was about two inches long and about a centimeter deep.

Her muscles were sore and stiff from lack of movement and the tight shackles. Her broken fingers hurt as she *slowly* felt them healing, the bones grinding together as they moved back into place. She looked down at her hand and saw the small cuts heal, the skin formed together again. As she looked at her broken finger, her eyebrows furrowed in confusion. Whenever the Leader broke her fingers, he always closed his eyes and turned his head away from her. She could feel his fingers shake and hear him breathe heavily. It was almost like he didn't want to hurt her.

She felt blood stream out of her mouth and nose, falling down on the side of her face. Rose looked to her side and saw the knife laying on a tray. She leaned a bit to to the side and tried to reach for it, her hand almost touching the handle. Right as her fingers touched the knife, she fell on the floor. She moaned in pain as she curled up into a small ball. Tears streamed down her face at the fact that she was so close.

She knew that she wouldn't be able to stand or crawl and the tray was just at the right position to where she couldn't kick it over. She closed her eyes and tried to rest, knowing that the pain was going to keep her awake. She was surprised that she wasn't used to the pain at this point; it was all she had known for years.

After a period of time, the Leader was back, and she started to breathe heavier as she saw him walk in the room. He took the apron off of the hook and put it back on, tying the straps around him. He walked toward her and stood next to her. He looked down at her curled up body. He sighed and picked her up, she slightly whimpered in pain. He placed her on the table before he shackled her wrists and ankles again.

He took the records, flipping almost halfway into the book. The other pages were filled with notes. He wrote: *Fingers have yet to heal fully*. He grabbed a ruler and put it on the cut on her stomach. She winced as he slightly pressed it down. He retracted the ruler and picked up the records again. *Over an hour and the cut has healed one inch.*

He scribbled down more notes as another one of her cuts healed. He paused halfway through scribbling down notes and checked if there was a scar on her leg. There was, but it also seemed to be slowly healing.

Cuts seem to heal along with the scar, but at different times, not at once.

He paused writing as he thought for a second. "What did you honestly think was going to happen? A human in love with a vampire and the vampire turns her into to one. You're a human – a *pet*. You're nothing more than that. You were stupid to think that you could be anything more," he said in a calm voice. Tears clouded her eyes. "You're even more pathetic than a human... Now, if you don't mind, I would like to try a few mental tests on you to see how different your will is from us."

He took a syringe and put the needle into a liquid, filling it halfway. He put the needle in her arm and injected the fluid. She got light headed, but it quickly subsided. She looked at him, but she saw someone else and screamed.

"Th-this isn't real." She was shaking in fear and in denial. She shut her eyes to block the vision.

"Oh yes, it is. It's *all* real. Look at me." She slowly opened her eyes and looked at him. "See? It's *all* real, everything and there's no changing that. Vampires can never love something like you."

Tears continued to stream down her face. He looked at her hand noticed something, a ring.

He lifted up her finger, and she winced in pain as it was one of the fingers that was broken. He took off the ring, which was now covered in blood and walked out of the room to wash it off. Leaving her in pain, one of her fingers popped back into place. She screamed and then the pain suddenly subsided. She focused on the few fingers that weren't broken to try and take her mind away from all the other pain.

He walked back in the room with the ring that Henry had given her for her birthday, it was clean. "Did anything happen while I was away?"

"M-my finger healed," she mumbled.

"Which one?"

"Left hand, pointer finger." She raised it a little.

He picked up the pen and paper and scribbled down notes, similar to the ones he had previously written. He looked at the ring. "Does this mean a lot to you?"

"Yes…," she said as she remembered that day.

He looked at the ring. "I take it that a vampire gave this to you?" She nodded her head. He tossed the ring in the pool of blood on the other side of the plastic tarp on the floor. He pinched the bridge of his nose. "You're a pet, and you shouldn't be allowed to have anything at all." He said more to himself than to her, there was a pause. "I have a few more experiments I want to try for today."

"Pl-please don't." She begged weakly. He sighed.

"I have to test these things on you several times to make sure that you heal at the same rate. We've only done everything twice. We need to test it multiple times…" He trailed off. Rose watched, as an emotion washed over his eyes that looked like pain. He closed his eyes for a second before he walked out of the room, leaving Rose alone.

~2 days later~

Henry still laid unconscious on the floor in a pool of his own blood. He slowly opened his eyes. A black haze surrounded his eyesight, and everything was blurry. A few seconds went by before his nose popped back into place. He sat up as he screamed. He held his nose with both hands. The blurry haze was now gone.

Shock set in all the sudden. *Where's Rose? They took her, they are going to hurt her.* He thought frantically as he quickly stood up and ran to the garage. He hopped in his white Porsche, revved the engine, and drove off. He was going to get Rose back. He didn't know how but he was going to get her back.

Chapter 23

Henry arrived at the police station. He knew that the Special Units Force operated on their own. He suspected they didn't tell the police anything. He walked in, and the police officer looked up a bit startled.

"Lord Henry, are you ok?" the man asked as he stood up from his desk. Many other people in the waiting room looked at Henry. Henry looked down at his shirt and saw his blood from being knocked out with the baton.

So only the Special Units Force must know what I did, Henry thought thankfully that his prediction was right. "Ah, yes, I am. I just drank out of my pet and forgot to change shirts." He lied smoothly as the man just nodded. "You wouldn't happen to know where they keep humans that have turned into vampires?" Henry asked as he leaned against the counter.

"No sir." *Yes,* the man thought. Henry smiled.

Why do people always think the truth when they lie? He thought to himself gratefully. In a split second, his hands were next to the man's head. He concentrated hard.

The man looked confused for a second, but before he could do anything, he closed his eyes and opened them, staring at

Henry blankly. Henry smiled. "You're going to take me to where they are," Henry demanded. The man nodded and walked out of the building. Henry followed, and the other people in the waiting room didn't bother looking as Henry led the police officer out of the station.

"In that car." Henry pointed to his car. The man sat in the driver's seat while Henry took the passenger's seat. He slumped back into the position; he was exhausted. He rarely controlled people because he needed to get close to them. It almost drained all of his energy, and it took a long time for him to regain all of his strength, days even. He leaned his head onto the headrest as he thought about trying to control his father when he was younger; to try and get him stop controlling Rider but to no avail. He hated controlling people; it made him feel like his dad. Henry closed his eyes as he rested.

They arrived at a place that seemed to be a warehouse. The metal on the outside was old and rusted. Clearly, they were rarely needed. Rose was probably the first one they had had in centuries. Henry got out of the car, and so did the man.

"I want you to walk back to the police station and forget that this happened." The man nodded and started to walk. Thankfully, after they had done the last thing that Henry told them to do, they forgot everything that had happened.

Henry looked through the glass on the door and saw three people standing there. He couldn't fight them all. He was too weak, and he couldn't control them. He knew he would pass out.

He walked to the side of the building and found a window. He jumped up and grabbed the edge of the window. His feet were a few feet off the ground. He looked through it; nobody was there. He opened the window with his left hand; his right hand barely holding his weight. He climbed through it and landed on the cold, hard concrete, making an echo sound.

He looked around nervously to see if anyone heard it. There were no signs of anybody coming, so he continued. He sniffed the air for the scent of Rose's blood. He found a very faint, sweet scent and he followed it.

After walking through several corridors and hallways, he was outside the door. The scent was really strong. He walked up to the door and peered through the glass. There was a plastic tarp blocking his view.

He heard Rose scream in pain. He laid his hand on the handle and almost walked in, but he remembered that he was too weak to fight. He didn't know how many people were in there and he was Rose's only chance at escaping. He couldn't afford to get caught too.

It took everything in him not to barge in there. Instead, he had to stand outside of the door and listen to her being hurt.

He had been standing outside the door for what seemed like an eternity. He had to sit down because he was too weak to stand, tears surrounded his eyes from having to listen to Rose be in pain for so long. His hands were over his face, and he brought his knees up.

He needed to be as strong as he could for Rose. All the sudden, the screaming ceased. He heard the sound of metal hitting a surface and a feet walking in his direction. He looked around, but there was no place to hide. He quickly jumped up onto the corner of two walls; each of his feet on every corner as well as his hands.

The door opened, and the Leader walked out. He stopped as he sighed and pinched the bridge of his nose. He grabbed a set of dog tags that hung around his neck before walked down the hallway. Thankfully, the scent of Rose's blood blocked out Henry's scent. Once Henry was sure that the Leader was gone, he jumped down from the corner of the ceiling.

He fell on the ground, landing on his feet, but he was barely able to support himself. He opened the door and saw something sparkling on the floor. He bent down to pick it up and realized that it was the ring he had gotten Rose for her birthday. He put the ring in his jeans and walked through the plastic tarp.

On a metal table lay Rose. Next to her were metal trays with knives, shots, and other equipment covered in blood. The curtain was pulled back allowing the sun to fall on her, burning her skin. Her head was turned away from the light. Henry could tell that the sun wasn't burning her like it had the first day.

Henry rushed over to Rose and tried to find any signs of life. He heard her breathing very faintly. He tried to pry apart her restraints, but they wouldn't budge; he was too weak. He looked around the room and saw a video camera. He removed the memory card and put it in his pocket. *Hopefully, nobody was watching*, he thought to himself.

He looked on the metal tray and saw all the notes that the leader had been writing down. He also put them in his jacket pocket. He looked over at the wall and saw the keys. He picked them up and unlocked the cuffs on Rose.

Henry carefully carried her, aware of the cut on her stomach. He couldn't go out the way he came. The window was too high for him to climb up with her and he might also get caught.

He put his jacket over her, protecting her from the sun. He opened the window and deliberately climbed through it. He made his way back to the car, laid her down in the passenger's seat, and buckled her in.

He hopped in the driver's seat and drove off toward his cabin. He looked at Rose. Her face was still burnt but healing. His jacket had fallen in her lap. Blood dripped from her face and everywhere else that she had been cut.

Hopefully she'll heal and wake up... I swear if I see any of them again I'm going to kill them. He thought to himself as he drove towards his cabin, somewhere that was hopefully safe.

Chapter 24

Rose's finger popped back in place, making a cracking noise. Henry's hands tightened around the steering wheel. It made Henry sick to even think that they could lay a finger on her, let alone break her bones. He looked down and saw that only one of her fingers was broken. A few of her cuts had not healed yet, especially the giant gash on her stomach. After what seemed like an eternity, they finally arrived at the cabin.

The cabin was like a miniature mansion, just in cabin form. The outside was wood – a light oak colored wood. The house was two-story high; windows were around the house, more than his other house. The windows took up most of the house, more so than the walls did. The roof was a dark grey metal, the sun shining on it.

He hopped out of the car and walked to Rose's side. He placed the coat over Rose to protect her from the sun. He carefully scooped her into his arms and carried her inside, carefully laying her on the couch. He stood straight up, breathing heavily, still exhausted from controlling the policeman.

He sat down and carefully laid her head on his lap. He looked around the house, it had been awhile since he had been at the cabin. The stairs were wooden and weren't curved like the last house. The stairs went straight up; the balusters were pieces of wood, not cut straight but looked natural, like a branch. The bedrooms were also upstairs – there were only four bedrooms. The kitchen was to the left, it was more of an enclosed kitchen. The doorway was the length of two regular-sized doors. This house was smaller and had fewer rooms, but it was still big.

He gently caressed her cheek with his hand. "I'm so sorry that this happened to you." Sadness was edged in his voice as he looked at her injured body. "I would have gladly taken your place in a blink of an eye." He closed his eyes, leaned back his head and started to relax, but not rest.

He felt her twitch a little and he looked down. She quivered again as she lightly whimpered. She slowly opened her eyes and looked around the unfamiliar house. *Wh-where am I?* She thought as her eyes landed on Henry.

Fear overcame her, and she sat up quickly, making the cut on her stomach open up again. She backed off the couch and into the wall.

"What's wrong?" Henry asked concerned as he slowly stood up and walked to her.

"Yo-you're not real, th-this isn't real," she stuttered as she tried backing further into the wall, scared.

"What are you talking about?" Henry furrowed his eyebrows.

"This is all just an illusion. You're not really you." She placed her hands on both sides of her head and started to rock back and forth. She was trying to break the illusion, convincing herself it wasn't real. Henry gently grabbed her arms, careful not to hurt her broken fingers, and she struggled in his grasp.

"I'm real. This is all real, you're safe," he said, trying to calm her down. She shook her head.

"No, this can't be real." She struggled even more. Even though Henry was weak, he could still hold Rose without much trouble.

"You were once my brother's pet. His name was Rider and he abused you. I bought you next. Your birthday is April thirteenth. I gave you a ring." He reached into his pocket and grabbed the ring. "This ring. My brother killed you, so I changed you into a vampire. We are together. You think that my mom's cooking is better than mine," he said as he rehashed her life and things that only the two of them would know.

She stopped struggling. "Henry?" She looked into his kind, red eyes. He nodded his head and she hugged him. "The-they drugged me, so whenever they hurt me, I-I saw..." she trailed off as tears escaped her eyes.

"Whenever they hurt you, you saw *me* hurting you," he said, finishing her sentence. Pain was edged into his voice. *They made her see me hurting and torturing her,* Henry thought. It made him sad and angry.

She nodded her head in sadness. "It was a mental test..." Another tear fell down her face as she went limp in his arms, passing out. Henry carried her back to the couch. He breathed heavier, exhausted.

He laid her down gently. As he did so, he saw more blood than before on her stomach. He looked at the cut on her stomach and saw that it had expanded a few centimeters. He had a first aid kit, but he couldn't sew it up, she would heal with the stitches still in her.

He put the ring back on her finger and moved the jacket under her head for a pillow. He felt something in his pocket; he reached into it and got the notes and video camera footage. He kissed Rose's head as he got up and walked to his office. He didn't like leaving Rose by herself, but he *had* to know what they had done to her.

He sat down in front of his desk; he opened a drawer and turned on his computer. He started to download the video footage onto his computer. While he was waiting, he opened the notes and started to read them. *Takes two hours for her broken nose to heal fully. Fingers have yet to heal fully... Over an hour, the cut has healed one inch... Cuts seem to heal along with the scar, but at different times, not at once...* The notes were pages and pages of how she healed, what the Leader had done to her, and how many times he had tested it. Henry threw the papers against the wall and looked at his computer to see that the footage had fully downloaded. He then played it.

The Leader picked up a syringe and put the needle into a liquid, filling it halfway. He put the needle in her arm and injected the fluid. She got light headed but it quickly subsided. She looked at him, but she saw someone else and screamed.

"Th-this isn't real." She was shaking in fear and in denial. She shut her eyes to block the vision.

"Oh yes, it is. It's all real. Look at me." She slowly opened her eyes and looked at him. "See? It's all real, everything and there's no changing that. Vampires can never love something like you."

Henry slammed his computer. He couldn't bare to watch anymore; it was too painful for him. *That must be when they drugged her to make her see me,* he thought to himself as he walked out of his office and went back to the couch. Blood continued to come out from the cut on Rose's stomach – she was pale. *She needs blood,* he thought for a moment, a sudden idea hit him.

He walked to the closet and grabbed the first aid kit. He opened it and found the IV. He walked back over to the couch, he put the IV into his arm and the other side into Rose's. He lifted his arm, with the IV in it, on top of the couch to get the blood moving faster to her arm. He watched as his blood came from his arm to hers; he laid her head on his lap and held her hand.

Henry knew that he was going to be *very* weak from losing blood, but Rose was in danger, and she didn't heal as fast as he could. He *had* to help her recover.

A few minutes had gone by, he heard a noise in the kitchen. He looked behind him but didn't see anything. He took out his IV and weakly stood up, rubbing the spot where the IV had been. He carefully walked to the kitchen. The first thing he did was grab a knife to protect himself, as he was too weak to fight off people with just his hands.

He heard the noise come from the pantry. He opened the door and saw a girl on the ground. She was frantically grabbing food, shoving it into a bag. She looked up at him, startled, and backed into the corner.

"I-I'm sorry. I didn't know that somebody lived here. Pl-please let me go, don't send me to the pet shop." The girl was frightened and continued to push her back into the wall.

She had dirty blonde hair that was fairly long; it went down a little past her shoulder blades. Her hair was badly tangled, but she had somehow gotten her hair into a braid. She had hazel eyes, a mixture of emerald green and dark brown. Henry recognized her from one of Rose's memories. "Are... are you Rose's sister?"

Chapter 25

She stayed silent as she scooted further into the corner. Henry slowly bent down and placed the knife on the ground. "I'm not going to hurt you," he said as he stood up and stepped back from the knife. "Are you Rose's sister?" He asked again.

"What...how-" she was cut off when Henry heard someone behind him. He quickly turned around and grabbed the person's arms. The person was a boy who was trying to stab Henry in the chest. Henry could have easily shoved him off if he wasn't as weak as he was now. Henry was pushed against the wall as he continued to try and push the boy off of him, his arms started to shake. "Joey, stop!" Rose's sister said as she grabbed Joey's arm.

"What, why?! He's a leech!" Joey pointed to Henry with his knife. Henry was leaning his hands on his legs, breathing heavily.

"He knows Rose," Lilly said as she got in between them, making sure that Joey didn't try to attack Henry again. Joey backed up and put his knife in his holster.

Henry looked at Joey – he had dirty blond hair that was shaggy, barely going past his ears. He had vibrant light blue eyes and looked around the age of thirteen, just like Rose's sister. "Lilly, how do we know if he's telling the truth? He's a vampire; they have *humans* for *pets!*" Joey yelled.

"He didn't want to hurt me. Look." She pointed to the knife that Henry had placed on the floor.

"I still don't trust him," Joey said as he looked at Henry. He was now standing up straight.

"I'm willing to take that chance. My sister was taken from me years ago. If he knows her, then I'm willing to somewhat trust him," she said as tears started to appear in her eyes, remembering the day that Rose was taken. She could still hear Rose's pleas and screams in her head. Joey sighed, and Lilly turned to Henry. "How do you know my sister? If it even is her...describe her," she said cautiously.

"She has brown hair and emerald green eyes, her birthday is April thirteenth, and she is now nineteen," Henry said as he listed it off on his fingers.

"How do you know my sister?" Lilly asked again.

"I...was her master," Henry said in a low tone, almost like he was embarrassed; he glanced down.

"You mean you bought her! Let me guess, you also abused her and treated her like a dog!" Lilly shouted at Henry.

"No, I treated her like a human, was kind to her, and actually got her away from abuse." He held up his hands. *Besides the time I lost control,* he thought to himself.

"How do I know you're telling the truth?" Lilly went beside Joey who was resting his hand on his knife holster.

"You can ask her once she wakes up, she's in the living room-"

"Then lead the way." Lilly interrupted him.

"There is something that you need to know-"

"All I know is that my sister who was taken away from me is alive." Lilly cut him off again.

Henry nodded his head as he led them to the living room, guessing that if he were to try and speak again, he would be interrupted. Once Lilly saw Rose, who was covered in blood and cuts, she immediately ran to her. "What did you do to her?!" Lilly was enraged. Joey pulled out his knife.

"I didn't do anything. I rescued her and am now healing her," Henry said as he sat down on the couch and inserted the IV into his arm again.

Lilly looked at the IV and saw that it went into Rose's arm. "That's vampire's blood. Won't that change her?" Lilly asked as she pointed to the IV.

"She's...she's already been changed." Henry scratched his head.

"What?!"

"She was killed, and I brought her back. Before she died, she told me to turn her into a vampire," Henry explained.

"Why would she ask you do to that?" Lilly said, her voice becoming calmer.

"We...we are together," Henry announced as he grabbed Rose's hand. Lilly was too shocked to say anything.

Joey stepped forward. "Why were you so weak? It's not just losing blood," he asked as he looked at Henry. "You're also paler than normal and look awful, like really awful." Joey looked closer at Henry.

"I can control people, but it weakens me. I had to use that ability in order to save Rose, then I had to give her some of my blood because she passed out from blood loss..." Henry trailed off.

"Why did you have to save her?"

"I had to save her because turning a human into a vampire, or even loving a human is illegal. Somehow, the Special Units Force found out, beat me up, and then did this to her." Henry stared at Rose in sorrow and gently caressed her hand.

Rose stirred a little before opening her eyes, they landed on Henry. "Henry?"

"Yes, it's me," he said reassuringly as he took his other hand and caressed her cheek. She smiled weakly. "You have a visitor," he said as he looked at Lilly. Rose's eyes followed his until her eyes also landed on Lilly. Her eyes started to tear up.

"Lilly?" Rose asked in disbelief. Lilly nodded her head as her eyes started to tear up too. Rose looked back at Henry.

"Is she really there or am I just imagining this?"

"She really is there," he said. Rose turned her attention back to Lilly.

"I...I thought you were dead," Rose said in total disbelief.

"I was on the verge of death before Joey stumbled upon the house, found me, and brought me back to health," Lilly said as she glanced at Joey, Rose turned her head and looked at the boy beside her sister.

"Thank you." Her voice was full of gratefulness.

"No problem." Joey nodded his head.

"I would hug you right now, but it'll probably hurt you." Lilly wiped away her tears with the back of her hand.

"Yeah, you're probably right," she said as she lightly laughed, trying not to hurt her stomach. Lilly also laughed a little. The next thing Lilly knew her face was pressed into Joey's chest as she continued to cry. She hadn't seen Rose in so long she didn't know what to say or how to act. It was overwhelming for her. Having had a dream like this several times she didn't even know if it was a real.

Rose looked down and saw the IV in her arm. "What's this?" she asked as she put one finger under the IV, slightly lifting it up.

"You passed out from blood loss so I'm giving you some of my blood," Henry simply responded.

"Henry, you look awful." she reached up her hand and brushed his face in concern.

"It's no big deal."

"Are you sure?" Rose asked, he nodded his head. There was a short silence "I'm...I'm tired-," she was cut off when she fell back into unconsciousness, her hand went limp in his.

"Rose?!" Lilly panicked.

"It's ok, she just passed out again. She'll wake up eventually," Henry said as he yawned. He realized how tired he was, but he needed to get food. He stood up, taking out the IV, and walked upstairs. In a second, he came back down wearing a new t-shirt. He grabbed his keys out of the pocket on his jacket. "I'm going to the store to buy food, I'll be right back," Henry said. The food in his pantry hadn't been touched in a year and he was not about to eat that. He opened the door and locked it behind him. Getting into his car he started to drive.

Joey slowly released his grip around Lilly. Lilly looked at Rose's unconscious body; more tears streamed down her face. She continued to wipe away the tears with the back of her hand. Joey looked at Lilly sympathetically.

"Why don't you talk to her?" Joey said. "She can still hear you." Lilly nodded her head as she walked to the couch. She sat down where Henry had sat and gently grabbed Rose's hand. Joey went to the kitchen to give them some privacy.

"Hi... um, I don't really know what to say, which is weird because I imagined what I would say to you if I ever saw you again." There was a short pause. "I really missed you, and I'm sorry that I wasn't stronger that day. I should have been stronger... I should have tried to fight back, but I was too scared to... I-I'm so sorry-" she was cut off as she choked on her tears. She laid her head on Rose's shoulder as she continued to cry.

Awhile later, Henry arrived at the house. He saw Lilly laying with Rose. When Lilly heard the door close, she sat up in a panic, but settled down when she saw Henry. She looked curiously at the bags he was carrying. He had five bags of groceries going up and down his arms. He walked to the kitchen as Lilly followed. Joey was laying down on the counter as he stared at the cabinets.

Henry laid the bags next to Joey as he started to unpack. Joey looked at all the different kinds of food inside the bags in awe. It seemed that every time Henry would take out one thing, Joey would take out two. Lilly would pick up what Joey had taken out and examine it. "Ok, I have bought food so you guys can eat," Henry said as he yawned again.

He went back to the living room and put Rose in his lap. Careful not to reopen any of her wounds, he wrapped his arm around Rose, and she naturally snuggled closer to him. "I'm going to go to sleep, so please don't break anything. And yes, you can have all the food that you want," he announced tiredly. Joey nodded as he opened a bag of chips with his knife. Lilly walked out of the kitchen with an apple in her hand and looked at Henry and Rose.

"So you really do like her?"

"Yes, I do."

"Treat my sister well."

Wow, this is coming from a thirteen-year-old, Henry thought to himself. Lilly walked back to the kitchen, leaving Rose and Henry resting on the couch.

***

Henry was awoken by Rose's last broken fingers popping back into place. He opened his eyes and saw black spots around his vision. Rose was still soundly asleep in his arms. He looked at her fingers and saw that every finger was healed. Suddenly, he got a bit dizzy. *I need blood, I think I have some in the pantry,* he thought as he carefully got off the couch. He had checked the store for blood but they were out.

He slowly and weakly made his way to the kitchen. He braced himself on the counter, regaining his balance; he was breathing heavily. "You look *awful.*" He heard Lilly's speak behind him.

So I've been told, he thought sarcastically. "I feel awful."

"There are these strange comfortable things upstairs. What are they?" She asked as she furrowed her eyebrows.

"Beds," he simply said. She nodded her head, there was a short pause "Can you open the very bottom shelf and grab me the remaining blood bags?" Henry pointed at the fridge.

"Sure..," Lilly said hesitantly as she reached down to the drawer.

Henry didn't use the blood bags on Rose because human blood only satisfied hunger. Henry's blood would heal Rose a lot faster and better than what humans blood could do.

She found only two blood bags left and handed them to Henry. He bared his fangs and bit into the bag, savoring it. He slowly felt some of his strength come back. Once finished with the first one, he moved on to the second. The second bag regained some of his strength, but he was still weak. Once he was done, he saw Lilly staring at him.

"What?" He asked as he wiped his mouth with the back of his hand.

"Nothing. It's just that you have two humans in your house, and you go for the bags."

"Believe it or not, but I don't like hurting humans. I like them actually," he said as he threw the bags away. There was silence between the two.

"What happened to my sister once she was taken?"

***

~jail~

Rider was resting on the uncomfortable bed in the cell; he got one all to himself because he was a Lord. He was awoken when he heard his cell being hit. He looked up to see the Leader. "What?" Rider asked.

"Does your brother have any other houses because we have checked his house inch by inch and nothing." There was a short pause. Rider looked at the Leader's eyes and saw that they were a dark red.

"What do I get out of it?" Rider asked. His eyes turned a darker red.

"I'll bail you out." Rider laughed, the Leader furrowed his eyebrows, confused.

"You're joking, right?"

"No, show us where your brother is and I'll bail you." Rider looked like he was thinking, even though he knew the answer.

"He has a cabin. If you give me a phone, I can lead you there." The Leader gave a faint smile as he walked off to grab a phone. "One more thing!" Rider yelled at him.

The Leader walked back. Rider was grasping the cell bars with both of his hands and had an unreadable look plastered on his face. "Don't... don't hurt him. I don't care about the girl, but please don't hurt Henry," Rider said. A small part of him was still the protective older brother for Henry. His eyes were now a brighter red and he looked almost confused and tired.

"You send me to your brother's cabin, yet you don't want me to hurt him. Why?"

"What he's doing is wrong. It's sad and somewhat pathetic to think he could love a human. I'm willing to do anything to show him what he's doing is wrong. He just needs guidance, that's all."

The Leader nodded as he walked away.

Chapter 26

Henry sat down on the chair on the island. "You want to know what happened to Rose after she was taken?" Henry asked.

"That's what I said," Lilly stated. Henry sighed.

"Ok." Henry thought about Rose's past. "She was taken to the pet shop and sold to a master," he paused, emotion stopping him from talking. "He... he was my brother. He abused her, beat her, whatever you want to call it. He returned her to the pet shop. Two weeks later, I went to the pet shop to buy a new pet. That was when I saw her. She was covered in cuts, scars, and bruises. I decided to buy her. When I first bought her, she was so scared; she thought that I was going to be like her old master. I was kind and didn't want to hurt her, until," he stopped again. "Until... I-I lost control and drank her blood, I almost killed her... Somehow, she still forgave me. Everything was going fine until my brother showed up again and killed her. *She died in my arms*... I brought her back to life, but as a vampire. Again, everything was going fine until the Special Units Force came. They knocked me out, took her away, and tortured her. I rescued her, then I found you."

There was silence between them. Lilly sat there speechless, too shocked to say anything. *My sister went through all that,* her started to tear up. Henry was in turmoil, thinking about all the pain that Rose had gone through.

Both their silences were cut off when Rose screamed. Henry used his super speed to run to her, Lilly wasn't too far behind him. Rose was clutching the couch tightly, she was still asleep.

~dream~

Rose ran through the woods. Her lungs burned, and her legs had gone numb; her naked feet were being cut by sticks on the ground. Please don't let him catch me, Rose pleaded with herself. She couldn't run anymore. She stopped at a tree and started to climb. She got to a branch that was big enough for her to sit on.

She took the collar off of her neck and threw it as far as she could. She tried to control her breathing; breathing in through her nose and out through her mouth

A minute later, she heard twigs break. She looked around and saw Rider running, he stopped around the area that Rose was in. He looked around and saw her collar. He walked over and picked it up. He tucked it into his pocket. "Rose, come out!" *he yelled. Rose flinched at his harsh tone.* "You can't hide from me. You were stupid to think that you could escape. You're a pet, you belong to me!" *Rider ran to the other direction, away from Rose. She breathed out deeply and relaxed all her muscles.*

Suddenly, she was pushed off the branch. She fell, crashing into twigs on her way down, and hit the ground as the air was knocked out of her.

She breathed out deeply, trying to regain some air. That didn't stop her from quickly standing up and starting to run. She ran into what felt like a wall, and fell backward, landing on her butt. Rider was standing over her, his fists clenched. She scooted back, away from him as his eyes became darker. He grabbed a fist full of her hair and punched her in the face several times. He stopped, standing straight up. Rose was curled in a ball, doing her best to protect herself. She was shaking at the thought of what was going to happen to her. Rider started to drag her, and she looked into the sky. She could only see the sun through her left eye as her right eye had swollen shut.

They finally made it to his house. He opened the door and threw her on the ground. He kicked her in the stomach and she rolled over on her other side. "I'm going to kill you!" He yelled as he stood over her. A girl got in front of him, blocking Rider from Rose.

"Master, please. Sh-she's new; she'll get the hang of things, j-just like I did." The girl was trembling in fear.

"Did you just tell me what to do, pet?" Rider shot a glare toward her. She seemed to shrink as he questioned her.

"N-no master, I-I would never-"

"I think that you did!" he yelled at her. The girl shook her head back and forth. In a second, Rider grabbed both of her arms and sunk his fangs into her neck.

The girl screamed in pain, blood trickled down her neck. She struggled in his grasp but he didn't budge. "Master, pl-please...," she trailed off as she went limp in his arms. Rider continued to drink her blood; purple bruises had formed on her arms from where he was grabbing her. A few seconds went by before he had finally run out of her blood.

Rider dropped the girl on the ground, dead. Rose tried to quickly rush to her, but Rider kicked her in the face. She screamed as she rolled across the ground. She got on her knees and held her nose with both hands, she crouched over in pain. Rider started to pace angrily. "If you could have just stayed, none of this would have happened," he said as he looked at the girl on the floor. "She was a perfectly good blood pet, and now I'm stuck with a worthless, pathetic pet like you!"

Rose continued to hold her nose in pain, blood was coming out of her nose. Rider walked over to her. "Come here." He grabbed her hair, forcing her head upright, and grabbed her chin with his other hand, making her look at him. While also making her sit up, her hands were resting on her legs.

"Look at me!" He tilted her head up harshly and stroked his right thumb along her cheekbone back and forth, smearing the tears on her face.

"What should we do about a pet that doesn't listen?" He asked as he looked down at her; she remained silent. He squeezed her face tighter and she whimpered as he did so. "I asked what should we do to a pet that doesn't listen?" This time, he gritted his teeth together. Rose knew that if she were to say do nothing, she would be beaten. But if she were to say whatever you want, he would beat her too.

"I-I don't know, master," she stuttered, scared.

"You don't know? Well, doesn't that always seem to be the fucking answer!" He smacked her face which turned a shade of red. She was now on her hands and knees. He took advantage of her position and kicked her in the stomach. She rolled over, coughing and gasping for air.

Before she could catch her breath, she felt something wrap around her neck – the collar that she had taken off. Rider fastened it as tight as it would go, making it even more difficult for her to breath. He grabbed the back of her collar and lifted her off the ground. Before she could react, her back was shoved against the wall, his hand was tightly gripping her collar. He lifted her collar up a little, her toes were now the only thing touching the ground. He stared at her angrily, his violent red eyes bore into hers. She avoided eye contact by staring at the ground. He slammed her down, her shoulder collided with the hard floor. She whimpered as she held her shoulder. He stood over her.

"Why can't you just be a good pet? I can't kill you, I just killed her. You also cost a lot of money." Rider talked more to himself. Then he stopped and started to think. Rose could see the wheels turning in his head, and it scared her. "I know what to do." There was a short pause. "I'll train you." He pinched the bridge of his nose. "Here's what's going to happen – I'm not going to kill you, I'm going to train you and you're going to do exactly what I say."

"Rose…" She heard a voice coming from somewhere. The voice was soft, kind, and concerned. "Rose, wake up." Black spots started to cloud her vision before it was replaced by light.

~end dream~

She sat up breathing heavily, hurting the cut on her stomach; sweat was drenching her face. She saw Henry in front of her and immediately hugged him. "Elizabeth," she said as a tear streamed down her face.

"Who's Elizabeth?" Henry asked.

"She... she was Rider's blood pet. He killed her because of me." She cried even harder onto his shoulder.

"It wasn't your fault." Henry held her closer to him.

"Yes, it was. I-I ran away, I had only been there for a few weeks. Rider found me and brought me back. He was going to kill me, but Elizabeth jumped between us. Rider didn't like the fact that a pet was telling him what to do so he...killed her. If I could have just accepted that I was his pet, she would still be here." Rose was sobbing; tears won't stop streaming down her eyes.

Henry comforted her. *First her parent's death; then Rider as her master; Rider killing her; the Special Units Force; and now this. She's been through so much pain,* he thought to himself, sadly. "Come here," he said as he picked her up and placed her on his lap. She started to cry into his chest, grasping onto his t-shirt with both of her hands. Lilly looked at the two.

"I'm going to find Joey," she whispered as she ran upstairs.

"Hey, look at me," Henry said gently. She looked up at him, he wiped away a stray tear with his thumb.

How can they say the same things, but the meanings are so different? Rose thought. She didn't understand it.

"Hey, that was in the past. Rider is in jail for a little while. He can't hurt you or anyone else, ok?" She nodded her head as she slowly stopped crying.

He grabbed her hand and rubbed small circles on it. She laid her head back on his chest, and he put his head on top of hers. Joey ran down the stairs and into the kitchen, loudly stomping as he ran; Lilly followed. "Sorry," Lilly whispered.

It's fine, Henry thought to her. Lilly seemed shocked to hear his voice in her head. After Joey and Lilly grabbed some food, they went back upstairs. Rose and Henry still continued to snuggle on the couch. Henry looked down and saw that the cut on her stomach was bleeding again from sitting up too fast.

Henry picked up the IV and inserted it into his arm. "I want food," Rose said into his chest.

"Ok," Henry said as Rose moved off of his lap. He stood up and helped Rose walk to the kitchen. Rose grabbed cheese puffs and started to eat them. Henry reached his hand into the bag and took a handful. She gave him a look.

What are you doing? She thought to him.

Eating, he simply said back.

But I chose the chips, they are now my chips.

Yes, but I want them too. I also bought them. Henry reached for the bag again but she moved the bag away from his hand. *Please.* He gave her cute look.

I hate you. She moved the bag to his hand.

You love me. He smiled.

Sure. Rose rolled her eyes. Henry laughed.

After they were done eating, they moved back to the couch and started to relax in silence. Their silence was interrupted by Joey and Lilly
running down the stairs.

"Guys, there are men walking toward the house," Lilly said. Henry took out his IV and ran to the window, out of breath by the time he reached it. He was still weak from having to control the man and having to give Rose his blood.

He looked out the window and saw the Special Units Force walking in their direction. *Not again.*

Chapter 27

Henry quickly rushed under the stairs, he opened a hatch that was an empty storage space that he never used. "Get in." That was all he needed to say. Lilly and Joey quickly ran to the space and went in, Rose followed before she stopped. "Get in." He repeated.

"Promise me that I'll see you again when I come out of here," she said quickly yet sadly.

"I promise." He kissed her on the forehead, not knowing what was going to happen. She went in, and he closed the door, it blended into the wall. *Don't come out no matter what,* Henry said to all of them.

Ok, Joey and Lilly responded. Rose didn't say anything. Henry quickly ran to the pantry and picked up the knife that he had placed on the ground. He grasped onto the handle tightly, knowing what he was about to do.

It's worth it to protect the people I love, Henry thought as he looked at the knife again.

He ran back to the living room right as the door was opened. Henry clasped and unclasped his free hand. The hand that was gripping the knife tightened, his knuckles were turning white. A man holding a baton ran toward Henry and aimed to strike him. Henry dodged and stabbed the man in the heart. He lifted the man over his head and threw the lifeless body on the ground.

Two more men rushed at Henry. One of the men swung his baton at Henry's head. Henry ducked and stabbed the man in the chest. The other man went behind Henry and aimed for his shoulders. Before the man could fully grab him, Henry evaded the attack and killed him.

Henry heard someone else behind him. He turned around and raised his knife, but he saw the Leader pointing a gun at his chest; Henry froze.

"You look awful," the Leader said. He took a step closer, looking at Henry's face while also placing the gun on Henry's chest. Henry had paler skin and dark circles under his eyes and was breathing heavily, exhausted from the fight. "Put down the knife," the Leader commanded. Henry was grasping the knife so tightly that it was shaking.

Henry let go of the knife and let it fall on the marble floor, making an echo sound as the metal bounced on the floor a couple of times before it finally settled. "Where is she?" The Leader asked. Henry bit his bottom lip, showing that he wasn't going to speak; he stayed silent. "I know that she is here. The blood on the couch has her smell," The Leader said as he looked at the bloody couch. The Leader looked around. Sighing heavily and with tears appearing in his eyes he spoke. He was slightly trembling like he was fighting something. "Come out, or your boyfriend dies!" The Leader slightly pressed the gun harder onto Henry's chest. The Leader's eyes became a dark red, like Rider's. The tears that were in his eyes disappeared.

Rose slightly furrowed her eyebrows together in confusion. Even though the Leader had hurt her, he was acting more sadistic than what she had seen. Even when he was experimenting on her, he was silent and never found enjoyment with what he did. If anything he became upset when he hurt her. Now, he seemed strangely sadistic.

Don't come out, Rose, Henry thought to her. Henry continued to look at the Leader, not giving away where she was. Rose looked through the small crack in the wall, she almost sprang out of there, but didn't; her hands were pressed on the door.

The Leader shook his head. "Ok, your funeral." He shrugged. He looked at Henry before he cocked the gun. "Three... two... one-,"

"Stop!"

Rose yelled as she ran out of the storage space, quickly closing the door so Lilly and Joey wouldn't be seen.

Lilly started to stand up and almost sprang out of the space, but Joey quickly grabbed her and pulled her back down. He wrapped one arm around the front of her body, holding her arms in place. His other hand was cupped over her mouth, and he pressed the back of her head into his chest.

Lilly started to cry, thinking about the day Rose was taken, how she didn't do anything to help her sister. It was happening again, and she couldn't help but think of what was going to happen. Joey felt her hot tears run over the hand that was cupped around her mouth. He felt terrible for holding her down, but he wasn't going to lose her.

Henry sighed as he looked at her.

What are you doing? He thought to her.

I can't let them kill you, she said back. The Leader uncocked his gun.

Two men grabbed Rose and forced her to her knees, hurting the cut on her stomach; she winced in pain. The Leader looked at Rose and Henry. "You both look awful." He laughed a little, both Henry and Rose rolled their eyes. "Ah... Henry is it?"

The leader asked as he looked at Henry, who nodded his head once. "Henry, it was good to know you because I'll never see you again." He looked at Rose. "She'll never see you again."

He cocked his gun again. "Stop, please! Just take me, don't kill him!" Rose begged as she struggled in the men's grasp, but to no avail.

"If I let him live, he'll just try to rescue you. I'm not letting that happen again," the Leader said as he looked at Henry.

I love you. Henry looked at her, focusing on her face. *You're beautiful,* he thought to her. He wanted Rose to be the last person he saw before dying; his eyes teared up.

I love you, too, Rose said as a tear fell out of her eye.

The Leader started to pull the trigger, but suddenly stopped midway. He began to breathe heavily. Henry's eyes widened when he saw that Rose was no longer being held by the guards; the guards looked around them. He turned his head to the Leader and saw the knife piercing through his chest; Rose was holding the knife. The Leader coughed up blood and fell to the ground, dead.

How did she do that? Henry thought. Rose vanished and reappeared in front of the two guards who were holding her. She stabbed one of them. Henry took the gun out of the Leader's hand and shot the other guard in the chest. Both of the guards were deceased.

Henry and Rose looked around to see if anyone was left; no one was. Rose dropped the knife and fell to the ground, exhausted. Henry ran to her and collapsed next to her. Henry wrapped his arm around her while Rose leaned her head on his chest. Lilly and Joey ran out of the storage space.

"What... what was that?" Rose asked, bewildered about what she had done.

"That was your special power – teleportation," Henry said. Joey and Lilly knelt down beside the two.

"Rose, are you ok?" Lilly asked concerned.

"Yeah, I'm... fine," Rose said as she shook her head like she was fighting something.

"She needs blood," Henry said, wanting some too. "I need blood," he whispered as he licked his lips.

Lilly and Joey both looked shocked and scared; they both stepped back a little. There was a long pause, Joey stepped forward. "Ok." Joey hesitantly went to Henry and sat down next to him. "Will it hurt?" he asked nervously.

"No, it'll be just a small pinch. You won't even feel anything after a second." Joey nodded his head. "You're sure you're ok with this?" Henry asked Joey.

"You didn't kill us. You let us stay here and just saved both of our lives. I owe you one," Joey said.

"Tell me when to stop." Henry grabbed Joey and pierced his neck. Joey winced before the pain subsided.

"Do it," Lilly said to Rose.

"Are you sure?" Rose asked her, concerned. Lilly nodded her head. "I don't want to hurt you."

"Rose, just do it." Lilly scooted closer to her. Rose grabbed Lilly and penetrated her fangs into her sister's neck. The blood tasted weird, yet it was so good – it was sweet.

"Stop," Joey said to Henry. Henry took his last gulp and retracted his fangs. He licked the wound, healing the holes in his neck. A few seconds passed before Lilly said the same thing. Rose took two gulps and licked her neck.

"Are you ok?" Rose asked Lilly, concerned.

"Yeah, I'm fine." Lilly shook her hand in the air.

"Are you sure?"

"Yes, Rose. I'm alright, I promise." Rose nodded her head. They all stood up and made sure that Lilly and Joey were ok.

Henry and Rose started to pick up the dead people and drag them outside. It was sundown. Henry carried two people while Rose carried one. They went into the woods and laid the bodies on the ground. Henry went back to the house using his super speed and came back with two shovels.

Rose grabbed one of the shovels and froze as she stared at the ground. Henry noticed. "What's wrong?" He walked to her.

"I... I killed him," she said as she looked at the Leader's dead body; her hands started to shake. A tear escaped her eyes and Henry wiped it off with his thumb.

"Rose, he tortured you and was going to kill me. You did what you had to do." A tear escaped his eyes; he didn't realize that he was crying. He dropped the shovel and hugged her; Rose hugged him back. They both fell on their knees and started to cry harder. They cried on each other's shoulder for a long time as they thought about what they had done.

After they calmed down, they left each other's embrace and dried each other's tears. They stood up and grabbed their shovels, both their hands shaking as they did so. They started to dig a giant hole to put the bodies in. "Will other people come?" Rose asked as she continued to dig.

"It's my best understanding that they are not allowed to have a family. They are not the police, so while they know of them they won't know if they died or not. We should be safe," Henry said as he scooped another pile of dirt. Rose only nodded.

After they had finished digging the hole, Rose and Henry dumped the dead bodies into it and made a grave.

They both breathed heavily, tired and exhausted. They walked back to the house and sat down on the couch, not caring that the blood was still on it. "How's the cut on your stomach?" Henry asked; he had assumed it had healed when she drank Lilly's blood.

"It's healed. Lilly's blood really helped," she said as she whispered the last sentence, not wanting Lilly to hear. She leaned her head onto Henry's chest; he wrapped his arm around her and kissed her head.

After a while, they heard the doorknob jiggle. They looked at the door as it was opened and stood up once they saw who the intruder was. It was Rider!

Chapter 28

Henry got in front of Rose, protecting her. "What are you doing here? I thought you were in jail!" Henry snarled.

"The Special Units Force bailed me out once I showed them where your cabin was," Rider said smoothly.

"You told them where my cabin was?!" Henry practically yelled at him, his voice echoed throughout the house. Rider nodded his head. "Since you are free, why are you here?!" Henry asked even though he knew the answer. He was just thinking of what his next move was going to be.

"Well, I couldn't let that *abomination* live." Rider pointed at Rose in disgust. She seemed to shrink back a little, forgetting that she was a vampire, as the fear of Rider overtook her. Joey and Lilly heard the commotion and ran out of the kitchen. They went behind Rose. "Who's that?" Rider asked as he leaned to the side, looking at Lilly and Joey. Rose and Henry stayed silent as both of their fists clenched. "Well, I could always use another blood pet, after the other pet died, trying to protect you," Rider said, looking at Rose. Rose became outraged. She disappeared and reappeared in the air in front of Rider.

She punched him hard in the face. Rider stumbled backward, holding his jaw with his hand. He looked up at Rose in rage; anger had taken over him. He tried to grab Rose, but she teleported back to Henry.

"Her name was Elizabeth, and you're not touching my sister!" she yelled.

Rider spat out blood. "She's your sister..." Rider said to himself, and laughed. "Its name was *pet*. *You* of all people should know this." He stared intensely at Rose. "Soon, your sister and its friend will know this too." His eyes were now a darker shade of red. This sounded and looked familiar to Henry. He reminisced his childhood and the way his father treated and thought about pets. It made him furious.

"You're not touching them." Henry stood protectively in front of the three of them. "Rose, take your sister and Joey; go somewhere safe," Henry said. He knew that if he were to go with Rose, Rider would eventually find them again. He also didn't want Rose to stay and fight Rider because of all the abuse he had but her through. Their fighting had gone back years and this had become too personal.

"I'm not going to leave you."

"You are their only chance of getting out of here. Now go!" Rose nodded and grabbed Lilly and Joey's hands.

I love you, Rose said to Henry as she teleported.

I love you, too, Henry thought back to her. Just like that, Rider and Henry were left alone.

Henry focused his attention back to Rider. "I don't want to fight you, we are brothers. I know that this isn't you, this is dad." Henry was trying to find a way out of violence, he was tired of it at this point. As well as trying to snap him out of the trance he was in.

"You stopped being my brother the day you decided to love a pathetic human – *your pet!*" Rider yelled. "If only you had just listened to dad, none of this would've happened."

"Can't you just please leave?" Henry begged.

"No, I can't leave. Don't you see? I'm trying to protect you," Rider spat.

Get a life, Henry thought angrily. "Since when is sending men to *kill* me being protective?"

"I didn't know they were going to kill you. I even made a deal with one of them. I was trying to save you from that pathetic waste of space!"

"Fine, let's fight!" Henry growled and balled up his hands into fists.

"When has fighting the older brother ever worked, especially for you?" Rider asked as he looked at Henry.

"The last two to three times." A small, thin smirk spread across his face. Rider balled up his fists in anger.

Rider used his super speed to rush at Henry and threw a punch at his face. Henry blocked the attack by grabbing Rider's hand. As soon as he did, Rider kneed Henry in the stomach. Henry crouched over in pain. But he quickly uppercut Rider in the nose, before Rider had a chance to hit him.

Rider stumbled away from Henry, giving Henry the opportunity to kick him in the face. He felt his foot hit Rider's face. Rider fell on the ground, landing on his back; he grunted in pain. Henry got on top of Rider. As soon as he did, Rider punched Henry in the face. Henry's head was knocked back. Rider flipped Henry over him. Henry landed on his back. Rider placed his hands on either side of Henry's head and rolled backward, aiming the soles of his feet at Henry. Henry quickly turned to the right to dodge. Rider's feet landed on the ground, creating a loud thud.

They both stood up, breathing heavily. The blood on their faces dripped onto their t-shirts.

"You're tougher than I thought," Rider said.

"There's a lot of things you don't know about me," Henry said as he wiped away the blood from his nose with his hand. In a split second, Henry charged at Rider and punched him in the stomach; Rider bent over. Henry grabbed Rider's and and kneed him in the face, cracking Rider's nose. Rider held his nose in pain. Henry swung his leg toward Rider's face, but Rider was able to dodge it.

Henry was pushed off the ground. Rider got on top of him and placed his knees on Henry's hands, holding them in place. He punched Henry repeatedly. Henry kneed Rider in the groin; Rider grabbed it with his hands in pain. Henry took both of his hands and pushed Rider off of him. Rider landed to the side, still in a fetal position. Henry stood up, but he was yanked back to the ground. Rider put his arm around Henry's neck, choking him. Henry heard the crack of Rider's nose pop back into place.

They were both sitting on their knees. Henry leaned against Rider as Rider continued to choke him, forcing the back of Henry's head into his chest. Henry knew he had to do something and fast, otherwise, he would be knocked out. Henry steadied his hands as he put them around Rider's arm. He flipped Rider over him, but Rider refused to budge. Henry was flipped over with the momentum he had created. They were both on their backs, Henry on top of Rider. Henry brought his head forward and slammed it into Rider's face.

Rider became dizzy, as his head slammed into the ground. Henry grabbed two of Rider's fingers and broke them. Rider let go of Henry's neck as he held his broken fingers with his other hand. Henry stood up weakly, coughing and regaining the air that he had lost. Henry's eyesight was blurry as he stared at the ground. Rider stood up as well, holding his fingers. Before Henry had a chance to react, Rider rushed at him. Rider wrapped his arms around Henry's waist and lifted him up. Henry tried to grab onto something, but he couldn't. Rider slammed Henry into the glass cocktail table next to the couch, breaking it.

Shards of glasses pierced into Henry's back. Henry's head hit the floor, making everything around him spin. Rider stood up, breathing heavily before his fingers popped back into place. Henry rolled on his side. A few feet away, he saw something that went from shiny to red – the knife. Henry tried to quickly rush towards the knife. Before he could reach it, Rider kicked him in the face. He fell on his back, almost knocked out.

Rider sat on top of Henry's stomach, both knees on each side. Rider was holding a wood formed into a spike and raised it to stab his brother. Henry's eyes widened, and he quickly grabbed Rider's arm, stopping the spike centimeters from his chest. He was still dizzy and weak.

Henry looked to his side and saw the knife a few inches from him. But to grab it, he would need to take one hand off the spike. Henry shifted the spike toward his shoulder, trying to move it away from his chest. He breathed in deeply, preparing for pain. As he did so, he looked into Rider's eyes. His eyes were so dark they were a burgundy red. He had totally lost control. Henry closed his eyes, he had seen this before when they were kids.

In a split second, Henry let go of the spike with his right hand, giving Rider the chance to thrust it into his shoulder. Henry screamed in pain. His left hand tightened its grip on the spike; his knuckles turned white. Henry's eyes turned a dark red, the same color as Rider's. He saw Rider grab a piece of glass. Henry took advantage of the little time and swiftly grabbed the knife beside him with his free hand.

Rider's eyes widened as he saw Henry grasping the knife. Before Rider could react, Henry pierced the knife into Rider's heart. Rider had a shocked expression on his face for a split second. The dark red eyes turned lighter before his eyes closed; all emotion was taken from his face. Rider's lifeless body slumped on top of Henry, pressing the spike even further into his shoulder. Henry winced in pain as his eyes went back to normal. Looking at Rider he realised what he had done.

No, no, no, no, Henry thought frantically.

Henry took the knife out of Rider, throwing it away from him. His hands shook as he pushed Rider off of him. Rider limply fell on the floor. Henry pulled the spike out of his shoulder and threw it to the side. Henry got on his knees and put his head on top of Rider's chest, blood from Rider's chest soaked Henry's forehead. Henry started to cry as he grasped Rider's t-shirt with his trembling hands. He knew that Rider had abused Rose, killed her, told the Special Units Force where they were, and tried to kill him, but they were still *brothers*. They had grown up together, had a few good laughs, and played without fighting a few times. When Henry was younger, he looked up to Rider as the 'cooler' older brother – always followed him around, bought similar clothes that Rider bought, watched the same movies he liked, and copied his body language.

Henry sat there and cried for a while before he stopped and raised his head from Rider's bloody chest. He slowly and weakly stood up, his legs shaking as he supported his weight. He groaned in pain as he picked up Rider's dead body. He walked to where the Special Units Force men were buried and laid Rider on the ground. He picked up the shovel and started to dig. Every movement hurt his injured shoulder and cut up body.

Once the hole was dug, he carefully laid Rider's corpse into it and started filling the hole. He watched as the dirt covered Rider's hand. Before he completely buried his older brother, a bright silver ring shone from Rider's finger. He took the ring and placed it in his pocket. He thought Lisa should have something of Rider's.

A tear fell from his eye as the grim realization hit him like a train – he had dug a grave for Rider, his brother.

Chapter 29

I did it for Rose. I was protecting Rose. Henry had been repeating this over and over, ever since he started digging. It also took his mind off the pain in his shoulder and back. His back couldn't heal with the shards of glass in it; his shoulder was recovering slowly.

I did it for Rose. I was protecting Rose. He said to himself again. He was still sad, and his eyes and cheeks were stained with tears. But at least Rose was safe, and they wouldn't have to worry about being hunted. However, everytime he thought those words a part of his heart was slowly chipped away at for the loss of his brother.

***

Rose had been pacing nervously ever since she had teleported. At first, she had teleported to the grave where the Special Units Force had been buried. Then they all ran deeper into the woods and stopped after a while.

Rose turned around for the hundredth time, her right hand was up. She was chewing on her forefinger nail. Her left hand was grasping onto her right elbow. She turned around again. Lilly looked at Rose worriedly, as did Joey. They knew that they needed to take Rose's mind off of it.

"So uhm..." Lilly trailed off thinking.

"Do you want to know how I saved your sister?" Joey asked. Rose nodded her head, still pacing. Joey breathed in deeply before speaking. "My parents left one day and never came back, leaving me alone," Joey paused thinking about the mystery and sadness behind his parent's disappearance. "I had to learn how to survive by myself, grabbing food and collecting water. I had a few supplies with me – not much but it would suffice. I was just walking in the woods, trying to find more food or water. I heard screams. I turned the other way, not wanting to involve myself in someone else's problem. But for some unknown reason, I couldn't bring myself to walk away. So I walked in the direction of the screaming. By the time I arrived, I saw vampires carrying a girl out of the house. She was kicking, thrashing, crying, and screaming – you were that girl," he said as he looked at Rose. She stopped pacing, lowering the nail that she was biting. "I waited for the vampires to leave before I entered the house. When I did, I saw three people lying on the floor, blood coming out of their necks. I checked the man's pulse first, then the woman, and finally Lilly's. She was barely alive, luckily I had an IV in my rucksack. I took a gamble and chose the woman. I waited a good amount of time before Lilly opened her eyes. Just as she started to regain consciousness, the woman's blood ran out. She had little blood to give to Lilly, but it was enough. I had some water and barely had any food. It took a few days, but she was slowly nursed back to health. Since then, we stayed together," Joey said, finishing his story.

Rose ran to Joey and hugged him, thanking him repeatedly. Joey hugged her back. Lilly joined in and hugged both of them.

Ok, it's safe. You can come back to the house. Rose heard Henry say.

"He's ok." Rose was overjoyed. She grabbed both of their hands and teleported back to the house.

They all looked around, the floor was covered in blood and shards of glass were spread across the floor. Henry stood in the middle of the room. Rider was nowhere to be seen. Rose quickly ran to Henry and hugged him.

"Ow, ow, ow, glass in the back." Henry winced in pain.

"Sorry." Rose stopped hugging him and dropped her hands to her sides.

"It's ok." He grabbed her arms with both his hands. He brought her closer to him and leaned down to kiss her.

"Ew." They both heard Lilly say. Rose looked up at Lilly, her tongue was out in disgust, and her face was contorted into an almost gagging face.

"Grow up," Rose said to Lilly as she rolled her eyes.

"*Never!*" Lilly yelled as she ran upstairs. Joey followed.

Rose looked around the room, wondering where Rider was. But her question was quickly answered as she saw the dirt on Henry's hands, the bloody knife on the floor, and the dried tears on Henry's cheeks. He even looked deflated and sad. She put her head on Henry's chest and stepped closer to him, closing the space between them.

"I'm sorry." She paused for a moment. "I know what it's like to lose a sibling too," Rose said into his chest. Truth be told, Rose wasn't upset that Rider was gone; she was upset because Henry had had to bury his own brother.

"It's ok. You're safe, and that's all that matters," Henry said as he rested his chin on top of her head. His grip tightened around her. "Can you do me a favor and remove the shards of glass from my back?"

She nodded her head. They left each other's embrace and walked to the couch. They both sat sideways on the couch.

Rose was sitting behind Henry. She reached up her hand and grabbed a piece of glass. She breathed in deeply as she pulled the glass out of his back. Henry winced in pain as he clenched his fists. "I can't do this," Rose said as she looked at the glass that was stained with blood.

"Yes, you can. Besides, you're not the one with glass in you," Henry said. She nodded her head as she pulled another shard out of his back.

They had been doing this for about fifteen minutes, and she had pulled out more than half of the shards. She grabbed the biggest piece. She started to pull the shard, but it wouldn't move. "Ow!" Henry arched his back in pain.

"Sorry, there's a shard that's stuck," she said as she braced her feet on his lower back.

"Pull it out on three. One-" Henry was cut off when Rose suddenly pulled it out. "Ow!" He looked back at her. "I said on *three*," he said as he winced.

"Yeah, and I decided on one," Rose said sarcastically. He reached back his hand and playfully smacked her on the arm. She lightly laughed. "The good news is the rest of the shards are tiny." Henry sighed in relief. Rose started to pull out the smaller shards.

"I think I got all the shards," she said as she looked closely at his back.

"What do you mean you think?" he looked back at her, his eyebrow raised.

"It's glass, it's hard to see."

"Just rub your hand over my back and feel," he said. She nodded her head as she did so, carefully. There were no more shards.

"I got all the shards," Rose said as she looked at Henry's back. His shirt was full of holes and was stained with blood. Henry sighed in relief as he turned around.

"Thank you." Henry wrapped his arms around Rose and lowered his head to her shoulder. She gently hugged back. "I need to go take a shower," Henry said, realizing that his clothes were stained with blood.

"Same," Rose said as she glanced at her clothes too. They both stood up and walked to their rooms.

Rose looked in the wardrobes and dressers, there were no clothes for her. She went out and knocked on Henry's door. "I need clothes," she said. Henry disappeared into his room and came back with sweatpants and a t-shirt. "Thanks," she said as she grabbed the clothes.

"No problem," Henry said. Rose walked back to her room and opened the door, she hopped in the shower. It had been so long since she had taken a shower, the warm water soothing her skin.

After showering, she dried herself and put on her new clothes, which were too loose for her. She walked out of her room and looked around. Henry wasn't there, he was still in the shower. She walked downstairs, careful not to step on the blood. She practically hopped every few feet.

She made it to the kitchen. She grabbed a rag and wetted it with water. She grabbed a dry cloth as well. She walked to a pool of blood and started to scrub it away. She watched as some of the blood absorbed into the rag while the rest was pushed around in the water.

This scene was so familiar to her. After Rider would beat her, he would throw a rag at her and make her clean up her own blood. It didn't matter if she was sore or half knocked out. He would make her do it right after he had stopped beating her. If she didn't do it right or missed a spot, she would be punished again.

She took the dry rag and wiped the wet area. She proceeded to the next pool of blood. Halfway through scrubbing the blood, a pair of hands grabbed her from under her stomach and lifted her off the ground. Her legs were still bent. Henry turned her over to where he was holding her bridal style.

"What are you doing?" Rose asked as she dropped the tow rags, letting them fall to the ground.

"The real question is, what are *you* doing?" Henry raised an eyebrow and sat down on the couch, placing Rose on his lap.

"I was cleaning." She pointed at the two rags on the ground.

"Why?"

"Because there is blood on the floor." Rose rolled her eyes.

"Yeah, but I'm here now. Don't worry about the blood, it's not important. I'm important," Henry said as he brought her closer to him.

"Ok." Rose held up her hands and laughed a little. "How's your back?" She asked as she snaked her arm around his back.

"Completely healed and feeling good," Henry responded.

"That's great." Henry nodded his head.

She looked at Henry, he looked tired and exhausted, having small dark circles under his eyes. There was also a hint of happiness and relief in his eyes. His hair was still wet from the shower, making his brown hair look darker and flat. It was the first time that his hair wasn't styled up. Rose laughed a little at the sight of it.

"What's so funny?" Henry furrowed his eyebrows in confusion.

"Your... your hair," Rose said in between laughs as she pointed at his hair. He flipped his hair and swooped it to one side of his head.

"Don't laugh at my hair!" Henry pouted, pretending to be upset.

"It looks good on you." Rose patted down his hair, straight. She ran her fingers through his hair before she patted it down again.

"Don't touch the hair, it's my money maker," Henry said, moving his head away from her hand. Rose rolled her eyes as she dropped her hand.

Henry started to rock back and forth slowly. Rose pressed her head into his chest as Henry wrapped his arm around her and pulled her even closer to him. Henry put his chin on top of Rose's head. The back of Rose's feet rested on Henry's lap.

"Is it finally over?" Rose mumbled into Henry's chest.

Henry nodded and closed his eyes. "Yeah, it's finally over." They both relaxed, relieved that they could finally rest, not having to look over their shoulders every second. Henry continued to sway gently. Rose closed her eyes as her other hand grasped onto his shirt.

Rose had fallen asleep to the steady rhythm of Henry rocking back and forth. Her hand that grasped to his shirt had fallen limply on top of her. Her shirt had slid down one of her shoulders, revealing a scar from the whip. Henry moved the shirt back over her shoulder. He pressed Rose closer to him, feeling sorry that she still had scars and memories from her old life. Henry stood up and carried Rose to her bedroom. A thin smile spread across Henry's face as he looked at Rose, sleeping peacefully on her bed.

He moved hair out of her face and tucked it behind her ear. "It's over," Henry whispered to her. He leaned his head down and kissed her gently on the cheek. "It's finally over," he said even though he had a twisted feeling in his stomach.

Chapter 30

"Rose, it's time to wake up." Henry rubbed her back gently.

"I don't want to get up," she said in a tired and annoyed voice. Henry stood up from the bed as he held his hands up in defense.

"Ok. I just thought that you would be more excited that we are – oh, I don't know – going back to the house." He smirked. In a second, she jumped from the bed and dashed through the bedroom door. Lilly started to run after her, but Henry stopped her. "Wait for it," Henry said as he stared at the door. Rose ran back into the room.

"How did we get here?" she asked as she leaned against the doorframe.

"My car," Henry simply responded. Rose ran out of the room again and came back in a few seconds.

"Where is your car parked?"

"Don't run." Henry held up his hands. "Follow me." He walked out of the room while Rose, Lilly, and Joey followed. Lilly and Joey carried the few things that they had with them and walked down the stairs. The blood that was on the floor was gone, as well as the broken table.

Henry must have cleaned it up while I was sleeping, Rose thought as she looked around the clean room. They made it to the garage. There, a shiny muscle car was parked; Lilly, Joey, and Rose marveled at the car for a few seconds. Rose hopped in the passenger's seat while Lilly and Joey sat in the back seat. Henry was driving.

"Buckle up," Henry said as he fastened his seatbelt.

"How?" Rose asked as she looked around the car.

"You've ridden a car before."

"Yeah, a limo." Rose looked at Henry with her eyebrow slightly raised. He reached across and grabbed Rose's seat belt and buckled her in.

Joey and Lilly mimicked what he did. Henry started to drive towards the house. "So, what do we do if people come over?" Lilly asked as she leaned forward a little.

"Act like pets..." Henry trailed off.

"How do we do that?"

"Uhm, Rose?" Henry pleaded.

"That's easy," Rose said. "Don't look anyone in the eye. Don't speak unless spoken to. When you do speak, speak timidly. Always call Henry master. Be respectful to everyone; do what they tell you to do. And don't ask questions... I think that I've covered all the basics. I'll remind you if I think of anything," Rose said as she counted the things off on her fingers.

Lilly and Joey looked at each other, both of their brows raised in disbelief. "Those are the basics?" Lilly asked; shock filled her voice.

"Yep," Rose said nonchalantly as those rules were like second nature to her. She naturally followed them when she was a pet. She didn't have to be told anything.

They arrived at the house. Rose got out of the car and quickly ran to the door. She tried to open it but it was locked. She teleported into the house.

Henry looked up and saw Lilly and Joey staring at the house in awe. Henry grabbed his keys and unlocked the door. They all walked in; Joey and Lilly now marveling at the interior.

"I'll show you to your rooms," Henry said to Lilly and Joey as they all walked upstairs. Lilly got the room to the left of Henry's door while Joey got the room next to hers. Henry looked at Rose's door and saw that it was opened. He walked into Rose's room and saw her lying on her bed with her face down. She was slowly sinking into the mattress. He laughed at the sight of her.

"It's good to be back," Rose mumbled. Henry laughed again.

"Wow." That was all he could say. Henry rested his right hand under his chin as he stared at her.

"I'm going to go to the garden." Rose stood up and looked at Henry, waiting for an answer.

"I'll be there in a few, ok?" Rose nodded her head as she walked out of her room. Henry went into his room. He grabbed his phone and called his mom. "Hey, mom," Henry greeted sadly.

"Hey sweetie, why did you call?" Lisa answered from the other line.

"I... I have so-something to tell you," he whispered as he rubbed his eyes with his free hand.

"What is it?" Lisa asked, a bit nervous at Henry's tone. She could tell something was wrong.

"Rider... Rider is dead," he announced regrettably, remembering what had happened.

"What?! How? How did that happen?!" she asked in disbelief. Hearing his mother's voice sound so hurt made him devastated.

"He attacked Rose and me, it was self-defense. He had a stake centimeters from my heart, I had no other choice." He looked down and brushed his hand through his hair. "I-I have his ring."

He heard his mom start to cry. "Ok, I-I'll come over and get it," Lisa said.

"You do-don't have to." Henry held back his tears that were threatening to fall any moment. "I-I'll bring it to you."

"No, no. I want to come over," Lisa said as she lightly cried. There was a short pause. "Bye..." Henry could tell that she didn't want to talk anymore, she just wanted to mourn for her dead son.

"...Bye." Henry hung up. He sighed deeply and rubbed his hand through his hair again. He wiped his eyes, drying the tears. He put his phone in his pocket and stood up from her bed. His eyes turned a dark red.

He grabbed a reading chair from the corner and threw it across the room. It smashed into the wall and broke apart on impact. He grabbed one of the broken legs of the chair and started to hit his dresser with it. The leg snapped in two. He then slammed his fist into the wall, creating a hole. He stopped as tears began to fall down his face. He didn't like the fact that his mom had to say goodbye to her own son. His eyes turned back to its natural color and he looked around the room at what he had just done.

He calmed himself down before he walked to the garden, hoping that Rose could take his mind off of his brother.

He saw Rose laying in her usual spot. He moved close to her.

"Hey," Henry said. Rose was startled by his presence. "Sorry," Henry held his hands up.

"Can you make sound when you walk?" she asked as she raised an eyebrow.

Henry chuckled. "Yeah, I'll stomp when I walk," he said sarcastically.

"Come on up." Rose patted the rock right next to her. Henry walked around to the other side of the rock. He jumped up, but only his chest got on top of the rock. He grabbed at everything as he slid off the rock and fell to the ground. Rose laughed at him. He nodded his head as he placed his hands on his hips.

"How did you get up there?"

"There are cracks and bulges on my side of the rock," Rose said.

"Why didn't you tell me this before I tried this side?" Henry asked.

"I wanted to see what would happen." Rose smiled.

He walked to the other side of the rock. "Scoot over," he said. Rose did as she was told. He climbed up and sat down next to her. They both laid down, facing each other. Rose stared at Henry and noticed his glassy eyes.

"Are you ok?" Rose asked as she looked at him. Henry knew what she was talking about.

"Yeah, I'm fine. Let's not focus on that. I'm with you now." Henry brushed Rose's face with his hand. He took his other arm and wrapped it around her. Henry interlocked their fingers and put his head on top of hers. "Have I ever told you that I love you?" Henry asked.

"Yes, you have." Rose nodded.

"Oh. Well, I'm going to tell you again. I love you," Henry said as he slid his body down to where his face was in level with hers. He leaned in and kissed her; she kissed him back. "Never forget that I love you." Henry pulled away and stared into her eyes.

"I'll never forget that," Rose said as she leaned her forehead against his. He started to rub small circles, with his thumb, on her hand.

Neither of them spoke a word after that, too comfortable in each other's arms to say or do anything. They both listened to the sound of the water. They both closed their eyes and continued to hold each other's hands as Henry rubbed small circles on hers. They were both finally in peace, they could finally rest.

Chapter 31

It was morning, and the sun shone through the glass. Luckily, it didn't burn Rose because the glass dimmed the sun. Rose's eyes were closed, as well as Henry's, but neither of them were asleep. Henry's hand was on Rose's head, massaging it.

"I'm hungry," Rose mumbled. Henry chuckled lightly.

"You're always hungry," Henry said as he laughed more.

"Well duh, I was barely fed when I was a pet. And you shouldn't be talking, you're always hungry too," Rose said sassily. She opened her eyes and looked at Henry.

"Ok, you have me beat there. I think I know what you want."

"What?" She looked at him skeptically.

They both sat up. Henry jumped off the rock and helped Rose get down. "Pancakes," Henry replied as they started to walk towards the kitchen.

"You're right."

"Of course, I am. It's one of your favorite food." Henry chuckled.

"You know me so well," Rose said as she laughed too. They walked into the kitchen and Henry started to make pancakes. Once the food was ready, they started to dig in. It didn't take long for either of them to finish. "Thank you, I needed that," Rose said.

"You're welcome. I needed that too," Henry said as they both went to the living room. They made themselves comfortable on the couch and turned the TV on. Just as they were relaxing, someone knocked on the door. Rose looked at Henry nervously.

"It's ok, it's just my mom," he reassured.

"What? You didn't tell me that your mom was coming. I love your mom!" She relaxed and became cheerful.

"Sorry, it slipped my mind." Henry shrugged. Rose hit him in the arm. "Ow," Henry rubbed his arm. "I'm sorry," Henry said as he held up his hands, protecting his face. He fell sideways on the couch. Rose only pointed to the door before Henry got up and walked toward it.

Henry opened the door. "Hey, Henry," Lisa greeted somewhat sad. Henry hugged Lisa as she buried her face in his shoulder. They pulled away from each other. Lisa looked Henry in the eyes. Her eyes were deep as if she needs to tell Henry's something important. *Sorry, but your dad is here,* Lisa said to him. He looked at her, a bit shocked and angry at the same time.

Why is he here? Henry asked back as Lisa hugged Rose. Henry looked at the car that they had come in and saw his dad getting out.

Rider was his son too. He has a right to be here, Lisa said.

"It's good to see you," Lisa said to Rose.

"It's good to see you too," Rose responded.

Henry pinched the bridge of his nose. He never really liked his father; he was the reason that Rider became the way he was. His father was a controlling, cruel, and stubborn man that manipulated Rider into what he was. Henry's dad had tried it with him, but luckily, Lisa had gotten him away from his father.

Rose, Henry said to her as he finally lifted his face from his hand.

Yes? She asked back, looking at Henry.

My father is here, his power is manipulation. Be careful of what he tells you.

Why are you telling me this? Rose asked as worry spread across her face.

Because... he's a lot like Rider. He was the one that made him the way he was. Rose's face fell. Henry's dad walked in the house. Rose looked at his thinning brown hair, his face was naturally set to look stern. He looked a couple years older than Lisa.

He hugged Henry. "Hey son, good to see you," Henry's father said as he patted him on the back.

"Good to see you too," Henry deadpanned.

"Who's this?" Henry's father asked as he looked at Rose. Her face was a little paler, and her hands had started to shake.

"Dad, this is Rose," Henry said in a protective tone. Henry's dad extended his hand to her. Rose hesitantly reached up her subtly shaking hand and shook it.

"I'm Phil," Henry's dad introduced himself. Rose only nodded, still in shock. Phil pulled his hand away. "Is she ok?" Phil whispered to Henry and Lisa.

Lisa looked at Henry, and he nodded his head once. Lisa wrapped her arm around Phil, and they turned around. Lisa whispered something into his ear. Phil turned back around, shock on his face.

"You did what?!" Phil asked Henry, a hint of anger edged into his voice. Rose subtly jumped at his outburst, remembering how Rider used to yell.

"I had no other choice," Henry said. Phil put his hand over his face, clearly disappointed.

"Yes, you did! You should have just let it die!"

"I couldn't let her die!"

"Yes, you could. Now, it's a vampire!"

"You sound just like Rider!" Henry said clearly upset and hurt.

"He always listened, unlike you!"

"Like it's my fault that you focused all your attention on him!" Henry yelled; silence fell between the two of them. Lisa had put her arm around Rose and was comforting her. "I don't need you to tell me what to do. I chose this, and I'm happy with my decision." He sighed deeply, calming himself down. Henry wrapped his arm around Rose as she wrapped her arms around his waist, burying her head in his chest.

Lisa looked at Phil. "He is a grown man, and he can make choices by himself. You should be happy for your son."

"It's hard when the son that's alive killed the other son." Phil's voice was filled with sorrow, his eyes clouded with tears.

"It was self-defense, he had no other choice. I saw Rider killing Rose. Henry told me that he attacked them. He tried to kill Henry as well. *Believe me*, he was telling the truth. It was either one son or the other... I'm not happy with either of them dying, but it was all to protect themselves," Lisa said as tears spread throughout her eyes.

Phil looked back at Rose and Henry. Henry was still comforting her. "Did Rider have a reason for attacking them?"

"No," Henry responded as he glanced at his father.

"Why did he kill it? Was it because you loved it?"

"He was her old master, and he also didn't like that I loved her," Henry said.

"He was its old master?" Phil asked and Henry nodded.

Can I show them the scars? Henry asked Rose, she nodded her head. He reached down his hand and lifted the back of her shirt, revealing the scars from the whip on her back. Phil looked at it. Henry let go of her shirt and tidied it.

"At least you didn't kill-"

"Phil!" Lisa interrupted.

"What? It needs to know that Rider and Henry may not be that different." Rose dropped her arms around Henry and moved away from him. Her eyes became slightly glossed over.

"What...what is he talking about?" Rose asked nervously.

"Nothing," Henry reassured as he glared at Phil. *Don't,* Henry warned his dad.

"It has a right to know," Phil said.

"Kn-know what?" Beads of sweat started to form on Rose's forehead.

"He hasn't told you?" Rose shook her head but with little to no emotion. "The kind and pure Henry you knew isn't all so sweet and innocent." Rose took a step away from Henry. "A few years ago, Henry had another pet, and he killed it."

"Wh-what?" Rose asked as she scooted farther from Henry as he took a step towards her. "Do-don't come near me!" She stuttered as tears appeared in her glossed over eyes.

"Rose, it's... it's not like that," Henry said as he held up his hands, showing he wasn't going to come near her. What was happening with Rose seemed too familiar to what happened to Rider.

"Then what?! Did you kill your last pet?" she yelled.

"Yes." Henry's voice was filled with remorse.

Henry had another pet, and he killed her; just like Rider did to Elizabeth and how he almost did to me. He lied to me, he's just like his brother. Henry furrowed his eyebrows at Rose's sudden outburst. He glanced at his dad and could tell that he was using his power on her. Phil stared at Rose, his eyes boring into her. Phil's hand shook a little form using his powers. Henry needed to get Rose out of the trance.

"Rose-"

Henry was cut off when Rose disappeared. He looked around, she wasn't there. Just like that, she was gone.

Chapter 32

Henry looked around the room in utter shock. Rose was gone. Henry became outraged at his father. "Get out," Henry said in a low tone as his teeth gritted together.

"Get out? We just got here," Phil said in shock, he furrowed his eyebrows.

"Get out!" Henry practically yelled at Phil, his voice echoed throughout the house. Hot tears started filled Henry's eyes out of anger. Phil stepped toward Henry and opened his mouth to say something, but Lisa interrupted, jumping in between the two.

"We should go." Lisa grabbed Phil's arms and started to push him towards the door. Phil looked back at Henry, anger written on his face at the fact that his son was getting away with talking to him like this.

Mom, you don't have to go, Henry said to her. He felt guilty for causing her pain.

It's fine, I need to make sure that your father doesn't do anything stupid, Lisa said.

Ok, thanks for stopping by. Love you.

Love you too. Oh, and go find Rose and set things straight.

I will.

Bye, Lisa said as she pushed Phil out the door. Before Phil was fully pushed out the door, he thought something. *I see that the police and Special Units Force were utterly useless.* Henry didn't process the words. He was so mad and worried. He even forgot to give Lisa Rider's ring.

Henry ran to the coat rack and grabbed a hoodie. He ran out the back door. He detected a *very* faint scent of Rose.

***

Rose ran through the woods, her naked feet were being cut from rocks and branches. She felt something within her start to fade as if the reason she was running away was fading. She slowed down as she stumbled and fell. She helped herself up and leaned against a tree as she started to breathe heavily. She felt sprinkles of water touch her skin. In a matter of seconds, rain started to fall. She sighed and could faintly see her breath, the thin cloud spread out before it evaporated. The rain felt like ice, each raindrop felt hard as it thudded against her skin.

He lied to me… The entire time, he lied to me, she thought to herself as she slowly sat down. She dug her fingers into the dirt, the ground warming her cold fingers. She leaned sideways on the tree, supporting herself as she cried.

A couple minutes had passed, somehow Rose hadn't passed out. The feeling that she had was becoming less and less noticeable, but it was still there. Lilly suddenly popped into her head.

I have to go back, she thought as she tried to stand up. She braced her hands on the tree, her legs shook before they faltered and she fell back to the ground. She was so weak that she couldn't even teleport.

She sensed something warm cover her back – a jacket. She stopped feeling the fresh drops of icy rain fall on her. She saw Henry's shoes from the corner of her eye, the cold earth cracking underneath his weight. She tried to move away but found that her muscles were cold and stiff.

"Rose... Please, just listen to me," Henry said softly. Rose didn't say or do anything – she *couldn't*. Henry continued. "Yes, I did kill a pet before, but there was a reason for it. I had gotten her when she was about nineteen, but she had a limp. No one wanted a handicapped pet. I knew that she would rot in a cage, so I got her. Years passed and she aged, but I didn't. She was old and near to death. Hospitals don't take care of humans well. I was her best option. She a-asked me to take her life. I... I drained all of her blood. It was painless for her..." Henry trailed off, tears fell from his eyes. "I waited five years before I got another pet – you."

Henry had only three pets in his life: the one when he was younger, the one with the limp, and Rose. He liked getting the pets out of pet shops, but he couldn't stand it when they aged and had to be put down. It was too painful for him.

He knelt down on one knee next to her and looked her in the eyes. The feeling that she had was completely gone now, now that the feeling was gone she felt all of her strength gone too. She didn't even remember teleporting out of the house or running through the woods.

"I-I..." Rose's body became numb. She felt all of her strength drain before she fainted. Henry caught her before she fully hit the ground, his hands wrapped around Rose's waist. Rose's body felt so cold. Apparently, her body hadn't adjusted yet to the coldness like his. He kept his house lukewarm, cold enough in the summer to cool off, and hot enough in the winter to warm up, even though he preferred coldness over warmth. The rain didn't affect Henry like it did Rose.

Henry lifted Rose off the ground, carrying her bridal style. One of her arms fell limply over the side while her other hand rested on her chest. Henry breathed out and saw his breath in the cold air like thin smoke. Henry muffled his jacket closer to Rose, trying to warm her, and ran back to the house.

By the time he was inside, he could feel Rose shivering in his arms. He carried her upstairs.

Lilly and Joey were outside of their rooms. "What-" Lilly was cut off by Henry closing the door. He wasn't trying to be rude, but he needed to focus on Rose.

He removed the jacket that was around Rose and dropped it on the ground, the wet jacket falling in a heap on the floor. He gently laid Rose in her bed and put the covers on top of her. She snuggled closer to the covers, still shivering. He looked at her lips and saw that they were pale, as well as her skin.

Henry ran to his room and grabbed all the blankets he could find. He went back into Rose's room and wrapped the covers around her. He also walked to the window and closed it.

Slowly but surely, Rose stopped shivering and just laid there. Henry sat down on the ground against the nightstand, like he had done before.

He brought his knees up and laid his head in between. He wrapped his arms around his legs and closed his eyes.

Why didn't I just tell her? Why did my dad have to be the one to tell her? Why does my dad have to be the way he is? Why did he make Rider the way he was? He sighed as he lifted his head from his arms, rubbing his hand over his face. He thought back to his childhood and how everyone became the way they are now.

~flashback~

Henry ran up to where Rider was in the living room, his feet stomping on the hard floor. Henry was a young boy. Rider was older than him by two years, he stood over Henry by about a foot. Phil was talking to Rider. He was standing up straight, intently listening to his father. Henry stood right next to Rider. He stood as straight as he could, holding his hands at his sides like someone from the military. He looked at Rider, making sure he was standing the way his brother was.

Sitting on the ground at Phil's side was a pet. She had blonde, tangled hair that went down to her mid-back, and a pair of light blue eyes. She had bruises on her, she was bracing her weight onto her hands on the floor. She was breathing heavily, exhausted. The dull grey collar around her neck was choking her.

"This is worthless," Phil said as he pointed to the pet on the floor. She subtly flinched as his hand went to her direction. "They are pets and nothing more. Do I make myself clear?" Phil asked sternly to both of the boys. Phil's free hand slightly moved and Rider jerked slightly at the gesture.

"Yes, sir," Rider said as he nodded his head.

"Yes, sir." Henry copied his brother.

"If a pet steps out of line," Phil grabbed the girl by the hair and pulled her off the ground. He let go of her hair as she shakily stood there, her legs were wobbling, barely supporting her weight. "You discipline it," Phil said as he slapped the girl across the face, hard. She started to fall, but Phil grabbed her collar, stopping her from hitting the ground. She wrapped her hands around his arm.

The girl whimpered as she made eye contact with him. Phil slammed the girl on the ground. The girl breathed heavily as the air was knocked out of her. She rolled to the side and Phil kicked her in the stomach. After he did so, she curled into a fetal position as she started to tremble.

"Henry," Lisa called from upstairs. Henry looked her way.

"Yes, mommy?"

"Can you please come up here? I want to talk to you."

"But mommy-"

"No buts, come up here now!" she said more sternly. Henry groaned out of annoyance and started to walk upstairs. Rider snickered that he could continue the 'lesson' with his father by himself.

Henry walked up to Lisa. "Yes, mommy?"

"I need to talk to you," Lisa said as she walked into Henry's room. Henry followed. She sat down on his bed, and he jumped up, sitting next to her.

"What do you need to talk to me about, mommy?" He asked curiously.

"Don't listen to what your father says."

"What? Why? What he's saying is right," Henry said sounding a little bit upset that his mother was questioning his father. A small look of concern came across Lisa's face as she thought Phil had already gotten to him.

"Would it be wrong if someone were to hit you?" Lisa raised an eyebrow, already knowing the answer.

"Yes, of course. But they're pets, and I'm not," Henry answered smugly, proud that he was following what his father had taught him.

Lisa sighed. "Sweetie, could you come here?" She asked as she motioned with her hand for the pet that was huddled in the corner of Henry's room to come to her. It was Henry's birthday present from his father, it was his first pet. He had had her for a week. The girl stood up and walked to them, she had a few bruises on her. Phil thought that he should get the pet into shape to make it easier for Henry.

"Yes, miss?" The girl asked weakly and shyly. The girl had dirty blonde hair, almost brown, and beautiful pair of green eyes. She was about seventeen. She looked down, avoiding eye contact like she had been taught to. Lisa put her finger under her chin and tilted her head up.

"Sweetie, what's your name?" Lisa asked. The girl looked confused for a second.

"My name is whatever master wants to call me," the girl said as she glanced at Henry, but she quickly averted her eyes.

"No, sweetie. What's your real name?" Lisa asked again, there was a pause.

"Melanie, miss."

"See, Henry? Pets have names. They are like us." Lisa told her son.

"No, they're not. They... they-" Henry was interrupted by Lisa.

"Melanie, do you feel pain?" Lisa asked her.

"Yes, miss," Melanie answered as she looked down at her blue bruises.

"See, Henry? They have names, and they feel pain like we do. Except that they don't heal like us. It takes a longer time for them to heal, so you have to be careful and not hurt them.'

"But, but..." Henry trailed off, not exactly knowing what to say.

"Look into her eyes," Lisa said. Henry tilted Melanie's head towards him and stared into her eyes. "What do you see?" Lisa asked him.

"I, I see... I see emotion and life. They're not empty and dead like what dad said, but full of life..." Henry trailed off, realizing something. His eyes slightly widened.

Now read her thoughts, Lisa thought to Henry. He closed his eyes and concentrated really hard.

Why are they being nice to me? What are they doing? Melanie thought as she looked at Henry and Lisa. Henry opened his eyes.

See? They are like us, they aren't less. Lisa said to him.

"I'm, I'm so sorry," Henry said as his eyes teared up. He hugged Melanie. She was confused, she hesitantly hugged him back.

"Don't be sorry, master," she said. Henry shook his head, no.

"No, I'm sorry that you were beaten and treated like shit." Lisa let the word slide even though she had no idea how he knew the word. "When no one else is here, call me Henry," he said as he pulled away.

"Call me Lisa." Lisa smiled at her.

Melanie stared at them. "Thank you mas - Henry," Melanie said, correcting herself. She smiled as her eyes teared up from happiness. Melanie was happy that she now had two people she could trust.

Why does father dislike humans so much? Henry asked.

That's a story for another day. There was a long pause before Henry heard a voice in his head: don't let your father manipulate you like he has done with Rider.

~end flashback~

Chapter 33

Henry sighed and rubbed his face with both hands.

Why couldn't mom have done what she did to me to Rider? Henry thought. Then he remembered how strict his dad was with Rider. He was always Phil's favorite and Phil had no problem making sure Henry knew that. His mom always liked Henry more, he was kinder and gentler then Rider. Lisa, however, only made sure that Henry knew that.

Henry straightened out his legs more, making his knees an inch or so off the ground. He put his hands to his side, supporting some of his weight on them. Breathing In deeply he sighed. Closing his eyes as he leaned his head back on the nightstand. He felt arms wrap around his neck. Rose slid off her bed and into Henry's lap, curling her legs on his lap. She buried her head into his shoulder.

"I'm sorry, I-I don't know w-why I left, yo-your dad-"

"I forgive you," he said as he buried his face into her shoulder. He knew what his father's powers did to people and he knew that Rose didn't leave on her own will. She continued to cry on his shoulder, not knowing why she had run away, only hoping that Henry wasn't mad. "Don't cry, it's ok," Henry said as he tilted her head up towards him. He wiped away the tear with his thumb. She stopped crying, as she did so Henry felt how cold she was. "You're freezing," He said.

"I don't care," she said as she shook her head into his shoulder. Henry grabbed a blanket off of the bed and laid it over Rose.

"You should care," Henry said as he wrapped his arm around her. He grabbed her hand. Rose grabbed the blanket and wrapped it tighter around her, she snuggled closer to Henry, burying her face deeper into his shoulder.

They continued to lay there in each other's arms. Henry slowly started to rock back and forth.

Time had passed and Rose had become a little warmer. "I'm hungry," Rose said, it came out mumbled into Henry's shoulder. He lightly chuckled into her shoulder.

"I thought you would never ask," Henry said as he smiled, hungry too. Rose slid off his lap and stood up. He stood up as well. Henry opened the door as he did so Lilly and Joey fell forward. Henry caught them, one with each arm, he stood them up.

"What are you doing?" Rose asked as she crossed her arms. She raised an eyebrow.

"We were listening," Lilly answered nervously. She rocked back and forth on her feet.

"Why?" Rose asked.

"Because Henry carried you upstairs, you were *passed out*," Lilly said. There was a pause.

"Fair point," Rose said as she nodded.

"You guys mentioned food," Joey said out of the blue. He rubbed his hands together.

"Yes we did, let's go," Henry said as he started to walk downstairs. He grabbed a hoodie off the coat rack and handed it to Rose.

"What's this for?" Rose asked as she held up the hoodie in her hand.

"To help keep you warm," Henry said, as he said it Rose realized that she was freezing. She put it on and it went down to her mid-thigh, she rolled up the sleeve to where her fingers were showing.

Henry, Rose, Lilly, and Joey walked into the kitchen. They all sat down at the island while Henry started to make food. Henry made salmon and grilled vegetables. Lilly and Joey wasted no time devouring their salmon and vegetables. Rose and Henry did take their time eating, making small talk as they ate. Once they were all done eating Henry put all the plates in the dishwasher.

Henry turned around and looked out the window. "It's snowing," Henry said a little shocked. Yesterday was the only indication that winter was coming.

"It is?" Rose said shocked too. She turned around and looked out the window. It was snowing, the huge white flakes falling rapidly. She thought back to all the times that her family had to put on all their clothes and huddle close to one another in order not to freeze to death. It shocked Rose every winter that they still had all their fingers and toes.

"Let's go outside and play in the snow!" Lilly said excited. She slightly jumped up and down.

"No, I'm tired. We'll do it tomorrow," Rose said as she waved her hand in the air, dismissing the idea.

"But what if the snow is gone tomorrow?" Lilly said as she looked at the window.

"Trust me, it's not going be gone by tomorrow," Henry said as he looked out the window again.

"Please, Rose," Lilly said as she gave her the puppy dog eyes.

"When has that face *ever* worked on me..? Never," Rose said as she mimicked Lilly's face. She then smiled and laughed. Lilly dropped the face.

"Fine," Lilly said as she stomped upstairs. Joey followed. Once they were both gone Rose and Henry started to laugh.

"Your sister is adorable," Henry said as he laughed more.

"Please don't encourage her, please," Rose begged as she held her hands together. Henry laughed.

"What happens if I tell her that?" Henry said in a 'what are you going to do' voice. Rose raised an eyebrow and crossed her arms, she started to tap her foot. She stared at Henry. There was a pause. "I'm sorry," Henry said. Rose remained in the stance. "I won't tell your sister," Rose didn't budge. "You're scaring me." She didn't move. "You're scary," Henry said as he sat down at the island, he hung his head. "I'm sorry."

Rose started to laugh. "You're too easy to crack," Rose said as she laughed more.

"Does that mean you forgive me?" Henry asked as he looked up, he gave her puppy dog eyes as he slightly made his bottom lip bigger.

"Yes, I forgive you," right as Rose said that Henry stood up and picked her up. He used his super speed to get to the couch, he laid her down on the couch. Before she could do anything he started to move the couch, she fell down sideways. The couch made a slight squeaking noise as it slid across the marble.

He stopped moving the couch once he was in front of a giant window. Rose sat up as he sat down next to Rose. He wrapped her arm around Rose and she leaned her head against his shoulder. They both looked out the window, watching as the snow fell. Rose tried to find a snowflake that looked alike, even though she could barely see. It was a game she used to play when she was with her parents and sister.

A long time had passed and it became so dark that they could no longer see the snow falling. "I'm tired," Henry said as he yawned, he stretched his arms.

"Same," Rose said as she yawned and stretched too. They both got up and walked upstairs, they hugged.

"Night," Henry said as he kissed her on the cheek.

"Night," Rose said as she snuggled her head into his chest. They left each other's embrace and went to their own room, they both started to rest.

"Rose," there was a pause. "Rose! Wake up it's morning. You said you would take me outside to play in the snow," Lilly said as she sat down in the bed next to Rose.

"Not now," Rose grumbled into her pillow. She waved her hand in the air, telling Lilly to go away.

"But you promised!" Lilly said as she laid her hands on Rose's arm. She shook Rose.

"Do you know how rare it is for me to not be knocked out, pass out, or have nightmares and actually have a good night's sleep?" Rose said as she counted on her fingers. She dropped her hand after she had hit three.

"But you PROMISED!" Lilly said as she shook Rose more. Rose didn't move, she only groaned into her pillow out of annoyance. Lilly sighed, she looked at the nightstand and saw one of the drawers was slightly open. She saw something blue and gold in it. "What's this?" Lilly said as she opened the draw and pulled out Rose's collar and leash. Rose turned around and looked at it, she rubbed her eyes, adjusting them.

"It's my collar," Rose said as she closed her eyes again.

"Collar?" Lilly asked as she furrowed her eyebrows.

"Yeah, pets wear collars. I was a pet, I wore a collar," Rose said with little to no emotion. Lilly just stared at it blankly.

"Can we go outside now?" Lilly asked as she shook Rose more.

"No."

"Please."

"No!" Rose said louder.

"PLEASE!" Lilly practically yelled.

"Fine," Rose said. Lilly clapped her hands excitedly. "Only if you drag me out of bed and outside," Rose said as she smirked. Lilly threw back the covers. "What are you doing?" Rose asked.

"I'm dragging you out of bed," Lilly replied as she grabbed Rose's wrist and pulled her out of bed. Lilly dragged Rose out of her room. Rose hit the floor with a thump.

"Henry," Rose said agitated. There was no response. "Henry!" She said louder. His door opened. Joey came out, he was dragging something, Henry.

"They got me," Henry said as Joey dragged him out to the hallway, following Lilly.

"What do you mean they got you?" Rose asked.

"I mean they got me."

"Why aren't you moving?"

"Because I'm tired. You?"

"Because I'm tired. Since when have you been tired, you're never tired?"

"Every once in a while I need to rest."

"So today of all days you choose to rest?"

"I didn't choose it, it just happened to be today. Besides you're always tired."

"I'm always tired, what is that supposed to mean?" She asked as she raised an eyebrow at him.

"Nothing," He said, some fear seeping into his voice.

"No it means something."

"No it doesn't," Henry said as his voice cracked.

They were so caught up in their 'argument' that they didn't know they were going down the stairs. They were now being dragged towards the door. Henry and Rose continued in their conversation. "Stop!" They both said at the same time. Joey and Lilly stopped.

"What?" Lilly asked.

"We need jackets, sunglasses, and shoes," Henry said. Lilly and Joey dropped their hands, grabbed the jackets and slid them onto their arms. They zipped up the jackets, grabbed the sunglasses and put it on them. They then put their shoes on their feet. Rose and Henry were both wearing sweatpants. Lilly opened the door and dragged Rose outside.

Once the snow touched Rose she yelped and jumped high in the air. Henry quietly chuckled to himself, he then felt the snow. He did the same thing that Rose had done. The snow was about two to three feet high, going up to below Rose's knee and to Henry's shins. The rain had made the roads icy, not a slush, but a hard, slippery ice. A steady flow of snow was still falling, adding to the already tall snow.

Rose and Henry stood next to each other. They both wrapped their arms around themselves. "We should have done something," Rose said as she looked around.

"Agreed," Henry said. There was a pause. "Duck," Henry quickly said to Rose. Right as she ducked a snowball flew where her head was, it flew past Henry. Rose looked at Lilly.

"Did you just throw a snowball at me?" Rose asked. Lilly picked up another snowball.

"Yes," She said as she threw it at Rose. Rose ducked and used her super speed to get in front of Lilly. She had a hand full of snow in her hand, she shoved in Lilly's face. Lilly fell backwards into the snow, landing on her back. The snow encased her.

Joey walked behind Henry with a snowball in his hand. He was tiptoeing towards Henry, taking huge steps. "Don't even think about it," Henry said, not even glancing back at Joey. Joey dropped the snow and stood next to Henry.

"Don't think about what?" Joey asked innocently.

"I heard you pick up snow and I heard the snow crunch under your feet as you walked," Henry said, still not looking at Joey.

"Oh," Joey said. They both looked at Rose and Lilly. Lilly threw another snowball at Rose. Rose caught it threw it back at Lilly, it hit her in the face. She fell backwards. Rose jumped on Lilly and continued to shove snow in her face. "Girls," Joey said as she shook his head while rolling his eyes.

"They're adorable," Henry said as he chuckled. There was a pause.

"Yeah, they are," Joey replied. Henry looked down at Joey and smirked.

"You like Lilly," Henry said. Joey's cheeks blushed a bright red.

"N-no I don't," Joey said badly lying. *Yeah, a little.* Joey thought. Henry laughed. Joey looked at Henry. "What?"

"I just read your thoughts," Henry said as he smirked again.

"You have to stop doing that," Joey said as he crossed his arms. He rolled his eyes again.

"Want to talk about it?" Henry asked even though he knew the answer.

"Yes," Joey said immediately. They walked off and started to talk.

"So...why do you like Lilly?" Henry asked as he put both of his hands in his pockets.

"She's... she's just... you know... I can't describe it, she's just perfect. Maybe not everyone else sees it, but I see it," Joey said as he blushed again. Henry was a little shocked that this was coming from a thirteen year old. But at the same time he didn't expect anything else, they had been together for years. "Do you know what I mean?" Joey asked as he looked up at Henry. Henry nodded his head.

"Yeah, I do, when I first saw her in that pet shop I could tell that no one else saw what I saw. I could tell that all they saw was a human, a pet that was evident by the bruises that covered her body. She was scared, abused, almost broken, but underneath all that I could see a diamond in the ruble," Henry said as he smiled. Just thinking about Rose made him happy. The boys continued to talk.

Rose was still on top of Lilly, she held Lilly's arm behind her back. "Ow," Lilly said as she squirmed.

Say it."

"No."

"Say it!" Rose said as she applied more pressure, pushing Lilly's arm further into her back.

"Uncle. Uncle!" Lilly said as she tapped the ground with her free hand.

"That's what you get for waking me up early," Rose said as she stood up. Lilly was breathing heavily as she held her arm. "Let's just walk," Rose said. Lilly nodded her head in agreement. They started to walk in the opposite way that Henry and Joey had gone. There was silence.

"What... what was it like to be a pet?" Lilly asked as she looked at Rose. Rose sucked in a deep breath, trying to look for the words.

"Depends," Rose simply said as she stared straight ahead.

"On what?" Lilly asked as she looked at Rose.

"On what kind of master you get. My last master was abusive and didn't value humans at all. Henry is kind and actually does value humans."

"What...?" Lilly trailed off, not sure if the question she was going to ask was ok to ask.

"What were you going to say?" Rose said, still staring straight ahead.

"What was your old master like..." Lilly asked in a quiet voice, she trailed off. There was a pause, for a few seconds the only noise was the wind blowing in the snow.

"Ah... like I said he was abusive, disobeyed him, he would beat me. Talked out of line or when he didn't ask me to, he would beat me. If he was mad for something that I didn't even do, he would beat me. If he was bored, he would beat me. There didn't have to be a reason for him to beat me and I couldn't say or do anything about it," Rose's eyes seemed to barely tear up as she thought back to Rider beating her within an inch of her life a couple of times.

"What... what was the worst punishment that he gave you?" Lilly asked, she could tell that it was upsetting Rose but she *needed* to know how her sister was treated. Rose turned around, her back facing Lilly. Lilly stopped walking as she looked as Rose's back. Rose lifted up her shirt to show the thirty whip marks on her back.

"The worst thing he did was whip me, it was actually the first day that he bought me. He wanted to literally whip me into shape," Rose said as she dropped her shirt. They continued to walk.

"I'm sorry," Lilly said as she looked at Rose.

"Don't be, that was a while ago. Besides Henry got me next so..." She trailed off. Lilly nodded head, understanding what Rose was saying. Rose was going to say something else but a noise cut her off, a car. "Do you hear that?" Rose asked as she looked around.

"No," Lilly said as she looked around, trying to find what Rose was hearing. Rose looked in the direction of the road and saw a car coming their way, it pulled up and stopped in the driveway. A person got out and started to walk to the front door.

"I'm going to bite you." Rose said quickly.

"What?!" Lilly said nervously.

"It's ok, I'm not going to drink your blood. But if the people see that we aren't feeding off our pets then they'll get suspicious. I have to do this," Rose said, trying to get Lilly to understand what and why she was doing this. Lilly nodded her head in agreement.

Rose leaned down to Lilly's neck and sunk her fangs into her neck, Lilly winced. Rose retracted her fangs, she let a little bit of blood run out of the holes, barely falling down her neck. Rose licked the wound healing it. Rose then took her forefinger and smudged some of the blood around the holes, she then licked her fingers.

They started to walk/run back the way they came. Henry and Joey were doing the same thing. As they reached the woman at the door Rose saw that Henry had done the same thing to Joey that she had done to Lilly.

They reached the woman at the same time. *Act like pets,* Henry said to both Lilly and Joey. They nodded subtly. The woman had blonde hair that went down to her mid back. She was wearing black skinny jeans with black UGG boots, a grey t-shirt, a black jacket, and a grey scarf. "Who are you?" Henry asked as he pointed to the woman.

"I'm Zoey," she said and looked at all of them. They looked lost. "I was Rider's fiancée."

Chapter 34

Can't we have two days a peace? Just two! Henry thought angrily. He didn't want any more reminders of Rider at this time.

Amen, Rose thought back. Rose subtly pushed Lilly behind her. Henry did the same with Joey.

"It's good to meet you," Zoey said as she extended her hand to Henry. He hesitantly shook it. Looking down at her free hand he saw the exact same ring that Rider was wearing on his finger.

"Good to meet you too, I'm Henry," Henry said as he eyed her up and down, trying to read her body language. Zoey then turned around and extended her hand to Rose.

"I'm... Rose," Rose said, forgetting her name for a second. They shook hands.

"And who are they?" Zoey asked as she pointed to Lilly and Joey. They were both hiding behind Rose and Henry.

"These are our pets," Henry said in a little bit of a protective tone. Zoey nodded her head in understanding. "So a... why are you here?" Henry asked as he realized she hadn't said why.

"Oh, right, sorry I almost forgot. I stopped by your mother's house, to ask where Rider was," she stopped choking on her tears. She swallowed back her tears. "She told me that he was... d-dead," Zoey stuttered as a tear fell from her eye and down her cheek. She wiped it away with the back of her hand. "When I asked where he was she said she didn't know, so I came here, hoping you could help."

Henry looked at Rose. *What should we do?* Henry asked.

I don't know, Rider must have dated her after he gave me up. She does seems nice.

What could be the harm of her seeing where Rider is buried?

Calling the police.

"Please I just want to know where Rider is buried. I won't tell anyone if that's what you're worried about. I just have to see for myself before I fully let go," Zoey said as another tear rolled down her cheek. Henry looked at Rose and she nodded.

"I think you should come inside," Henry said. He opened the door and they all walked in. "Pets, go upstairs until further notice," Henry said sternly to Joey and Lilly.

"Yes master," They both said at the same time. They walked upstairs and into their rooms.

"They're well trained pets aren't they?" Zoey asked as she saw Lilly and Joey follow orders without a second thought.

"We hadn't had to discipline them yet," Henry said, sounding proud. "Please, sit," Henry said as he gestured towards the dining room table. They all sat down. "So what do you want to know?"

"I want to see Rider, where he is buried," Zoey said. Henry sucked in a tight breath.

"Ok... We can take you there. Rose if you don't mind," Henry said. He didn't want to drive there and back in the uncomfortable silence, tears, maybe shouting, and he didn't know if she would lash out at them while he was driving. He would rather be there in a second and come back in a second.

Rose stood up and extended her hands to both of them Henry took hers and Zoey hesitantly took her hand not knowing what to expect. Once she grabbed Rose's hand, Rose concentrated on Henry's cabin. Within a second they were there.

"Where are we?" Zoey asked as she looked around.

"My... my cabin." Henry hesitantly said.

"*Your cabin,* you mean he's buried here. Where?" Zoey asked. Not liking the fact that Rider was here.

"Follow me," Henry said as he started to walk into the woods. Rose was at his side and Zoey was a foot or so behind them, looking around the woods as she walked. After some time of walking they came across two patches of earth where the dirt was above the ground a little and the dirt was loose.

One of the piles of dirt was marked with a rock formation in the letter R, the snow turning the rocks icy. Henry opened his mouth to say something but his tears choked him. He couldn't speak, all he did was point and look away.

Zoey stared at the grave for a few seconds before she dropped on her knees and started to cry. She reached out her hand and grabbed the dirt, squeezing it. The frozen dirt cracked as she crushed it. "It was s-self-defense," Henry managed to choke out. Rose grabbed his hand. "I-I'm sorry," Henry said as a tear fell down his cheek. Rose wiped it away.

Zoey cried even harder. Rose let go of Henry's hand and walked to Zoey. She knelt down next to her and placed her arm around her. "I'm sorry. I know what it's like to lose someone close to you," Rose said, her words barely even audible.

"Who?" Zoey asked as she continued to cry.

"My parents," Rose said as she just stared at the R. Tears started to appear in her eyes, thinking back to the day that she was taken and her parents were killed. Zoey looked up and around at Henry. He had his back turned to them.

"Guess we've all lost someone close to us," Zoey said. There was a short pause. "Henry come here, please," Zoey said. Henry turned around and walked towards them, he knelt down next to Zoey. He somehow managed to look her in the eyes, there was a pause. "H-how?" She managed to choke out.

"He attacked me, he had a broken piece of wood above my heart and he tried to stab me with glass. He was trying to k-kill me. I had no other choice," Henry said as another tear rolled down his face. Zoey embraces Henry in a hug. Henry was silent for a few seconds as he hugged her back. They pulled away from each other. "L-let's just go back," Henry said, not wanting to stare at his brother's grave anymore. Zoey nodded. They all stood up and Rose teleported them back to the house. They were now in the kitchen. Henry grabbed a box of tissues. They all dried their eyes.

Henry went to a cabinet and grabbed a glass of wine and two wine glasses, he knew that Rose had never drunken wine before and she would probably find it bitter, that and she was nineteen. He poured Zoey and himself a glass and then put the wine back in the cabinet.

He handed Zoey her glass. Rose looked at it questioningly. Henry handed her the glass she took a small sip. As she pulled the glass away from her she made a sour face and shook her head back and forth, no. Henry chuckled as he took the glass away from Rose. She stared at the glass as if it was evil.

They all sat down in the living room. Zoey sat in the chair, while Henry and Rose took the couch. For the first time since she was here Zoey looked around. "You have a really nice house."

"Thank you," Henry said. A long awkward silence fell over all of them.

"So... how long have you to been together?" Zoey asked as she pointed to Henry and Rose. They looked at each other. Rose shrugged her shoulders.

"To be honest I don't know, *so much* has happened," Henry said. Zoey nodded her head.

An hour or so had passed and they had all made small talk. They had not talked about Rider or anything like that. Zoey stood up, laying the wine glass on the table. "It's getting late, I should go," Zoey said as Henry and Rose stood up. Henry extended his hand and they shook hands. So did Rose.

"It was good talking to you," Henry said. Zoey nodded as she walked out of the door and drove off.

Rose leaned against Henry and he put his head on top of hers. "You ok?" Rose asked.

"Yeah, I'm fine. Let's not dread on the past, I'm with you," Henry said. Rose pulled her head up from his shoulder and looked at him. She ran her fingers through his hair, Henry smiled. She ran her fingers through his hair again.

"What are you doing?" Henry asked as he looked up at her hand.

"I'm playing with your hair," she simply said as she took her other hand and parted his hair down the middle. She let go of his hair and it naturally went back into place. It was a little messed up.

"Why?" Henry asked as he furrowed his eyebrows.

"I don't know it's just so... poofy," Rose said as she took her hands and pressed down the hair. It naturally bounced up again.

"You make fun of and play with my hair when it was wet and now when it's normal. You have a problem," Henry said as he pointed to Rose.

"I do not."

"Do to."

"Do not."

"Do to." Henry said, there was a pause. "We sound like five year olds," Henry said as he laughed. She pulled her hand away from his hair and sat back. "What are you doing? Don't stop, it felt like a massage," Henry said as he grabbed her hand and laid it on top of his head. She pulled her hand away.

"You criticize me when I'm playing with your hair but when I stop you want me to continue?" She asked as she furrowed her eyebrows.

"Yes."

"You're unbelievable," she said as she rolled her eyes.

There was a pause. "Should we tell Lilly and Joey that they can come out of their rooms now?" Henry asked as he looked upstairs.

"No, that's an awful idea," Rose said as she shook her head, no.

"Fair enough," Henry said as he shrugged. They both leaned back. Henry grabbed the remote and turned on the TV.

They had been watching TV for half an hour. Henry had had something on his mind for a while but he couldn't seem to think of it. Then he remembered something that his father had thought right after Rose disappeared and Lisa had to push him out the door.

'I see that the police and Special Units Force were completely useless,' Henry then thought about what the police officer had said to him when they visited them.

'The man that reported it must have worked up enough courage to tell on a Lord.*'* Henry's eyes widened, now everything made since. The man that reported it didn't work up enough courage to tell on a Lord, but to tell on his own son.

Henry stood up. "I'll be right back," Henry said quickly.

"Where are you going?" Rose asked as she stood up.

"To talk to my father," Henry said as he grabbed his keys off the coat rack. Rose only nodded, not wanting him to go to his father's house. He hugged her and she hugged back. He kissed her head and she buried her face into his chest. "I love you," Henry said.

"I love you too," Rose said into his chest. He finally let go of her.

"I'll be back," Henry said to her. She nodded her head again. He walked out the front door and to his garage. He hopped in his car and started to drive.

I can't believe my father would stoop to this level.

Chapter 35

Henry drove as fast as he could, the roads still icy. He was clutching the steering wheel so tightly that his knuckles were white. His eyes were fixed on the road. He couldn't believe that his own father would do something like this. He knew his father hated humans, but he didn't know his father hated them to this extent.

By the time he reached his parent's house most of his anger had worn off, but not all. He parked his car. His hands slowly unclenched the steering wheel, slightly shaking from grasping it so hard. As he got out he saw his mom being shoved out the door. She stumbled down a few steps, nearly falling. The door slammed behind her. Henry rushed to her, her eyes widened as she saw Henry. She was shocked to see him. Her eyes and cheeks were stained with tears. She quickly wiped them away with her hand, not wanting Henry to see his mom in a wreck.

"Mom, are you ok? What happened? Did he hurt you?" Henry asked as he looked at his mom up and down, worried.

"No, he didn't hurt me. Don't worry I'm fine," Lisa said as she waved her hand in the air, dismissing it. She wiped the back of her hand over her eyes and part of her face, wiping away more tears

"What happened?" Henry said more slowly. He bent down to her level, looking Lisa in the eyes. "And don't try lying to me," Henry said as he nodded his head, yes. Asking if she understood. Lisa lightly laughed at Henry's 'don't try lying to me,' line. She stopped laughing as she raised her eyes to meet his.

"We had a fight and I... ended it," there was a pause. She wiped away more tears. "I told him that he had to stop being so mean and heartless to humans and vampires, aka his son. He told me that he would change but of course I *knew* he was lying so... one thing led to another and now I'm out here. He won't let me grab my stuff," she said as she glanced back at the house.

Henry nodded his head as he pursed his lips. He walked up the stairs to the door. He took a deep breath as he lightly knocked on the door like a true gentleman.

A few seconds passed before the door was roughly opened. "What-" Phil was caught off when Henry punched him. Phil fell down backwards. Henry grabbed him by the shirt and lifted him off the ground, he slammed him into the wall. "Henry, what are you doing?!" Phil practically yelled at Henry as he struggled in Henry's grasp. Henry's grasp wouldn't budge, his muscles flexed through his shirt.

"You are to let mom grab her things," Henry said in a low tone. Trying to contain his anger at the way Phil was treating his mother.

Lisa walked into the house and looked at Phil and Henry and gave a faint smile at Phil, as if to say 'that's what you deserve.' *Thank you, Henry,* she said as she walked upstairs and into her room.

No problem, mommy, Henry said as he watched Lisa enter her room. The old habit of calling her mommy instead of mom came back.

"What are you doing here?!" Phil demanded as he struggled more. His voice echoed throughout the house, snapping Henry out of his thoughts.

"*You* told the police that Rose and I were hugging in the store. You were probably the one who manipulated the Special Units Force as well. *You started* all of this!" Henry said as he raised Phil off the ground even more. His voice echoed throughout the house.

"So what if I did? It's illegal. I was helping you," Phil said trying to manipulate Henry. He stared at Henry. *All I have to do is get him to slightly believe what he's doing is wrong,* Phil thought as he continued to try and manipulate Henry.

"No, you weren't. You hurt my family and me!" Henry said.

"It's not your family," Phil said as he continued to try and use his power. "It's just a pathetic human."

"She is my family and if you hurt my family again... you'll regret it," Henry said as he started to grit his teeth together.

"Henry, listen to yourself. I'm your family not that *pet.*"

"She's more of my family then you ever were!" Henry practically screamed as his eyes started to tear up. He swallowed back his tears, not allowing Phil to see. "If you try to hurt *my* family *ever* again," Henry paused again. "Don't hurt my family ever again."

Phil nodded his head, understandingly. He had stopped trying to manipulate Henry. Henry's power was getting into people's mind, it was pointless. Lisa walked down the stairs with three bags. One was rolling down the stairs, the other two were criss crossed over each other, one on each arm. Henry heard her walking down the stairs, the suitcase thumping as it hit each stair. Henry released his grip on Phil's shirt. Phil fell on the ground, sliding down the wall and onto his butt, too shocked at the way Henry had just treated him to do anything. Henry grabbed two of

Lisa's bags and walked outside. They walked to her car, a grey mustang, and put the bags in the trunk. Henry rolled his eyes as he saw that his mom was still driving a sports car.

She needs an old person's car, Henry thought to himself. Lisa slammed the trunk shut

"Are you ok?" Henry asked as he turned and faced Lisa.

"Yeah, I'm ok... it just, it just wasn't working out," she said as she shrugged. There was a pause.

"Do you need a place to stay?" Henry asked her. She shook her head, yes.

"Yes, I doubt that Phil will allow me to use one of our spare houses," Lisa said. Henry nodded his head. Lisa took a step closer and cupped his face in her hand. "My sweet baby boy," Lisa said as she smiled. "Thank you."

"It's no big deal," Henry said as he shrugged. Lisa hugged him. "I love you, mommy," Henry said as he hugged her too.

"I love you too, Hen," Lisa said using the nickname that she had given him while he was young. He pulled away and looked at her.

"Mom, I thought that you agreed to *never* call me that again," Henry said as he looked at her. He raised an eyebrow. She laughed as she took one hand, grabbing Henry's face, and squashed Henry's cheeks together. He moved his face away and out of her hand. He rubbed his face with his hand.

"I just wanted to see how you would react," Lisa said as she laughed more.

"You're unbelievable," Henry said as he sighed and put his face in his hand.

"No, I'm not. I'm funny," she said as she crossed her arms.

"Keep telling yourself that," Henry said. His face in his hand still.

She put her hand on her hips and raised an eyebrow. "Who's the better cook?"

"Me," Henry replied. Lisa shook her head, no. She knew it was a lie. There was a pause. "Do you have to bring up 'who's the better cook' every time you're losing an argument?" He asked as he lifted his face from his hand, looking at her. She laughed and nodded her head. He sighed. "I should head out Rose is expecting me," Henry said as he looked at his car.

"Ok, tell her I said hi. You can head out without me. I need to make sure that the suitcases are secure."

"Ok, love you," Henry said as he leaned down and placed a kiss on her cheek.

"Love you too, bye Hen," Lisa said as she kissed him on the cheek.

"Mom, stop calling me that," Henry said as his cheeks blushed out of embarrassment. She only laughed again. He walked back to his car. *You're unbelievable,* Henry thought to her as he hopped in, before she could respond he drove off. *Bringing up who's the better cook, that's just stupid, she didn't have a good argument. Why does she always pull that card? I'm a good cook, I'm probably better than her... Who am I kidding she's a human lie detector, even Rose said that she was a better cook than me. I have to step up my game,* Henry paused thinking. *Hen? What kind of a nickname is that, a stupid one,* Henry said as he rolled his eyes.

His thoughts were interrupted when he saw headlights on a car, the car looked like a black Hummer. The way to his parent's house way secluded, it was rare to see a car. Right before the cars started to pass each other the other car switched lanes into Henry's. Henry quickly turned the wheel to get to the other lane. Since the roads were icy his car spun out. His car spun around completely and hit the other car.

The other car hit Henry's car in the top left side. Since Henry's car was a Porsche his car was destroyed. The left side of his car folded back as the other car crashed into his. Henry's head slammed into the window, cracking the window and knocking him out. Before his head hit the steering wheel the airbag went off.

Henry's head fell on the steering wheel as his hands went limp at his sides. Blood leaked out of the cuts on his forehead that he had gotten when he hit the window. Blood came out of his nose, running down his face.

The person got out of their car and walked to Henry's, they opened the door. They grabbed Henry and sat him back, the person unbuckled Henry. They grabbed his arms and tried to pull him out of the car, he was stuck. They looked down and saw that the car was pinning Henry's leg against the seat. They scooted his seat as far back as it would go, once it was scooted back the person saw that a bone was creating a bump against his skin. They grabbed his arms and pulled him out.

Henry fell on the ground, limply. The person stepped down on the bone. They grabbed Henry's arms and dragged him to their car, a streak of blood rubbed off on the road as he was dragged. After they had managed to get Henry in the car they drove off.

Some time had passed when Lisa drove to where Henry's car was in the road. Her eyes widened at the sight of the destroyed car.

It can't be, Lisa thought as she stopped her car and got out. She recognized the car, she put her hand over her mouth. *It can't be,* Lisa thought again. She looked in the open door of his car and saw the blood on the window, it smelt like Henry. She looked at the seat divider and saw a wallet. She picked it up, in it was Henry's driver's license. She dropped the wallet and looked at the drag marks and the blood from where he had been dragged across the gravel. She fell to her knees and started to cry. *Not my baby, not my baby boy. Not Henry.*

It took her a long time to compose herself. She called someone to tow his car. She hopped in her car and drove towards Henry's house.

Rose was sitting in Henry's office, reading. She was trying to pass the time.

Henry's been gone a long time, Rose thought as she turned the page. She sighed as she did so. As she sighed the door burst open. Rose quickly closed the book and she stood up. She rushed towards the door, it was Lisa. Lisa's face was stained with tears again.

"W-what's wrong, where's Henry?" Rose stuttered. She could tell that something was seriously wrong just by the sight of Lisa.

"I don't know, he's been kidnapped."

Chapter 36

"Wh-what do you mean he's been kidnapped?" Rose asked as tears started to appear in her eyes.

"I found his car smashed and his blood and drag marks on the road," Lisa said as a tear rolled down her face. A tear rolled down Rose's face too. They locked each other into a hug and cried on each other's shoulders.

They then made their ways to the couch. Lisa sat down in the chair and Rose at the couch. They both stared down as Rose started to form a game plan in her head. Lilly and Joey walked down the stairs. They saw Rose crying and Lisa.

"Who's this?" Lilly asked Rose as she looked at Lisa, Rose stayed silent as she continued to think. Lisa answered for her.

"I-I'm Lisa, H-Henry's mother," Lisa said as another tear rolled down her face.

Joey and Lilly could tell that something was terribly wrong. "What's wrong?" Lilly asked. Her voice came out cracked, she glanced between Rose and Lisa. Joey did the same.

"H-Henry's been kidnapped," Rose said as she continued to stare blankly at the wall.

"Who could have done this?" Lilly asked as her eyes teared up. Rose looked at Lisa. "He went to go visit Phil, d-do you think that he..." Rose trailed off. Lisa shook her head, no.

"I left after Henry did. Phil never came out of the house, it couldn't have been him," Lisa paused. "Did anyone come over before he went missing?" Lisa asked as she looked at Rose. She looks at Lisa, her face already having the answer.

"Yes, actually Rider's fiancee, Zoey... But she left before he did and the time that she was here she was nice," Rose paused. "Should we tell the cops?" Rose asked, she already knew the answer. Lisa shook her head, no. Another tear rolled down her face.

"If they investigate then they might find out the truth about you. They'll take you away, probably me, and those two," Lisa said as she pointed to Lilly and Joey. "Even if they do find Henry there's no telling what will happen to him and what they will do to him if they find out," another tear rolled down her face at the thought of Henry being rescued only to be taken away again.

Rose only nodded as she went back to staring at the wall. Joey grabbed a blanket from the couch and put it over Lisa. He started to walk away when Lisa grabbed his arm.

"Thank you," Lisa said as she let go of his arm. She brought the blanket closer to her. Joey nodded as he walked back upstairs.

"Lilly?" Rose asked. She was still staring at the wall.

"Yeah?" Lilly asked as she looked at Rose.

"C-can you please hand me one of Henry's hoodies?" Rose asked as she looked at the coat rack. Lilly nodded her head as she walked to the rack. She grabbed a hoodie and gave it to Rose.

Rose laid her head down on the arm of the couch she brought the hoodie to her face and breathed in his warm vanilla scent. She was trying to breathe in his scent enough to where she went out she could easily pick it up.

Lilly laid down next to Rose and started to comfort her.

"Don't worry we'll find him," Lilly said to Rose. She wrapped her arm around Rose, comforting her.

"How can you be so sure?" Rose asked as she glanced back at Lilly.

"Because you were taken away from me and now we are together," Lilly said as the memory and all the years of questions came back into her mind. Rose nodded, it was the only hope that she had. She laid her head back down on the hoodie.

We have no clues to who it is, even if it is Zoey, there's no way of finding her. Why do things like this always happen to me or the people I love? Rose thought as a tear fell down her face. She became cold at the thought of it. She sat up and put on Henry's hoodie, it went down to her mid-thigh, it covered up her hands. She laid back down.

She glanced at Lisa and saw her face buried into the blanket, her shoulders rose and fell as she cried. Rose felt sorry for Lisa, she had recently lost one of her other sons and now she was losing the other. Not to mention the divorce. Rose looked back at the wall as she formed a plan.

It was late at night and Lilly stood up.

"I'm going to go to bed. Will you two be ok?" Lilly asked as she looked at Rose and Lisa. They both nodded. Lilly walked upstairs. Joey was at the top waiting for her, once she made it to the top he grabbed Lilly's arm.

"Are they ok?" Joey whispered to her, he released his grip on her arm.

"Honestly, I don't know, they're both really sad," Lilly said as she looked down at Lisa and Rose. Rose had her face buried into Henry's hoodie. Joey only nodded. "I should go to bed, I have a feeling that we'll have our hands tied tomorrow,"

Lilly said. Joey nodded again. They walked into their rooms and fell asleep.

Rose stared at the wall, her hands were near her face. She was breathing in his scent again, it calmed her down. She was going to go out soon to look for him. The reason she had waited until it was night was so she didn't attract any unwanted attention. Rose stood up and teleported as one thought raced through her mind.

Please let me find Henry, please, Rose begged.

~where Henry is~

Henry slowly opened his eyes, all he saw was blackness. He started to lift his arms and move his legs, but couldn't. His hands and feet were handcuffed. A pair of handcuffs held his arms behind his back, he felt as his hands touched the cold wall. A pair of handcuffs were cuffed around his ankles. He felt the cuffs rubbing against his ankle bone. He had a huge headache and his leg hurt from being crushed, even though he couldn't feel his leg with his hands he could feel that something was out of place inside his leg.

What happened? He thought to himself, as he did so he saw the memory of his car being smashed and his head being slammed into the window.

His headache increased at just the thought of it. His eyes had adjusted to the blackness. He was just in a room, no furniture, no anything, just him.

I need to get out of here, he thought as he tried to sit up. His head and leg screamed at him to stop moving. The rest of his body was sore and stiff, not wanting to move either.

He finally managed to sit up. He started to try and wiggle his hands out of the cuffs. He felt his skin being cut. He felt blood dripping down his hands so he stopped. He knew that he needed blood in order for his leg to fully heal and for his headache to go away.

His thoughts went to Rose and his mom. He imagined Rose and his mom crying on each other's shoulders, the thought made his eyes water. Thinking about the two people that he loved most, being so miserable.

I'll find a way out of here, I promise Rose and mommy, Henry thought to himself. Calling Lisa mommy comforted him, it took him back to when he was a kid and Lisa would always cheer him up after Phil would ignore him and only talk to Rider.

He heard footsteps outside of his door. He heard a key go into a lock and the handle turned, as soon as the door was opened a bright light shone through. Henry closed his eyes and turned his head away. His eyes adjusted to the light, he looked up and saw blonde hair, Zoey.

Chapter 37

She propped the door open, letting in light. She saw Henry sitting up. "You're awake," Zoey said. Her face and eyes were stained with tears. However, her eyes were different than they were the first time Henry had seen her. They were now a very dark, familiar red.

"Why?" Henry asked. His voice came out hoarse and slightly cracked.

"Why, *why*?!" She almost yelled. Her voice echoing through the small room. "Because you killed Rider, my fiancé. You *killed* him," Zoey said as a tear escaped her eye, she quickly wiped it away with the back of her hand.

"It was self-defense," Henry said. The memory of him killing Rider entered his mind. He closed his eyes as he sighed deeply. When he opened his eyes he saw her standing a few feet in front of him.

Within a second, she punched him in the face. He fell over as he landed on his side. He groaned in pain his leg moved and his head slightly hit the floor. She kicked him in the face and stomach multiple times.

When she finally stopped she was breathing heavily, exhausted from beating him up. She put her hands against the wall, propping herself up. She was standing over him.

Henry had blood coming out of his nose and mouth. He could feel bruises forming on his face and stomach. Now his entire body hurt.

"Don't say that. Rider would never do something like that," Zoey said as another tear rolled out of her eye. "He wouldn't," she said again.

"But he did," Henry said. His voice was weak, he spit out blood. Zoey shook her head.

"He wouldn't, I knew him he wouldn't do something like that."

"I knew him too. He was my brother he tried to *kill* me." Zoey only shook her head, there was a long silence. "Why did you kidnap me?" Henry asked again. He knew that him killing Rider wasn't the only reason and he had a theory as to why she did it and was just testing it. Zoey took a deep, shaky breath.

"You killed him," she said almost robotically.

" Zoey, this isn't you-"

"Yes, it is!... So I'm going to give you four days then..." Zoey trailed off. Henry knew what she was going to say.

"Please don't do this to Rose, please," Henry begged. She grabbed his hair and made him sit up. He groaned in pain as his leg was quickly moved. Pain shot into his head as she grasped onto his hair. He stared into her dark red eyes.

"Don't try and play the victim card now. You lost your chance when you killed him." Zoey pushed him back on the ground again. He winced as he hit the ground. She walked out of the room before he could say anything else. She closed the door behind her. He heard her lock the door again.

He was in complete darkness again, his thoughts once again trailed off to Rose. *I promise I'll get out of here, for you.*

~Henry's house~

Rose laid on the couch with her eyes closed as she clutched her stomach. She had thrown up several times. She still had Henry's hoodie on and she was curled up in a ball. Her head rested on the arm of the couch. She had only been thinking about where Henry was and who took him. She had stayed up the entire night looking around the cabin, but had found nothing.

Lilly and Joey walked downstairs to Rose. Lisa wasn't in the chair that she was in yesterday, her blanket was in the chair.

"Where's Lisa?" Lilly asked Rose worriedly.

"She went to Henry's room," Rose said.

Last night Lisa had tried to track Henry's phone, but it was shut off. She had called the phone company to see if they could turn it on, but they couldn't.

Rose had teleported everywhere she could think of. She had went to the cabin and had run around for two hours trying to catch his scent. Lisa even gave Rose her address so she could go there. Rose had gone there and explored. She found Henry's blood in the road and with that his scent, but it was gone as soon as she would walk away from it. She had tried to find out which way the car went and had even walked until she got to the main road, but found nothing.

Joey quickly walked upstairs to Henry's room. Joey opened the door to see Lisa in Henry's bed. She was hugging one of his pillows. Her face was stained with tears.

"Is there anything you need?" Joey asked. Lisa shook her head.

"No, I don't want anything," Lisa said quietly. Joey sat down on the bed next to her.

"You need something to eat, or at least drink. I'm not leaving until you do," he said as he crossed his arms, showing that he could be a stubborn teenage boy.

"I'd like a water," Lisa said. Joey nodded as he got up and walked downstairs. He grabbed a cup of water and walked back to Henry's room, he handed her the glass. She drank some of the water and laid it down on the nightstand. "Thank you," Lisa said to Joey. He nodded his head. "You look a little like Henry when he was little," Lisa said as she looked at Joey's face more.

"Do I?" He asked. She nodded her head and they started to talk.

"Please, Rose you have to eat something," Lilly begged.

"I'm. Not. Hungry," Rose said for the hundredth time. Lilly sighed.

"Will you at least drink something?" Lilly asked. Rose nodded her head. Lilly sighed out of relief. She walked to the kitchen and grabbed a glass of water. She handed the glass to Rose. She took a few sips of it before she laid it down on the table. Lilly sat down next to Rose. "Is there anything else that you need?" Lilly asked as she looked at Rose.

"Maybe my book, it's in Henry's office," Rose said as she pointed to the dark brown door that was Henry's office.

Lilly stood up and walked to the office. She looked around the office for the book. She looked down and saw it on the ground from when Rose had thrown it on the ground when Lisa burst through the door. The book was laying on the ground, split open in the middle. She picked up the book and the bookmark. She walked back to the couch.

She handed Rose the book, Rose placed the book on the table next to the water.

"Thanks," Rose said.

"No problem," Lilly said. There was a pause. "If you need anything just ask, ok?" Rose nodded her head. Lilly wrapped her arm around Rose. "Don't worry we'll find him," Lilly said reassuringly.

Rose knew that the chance of them fining him was *very* slim. They couldn't contact the police, didn't know where he was, and didn't know who took him. They could only think about where he was and who took him. They had nothing to go off of.

"I hope so," Rose said. Her eyes were fixed on the wall. Lilly needed to get Rose's mind off of Henry.

"You want to watch a movie?" Lilly asked as she grabbed the remote.

"Sure," Rose said, not caring what they did. She needed to think of another game plan.

Lilly turned on the TV. Rose had to help her figure out which buttons did what. "What do you want to watch?" Lilly asked.

"I don't care," Rose simply said as she shrugged.

"Ok, I'm going to pick a girly movie," Lilly warned. "What's *Bitchy High Schoolers?*" Lilly said to herself, she read the description. "Looks good," Lilly said. She then looked at the date. She pressed play.

Rose laid her head back on the arm of the couch, a tear fell out of her eye.

Don't worry Henry I'll find you, I promise, Rose thought to herself. Even though she didn't know where he was or who took him. She started to think about those things and where she would teleport next. She just had to wait until Lilly wasn't paying attention then she would teleport.

Occasionally her thoughts trailing off to the good times she and Henry had experienced.

Chapter 38

~day two~

"That was such a good movie!" Lilly said excitedly. They had stayed up the entire night watching the movie, it was now 2:30 AM. "What did you think?" Lilly asked as she looked at Rose. She was sitting up and her knees were up and her head was in between them. Her arms were wrapped around her legs, and she was looking at the TV. The area under her eyes were red and her eyes seemed to be bloodshot, no doubt from being sick not too long ago when she went out looking for Henry.

"It was good," Rose said as she shrugged. She had only seen about fifteen minutes of the movie. She understood what Lilly was trying to do to her, but she couldn't get her mind off of Henry.

"That's all you have to say about it?" Lilly asked, shocked.

"Yep," Rose simply said. Lilly's mouth hung open, shocked.

"That movie was a masterpiece!" Lilly said practically yelling.

Joey came down the stairs, out of Henry's room. "Hey guys, Lisa is asleep so please don't yell," Joey said in a whisper. They both nodded.

"You two should go to bed, it's late," Rose said as she looked at Lilly then to Joey.

"Will you be ok?" Lilly asked. She grabbed Rose's hand and gave it a slight squeeze.

"You're my little sister, you shouldn't worry about me. Just go to bed," Rose said. She just wanting to be alone.

"Ok," Lilly said as she let go of Rose's hand and walked upstairs. Joey stayed.

"Don't worry we'll find him," Joey said. "He's a tough guy, he'll be ok," Rose nodded her head.

"I hope so," Rose said. Joey nodded his head and patted her back. He walked upstairs and into his room.

Once Rose was sure that they were both in their rooms Rose stood up from the couch. Her legs were shaking, she braced herself on the couch. Her arm was shaking from having to hold herself up. She took a small step forward and fell on the ground. It felt like she weighed a ton. She stayed on her back for a few seconds, breathing heavily, exhausted. When she finally caught her breath she slowly stood up again.

She knew that she was this way from lack of food, stress, and the thought that she might never get to see Henry again. She thought that Lisa was probably in the same state that she was in, weak and miserable.

She teleported to the road where Henry was taken. She crouched down and ran her hand over the gravel that now had Henry's dried blood on it. She looked at the end of the tracks and the beginning as she tried to figure out which way the car had gone. It looked like it was heading towards Phil's house, but she had already looked there.

She stood up and started to walk, something was telling her not to teleport. As she walked her eyes scanned from side to side. She suddenly stopped as she saw something. In the side of the road were tire tracks. Her eyes followed in the direction that they went. She looked on the other side of the road and saw tire tracks, the car had turned around. Rose looked back before she took off in a full on sprint.

She finally stopped as she made it back to the drag marks. She grabbed the sleeve of the hoodie and sniffed it, picking up his scent. She started to walk in other directions as she prayed this would lead her to him.

She thought back to her birthday, her and Henry laying in the grass. His arm around her and his face in the crook of her neck. She smiled faintly at the memory. She looked down at her ring and brought the ring up to her lips and kissed it softly. A tear fell out of her eye, trailing down her cheek and fell onto the ground.

I'll find you, Rose thought as she continued to walk.

~where Henry is~

He laid on the ground. His throat was dry from lack of water and he was hungry too. The cuffs had cut into his ankles and wrists and felt like they were touching his bones. His leg still hurt from the crash and he still had a headache. Dry blood was on his face, arms, and legs. It hurt him to move and it felt like he weighed a ton. His thoughts were all about Rose and his mom. He knew that his time was running out.

Zoey hadn't come back since the last time she left, leaving him alone in complete darkness, unable to move. Every second felt like a minute and every minute felt like an hour. The slowness was almost unbearable for him. His thoughts could only keep him occupied for so long.

He had tried to start to rest but the pain kept him from it, the thudding in his head, the cuffs rubbing against his irritated skin, red, cut up skin. He had stiffness from lack of movement and the soreness that spread throughout his body. His new plan was to become so tired that he would pass out. He just needed to escape this dark room and go into his thoughts.

Hours had passed and his eyes had become heavy, he closed his eyes. Hopefully now he could fall asleep. He breathed out deeply and relaxed. He let his imagination run wild as he drifted into his darkness, not the darkness that the cold room had to offer, but the peaceful darkness. He slowly started to rest.

He woke up and slowly opened his eyes, after a few seconds he felt pain in his wrists. He winced in pain. In his sleep he and turned over on his back. The handcuffs had cut into his wrist and his hands were being crushed from his weight. He groaned in pain as he turned back on his side. His hands were numb and it hurt when he moved his fingers.

Zoey walked in and propped the door open. Henry closed his eyes and moved his face into his shoulder, blocking out the light.

"Day three," Zoey said. Henry had rested through an entire day. He was glad that he got sleep but the time was now closer.

He moved his head away from his shoulder, the light stung his eyes before he got used to it. He looked up at Zoey.

"Why are you telling me this?" He asked her. His voice was hoarse and dry from lack of water.

"I'm telling you this because I didn't have a warning. The least I could do is tell you," she said blandly. The way she sounded made her seem like she had no emotion but at the same time was fighting herself.

"You are a nice and good person, you don't have to do this," Henry said as he shook his head. Trying to snap her out of whatever she was in.

"That person that you are talking about died when Rider did. I've already made up my mind," Zoey said as she started to walk away. The door started to close.

"Wait, can you please tell me where I am, you know where Rider is. Please, let me know where I'm going to die," Henry begged her. She turned back around as she looked at him, deciding. After a few seconds her eyes became slightly lighter.

"You're at your brother's house," Zoey said. Before Henry could respond she closed the door behind her.

I now know where I am, but how is that going to help me? He thought. He couldn't get out of the cuffs, he couldn't move, he couldn't do anything. He closed his eyes as tears rolled down his face. The thought of Rose and his mom being lonely was unbearable. Rose had been alone for so many years. He didn't want her to be alone again. *I only have a day left, I have to think of something,* Henry thought as he tried making a plan. *I'll get out of here for you, Rose,* Henry thought as he closed his eyes. Another tear rolled down his cheek. *I'll think of something, I have to.* Henry knew they couldn't contact the police. They didn't know where he was, or who took him.

He had already tried talking to Rose, but it had no effect. He was too weak to use his powers. He couldn't concentrate fully, all he could concentrate on was the pain. He couldn't talk to Rose and Rose needed to know a location in order to teleport. He had to do this all by himself, no powers, just himself.

Chapter 39

Henry's eyes started to close. He had spent hours thinking of a plan, he had come up with one and if that plan failed then he was going to die. He closed his eyes and breathed out deeply.

This has to work, it has to, Henry thought as he clenched and unclenched his fists. He was so anxious that his hands were shaking, making the metal on the cuffs make a small clinking noise.

He heard footsteps outside of his door. He breathed out deeply as he prepared himself.

Please let this work, Henry thought as the door was opened. He closed his eyes, blocking his eyes from the harsh light. When he opened his eyes he saw Zoey. It looked like she hadn't slept in days. He looked down at her hand and saw a gun. Her hand was slightly shaking like the Leader's hand was at the cabin.

She took a step forward and crouched down to Henry's level, placing one knee on the ground. She placed the gun on Henry's chest, where his heart is. Henry looked into her eyes and saw that they were a dark red. The same color Rider's were before he was killed.

"Please, just let me call them. Let me tell them that I love them before you kill me, please," Henry begged. He needed this to work. Zoey just stared at him for a few seconds before her eyes changed to a lighter red. Henry closed his eyes in slight relief.

She removed the gun from his chest and pulled Henry's phone out of her pocket. It was cracked, but still worked. "Passcode?" She asked as she went to the dial pad.

"One, nine, three, seven," Henry said slowly so she could put in each number. She put in the combo and went to his contacts. Rose wasn't in his contacts because she didn't have a phone.

"Who do you want to call?" She asked as she turned the phone in his direction. He looked at his contact list.

"My mom," Henry said. She pressed the call button and it started to ring.

"You get three tries, no more after that," she said. Henry nodded his head, understandingly.

Hopefully mom will pick up the phone, this is my only hope.
~Henry's house~

Lisa's phone vibrated on the nightstand. Her phone was turned over, blocking her from seeing the screen. She watched as her phone vibrated again and again. She didn't want to talk to anyone. The phone stopped vibrating.

Rose had come back early in the morning and the news that she had found nothing saddened Lisa.

A few seconds later it started to vibrate again, she sighed out of annoyance. She let it vibrate a few times. After a few seconds she had a feeling that she should pick up the phone to see who was calling.

She reached to the nightstand and grabbed the phone. Her eyes widened as she saw Henry's name on the screen. She went to press answer when the call ended.

No, no, no, no, please call back, please, she begged as she stared at her phone. A few seconds passed before it rung again.

She immediately pressed answer and put the phone on speaker. "Hello?! Henry is that you?!" She asked hopefully.

"Hey mom," Lisa heard Henry's hoarse, weak voice come through. She put her hand over her mouth in shock of the way that her baby sounded. Her eyes filled with tears.

"Henry are you ok?" She asked even though she knew the answer.

"No... I just called to say that I love you. Thank you for always being there for me. I couldn't have asked for a better mother," Henry said sounding like he was on the verge of tears.

"Henry what are you saying?" Lisa asked as a tear rolled down her face.

"Today," Henry paused, swallowing back his tears. "I'm going to die," Lisa shook her head back and forth.

Not my baby, Lisa thought as she cried harder.

"I called to say that I love you so much," Henry sounded like he was going to cry.

"I love you too," there was a short pause. "W-would you like to speak to Rose?" Lisa asked.

"Yes," Henry said. Lisa quickly jumped out of bed and ran downstairs, regaining her strength. Rose wasn't on the couch. She saw Lilly.

"Where's Rose?!" She asked as she looked around.

"In the office," Lilly said, not comprehending what was happening. Lisa rushed in the office and saw Rose resting. Her arms were around her head and her face in the open book. It was the first time Rose had rested since Henry went missing.

"Rose!" Lisa said. Rose sat up quickly, shocked. Her eyes were still bloodshot and it looked, and smelled like, she had thrown up some more. She looked around until her eyes landed on Lisa. Lisa's face looked worried.

"What's wrong?" Rose asked, expecting the worst news. Lisa handed the phone to Rose. She looked down and saw Henry's name on the phone, her eyes widened.

"H-Henry?" Rose stuttered like she always did when she was scared.

"It's so good to hear your voice," Rose heard Henry's weak voice on the other line. A tear fell out of her eye as she placed a hand over her mouth, shocked.

"It's good to hear yours too," Rose said as she cried more.

"Can you do me a favor?"

"Yes," Rose said as she nodded her head.

"Go into my office, reach down to the second drawer on the left and open it," Henry said. She did as she was told and opened the drawer. In it was a picture of a girl and behind that was a name, blood type, age, gender, and so forth.

Some pet shops did this and others like the one Rose was in, had the owner tell you.

"You know that girl that I told you about that had the limp?" Henry asked.

"Yes," Rose said as she nodded her head. Still staring at the picture.

"That's her, her name was Mckenzie. I should have thrown it away and told you sooner. I felt so guilty after I killed her, I'm sorry," there was a short pause. "And don't worry I didn't like her the way I like you."

"W-why are you telling me this?" Rose stuttered again.

"Because today I'm going to die and I don't want there to be any misunderstandings between us, because I love you so much," Henry said. He sounded like he was crying. "Please throw it away," Henry said. Rose tossed it into the trash can. "I hope you can forgive me."

"There's no reason to apologize," Rose said as she shook her head. Another tear rolled down her face.

"Thank you," he said.

"No...no problem," Rose said as she cried more.

"That's another reason why I love you so much," Henry said as he cried more.

"I love you so much," Rose said. Lisa hugged Rose, crying on her shoulder.

"Rose there's one more thing I need to tell you," Henry sucked in a deep breath. "I'm at Ri-" Henry was cut off as Zoey slammed the bud of the gun on Henry's head.

"Henry? Henry?!" Rose heard the other line go dead. Rose looked at Lisa for a split second before she ran to the kitchen, she grabbed a knife.

She thought about going to Rider's house, the one place that she never thought she would see again. The place where she was tormented for years, Rider's house.

Chapter 40

Henry lay unconscious, blood came out of his nose from where she had hit him. Zoey pointed the gun at Henry's chest. She couldn't pull the trigger. She couldn't bring herself to do it and she didn't know why. Her brain felt like it was fighting her body and while her brain wanted her to do it her finger wouldn't pull the trigger. Feeling her brain fight with her body made her dizzy.

Once he wakes up, I'll kill him, Zoey thought as she walked out of the room. She locked the door and was barely able to walk into Rider's room. She laid the gun on the nightstand and put his pillow to his face and breathed in his scent. She closed her eyes as she cried into the pillow. Without warning her body shut down and she passed out.

Rose teleported in the living room of Rider's house. She looked around to see if anyone was around. She looked at the too familiar house. While Henry's house was light and kind, Rider's house was dark and almost unsettling. She smelt a warm vanilla scent, Henry's scent. It was coming from upstairs almost breathed out a sigh of relief. She had wanted to smell a fresh scent for days now. She carefully started to walk upstairs as she followed the scent. As she did so images from being Rider's pet entered her mind.

  Rider grasped onto the back of Rose's collar as he dragged her by the collar up the stairs and away from Elizabeth's dead body. Rose's feet tried desperately to land on the stairs to stand her up. Her hands were around her collar, trying to release the pressure so she could breathe. When they made it to the top of the stairs he let go of her collar. She fell on her hands and knees, coughing and gasping for air. He grabbed her hair and made her stand up. She grasped onto his arm as she tried to release the pressure.

  "Stop struggling!" Rider said through gritted teeth as he slightly shoved her against the railing. She remained silent as she closed her eyes. "Do you understand?!" He yelled at her. She whimpered at his harsh tone.

  "Yes m-master," Rose stuttered. He dragged her to a room as his hand was still grasping onto her hair. He opened the door and threw her in. She rolled across the floor. He slammed the door shut and locked it. She crawled to the door and tried to open it.

  "Master, please, I'm sorry!" She begged as she hit the door. In a second the door was opened. Rider slapped her before she could even blink. She fell sideways from the force. He grabbed her collar again and lifted her off the ground, slamming her into the wall.

  "Shut up you stupid bitch!" Rider yelled in her face. She only nodded her head as best she could. "Do you understand?!" He yelled in her face again.

  "Yes, m-master," Rose stuttered. He let go of her collar. She limply fell on the floor. He once again slammed the door shut and locked it. She looked around her surroundings. She was in a pitch black room with nothing in it. She held her hand in front of her face and could barely see that. She crawled to a corner in the small room, she lightly touched her swollen eye. She flinched at her own touch. She brought her knees up and laid her head in between them.

  She started to cry, knowing that she was going to be in here a long time. She probably wasn't going to get fed in the time that she was locked in *this room. She cried harder as she realized the only way she was going to survive was by following her masters' orders.*

Rose stopped outside a door. Henry's scent seemed to be coming from inside the room. She recognized the door, it was the one that Rider had locked her in after Elizabeth had died. She laid her hand on the doorknob and tried to turn it, it was locked.

She teleported into the room and she was encased in darkness. It took her a few seconds for her eyes to adjust. She looked around the familiar room before she looked down and saw Henry. His hands and feet were handcuffed and he had blood on and around him. She knelt down next to him. He wasn't moving.

Please don't let me be too late, Rose begged herself silently. She leaned down near his face to listen if he was still breathing. She barely heard him breathing. She placed her hand over his mouth to prevent him from making any noise, just in case he thought she was Zoey. She allowed him to breath out of his nose.

"Henry," she whispered loudly. There was no response. "Henry," she said a little louder into his ear. His eyes shot open. Fear was plastered on his face from thinking it was Zoey. His face softened when he saw it was Rose. She removed her hand from his mouth. She buried her face in the crook of his neck and gently wrapped her arms around him, in fear of hurting him. He buried his face into the crook of her neck. "I-I missed you so much," Rose said into his shoulder.

"I missed you too," Henry said into hers. He closed his eyes as for once in the time he had been here he relaxed. There was a short pause.

"Where are the keys?" Rose asked. She moved her face out of his neck.

"Zoey might have them," he said as he looked at her.

"Where is she?" Rose asked, a hint of anger was edged in her voice.

"I don't know. Wait for her to come back," Henry said. Rose nodded her head. Rose moved to the side of the room and even though Henry knew she was there he felt alone again.

Zoey's eyes opened. Slowly she sat up and her gaze traveled to the gun. She felt as something washed over her and invaded her brain. Grabbing the gun she walked out of the room. She walked to the room.

They heard the door being unlocked. Zoey walked in and without saying anything she pointed the gun at Henry's chest. Her eyes were so dark they were almost black. Rose tackled her as Zoey pulled the trigger. The bullet shot into the wall right above Henry's head.

Both Rose and Zoey fell on the ground, both landing on their sides. They were now facing each other. Rose sat up, she went to grab Zoey. Zoey swung her gun, hitting Rose in the face with it. Rose stumbled backwards, landing on her back. She quickly stood up. Zoey pointed the gun and fired, the bullet skimmed Rose's arm. Rose held her arm as she disappeared. She appeared in front of Zoey, the knife in her hand. She swung the knife at Zoey but Zoey moved backwards. The knife did manage to cut her shoulder. Zoey didn't even seem to feel the knife as she blankety stared at Rose.

Zoey rushed at Rose and tackled her. Zoey had Rose pinned to the ground. Zoey put the gun on Rose's chest and fired.

Right as she did so Rose disappeared again, she appeared in the air. The knife was in her hand. Rose brought the knife down into Zoey's back and pierced her heart. Zoey slumped over, dead. Rose put her hand over her mouth and swallowed back the vile that was rising in her throat.

After she had calmed down she started to search Zoey for the key, reaching her shaky hands in her pockets. Rose couldn't look at Zoey's face as she searched, she focused her attention on her hands. She found the key and walked to Henry. She put the key into the handcuffs around his ankles first, the cuffs fell off his feet and onto the floor. Henry moved his legs slightly, pain shot into his hurt leg and his other leg popped from lack of movement.

She moved on to his hands. The cuffs fell to the ground as they made a loud clink noise as they hit the floor. Henry moved his arm to go in front of him. His shoulder popped and he used his arm to support his weight on.

"Help me sit up," Henry said to Rose. She grabbed his shoulder and got him to sit up. He moved his legs in front of him and leaned against the wall.

Henry looked around the room. "Why would Rider have a room like this?" Henry asked. The question had been on his mind ever since he came here.

"To put pets that he didn't feel like dealing with in," Rose said as she looked around the familiar room. Despite being weak he picked Rose up and placed her on his lap. She buried her face into his chest. He wrapped his arm around her as he breathed in her scent. It had felt like ages since he had held her in his arms.

"It's ok, you're safe," Henry said. He had only spent four days in the room. He couldn't imagine what it would have been like to be in here whenever Rider didn't feel like dealing with you. A tear fell out of her eye as she thought about it. It fell on Henry's chest. He placed his fingers under her chin and tilted her head up. He wiped away the tear from her cheek with his thumb. He cupped her face with his hand. "You look like you haven't eaten in a while," Henry said to her. She didn't say anything. "You can't do this to yourself, ok?" He asked. She nodded her head. He then looked at her arm that had been skimmed by the bullet. "You're hurt," Henry said as he watched the gash start to heal.

"I'm fine, it's just a scratch. Don't worry about me. Besides you were the one that was trapped in here," Rose said as she looked at the blood that covered Henry's face.

"But, I care about you more than me. Besides you've been through more than I have," Henry said as he rubbed her cheek with his thumb. She remembered when this motion brought fear, now it brought comfort.

Rose looked at Henry closer and saw that he was pale, like the time he lost control. "You need blood, don't you?" Rose asked. He shook his head, but as he did so his fangs descended and pierced his lip. A drop of blood fell from his lip and onto his shirt. "Hey, it's ok," Rose said as she ran her fingers through his hair.

"Are you sure?" He asked. She nodded her head. He took his hand and moved her hair away from her neck. He took two fingers and tilted her head slightly. He leaned his head down and pierced her neck. Her blood tasted so good. He felt his leg heal more. He felt the soreness in his body fade as his strength returned. His wrist and ankles healed and his headache faded. When he had finally had enough he retracted his fangs from her neck. "Are you ok?" Henry asked concerned as he looked at her.

"Yeah, I'm fine," she said as she leaned her head against his chest. He laid his head on top of hers and wrapped his arm around her, bringing her closer to him. He slowly started to rock back and forth.

After a good period of time Rose remembered something. "We should go, your mom is probably worried," she said. Henry nodded, he had forgotten about his mom because he was so happy to see Rose. She got off his lap and helped Henry stand up. They both looked at Zoey's dead body.

"Let's go bury her," Henry said. They walked to Zoey's lifeless body. Rose grabbed Zoey's hand and Henry grabbed her ankles. She thought about going to Henry's cabin to bury Zoey.

Hopefully she would be the last person they would have to bury.

Chapter 41

They arrived at the cabin, where the graveyard was. The snow had stopped falling but was about a foot high. Rose breathed out and her breath showed in the cold air. The thin ice spread out before it evaporated. Henry squinted his eyes shut, blocking out the sun and the whiteness of the snow. He had been in a dark room for four days, seeing light was like staring directly into the sun.

Once Henry's eyes adjusted to the light he looked around, he bent down and scraped away the snow as he tried to find Rider's grave. His hand hit a rock. He moved the snow to reveal the R.

"I'll go get the shovels," Henry said as he walked towards the cabin.

Rose stared at Zoey's body, she got nauseous and had to look away. Henry walked back with two shovels in his hand. He handed one to Rose. She just held it. Henry put his shovel into the cold, icy dirt and scooped it out, making a small pile. Rose got out of her daze and started to help Henry.

Once they had a big enough hole Henry grabbed Zoey's ring and pulled it off her finger. He placed it into his pocket. He grabbed her wrists and Rose grabbed her ankles. They lifted her into the grave. They picked up their shovels again and started to fill the hole.

Rose continued to fill in the hole. Rose watched as the dirt covered up Zoey's fingertips. The last bit of her was covered up by the icy dirt.

Once the last scoops of dirt were put on the grave Henry and Rose dropped their shovels. They started to dig in the snow with their hands, looking for rocks. They grabbed the rocks that they found and put them on Zoey's grave, making a Z. They both looked at the graves, the Z next to the R.

Henry sighed, as he did so his breath showed in the air, showing how cold it was outside. He looked at Rose, to see if she was cold.

"Are you wearing my hoodie?" Henry asked.

"Yes," Rose simply said.

"Why are you wearing *my* hoodie?" He asked. "It's mine."

"I wanted to wear it because it's comfortable and smells like vanilla."

"Are you saying that I smell like vanilla?"

"Yes," Rose said. There was a short pause.

"Awesome," Henry simply stated, as he did so it started to snow again.

"Your mom is probably waiting," Rose said as she hopped from one foot to the other. "And my feet are freezing."

"Good point," Henry said as he grabbed Rose's hand. She thought about going to Henry's house.

Lisa paced back and forth nervously, her right index finger was in her mouth as she chewed her nail. "Don't worry, Rose will bring him back," Lilly said reassuringly.

"I know, but what if-"

"Don't think like that," Joey said, interrupting her before she could finish the sentence.

"I know, but he's my baby. I can't help but worry," Lisa said as she started to chew her right thumb.

Rose and Henry appeared in front of her. Lisa stopped chewing on her nails, she ran to Henry, jumping up into his arms. He wrapped his arms around her and hugged tightly, as did she. "I missed you so much," Lisa said as she cried into his shoulder.

"I missed you too, mom," Henry said into hers. Lisa pulled away and looked at Henry's face. His face had blood and some dirt on it. Lisa licked her thumb and started to wipe away the blood on his cheek. "Mom, please stop. I have a shower upstairs that works perfectly fine and you just ruined the moment," Henry said as he moved his face away from her hand. She removed her hand.

"Fine *Mr. Prissy*, I'll leave you to it," Lisa said sarcastically. Lisa walked to Rose and hugged her. "Thank you for bringing my baby back."

"No problem," Rose said as she hugged her back, they stopped hugging. Without warning Lilly jumped on Rose, hugging her.

"I'm glad that you're back," Lilly said as she hugged Rose tighter. She stopped hugging Rose and went to Henry. She wrapped her arms around him and hugged him, tightly. "I'm glad that you're ok." Lilly said as she squeezed him tighter.

"My... spine," Henry said as Lilly squeezed even tighter. "Please... stop... my... spine...is... going... to... break... and... I... can't... breath," Henry said as he arched his back in pain and gasped for air. Lilly released her grip on him. "Thank you," he said as he breathed out. Joey walked up to him and held his hand out, Henry high five him.

"It's nice to have another boy in the house." Joey said to Henry. Both the boys looked at the girls.

"I can only imagine," Henry said as he continued to look at Lilly, Rose, and his mom.

"Hey, Mr. Prissy you want to go take a shower, you still have spit on your face," Lisa said. Henry turned his head, slowly, looking at her.

"I feel so loved, please note my sarcasm. But spit is disgusting so I'll take your advice," Henry said as he walked upstairs.

"I should go take a shower too," Rose said as she looked at herself. She walked upstairs and to her room.

Henry walked out of his room and down to the sofa, he sat down. It had been awhile since he had sat on furniture, he sank into the couch and leaned back into the cushion. He sighed and closed his eyes and he started to relax. A few minutes went by before Henry felt hands in his hair.

He opened his eyes and looked up, he saw Rose above him. She was wearing another one of Henry's hoodies. Rose came around the side of the couch and sat down next to him. She continued to play with his hair.

"What are you doing with my hair this time?" Henry asked as he raised an eyebrow.

"Can't say," Rose said as she continued to play with his hair. A few seconds went by before Rose pulled back her hands.

"Now will tell me what you did?"

"Yes, I did a mohawk."

"What?!" Henry said as he looked in his reflection on the TV. He started to reach up his hands to fix it.

"Don't touch the hair, it looks good on you," Rose said. She gave him puppy dog eyes. Henry sighed as he put his hands at his sides again. Henry wrapped his arm around Rose. She leaned her head on his shoulder.

Lisa came down stairs and sat down next to Henry. He wrapped his other arm around her. "What happened to your hair?" Lisa asked.

"Rose, Rose happened," Henry said as they both looked at Rose. She gave a toothy grin.

"It looks good doesn't it?" Rose asked. She could tell that a Mohawk didn't suit Henry, but it was funny.

"I have to agree, it does look on you," Lisa said, playing along with Rose.

Joey and Lilly came down shortly after. They paused as they saw Henry's hair. After staring at his hair for a few seconds they both sat down on the floor. Henry smiled to himself as he looked at everyone, they were all together. They could finally relax and be happy now.

Henry kissed the top of Rose's head and closed his eyes, he rested his head on hers. He started to rest.

Chapter 42

Lisa's head fell on Henry's shoulder. He looked over at her. She was peacefully asleep. Her head was on the edge of his shoulder, about to roll off.

"I'm going to take mom upstairs," Henry said to Rose in a whisper, trying not to wake Lisa. Rose nodded her head as she looked at Henry then Lisa. Henry removed his arm from around Rose. He picked up Lisa and carried her up to the guest bedroom. The one that she always slept in when she visited.

He laid her in the bed. She had snaked her arms around Henry's neck. "Mom, you have to let go," Henry said in a whisper. She didn't budge. He grabbed her hands and gently pulled them apart. He put the covers over her, going up to her shoulders. She snuggled to the covers. He placed a soft kiss on her forehead. "I love you, mommy," he said as he walked out of the room. He walked down to the sofa again, Lilly and Joey were still sitting on the ground next to each other as they rested backwards on their hands. Rose was on the couch as she leaned against the armrest. Lilly had switched the TV to *Mean Girls*.

Henry sat down on the couch next to Rose. He criss crossed his legs on the couch. He picked up Rose and laid her in his lap. She sunk in between his legs, the circle that his legs made when he was crisscrossed. Her legs were over the front of his and dangled off the couch, a few inches above the floor. Henry wrapped his right arm around Rose's waist, going across her stomach. He laid his head on her shoulder, his chin going into her neck. Rose grabbed Henry's hand that was around her waist.

"Get in loser we're going shopping," Lilly mimicked the TV. Henry and Rose lightly laughed at Lilly.

That's adorable, Henry thought. There was a pause. *Hey, look,* Henry said to Rose as he pointed to Joey and Lilly. Joey gently moved his hand onto Lilly's. She leaned her head on his shoulder.

That's so adorable! Rose thought as she golf clapped her hands and lightly squealed. It was only audible to her and Henry.

It's about time he made a move, Henry thought as he looked at them.

Wait, you knew that Joey liked Lilly and you didn't tell me?! Rose thought as she looked back at Henry. Her eyebrow was raised.

In my defense that was the day that Zoey came so... yeah, he thought as he held his hands up in defense. He lightly shrugged as if to say 'what can you do?'

Ok, that's a good excuse, Rose said as she shrugged. She turned her head back to the TV.

"Four for you Glen Coco! You go Glen Coco!" Lilly mimicked the TV again, showing the enthusiasm of a little kid about to get candy.

How does Lilly know this? Henry asked.

She watched it when you were gone, trying to take my mind off you, Rose thought. Henry nodded his head, thinking about how hard Lilly and Joey must have tried to get Rose's and Lisa's minds off of him. He wrapped his arm around her waist again. Rose grabbed his hand. He gave Rose's hand a little squeeze as he put his face next to hers.

The movie had finished. "I love that movie, so much!" Lilly said excited. Joey only nodded, not knowing what to think of the movie. Lilly looked back at Rose and Henry. "What did you think?" She said as she pointed to Henry dramatically.

"Um, it was good, a little girly, but good," Henry said simply. A small hint of nervousness in his voice.

"You take that back!" Lilly said angrily.

"Fine, I'm sorry, it was the best movie I've ever seen. Better?" Henry asked as he raised an eyebrow.

"Yes, thank you," Lilly said losing the hint of anger that she had.

Joey yawned. "I'm tired," he said, nearly falling over from sleepiness. It hit Lilly how tired she was too. Lilly nodded her head in agreement. They both stood up and walked upstairs.

Henry and Rose watched as they walked upstairs. Joey hugged Lilly. When they pulled away Joey lightly kissed Lilly on the cheek. Lilly's cheeks blushed a bright red. *That's adorable,* Henry said to Joey.

Stop reading my mind! Joey thought as he looked at Henry.

No, Henry thought as he smirked.

Henry, tell Joey I think they make a cute couple, Rose said to Henry as she slapped his arm repeatedly.

Joey, Rose said you two make a cute couple. Joey's cheeks blushed. Lilly had already walked into her room. Joey looked back at Henry and Rose, he rolled his eyes. Henry and Rose both smiled at him, both giving him a toothy grin. Joey walked into his room.

Henry tightened his arm that was around Rose's waist. He reached down on the ground and grabbed the remote, he started to browse through the TV. He went to the *What's New* section. "Oo, a new show," Henry said as he pressed it. The name of the show was *Roses Are Red, Violets Are Blue, I Hate You*.

Henry read through the description: *a man comes home to find his wife dead. He tries to figure out who could have done this. As he investigates further into his wife's death he thinks he may have found something, the wife's boyfriend.*

"You want to watch it?" Henry asked as he looked at Rose. She nodded her head. He pressed play as he laid his head on her shoulder. She tilted her head to where their faces were touching. She leaned back to where her back was on his chest. Rose grabbed the hand that was around her waist. He started to rub small circles on her hand. She immediately realized that the picture was much clearer and better looking than the older TV shows.

They were part way through season one and Rose was crying. "Why would she cheat on him? He was so kind, a good husband, and hot. Why would she do this?" She asked as she cried more. She wiped away her tears with the back of her hand.

"We'll get our answer when the show is over, don't worry. There's no reason to cry."

"There is a reason to cry, it's *her* fault," Rose said talking about the wife.

"Do you want me to turn it off?" Henry asked.

"No, I like this show."

What? That makes no since, Henry thought as he looked at Rose, trying to read her. There was a pause. "Wait, did you say he was hot?" Henry asked as he looked at Rose.

"No," Rose said quickly.

"Yes you did. How could you say that? I'm way hotter than he is," Henry said as he pointed to the man on the TV. The man had dirty blonde hair that was styled like Henry's. His eyes weren't a dark red but a light red, the man was an inch or so taller than Henry. Henry continued to look at the man, there was another pause. "I'm turning it off."

"No!" Rose said as she quickly grabbed the remote from his hand. She crouched over it, turning into a ball, protecting the remote.

"Ok, ok, I won't turn it off," Henry said as he held up his hands.

"I don't believe you," Rose said, not moving.

"Would I lie to you?" Henry asked as he turned her head towards him. He kissed her on the lips, he tried to reach for the remote. She noticed and moved it farther away from him, falling off his lap and onto the couch cushion next to him. She turned around and slapped him on the arm, hard. "Ow, I'm sorry," Henry said as he held up his hands, protecting his head.

She moved the remote farther away from him. He wrapped his arm around her waist and moved her back on his lap, she struggled a little. "I'm sorry, I won't try that again. Do you forgive me?" He said into her neck. When she didn't answer he looked up at her and gave her puppy dog eyes. "I'm swory," Henry said sounding like a five year old. She still didn't say anything. "When I was captured I only thought of you," Rose sighed.

"I forgive you," Rose said with little to no emotion. He kissed her on the cheek quickly before he moved his face back in the crook of her neck. They went back to watching the show. Rose still had the remote in her hands, grasping it tightly. *I can't let my guard down, any minute he could try to take the remote,* Rose thought as she stared at the TV.

Rose had fallen asleep in his arms. Henry reached over her and grabbed the remote from her hands. He paused the show then turned off the TV. He was exhausted, he fell over with Rose. Rose was on the outside of the couch while he was on the inside. His arm was still around her waist and her hand was still grasping his. Henry moved his face in the back of her neck, like on her birthday when they laid on the grass.

Henry closed his eyes as the remote fell out of his hand and onto the floor as he started to sleep.

Chapter 43

Rose's hand went limp in his and the hand that was on his face fell on the ground. She closed her eyes. "Rose! Rose please don't leave me!" Henry begged as he started to cry.

Henry's eyes shot open. He looked around worried. He saw Rose laying next to him, resting. He tightened his arm around her waist and brought her as close as he could to him. He laid his face in the back of her neck and he closed his eyes. *I'm never going to let you go again,* Henry thought as he snuggled closer to her. He closed his eyes and started to rest again.

Rose twitched beside him before she whimpered as if in pain. Henry opened his eyes and looked at her. Even though she was eating she was still skinny, every time she twitched or flinched he felt her spine rubbing against his stomach. It pained him that she still had the scars on her back and the skinniness from her old life. He hated that she could never fully forget her old life. He slightly moved his head to look at her face. She was resting, another nightmare.

"Be a good pet while I'm gone," Rider said as he walked towards the door.

"Yes, master," Rose said as she stood in the middle of the open room as he walked to the door. It was like Henry's house, in terms of openness. "Master?" Rose asked before he reached the door. He turned around facing her, a small look of annoyance was on his face. "M-may I grab my pillow?" Rose asked as she pointed to Rider's room, upstairs. Rider had given her a pillow because she hadn't done anything wrong in a while.

In a split second he was in front of her. She quickly looked down, avoiding eye contact. He put his fingers under her chin and tilted her head up. Her bottom lip started to slightly quiver. "Yes, you may, but remember it's my pillow. You don't own anything. Understand, pet?" Rider asked her.

"Y-yes master, I'm sorry, m-my mistake," Rose said apologizing. A thin smile spread across Rider's lips.

"Good, pet," Rider said. "And remember to stay in that spot," Rider said as he pointed to the middle of the room, not wanting her in his room or any other room. Rose knew it was a test to see how obedient she was. Rose nodded her head.

"Yes, master," she said. He nodded his head as he walked back to the door. He opened it, looked back at Rose one last time and closed it. She ran up the stairs and entered Rider's room. She looked around the room, trying to find the pillow that Rider had kicked away when he woke her up.

The walls were a dark grey, but not to a point of looking black. The shelves, wardrobe, nightstand, and dressers were white. The bedspread was a dark grey as well. His floor, as well as the rest of the house, was a dark brown, wooden floor. She walked around the other side of his bed and found the pillow.

Rose picked up the plush pillow, hugging it closely to her chest. She walked back down the stairs and into the middle of the room. She laid down on the hard wooden floor that she had since gotten used to since her arrival. She wrapped her arms around the pillow as she laid her head down on it. She closed her eyes as she got some much needed rest.

She was awoken as she heard the door open. It was opened so roughly that it slammed into the wall. Rose quickly sat up and looked at Rider. His hair was a mess, his once neat, tucked in shirt, was untucked and wrinkled, and a liquid coated the top of his shirt. He was missing a shoe, he swayed back and forth as he walked. It shocked Rose that he didn't fall over. She stood up. "Master, you're home," Rose said. He pushed passed her, his arm pushing into her.

"I need-ed, need... whiskey," Rider said. His speech was slurred and it seemed as though he didn't know what he was saying. Rose smelt a strong smell coming from his breath. She somehow knew he was drunk even though she had never seen anyone drunk before, she had never even laid eyes on alcohol. Rose followed Rider into the kitchen.

"M-master, you're drunk," Rose said as he pulled out a bottle of whiskey. He grabbed a glass from the cabinet. He started to pour a glass of whiskey, his hand shook and swayed everywhere, spilling the whiskey onto the counter. He laid the bottle down on the counter. "M-master, please y-you're drunk," she said. He turned around, his arm extended, he backhanded Rose in the face. She fell on the ground, holding her face with her hand.

"No... do... don't-not tell-order... me what I-me am... pet," Rider said as he swayed more. She didn't respond. He grabbed his whiskey glass and threw it at Rose, thankfully his aim was off. The glass hit the island, a few feet beside her. The glass flew everywhere. Rose covered her face with her hands as the whiskey spread out across the floor. Rose scooted away from the whiskey. Rider grabbed her collar and dragged her across the floor. He stopped next to her pillow. He grabbed the pillow. "You... pet-you're... gona stay there-here," Rider said as he pointed his finger and circled it. He swayed more.

"Yes, master," Rose said in a soft voice. He nodded as he started to walk upstairs, the pillow in his hand. He tripped a few times on the stairs, nearly falling on his face. He walked into his room and slammed the door.

A few hours later Rider came out of his room. His hair was still a mess, but he looked sober. He walked down the stairs, rubbing his face with his hands. He walked into the kitchen and grabbed two pills and water for his headache. He drank down the medicine, as he walked back he stepped in something wet. He looked down and saw the broken glass and whiskey on the floor. The spread out whiskey looked clear, like water.

He walked to Rose. She hadn't moved an inch like he had told her to do. He grabbed her hair and stood her up. She whimpered as he did so. "What is that?!" Rider yelled as he pointed to the broken glass.

"M-master, you w-were drunk, you th-threw the glass," she said, knowing she was going to get punished. He jerked her head, his hand still grasping her hair. She whimpered.

"Don't try to blame me, tell the truth, pet!" He yelled in her face.

"It was an a-accident m-master," Rose said, knowing that telling the truth was only going to anger him more. He slapped her in the face with his free hand.

"Didn't I tell you not to move from that spot?" Rider asked as he pointed to the spot. "Didn't I?!" He yelled at her.

"Yes, master," she said. He sighed.

"Why can't you just obey me?!" Rider continued to yell, without waiting for a response from Rose he spoke again. "I can't have a pet that refuses to obey me," he said more to himself. "Stay there," he said sternly. She nodded her head. He quickly ran upstairs and came back down. In his hand was the leash. He clipped the leash onto her collar. He quickly jerked her out the front door and into his garage. He was too angry to wait for a driver. He opened the trunk, not wanting Rose to touch the seats in his car. He threw her in the trunk and slammed it shut.

He arrived at the Pet Shop and he opened the trunk. She blocked the sunlight from her eyes. He grabbed both her hands with one hand. He dragged her out of the trunk and she fell on the ground. He wrapped the leash around his hand several times and started to practically drag her onto the Pet Shop.

She fell on the cold cement. Rider stood over her. Her leash was wrapped around his hand, his knuckles were white. "Lord Rider, what brings you here?" The Shopkeeper asked as he looked at Rose, he knew the answer.

"I don't want this pathetic thing," Rider said as he kicked Rose in the stomach. She whimpered in pain as she held her stomach.

"Of course sir, I need you to sign some paperwork and then I'll take it off your hands," the Shopkeeper said as he glanced at Rose. She was still laying on the ground, slightly shaking in fear. Rider nodded in understanding the Shopkeeper started to walk to the back room. Rider yanked her leash up, pulling her onto her knees. He started to walk as he wrapped the leash around his hand a few more times. She only had about a foot between her and him, he had to practically drag her to the room.

The Shopkeeper had the papers on the table. He was holding a pen, ready for Rider to take it. Rider shoved her to the ground again. He grabbed the pen and started to sign the papers.

When he was done he laid the pen on the table, he turned and faced the Shopkeeper. "Is that all?" Rider asked, clearly annoyed.

"Yes sir," the Shopkeeper said. "Would you like to keep the leash and collar or shall I take it?" The Shopkeeper asked.

"I want to keep it, it's the only money I've spent that hasn't gone to waste," Rider said as he looked at Rose. She averted her eyes. Rider removed the collar from her neck. Rose fell on her hands and knees, taking deep breaths, seeing as how the collar was as tight as it would go.

Rider walked out of the shop. Leaving Rose with the Shopkeeper. He quickly grabbed her hair and started to drag her to the cages. She only put her hands on his arm to try and release the pressure. When they reached an empty cage her threw her against the wall. She fell on the ground. He kicked her in the stomach multiple times. She didn't struggle she only whimpered in pain.

He noticed that she wasn't struggling like she used to, but just sat there taking it. He stopped for a second. He grabbed her hair and threw her into the open cage, she rolled across the floor and hit the back of the small cage. She looked around at the familiar cage. The three walls of cement brick and the old cage door. He grabbed the metal collar that was attached to the wall and threw it in the cage next to Rose. A small dirt cloud accumulated around the collar before it settled.

"Put it on," he simply stated as he looked at her.

"Yes, sir," she said as she picked up the metal collar, rubbing her hands around the familiar collar. She placed it around her neck and clamped it shut. He grabbed the collar, making sure it was on. Once he confirmed it was on he pushed her back into the cage. He slammed the door shut and walked away.

Rose leaned against the wall. "Why?" She heard a voice say. She looked around. In the cage across from her was a young girl. She was looking at Rose. Rose furrowed her eyebrows in confusion. "Why did you let him beat you up? You didn't even put up a fight," the girl didn't have any visible bruises. She probably hadn't even been hit yet.

"When you get abused every single day for over a year, then you can talk to me," Rose said bluntly. She closed her eyes as she leaned her head against the wall. A tear fell out of her eye. I've finally been broken, she thought as she lightly started to cry.

"Hey, hey, it's ok. Wake up," Henry said gently as he ran his fingers through her hair. Her eyes shot open. She looked around frantically. She struggled in his grasp, but relaxed as she realized she was in Henry's arms. "It's ok, I get them too," Henry said as he placed a soft kiss on her cheek. She turned around in his arm, now facing him. She buried her face in his chest as she wrapped her left arm around him. His right arm was still around her. "It's ok," Henry said as he kissed her head. He felt her smile into his chest.

"You smell like vanilla," she said. He lightly chuckled.

"So you've told me," Henry said as he tightened his grip. She tightened her grip, burying her face deeper into his chest. He leaned his head on her head. He closed his eyes again as he started to rest.

A few minutes later Henry was being shaken. He opened his eyes to see Lilly. "Joey and I need clothes," Henry furrowed his eyebrows.

"What have you been wearing this entire time?" Henry asked.

"We had some spare clothes but I would borrow Rose's clothes and Joey would borrow yours," Henry looked at Joey and saw that the clothes were huge on him.

"Maybe later. I'm relaxing right now," Henry said as he pointed to Rose.

"Please we need clothes," Joey said as he rolled the sweatpants up again.

"Maybe in," Henry looked at his watch. "An hour," Lilly reached for Rose. Trying to get her away from Henry. Henry turned over and placed Rose on the inside of the couch and him on the outside.

"I'm going to call your mom," Lilly said as she crossed her arms.

"You wouldn't dare," Henry's voice was muffled into Rose.

"Lisa!" Lilly yelled. In a second Lisa was down stairs.

"Yes, sweetie?" Lisa asked.

"Henry won't take us to get clothes," Lilly said as he pointed to Henry. Lisa crossed her arms.

"Hey Mr. Prissy don't make me count to three," Lisa said as she raised her eyebrow.

"Mom, I'm an adult that won't-"

"One... Two... Three," on three she raised her hand to smack Henry on the arm. Henry quickly turned on his back. Rose on top of him, blocking him from Lisa. "Wow, that's sad," Lisa said. Henry chuckled, it came out muffled. Lisa sighed. "Hey, Mr. Prissy your hair is still a Mohawk," Lisa said.

Henry quickly sat up, making Rose fall on the ground. He quickly ran upstairs. Rose laid on the ground for a few seconds. "And I'm up," Rose said as she sighed. She stood up and walked upstairs. Lisa and Lilly high-five each other.

A few minutes later Henry walked down the stairs wearing blue jeans and a black muscle t-shirt. His hair had a tiny Mohawk on the top and in the center of his head, it stood up about a centimeter. The rest of his hair looked normal, he couldn't get that part out. He was carrying a black collar and leash. *Rose, grab your leash when you're ready,* Henry thought to her.

I hate you, Rose thought back to him. He slightly laughed. He walked down stairs. He gave the collar and leash to Joey. He blankly stared at it. "You're a human, we are going out in public, you guys are my pets," Henry explained to both of them. They both nodded.

"Why do you even have a second collar?" Joey asked as he put it on.

"Sometimes my pets would throw away or lose their collars and my brother or father would come over, so I would let them use this," Henry explained as he finished texting the driver. Both Lilly and Joey nodded.

A few minutes later Rose came down the stairs. She was wearing a dark red t-shirt and black blue jeans. "Nice hair," Rose said. It didn't look bad but it wasn't what she was used to. She handed the leash to Henry and he handed it to Lilly who put it on.

"It kind of suites Mr. Prissy," Lisa said.

"Mom, stop calling me that," Henry said as he gave her the death stare.

"Fine I'll use your other nickname-"

"Please don't," Henry interrupted her.

"Hen," Lisa said. Henry sighed out of frustration as he placed his hand over his face.

"Hen?" Rose asked. There was a short pause. "Isn't that a chicken?" Rose asked. Lisa nodded her head. "I like the name,"

"Oh please, not you too," Henry begged. Rose smirked, giving him the answer. "Fine if you get to give me a nickname, I get to give you one," Henry said, there was a pause. "Short Stack."

"Short Stack?" Rose asked. l Henry nodded his head.

"You like pancakes and you're short," Henry simply said.

"I'm not that short," Rose said as she looked down at herself. Henry walked to her. He placed his hand on her head and pushed her face into his chest.

"I'm like a foot taller then you," Henry said as she struggled in his grasp. Her hands pressed against his chest as she tried to push off. He finally let go.

"You suck," Rose said as she crossed her arms. He slightly laughed. Henry's phone vibrated and he read the text.

"Ok, our driver his here," Henry said as he grabbed Joey's leash. Rose grabbed Lilly's. They walked out to the limo. The driver was holding the door open for them. They all hopped in and the driver shut the door behind them. He ran to his side and got in. He turned on the car and looked back at Henry through the small window. "Take me to the mall," Henry simply said. The driver nodded as he started to drive. Henry pressed the button that closed the window and it locked in place. He leaned back as the only sound was the wind against the car. Rose leaned her head against his shoulder. He faintly smiled.

Chapter 44

Rose's head was still leaning against Henry's shoulder and his arm had wrapped around her waist. Joey, Lilly, and Lisa had started to talk. "Hen?" Rose asked. Her eyes were still closed.

"Yes, Short Stack?" Henry asked. His eyes were still closed. He faintly smiled at the fact that they were calling each other by their nicknames.

"Will Britney be there?" Rose asked. She finally opened her eyes and glanced up at Henry. Henry nodded his head.

"Yes, she will be there," Henry said as he opened his eyes.

"Will she...?" Rose trailed off as she looked at Henry. Awaiting an answer.

"No, she won't care that you are a vampire," Henry said, answering her question. Rose nodded as she leaned her head back on his shoulder. He leaned his head on top of hers. They both closed their eyes again.

The car stopped. Henry and Rose jolted forward about an inch. "And I'm awake," Henry said as he rubbed his eyes. Rose looked around, remembering where she was. The driver opened the door.

"Sorry sir, the roads don't seem to be in the best conditions to drive in," The driver said a little nervous.

"Don't I know it," Henry mumbled to himself. "It's fine," Henry said to the driver. He nodded. After they all got out Henry grabbed Joey's leash and Rose grabbed Lilly's. "I don't care what you do," Henry said to the driver. The drive nodded as he got back in the car and drove off. The roads had been salted making the snow and ice a slush.

They walked into the mall. "Hey, Hen?" Lisa said. He rolled his eyes and groaned. "I'm going to go buy some things so I'm going to go now," Lisa said as she walked off. They started to walk towards the store. Rose looked around the mall, everything was green and red.

"Why is everything red and green?" Rose asked. She didn't understand why they were doing this. She furrowed her eyebrows in confusion as she saw a giant tree in the middle of the mall, ornaments and streamers were on it. Some of the streamers sparkled and others were plain.

"It's like that because it's December, near Christmas," Henry said. He looked down at Joey and Lilly. They both looked around in amazement.

"Christmas?" Rose asked.

"Yes, there are other holidays before this but we were busy. Aka trying to survive. So now it's Christmas. This holiday involves gifts and other stuff like that," Henry said. He didn't really know how to describe it to someone who had never heard of Christmas. "Did Rider not celebrate Christmas?" Henry asked.

"I don't know. He would lock me in a room and go somewhere. The only thing that looks familiar is the tree," Rose said. Henry nodded his head. He was sad that he hadn't had the chance to celebrate the other holidays with Rose. He turned to the right and Rose glanced up and saw the store that Britney worked at. They walked up to the cashier.

"Is Britney here?" Henry asked like he did the last time he was here. The cashier looked up.

"Yes, I'll call her now," she said as she reached for the intercom. The cashier looked back up at Henry. "I called her, she'll be here any minute now," the cashier said.

"Henry!" Britney yelled across the store. A few customers looked to see what the noise was. Henry squinted his eyes, trying to find her in the shelves and racks of clothes. In a second she had emerged from the clothes. She jumped into Henry's arms which caused him to nearly fall over. "Oh my gosh it's been so long since I've see you," there was a short pause. "Nice hair." She said looking at the miniature mohawk.

"Thanks, she did it," Henry said as he pointed to Rose. She looked down at Rose.

"Rose!" She said excited. She hugged Rose tightly. When she pulled away she looked at Rose. "Wait," there was a pause. "Are you a vampire?" Britney asked in a whisper. She looked at Rose's red eyes.

"Yes..," Rose trailed off, not sure how she was going to react. Britney squealed as she jumped up and down. She clapped her hands together.

"Does that mean that you two are together?" Britney asked as she glanced from Henry to Rose, back to Henry, then back to Rose. Henry nodded his head as his cheeks turned a light shade of red. Britney squealed again. She tightly hugged Rose then hugged Henry. "Oh my gosh, it's about time that my ship sailed," Britney said excited.

"Wait, are you saying that the second you saw us you shipped us?" Henry asked as he raised an eyebrow. Britney nodded her head up and down, very fast.

"You two were just so cute that when I saw you I had to ship you guys," Britney said. Henry buried his head in his hand. "You two are *so cute*," she said as she looked at Rose. Her cheeks were a bright shade of red. "I'm so happy for you," Britney said excited. There was a pause. "What brings you guys here anyway?" Britney asked.

"They need clothes," Henry said as he pointed to Joey and Lilly. His head still in his hand. Britney squealed at the sight of them.

"Oh my gosh, they are so cute. What are their names?" She said as she looked at both of them.

"This is Joey," Henry said as he pointed to Joey. He finally lifted his head out of his hand. "And this is Lilly, Rose's sister," Henry said. Britney squealed again.

"Rose! You have the cutest sister I've ever seen!" Britney said as she looked at Lilly.

"Thanks," Rose said.

"So I'll take them around the store and you two can do whatever," Britney said as Rose and Henry handed her the leash. Britney, Joey, and Lilly walked into the back of the store. Henry and Rose sat down on the couch. He wrapped his arm around her as she leaned her head on his shoulder. They started to relax.

A few minutes went by. "Hen?" Rose asked, her eyes were still closed.

"Yes, Short Stack?" Henry asked, his eyes were still closed.

"I'm hungry," Rose simply stated. She opened her eyes and gave Henry puppy dog eyes. He opened his eyes and looked down at Rose. She was still giving him puppy dog eyes. He sighed.

"Fine. Are pretzels ok?" Henry asked as he stood up. She nodded her head. "What kind of pretzels?" Henry asked.

"What kind do they have?" Rose asked. She didn't know there was more than one kind.

"Plain, cinnamon, cheese... that's all I know," Henry said as he shrugged. Rose thought for a second.

"Cinnamon," Rose said. He nodded his head as he walked out of the store. Rose laid down on the couch. Rose closed her eyes and started to rest, waiting for Henry to return.

It had been some time now. Rose sighed as she sat up. She walked to the cashier. "What time is it?" Rose asked. The cashier looked at the clock.

"It's 3:30," The cashier said. Rose sighed as she made her way back to the couch.

Where is he? I'm hungry and want my pretzels! Rose thought as she looked around. She sighed as she laid down on the couch again. After a few minutes she opened her eyes. Henry walked into the store with a cup of pretzels in his right hand. The small brown sugar cubes, that was the cinnamon, was sprinkled over the pretzels. Rose immediately sat up as she rubbed her hands together.

"Sorry, there was a *really* long line. It was unbelievable," Henry said as he reached in the cup and took out one pretzel. They were bite sized. He put it in his mouth. "Wow, this is good," he said with food still in his mouth. Rose reached for one. He moved the cup away from her hand and held his arm in the air. "What are you doing?" Henry asked as he furrowed his eyebrows.

"Getting a pretzel that you got for *me*," Rose said as she pointed to the cup in the air. Henry shook his head back and forth. She jumped up, grabbing his arm with both her hands. His arm didn't budge. She started to slowly climb up his arm. He laughed as her feet went higher off the ground.

She moved her right hand up as she unattached her right hand. Her left hand couldn't hold on. She fell on the ground and landed on her feet. She teleported in the air. She snatched the cup out of his hand before she fell on the couch, sitting down. She laughed in victory. She took a pretzel out of the cup and started to eat it. Henry laughed as he moved his other hand away from behind his back, there was another cup of pretzels in his hand.

He sat down next to Rose as he ate his pretzels. Rose stared at his cup. She glanced at Henry, the cup, Henry, then the cup. Henry glanced at her as he smiled, without showing his teeth, it came across like a huge smirk. Rose sighed as she went back to eating her cup of pretzels. Britney walked towards them, Joey was wearing blue jeans, a loose fit t-shirt and a beanie. Lilly was wearing blue jeans and a pink shirt.

Britney reached over to Henry's cup and she took a pretzel. Henry held up his hands as if to say 'what the heck?' "Ok, with Joey I kind of went for a hipster look and with Lilly I went more with a girly girl," Britney said as she looked at both of them. Henry and Rose nodded. Henry took another bite of his pretzel. He stood up and walked to the cashier.

"Rose do you want anything?" Henry asked as he glanced back at her. She shook her head no. "Britney, can you please go get their clothes?" Henry asked as he pointed to Lilly and Joey. Britney nodded as she went back to the changing room. A few seconds later she came back with an arm full of clothes. They were falling over her arms and almost blocking out her face.

Britney laid the clothes down on the counter as the cashier looked at the clothes, her eyes widened. She quickly got out of her shock and started to scan the clothes. Britney came back with a smaller arm full of clothes and she laid them down on the counter. She wiped her hands together as she breathed out deeply.

The cashier continued to scan the clothes before placing them in the bag. Henry twirled his credit card in his hand as his pretzels were in his other hand. Rose ate the last pretzel in her cup. She threw it away in the trash can. She looked at Henry's cup of pretzels. She teleported right in front of him. He jumped back about an inch, scared. She quickly grabbed his cup and teleported next to Britney. Britney reached her hand in the cup and ate a pretzel.

Henry stared at them, his eyes were wide and his mouth slightly open. He opened his mouth to say something. "Um, sir?" The cashier asked. Henry glanced towards her. "I'm ready for you to swipe," she said as she looked at the scanner. Henry swiped his credit card. Henry and Rose grabbed the bags. Britney waved enthusiastically at them as they left. She cupped her hands together and tilted her head to the side.

They're so cute together, Britney thought as she skipped into the back of the store. Rose and Henry walked out of the store, bags in their hands along with the leashes. Lilly and Joey trailed behind them.

Chapter 45

They started to walk towards the exit. "I feel like I'm forgetting something," Henry said as he tried to think.

"Henry!" He heard across the mall, it was coming from behind them. It was Lisa.

"Oh, yeah. That's what it was," Henry said as he turned around. A huge toothy smile was spread across his face. "Hey mommy, we were just going to wait at the exit for you," Henry said as she walked up to him. She had shopping bags hanging off of her arms and she was carrying a miniature Christmas tree in her hand. It had miniature ordainments and small streamers laced around it.

"Don't you 'hey mommy' me, you forgot I came here with you," she said as she raised an eyebrow.

"What? Me forget *you*, that's... that's impossible," he said very badly lying. He scratched his head. Lisa rolled her eyes. There was a pause. "Wait, why do you have a miniature Christmas tree?" Henry asked as he pointed to the tree.

"Because it's *so cute*," she said as she shook the tree in his face. He backed away from the tree. "Besides it's very unlikely that Rose celebrated Christmas so she needs to see miniature

Christmas trees even though we're going to get an actual size tree," she said.

"Does that mean..?" Henry trailed off, he knew Lisa knew what he was asking.

"Yes, we are getting an actual size tree, today," she said as she started to walk. Henry sighed.

"But, we have a limo. We can't carry a Christmas tree home in that car," Henry said as he started to walk too.

"We'll just tell the people to follow us," Lisa said as she shrugged. Henry sighed again. They walked outside. The limo driver was there waiting. He opened the door as he saw Henry walking towards him, he bowed his head. Henry, Lisa, Rose, Joey, and Lilly hopped in the car. The driver closed the door behind them before he walked to the driver's seat. He looked back, awaiting Henry's order.

"Take me to the..." Henry paused forgetting the name. "Christmas tree place, thingy. I don't know, that place you buy Christmas trees," Henry said as he pinched the bridge of his nose. The driver nodded, somehow understanding what Henry was saying. Henry closed the window that allowed the driver to hear and see them and it locked into place.

"Christmas tree place, thingy?" Lisa asked as she looked at Henry. Her eyebrow was raised.

"I couldn't think of the name," Henry said as he held up his hands in defense. Lisa sighed. Henry leaned back, placing his arm around Rose. She leaned her head on his shoulder as she smiled into his shoulder. Joey subtly moved his hand onto Lilly's, her cheeks blushed a bright red. She looked away, not wanting anyone to see it.

After a while the car stopped. The driver got out and opened Henry's door. They all hopped out of the car. "I need you to wait here," Henry said. The driver nodded his head as he leaned in through his door, twisting the key and turning off the car. The driver opened the door and sat down in his seat. He got out his phone from his jacket pocket and started to play a game. Bringing his thumb back and releasing his thumb from the screen. He leaned his body to the left, as if his motions would help him.

"Henry, come here," he heard Lisa yell to him. He walked over to her as his feet created footprints in the freshly fallen snow. Lisa was looking at two trees, turning her head between the two. She was talking to Rose. "Now this one is bigger, but this one has more branches," Lisa said as she looked at the branches of the trees. She stepped back and looked through the two trees and saw something. "But that one is beautiful," Lisa said as she grabbed Rose's arm and ran towards the dark green tree.

Henry sighed, he knew this was going to take longer than expected. He walked to the driver and he tapped on the window. The driver stopped playing his game and rolled down his window. "This is going to take longer than expected, so... here's your tip..." Henry opened his wallet and pulled out a twenty dollar bill. The driver took the money, folding it and tucked it into his pocket. "It's going to take a long time," Henry said as he patted the car. He walked off as the driver continued his game on his phone.

Rose walked to Henry. "I don't understand what she's talking about," Rose said in a whisper. Henry wrapped his arm around her.

"I've had to deal with this for years... I still don't understand.., but if we wait in the car she'll talk to herself," Henry said as he lead Rose to the car. He opened the car door and Rose slid in. Henry shook his head and snow fell from his hair. He hopped in and closed the door behind him. "We'll be safe in here," Henry said as he looked out the window. Lisa was talking to Lilly and Joey about the structure of the tree, both of their leashes in her hand. "I feel sorry for them, they can't escape," Henry said as he turned back around. Rose looked out the window. She quickly turned around as if she didn't see anything.

A few minutes later Joey tapped on the window. Henry opened the door. "We, we need a place to hide. I don't understand the difference between the trees, they all look the same," Joey said. Henry motioned his hand for him to come in. Lilly followed him. Henry shut the door behind them. They all leaned back onto the seats. Joey looked out the window. "Now she's talking to the people that own the store," Joey said as she looked at Lisa. She moved her arms, outlining the tree, the men with her just nodded.

"Ma'am are you going to buy this tree?" The man asked as he scratched his head. There was a long pause as Lisa stared off into space.

"I think I'll take it, but will you fine gentlemen follow us. Our car can't carry a tree," she said as she motioned towards the limo. The men nodded. Henry opened his door and walked towards them.

"How much?" Henry asked as he pulled out his checkbook. Lisa looked around, realizing that Henry hadn't been with her. She also realized that Joey, Lilly, and Rose weren't with her.

"That will be fifty dollars, my Lord," the man said. Henry signed the check and gave it to the man. "We'll wrap this up, load it on our truck, and follow you," the man said. Henry nodded his head. Lisa grabbed Henry by the arm.

"Where were you," she whispered. Henry laughed nervously.

"We all got cold so we decided to wait in the car," Henry said. His time smoothly lying. He knew that that was somewhat of the truth so Lisa wouldn't detect it. Lisa's face expression changed, turning soft.

"Ok," she said as she walked to the car Henry sighed out of relief. They all hopped in the car, the driver turned off his phone and looked back, awaiting his orders.

"Take me home," Henry said as he sighed out of relief. The driver nodded as he started to drive. Henry pressed the button. Henry turned his head and looked backwards. He saw the truck following them, carrying their 'perfect' Christmas tree. He looked around. Lilly and Joey were sitting close together, their shoulders were touching. Lilly's face was red and Joey's was a lighter shade of red, Henry glanced down and saw their hands touching. *Way to go,* Henry thought to Joey. Joey looked at Henry.

Stop, Joey said. Henry lightly chuckled to himself as he looked at Rose. Her head was against the window, looking out of it. Henry scooted closer to her. He grabbed her shoulders and moved her head off the window and onto his chest. She wrapped her arms around him. He wrapped his arm around her shoulders as he leaned his head down onto hers. He took his free hand and grabbed hers. He smiled to himself.

We're finally going home, Henry thought as he closed his eyes.

Chapter 46

Rose heard a tap on her window. She opened her eyes and looked in the direction that the noise was coming from, it was the driver. "Sorry to wake you, ma'am, my Lord, but we are at the house," the driver said talking to Rose and Henry. Henry nodded his head as he rubbed his eyes with his hands. Rose stretched as she arched her back, relieving the soreness.

Rose slid out of the car and nodded at the driver, saying thank you. He returned the nod. Henry slid out of the car and thanked the driver as well. Lisa finally slid out of the car, holding Joey's and Lilly's leashes. They both bowed their heads as they passed the driver. "Do you need help with the bags, my Lord?" The driver asked Henry.

"No, that won't be necessary," Henry said as he and Rose grabbed the bags. Lisa held Joey and Lilly's leashes. "You can go home now," Henry said to the driver, he nodded his head as he got back in the car and drove off. The men that had the Christmas tree carried it up to the front door, where Henry, Rose, Lisa, Joey, and Lilly were.

"Do you want us to set this up, my Lord?" The men asked as one of them grunted from the heaviness of the tree.

"Yes, please," Henry said as he opened the door for the men to enter. The men walked in as did everyone else. Henry took his shoes off and laid them next to the couch. The men looked around Henry's house in amazement. Rose subtly smirked, thinking that her face probably looked like that when she was first brought here. She sat down on the couch.

"Does it matter where you want the tree, my Lord?" The man said, finally snapping out of his daze.

"No-"

"Yes," Lisa said as she interrupted Henry. She gave Henry the death eyes. Henry held up his hands in surrender, as if to say 'fine, do what you want.' Lisa nodded her head thankfully at Henry. Henry sat down on the couch, next to Rose. "Ok, so I want the tree over here," Lisa said as she pointed in the general area between the kitchen and office. The men followed her to the area. Henry sighed as he watched his mom try and describe where she wanted the tree. The men just nodded their heads, even though they were both lost.

Henry reached his hand into his pocket. "I'll be right back," Henry said as he stood up. Rose nodded. He walked upstairs and into his room. A few minutes later he came back wearing a button up shirt and dress pants. His shoes were off, he sat back down on the couch next to Rose. He turned his head around. Lisa had finally made up her mind where she wanted the tree. The men were finally situating the tree, once they had screwed in the screws. Lisa looked at the tree.

"Henry, does that look crooked to you?" Lisa asked as she continued to look at the tree.

"No, it looks fine," Henry said, not even looking at the tree.

"Henry you have to look at the tree," Lisa said as she looked at him. He sighed as he turned her head back around. He looked at the tree for a second. "No, it's not crooked," Henry said again.

"Ok, thank you gentlemen," Lisa said to the two men. They nodded and subtly sighed out of relief. They started to walk towards the door. Henry stood up and walked to the men and shook their hands.

As Henry shook their hands Henry whispered into their ears. "I'm sorry," the men only nodded and walked out of the house. They hopped in their truck and drove off. Henry sighed, he started to unbutton his shirt to reveal a muscle-t underneath it. He slid down his pants to reveal sweatpants. He threw his clothes on the stairs as he walked back to the couch. He wrapped his arm around Rose.

"Hen?" Rose asked as she looked at him.

"Yes, Short Stack?" Henry asked as he looked down at Rose.

"Can we watch RARVABIHY?" Rose asked. Henry furrowed his eyebrows.

"What's that?" Henry asked, confused. Rose sighed.

"*Roses are Red Violets are Blue, I Hate You*, duh," Rose said in a 'duh' tone. Henry held up his hands.

"I'm sorry, I didn't know we were calling it R... A... R... V... A... B... I... H... Y," Henry said thinking about what letter to use. "But, yes, we can watch it," Rose golf clapped her hands. Henry looked around for the remote. "Where's the remote?" Henry asked. Rose reached to her side and grabbed the remote. She held it up to Henry. "You had it the entire time?" Henry asked as he continued to stare at the remote. She simply nodded her head. Henry reached for the remote but Lisa quickly grabbed it out of Rose's hand. They both looked up at Lisa, their faces reading 'what are you doing?'

"You two watch too much TV, go outside," Lisa said, sounding like a mother talking to a six year old.

"But, mommy," Henry said, using the mommy card to try and act sweet and innocent. Lisa raised an eyebrow.

"Don't you 'but mommy' me," Lisa said, mimicking a six year old. She pointed to the door. "It's a beautiful day, it's snowing, go outside," Lisa said, still pointing to the door.

Is there any way to win this? Rose asked Henry.

No, we better do what she says, Henry said, in unison they both stood up from the couch. Rose ran upstairs and into her room. A few minutes later she came back down wearing a t-shirt and sweatpants. Henry was by the door, holding a hoodie and sunglasses for Rose. He had already put on his hoodie and sunglasses. Rose grabbed the hoodie and put it on, she grabbed the sunglasses from his hand and put them on as well. They both walked outside, Lisa closed the door behind them and locked it. "And she locked us out... great," Henry said as he shrugged and sighed. Rose sighed as well.

"So... what do you want to do?" Rose asked as she looked at Henry. He grabbed his hood and placed it on top of his head, stopping the snow from falling in his hair. Rose did the same with her hood.

"I guess walk," Henry said as he shrugged. Henry started to walk as did Rose. They were side by side. They turned right and started to walk down the side of the house. A little down halfway Rose started to fall behind Henry. He turned around facing her. "You're slow," Henry said as he continued to walk backwards.

Rose stopped walking and looked at Henry. "Hen, you are a foot taller than me, the snow goes up to your shins," she said as she pointed to his shins. "And the snow goes up to my knees," she said as she pointed to her knees. "How am I supposed to walk with only one third of my body?" Rose asked, she raised an eyebrow.

Henry held up his hands in defense, he walked to her. Her eyebrow still raised. When he reached her he turned around and squatted. "Hop on, Short Stack," Henry said as he motioned with his hands for her to jump. She placed her hands on his shoulders and jumped on his back. He wrapped his arms around each of her legs. She wrapped her arms around his neck, holding tightly, but not choking him.

He started to walk again. Rose leaned her chin on his shoulder, next to his face, she took her left hand and ran it through his hair. Henry laughed as she did so. "Wow, you are short," Henry said as he laughed more.

"Hen, don't tell me something I already know," Rose said with a hint of sassiness in her voice.

"Ok, I'm sorry," Henry said as he turned his face to the right. His was only a few centimeters away from Rose's face. "Do you forgive me?" Henry asked.

"I'll have to think about that," Rose simply said. He nodded his head in understanding. He continued to look at Rose's face when he saw something behind her face, his mom. Lisa was staring out the kitchen window, when she and Henry made eye contact Lisa formed her hands into a heart.

Henry quickly looked away from the window, they passed the kitchen window, which was the last window on the right side. They were alone. "You're heavy," Henry said, jokingly. In a split second Rose had swung her left leg out of his arm, placing it on the ground. She used her other leg and her hands that were around his neck, to flip him sideways onto the ground.

Henry fell in the snow, before he could react Rose was shoving snow in his face. She pulled off his hood and shoved snow in his hair and down his back. Henry tried to fight her off. "I'm sorry, I'm sorry, it was a joke, I'm sorry," Henry said as he continued to try and protect himself.

"It wasn't very... funny," Rose said as she shoved a huge amount of snow in his face and hair. She went to shove more snow in his face when he grabbed her arm, he rolled over, still holding her arm. Rose was now on the bottom while Henry was on top of her. His legs on either side of her. He took his free hand and grabbed her free hand, he moved her hand to his hand, he was now holding both of her hands with his one hand so she couldn't shove more snow in his face and hair.

He leaned down his face and kissed her on the lips, he pulled away. His lips a centimeter away from hers. "I'm sorry, I shouldn't have said that," Henry said as he kissed her on the lips again. He pulled away, keeping his lips the same distance as before. "How come you're not teleporting?" Henry asked. There was a short pause.

"Because, that kiss felt nice," Rose said as she smiled.

"Does that mean you forgive me?" Henry asked as he gave her puppy dog eyes.

"In time, but not now," Rose said. Henry nodded his head in understanding. He released the hand that was holding both her hands. She reached over and shoved more snow in his face. He quickly turned around. She was on top of him. He wrapped his arm around Rose, holding her down.

"Stop shoving snow in my face," Henry begged.

"Don't make a remark like that again," Rose said as she gave him the death stare. He nodded his head fast, understandingly.

She ran her fingers through his wet, snowy hair. She leaned her head on his chest and he kissed the top of her head. They both closed their eyes as they laid in each other's arms, the snow continued to fall on and around them. Henry smiled as he felt Rose smile into his chest.

I'm glad that mom sent us out here, Henry said.

I agree, Rose said as she smiled into his chest again. He smiled again as well.

Chapter 47

A thin coat of snow had coated over them. Rose's head was still on Henry's chest and she continued to run her fingers through his hair. Henry's head was leaned back, allowing Rose to run her fingers through his hair

Neither of them felt cold, even though their clothes were both wet from the snow and they were both deep in the high snow. "You know that you only weigh like ninety pounds, so when I called you heavy it was a lie," Henry said. Still trying to make up for his earlier comment.

"I know, but it still wasn't funny and you'll have to wait till I forgive you," Rose said as she talked into his chest.

"That's understandable," Henry said as he nodded. By the way Rose had beat him up when he first said she was heavy, he wasn't going to push it.

They both heard the crunching of the snow. Henry opened his eyes to see Lisa standing over them. She had many jackets on, leggings, high boots, and her arms were crossed as she tried to warm herself up.

"Why don't you two come inside?" Lisa asked as she shivered more.

"Because you were the one that *locked* us out," Henry said as he closed his eyes again.

"I unlocked the door over an hour ago," Lisa said as she glanced back at the door. "You've been out here for three hours,"

"But we're so comfortable," Rose said. Her face still in Henry's chest, making her voice muffled.

"I made dinner," Lisa said. Henry and Rose both opened their eyes.

"Rose," Henry said as he looked at her. She knew what he was saying. She teleported both her and Henry out of the snow and into the house. Lisa lightly laughed to herself as she turned around and started to walk to the door.

Rose and Henry both took off their wet hoodies and threw them on the coat rack. They took of their shoes and laid them under the coat rack. They quickly went to the kitchen, both of them hungry. Rose rubbed her hands together as she saw that Lisa had prepared grilled steak and French Fries. Joey and Lilly were both sitting at the table, already eating. Rose and Henry both sat down at the table and started to eat as well. A few seconds went by before Lisa walked through the door. She took off her boots, top coat, and jacket. She walked to the dinner table.

"It's nice to see that my *beloved* son waited to eat until his *amazing* mother got there," Lisa said as she grabbed her food and sat down.

Henry shoved a fork full of steak in his mouth and looked up at Lisa. "What did you say?" Henry asked, food still in his mouth.

Lisa sighed. "I thought I raised you better than this," Lisa said. Henry swallowed his food as he shook his head.

"No, this is the outcome," Henry said as he motioned to himself. He gave a toothy smile. Lisa sighed again then she looked at Rose.

"Rose you're my new child, Henry is no longer mine," Lisa said bluntly.

"What?! That's not fair," Henry said upset.

"No, this is fair. You said that *you* are the outcome. *I* want a new outcome," Lisa said as she wrapped her arm around Rose and brought her closer. Henry grabbed Rose and brought her closer to him. He picked her up and placed her on his lap.

"If you choose me I'll watch RARVABIHY," Henry said, there was a short pause. "I've been practicing how to say that just for you," Henry said. She looked up at him.

"Ok," she said. He smiled a toothy smile at his mom, as if to say 'ha, I won.' Lisa rolled her eyes and Henry stood up as he carried Rose. Rose reached down and grabbed both of their empty plates. Henry walked to the dishwasher, she took her free hand and opened the dishwasher. Henry bent down to allow Rose to place the plates in the dishwasher. Henry stood up as Rose closed the door. Henry walked to the couch.

Henry sat down on the couch with Rose on his lap. She wrapped her arms around him as he grabbed the remote and turned on the TV.

Lisa looked at Joey and Lilly, they were all still sitting at the dinner table. "You two are my new children, Henry and Rose are not mine," Lisa said bluntly as she stood up and placed her plate in the dishwasher. She turned around, facing Lilly and Joey. They both nodded in agreement. Lisa clapped her hands together in excitement. She grabbed foil and started to wrap up the leftover food.

"Why, why would she do this? I loved her. She was my everything," William, the husband, said as he started to cry.

"No William, she cheated on you!" Rose practically yelled at the TV. She was crying as well. Henry wiped away the stray tear with his thumb.

"It's ok, don't cry, it's ok," Henry said as he continued to cradle Rose. He was sitting criss crossed again and Rose was sitting in his lap as his arm was across her waist.

"No it's not. He doesn't know that she was cheating on him," Rose said as she pointed to the TV. "He's hot, this shouldn't be happening to him," Rose said as she looked at William. He had brown hair that was styled like Henry's, but it had a few blonde streaks in it, he was as tall as Henry too. The only difference was the eyes, they were once the kind red like Henry's, but now they were a dark red as he searched for his wife's killer.

Rose grabbed the remote and clutched it tightly, knowing that Henry would try and take it after the 'he's hot' remark. Henry, with the arm that was across Rose, tapped his pointed finger in anger.

"He's not that hot," Henry said as he pointed to the TV. His voice cracked as he did so. Rose looked back at him and nodded her head. Henry sighed as he placed his face in the crook of her neck. "I think I'm hotter than he is," Henry said. Rose just shrugged.

Henry fell sideways with Rose on his chest. His arms were wrapped around her. She was still grasping the remote. Henry kissed her on the lips. "I think I'm hotter," Henry said as he kissed her again.

Rose kissed back. "I think just this time you are," Rose said as she pulled away.

"I'll take any points I can get," Henry said as he kissed her again.

"Ew," they both heard Lilly say. Rose and Henry continued to kiss. Rose reached up her hand and swooshed her away. Lilly, Joey, and Lisa all walked upstairs and into their rooms. Henry and Rose pulled away and they both turned their attention to the TV. Rose rested her head on Henry's chest and Henry propped his head on the arm of the couch.

Rose had closed her eyes with her head still on his chest and her arms had wrapped around the back of his neck. Henry's head was still rested on the arm of the couch. He moved his body down, his head now on the couch. He grabbed the remote out of Rose's hands and turned off the TV.

"I'm hotter than he is," Henry said to himself. He closed his eyes as he felt Rose snuggle closer to him. *How did I get so lucky?* Henry thought as he kissed the top of Rose's head.

He closed his eyes as he started to rest.

Chapter 48

Henry slowly opened his eyes. Rose was curled up on his chest and her hands were wrapped around the back of his neck. Her face was nudged into the crook of his neck. Her legs, along with the rest of her body, was curled up in a small ball on his chest. Henry's arms were wrapped around her waist. Henry removed one of his arms from around her waist and looked at his watch. Rose groaned, he had awoken her.

"Hi," Henry said as he placed his arm back around her. His voice was rough from just waking up.

"Hi," Rose said into his neck. Her voice was low and tired, it came out a whisper.

"Any nightmares tonight?" Henry asked. Rose shook her head. "That's good," Henry said as he placed a soft kiss on her head. She smiled as he did so. There was a short pause. "Are you hungry?" Henry asked. Rose just simply nodded her head. "Ok, you have to get off of me," Henry said as he lightly sat up, propping his lower back on the arm of the couch.

"No," Rose said as she shook her head. The arms that were around the back of his neck tightened. She nudged her face further into the side of his neck.

"Ok, I'll just... carry you?" Henry asked if that's what she wanted. She nodded her head in agreement. Henry stood up from the couch. Rose was still curled up in a ball on his chest and her arms still around his neck. Henry moved one of his arms under her legs for support. He lightly chuckled. "You're adorable," Henry said as he started to walk towards the kitchen.

"I know," Rose said into his neck, still sounding half asleep.

"You know?" Henry asked, making his voice sound like he was talking to a young child. Rose nodded her head. "Well then, why am I here?" Henry asked.

"To remind me," Rose said into his neck.

"I'm here to remind you?" Henry asked. She nodded her head. He walked into the kitchen. "Let me guess, you want pancakes?" Henry asked even though he knew the answer.

"No," Rose said as she shook her head into his neck. Henry froze at her answer, his eyes widened in complete horror. He couldn't believe what he had just heard. He thought this day would never come.

"No?" Henry asked, shocked. "Look at me," he said. She lifted her head from his neck and looked at him. He reached up his free hand and felt her forehead. "Are you sick, do you feel well?" Henry asked as he continued to feel the temperature on her forehead.

"I'm fine, I'm just in the mood for chocolate," Rose said.

"I can put chocolate in the pancakes," Henry said to her. Her eyes slightly widened.

"You can do that?" She asked still sounding asleep. Henry shook his head as he lightly laughed and looked at Rose's face. The awe and wonder of just putting chocolate chips in a pancake.

"Yes, I can put chocolate in the pancakes. Would you like chocolate pancakes?" Henry asked. She nodded her head.

"Ok, but I can't cook with one hand," Henry said as he looked down at the hand that was supporting Rose. Rose moved her legs around Henry and locked her ankles together. "That works too," Henry said as he grabbed the pancake batter. He started to make the pancakes. Rose put her face in the crook of his neck again, breathing in his vanilla scent.

Henry walked to the stove as he turned sideways so Rose wouldn't touch the stove. He put the chocolate chips in the pancake. Rose reached down to the bag and grabbed a few, eating the chocolate chips as Henry continued to cook.

Henry flipped over the four pancakes. After a minute or so he turned off the stove and walked to a cabinet and grabbed two plates. He walked back and laid the plates next to each other on the counter. He took the spatula and laid two on one plate and two on the other. He walked to the fridge and grabbed the butter and syrup. He spread the butter over the pancakes, then the syrup.

He picked up the two plates and walked back to the couch. When he was in front of the couch. Rose unlocked her ankles and dangled from Henry's neck, too small to reach the ground. Henry sat down on the couch and Rose curled up on his lap. Henry handed her plate and a fork. Henry leaned against the corner of the couch and rested his plate and arm on the arm of the couch. They both started to eat. Henry grabbed the remote and turned on the TV and switched it to *RARVABIHY*.

They had both finished their pancakes. "Thanks Hen for making the pancakes," Rose said as she looked back at him.

"No problem Short Stack," Henry said as he laid his head on her shoulder. He turned his head and kissed her lightly in the cheek. Her cheeks turned a bright red as she leaned her head against his. William popped up on the screen, Henry looked at Rose. She was staring intensely at him. Henry took his hand and covered her eyes.

"Hen!" Rose said as she tried to pry his hand off his eyes. His hand didn't budge. She struggled more.

"You're not allowed to like anyone, except for me," Henry said. William disappeared from the screen. Henry removed his hand from her eyes. She looked back at Henry and gave him the death stare, she opened her mouth to say something,

"Henry," Lisa said from the top of the stairs. Henry smirked at Rose and turned his attention to Lisa.

"Yes, mom?" Henry asked.

"We need to go shopping," Lisa said. Henry's mouth dropped opened.

"But... but, we went shopping the other day," Henry said, sounding like a small kid. He hated going shopping multiple times in a short amount of time.

"I don't care, we are going shopping. I've already asked Joey and Lilly what they want for Christmas." Lisa said more sternly. Her face softened as she looked at Rose. "Honey, would you like to come too?" Lisa asked Rose. She just kind of shrugged.

"I think that Short Stack is having a lazy day," Henry said as he looked at Rose.

"I love those days... Rose would you like any Christmas present?" Lisa asked. Rose shook her head and there was a pause. "Henry, go get dressed," Lisa said as she pointed to his room. Henry sighed as he started to stand up, Rose grabbed him and pulled him back down. Henry faced Rose and he took one hand and caressed her face.

"I have to go get dressed or my mom will kill me. I don't want to be killed, so will you be so kind as to let go. I'll be back before you know it," Henry said as he placed a quick kiss on her lips. Rose reluctantly let go of Henry. He stood up and walked up to his room.

A few minutes later he came back down. He was wearing a dark blue muscle t-shirt, a black winter coat, a mixture of grey and black jeans, and winter boots. He ran his fingers through his hair as he walked to Rose. He kissed Rose on the head.

"I'll be back soon," Henry said as he started to walk away.

"Wait," Rose said. He stopped and turned back around. She motioned for him to come to her. He walked back to her. She ran her fingers through his hair. "Ok, you can go now," Henry's face dropped a little, thinking she was going to kiss him, but he only got a hand through the hair.

Henry walked to the coat rack and threw a hoodie at Rose. She caught it as she smiled. Henry and Lisa walked out of the house. Lisa pointed to her car, a grey mustang. Henry rolled his eyes, still thinking that she shouldn't have a sports car. He reluctantly got into the passenger's seat and let Lisa drive.

Rose slightly smiled as she thought about Henry's and Lisa's relationship, wanting, wishing to have had one with her mom or dad. The thought of what she could have had with her family was slightly sad. Even though she considered Lisa to be her mom she still wanted one with her actual parents. Wanting her parents to give her a nickname, to go places, to joke around, and so much more.

She needed to take her mind off of all the thoughts. She reached for the remote, almost if on cue she heard Henry's voice in her head.

Don't watch RARVABIHY, Henry said warningly. Rose knew that somehow he would find out if she were to watch the show. She stood up from the couch and walked to the library. She picked up the fourth book in the series that she had been reading throughout the year. She sat down on the plush, circular chair as she sunk into it.

Rose heard Lilly and Joey talking. She glanced up from her book and looked at the time. Her eyes widened as she saw that she had been reading for two hours straight. She looked down at her book to see how much she had read. It was a little less than half the book. She thought she had only been reading for a couple of minutes. Her thoughts were interrupted when Lilly and Joey walked into the room.

"We're going to go outside," Lilly stated as they both put on their coats and shoes. Rose simply nodded. They both turned around and walked out of the office. Rose heard the entrance door closing behind them. She glanced back down at her book and continued to read.

~mall~

"Ok, so I need to go to that store, that store, that store, and that store," Lisa said as she pointed to four stores. Henry had his head buried in his hand. He sighed as he lifted his head up, looking at Lisa.

"Why... why did you bring me along?" Henry asked. His voice sounded like he was about to cry.

"Because I wanted to spend time with my son and talk to you," Lisa said. Henry raised an eyebrow, not entirely believing in what she was saying. *I have something that I want to ask him,* he heard Lisa think.

"What do you want to ask me?" Henry asked. Lisa looked a little shocked before she remembered that he could read minds. She took a deep, nervous breath.

"I... I want Rider to be properly buried," Lisa said. Henry was taken back by her statement. There was a long uncomfortable silence as he thought. Lisa's eyes pleading with him to bury her son properly.

"Ok, I'll work something out. I'll do the same for Zoey," Henry said. He knew that burying them in the woods near his cabin was not ok. Every time he thought about it he got a sick, weird feeling, thinking that no one should be buried like that. *They deserve respect and a proper burial.*

Lisa wrapped her arms around Henry, overfilled with joy that her son would finally be at peace. She hugged him tightly. "Thank you, Henry," Lisa said. Henry kissed the top of her head as he hugged her back.

"No problem, mommy," he said. He made the mommy part more silent so that people passing by wouldn't hear. Lisa pulled away from Henry.

"Now let's go shopping," Lisa said as she grabbed Henry and started to drag him into a store. The store was filled with fragrances, candles, sprays, body washes, shampoo, conditioner, soaps, wallflower fragrance, wallflower holders, hand sanitizer, and scent portables. Henry closed his eyes as he placed his head in his hand. He hated these stores. Lisa ran off into the store, smelling all the fragrances.

"Henry!" Henry heard a high pitched squeal basically shout. He recognized the voice. He slowly lifted his head out of his hand, he saw straight blonde hair and a huge smile plastered on the face.

"Hey Britney," Henry said. She hugged him tightly and he hugged back. She had two shopping bags hanging off of her right arm, they were filled with fragrances. It looked like she had bought one of everything in the store. "How come you're shopping and not working?" Henry asked.

"It's my day off," Britney said. Britney looked around, her eyebrows furrowed in confusion.

"Where's Rose?" She asked. Henry opened his mouth to say something. Britney grabbed his jacket with both of her hands, she pulled Henry down where they were eye level. "And if you have hurt her I swear that I will avenge-"

"She's having a lazy day," Henry said scared. He had never seen Britney get mad before. She unclasped her hands from his jacket. Henry stood straight up again.

"Oh, ok," she said cheerily. "When you get home tell her I said hi," she said. Henry nodded his head, still shocked at Britney. "So what are you doing here?" Britney asked. Henry just pointed to Lisa. Britney's eyes widened and she quickly ran to Lisa and hugged her tightly. Lisa motioned for Henry to come to her. He reluctantly walked to her. His hands deep in his pockets. Lisa shoved a candle in his face.

"Does that smell good?" Lisa asked. He moved his head away from the candle, shoving Lisa's hand back.

"Yeah, I guess," Henry said as he shrugged. The reason he hated these stores was because they had too much fragrances. They were not cheap, and finding one that you liked that exceeded every other fragrance was next to impossible.

"I'm getting it," Lisa said. Henry sighed, not knowing why she had him smell the candle.

Why did she need me to smell it? Henry thought. He sighed deeply, knowing this was going to be a long day.

Henry looked at his watch as he sighed. They had been at the mall for four hours. He just wanted to get Rose a Christmas present and leave, but his mom and Britney had to go to every store that had something remotely cute. However, they had made progress, he was now walking to the store that he had been wanting to go to.

He walked in the store and looked around. The store was a designer store. It had blankets, bags, suitcases, t-shirts, wallets, and purses. He walked to the section that had the blankets. He looked for a dark blue blanket, one that Rose would like. He pulled back a blanket and saw a blue blanket with black swirls on it. He picked it up and walked to the cashier.

"Can I have something written on this?" Henry asked. The cashier nodded.

"So why did you drag along Henry?" Britney asked as she shifted all ten of her bags to a more comfortable position on her arm. Lisa shrugged as she did the same with her eight bags, most of the bags held Joey and Lilly's presents.

"I just wanted to spend time with my son," Lisa said. Britney clasped her hands together and tilted her head to the side.

"Aw, mother and son bonding time, that's adorable," Britney said as she lightly squealed. Henry walked out of the store carrying one bag.

"Ok, I got what I need. Can we please go now?" Henry asked, sounding tired and exhausted. Lisa nodded her head and Henry sighed out of relief. Britney hugged him tightly and he hugged back.

"Bye Henry, don't forget to tell Rose I said hi," she said as she stopped hugging him.

"Ok, I will, bye Britney," Henry said as Lisa and him started to walk out of the mall.

Henry opened the trunk for Lisa and they put their bags in the trunk and Henry closed it. They hopped in the car as Lisa revved the engine. Henry rolled his eyes as she did so. He crossed his arms and closed his eyes. He lightly smiled at the thought that he'll get to be with Rose after this long, tortures day.

Chapter 49

Henry felt a slap hit his arm. He opened his eyes and looked at Lisa. "Hey Mr. Prissy we're here," Lisa said as she walked away from Henry's door.

He rolled his eyes at the fact that she was calling him Mr. Prissy... again. He got out of the car, closing the door behind him. He grabbed his bag as Lisa grabbed all of hers. "Get Rose to come and decorate the tree," Lisa said. Henry knew that he didn't have a choice.

Henry walked up to his room and laid the bag down on the floor. He walked back downstairs to the office where he guessed Rose was. He knew that Joey and Lilly were outside playing in the snow.

He walked into the office. Rose was hanging upside down in the chair, her head was touching the ground. The book was on top of her hand, keeping it opened. Her eyes were closed, she was resting. No doubt she had gotten so bored that she decided to read upside down and had started to rest while doing so.

Henry grabbed Rose, laying one of his hands under her neck and the other around her waist. He sat her upright, her hand still grasping the open book. Her head resting on his shoulder. "Hey, I'm home, it's time to wake up," Henry said gently. He ran his fingers through her hair.

Her eyes shot opened as she heard his voice, she glanced up at him. She wrapped her arms around him, tightly hugging him. She stopped hugging him. She grabbed a fistful of his hair and forced him backwards on the chair. He was laying on his back. "You lied to me, you said you would be back before I knew it. That took forever, it was torture," she said as she repeatedly slapped his chest with her free hand.

He held up his hands in defense, trying to block off her attacks. His face held a shocked expression.

Why are all the girls beating me up today? Henry thought. "I-I'm sorry m-my mom met Britney and had to go into every store they saw. I'm sorry," Henry said scared as he continued to try and block her hand. Rose's face softened and she stopped hitting him.

"Oh, ok," Rose said as she released her grip on his hair. She sat up straight again. He hesitantly sat up. "All you had to do was say that."

"All I had to do was say that... you didn't let me speak before you attacked me," Henry said as his eyes widened.

"I didn't attack you," Rose said sounding like a small kid.

"What would you call hitting me multiple times and holding me down?"

"Attacking you," she said in a very small voice.

"Thank you," Henry said as he threw his arms and hands in the air. There was a short pause.

"I had a reason to do it," Rose said, sounding like a small kid. Henry raised an eyebrow. "The indoor garden died," she said.

"Yeah, it's a garden, it's going to die in the winter," he said in a duh tone.

"But I loved that garden," Rose said upset. Henry started to smirk.

"Since you hit me and your only reason is because of plants. It's my turn to let you go through my own form of torture," Henry said. He was talking about decorating the Christmas tree with Lisa. In a split second he had thrown Rose over his shoulder.

She hit his back with her hands. "Hen, let me go! Put me down! Where are you taking me?!" Rose practically screamed as she continued to hit his back.

"You'll have to wait," Henry said as he walked out of the office. He walked to the Christmas tree and laid her down on the ground. "She's all yours," Henry said to Lisa. He started to walk away.

"Young man, where do you think you are going?" Lisa asked. Henry stopped in the middle of the room, his smirk disappeared. "You are helping us with the tree," Lisa said. Henry silently cursed under his breath.

He put on a fake smile as he turned back around. He clapped his hands together. "I'll be happy to help, mother," Henry said as his teeth barely gritting together. He looked down at Rose. A huge smirk was on her face. She subtly stuck out her tongue, like a small child.

Ha, Rose thought to him.

Shut up, Henry said as he sat down next to her.

Don't tell me to shut up. You shut up, Rose said as she glared at him.

Ok, I will. I'm sorry, Henry said as he hung his head, realizing his fatal mistake. He wrapped his arms around Rose and brought her head into his chest. He leaned back falling on his back. Rose was on top of him. *I'm sorry.*

"No, you two help me with the tree," Lisa said as she looked at Rose and Henry 'cuddling' on the ground. Rose pushed on Henry's chest and sat up. Henry internally groaned as he sat up. He knew his torture was about to begin. "Ok so the ornaments need to be evenly spaced, not too close and not too far away," Lisa said as she hung two ornaments on the tree, demonstrating.

Henry sighed as he picked up two ornaments and hung them. "Not there," Lisa said to him. Henry's hand, that was grasping the ornament, moved up. Lisa shook her head. He moved it to the left, she shook her head. He sighed as he moved it to the right. Lisa nodded her head. Henry sighed out of relief, he hung the ornament on the tree.

Rose was somehow hanging all the ornaments the way that Lisa wanted. Henry watched her in utter shock. He had been doing this for years and he still couldn't do it. How can Short Stack get this?

This is her first Christmas for goodness sake! She didn't even know what Christmas was! Henry yelled to himself in utter frustration. He didn't understand it, it was unfair.

He grabbed two more ornaments and hung them on the tree. All the while looking at Lisa, she shook her head. He continued to move them until she nodded her head. He sighed, this was going to take a while.

Henry lifted Rose on top of his shoulders. His hands were holding her legs, keeping her from falling off his shoulders. Rose placed the star on top of the Christmas tree. She looked down at Lisa who nodded her head. Rose teleported off his shoulders and onto the ground.

She started to walk to the kitchen, but Henry grabbed her. He wrapped his arms around her waist. In a split second they were on the couch, Henry's arms were still wrapped around her. His head was on the arm of the couch. Rose's head was on his chest. She struggled in his grasp, but his grip didn't loosen. He smiled at the fact that she wasn't teleporting.

"I'm sorry," Henry said as he gave her puppy dog eyes. Rose stopped struggling as she saw his face. "Can you ever forgive me?" Henry asked as his bottom lip stuck out. "Tomorrow is Christmas Eve and I don't want you to be mad at me."

Rose's eyes furrowed in confusion. "What's Christmas Eve?"

"Christmas Eve is the day before Christmas."

"Oh."

"So... do you forgive me?" Henry asked again. Rose raised an eyebrow and shrugged. "I'll let you look at William," Henry added blandly. His voice held no emotion. Rose's face perked up at the mention of William.

"Ok, I forgive you," she said as she grabbed the remote and turned on the TV. Henry didn't know whether to be excited or sad.

William appeared on screen. Rose immediately perked up, her eyes widened as she looked at him. Rose glanced down at Henry, his arms were crossed over Rose and he had a huge frown on his face. His mouth was going down as far as possible, and he was giving William the death stare. He hated not being able to block Rose's eyes from looking at William. Rose sighed, looking at Henry's face made her sad.

"Fine, I won't look at William," Rose said blandly. Henry's face lightened up and his frown disappeared, turning into a huge smile. The arms that were crossed over her became uncrossed.

"Really, you would do that for me?" Henry asked her. She nodded her head. Henry kissed her multiple times. "You're the best," Henry said as he continued to kiss her.

"I know," she said once he had pulled away.

"I know that you know," there was a pause. "You know what this calls for?" Henry asked. Rose shook her head. "Food," Henry said. Rose's eyes widened. She hugged Henry tightly.

"You're the best," she said as Henry stood up. He was carrying her. Her arms were wrapped around his neck and he was using one of his hands to hold her up. They reached the kitchen and Henry started to roam through the refrigerator and all the cabinets.

"What do you want, Short Stack?"

"Um..." she trailed off for a few seconds. Henry stood there with his eyebrow raise. "Popcorn," Rose said finally. Henry nodded his head as he grabbed a bag of popcorn, he put it in the microwave and hit the popcorn button. "So what is Christmas Eve?" Rose asked as she waited for the popcorn. Henry jumped up on the counter. Rose was still on his lap.

"Well it's when you and your family get together and just hang out, maybe have dinner and a few other things," Henry said, there was a short pause. "And I was wondering if my family, aka you, would like to go out on a date with me tomorrow?" Henry asked. Rose looked back at him, a small shocked expression was on her face before it was quickly replaced with a smile.

"I would love to," Rose said as she wrapped her arms around him, hugging him tightly. He hugged her back. "But..." Rose trailed off. Henry pulled away and looked at her. "You consider me your family?" Rose asked. He softly caressed her cheek.

"Of course," Henry said as he quickly kissed her. Rose buried her face into his chest. She hadn't felt, or even been told, that she had a family in years. This all felt new to her, like she was learning something all over again, it felt nice.

"Is the popcorn ready?" Rose asked with her face still in his chest.

"No, not yet," Henry said as he shook his head.

The microwave beeped and Henry stood up in a blink of an eye. He grabbed the popcorn and started to walk back to the couch. Rose reached for the bag, Henry moved it away from her hand.

"Hen," Rose whined. "Come on, it was my idea to have popcorn. Give me the popcorn," Rose said as she hit his chest like a small child. He shook his head as he took another bite of popcorn. Rose gave him the death stare. *Fine, if he wants to play dirty, I'll play dirty.*

Rose teleported out of his arms and she appeared in the air, grabbing the popcorn bag out of Henry's hand. She disappeared again before Henry could grab her. Rose appeared on the balcony, in front of the bedrooms. "Ha," she said as she pointed at him, she disappeared again, reappearing in the kitchen. "Ha," she pointed at him, she disappeared and reappeared in front of him. "Ha," she said as she pointed at him again.

Henry ran at her, she disappeared before he could grab her. He knew it was pointless, he fell on his knees.

"Ha," he heard Rose say behind him. Henry fell face first into the floor, his face slid down the floor until he was fully laying on it. He turned over on his back.

"I... I just wanted popcorn," Henry said, whining. Rose appeared in front of him.

"Do you promise to never taunt me with food again?" Rose asked as she raised an eyebrow.

"Yes, yes, I promise," Henry said as he pathetically reached for the bag of popcorn, still laying on the ground.

"Ok, I'll share the popcorn," Rose said as she held out a hand for Henry. He reached up, grabbing her hand. She pulled him off the ground. They both sat down on the couch, Henry reached over and grabbed a handful of popcorn. "What are we doing tomorrow?" Rose asked as she looked up at him.

"You'll have to wait and see," Henry said as he smirked.

"No! You made me wait on my birthday and now this?" Rose asked as she stuck out her bottom lip. Henry quickly looked away, not wanting to be manipulated by Rose's face.

"Not only do you have to wait tomorrow, but for Christmas too," Henry said as he continued to smirk. He continued to look away from her adorable face. She stuck out her lip further. "But, but, but, but-" Rose was cut off as Henry grabbed her face, squishing it.

"No buts, you'll have to wait."

"Bwut," Rose said, her words were mumbled as Henry continued to squish her face.

"No buts, ok?"

"Okw," Rose said. Henry released her face. "Can we watch RARVABIHY?"

"Of course," Henry said as he turned on the TV. William appeared on screen and Henry covered her eyes. She grabbed his hand and tried to pry it off her face. "You never said I couldn't cover your eyes," Henry said as he cradled Rose close to him.

William finally left the screen and he removed his hand. Rose looked back at Henry. "Are you jealous about a fictional character?" Rose asked. Henry nervously laughed.

"What, ha, no... no. I'm not, no," Henry said nervously. Rose raised an eyebrow. She knew that he was from his bad lying. She rolled her eyes as she faced the TV. She leaned back, Henry's chin on top of her head. He wrapped his arm around her waist, Rose closed her eyes and breathed in his vanilla scent. She reached up her hand and ran it through Henry's hair. Henry positioned her to where he was holding her bridal style in his lap. She continued to run her fingers through his hair.

She soon fell asleep, Henry cradling her, and her hand resting on his head. Thinking that this is where she wanted to be for the rest of her life, in Henry's arms.

Chapter 50

Henry gently moved Rose off of his lap, she whined and moved her hand around, looking for something to hold. He grabbed a pillow and gave it to her. She snuggled closer to the pillow, thinking it was Henry. He lightly kissed her forehead, a small smirk appeared on Rose's face. "I'll be back soon," Henry whispered to her.

He walked upstairs to his room. He grabbed black jeans, a dark burgundy t-shirt, black combat boots, and his jacket. He walked into the restroom and fixed his hair. Rose's hand had created a miniature handprint in his hair. Once he fixed it, he quietly walked downstairs. He walked into the garage and hopped in his extra car, a grey Corvette.

He pulled his phone out of his pocket. He dialed Britney's number. He put the phone on speaker. "Hello?" He heard Britney's happy, perky voice on the other end.

"Hey, are you at the mall?"

"Is my hair blonde..? Yes of course I'm at the mall," she said in a 'duh' tone. Henry mentally slapped his face, of course she was at the mall she worked there.

"Ok, ok," Henry paused. "Do you know Rose's size?" He asked, Rose hadn't gained a lot of weight and her clothes still fit her. Since Britney helped find Rose's clothes he thought she could help. There was a long silence. Henry's eyebrows were raised.

"Why?" Britney finally said.

"Because we are going on a date tonight and I wanted to get her a dress," Henry said as his cheeks turned a very bright red.

"Aw! That's so cute!" Britney practically yelled, her voice becoming very high pitched. "Yes, come over now! Hurry!" Britney yelled. Henry heard her heels hit the ground as she jumped up and down. He also heard her hands clap together.

"Ok, I'm on my way. Bye," Henry said as he started his engine.

"Ok, bye," Britney said, she hung up. Henry started to drive to the mall.

He arrived at the mall, he got out of his car and walked in. He started to walk to *Rue 21* but saw Britney at the entrance. "Please don't tell me you're skipping your job to help me," Henry asked, he didn't want to be responsible if she got in trouble.

"Oh don't be silly... I have people covering for me," she said. Henry buried his head in his hand. Britney grabbed his arm away from his head. "Now come on we're wasting time, it's Christmas Eve, everyone wants everything," she said as she started to drag Henry through the crowds of people. They finally made it to a store that Henry had never been in.

There were dresses everywhere, sparkles shone in the light. There were people everywhere. "Ok," Britney said, Henry snapped out of his daze and looked at her. "What color were you thinking?" Britney asked him.

"A dark, almost midnight blue," Henry said, in a second Britney had dragged him to the dark blue color section. She started to slide the dresses to the side, looking at them. "What kind of dress?" She asked, there was fancy, prom, simple, lace, sexy, and about fifty other styles of dresses.

"Uh... something elegant yet simple," Henry said as he continued to look through the dresses.

"Why that kind of dress, why not something tight fitting and sexy?" Britney said as she moved her eyebrows up and down, Henry cheeks turned a bright red again at that thought.

"Because Rose is beautiful, she doesn't need something tight fitting or... sexy," he said, having a hard time saying the word. "Rose is perfect the way she is and a simple dress will do more than enhance her beauty," Henry said, he continued to look through the dresses. Britney stopped.

"That's one of the sweetest things I've ever heard!" She practically yelled. People stopped and stared at her. Henry put his finger over his lips, shushing her. Britney rolled her eyes as she started to look through the dresses once more. Britney pulled one off the rack. "Do you think Rose will like this one?"

Henry looked at the dress. It was a dark blue, it had long sleeves which were lace the neckline was also lace. The lace was see through in those places. The lace pattern was flowers, scribbles were in between each flower, connecting to the other. The lace went from see through to going over a dark blue underdress, the lace pattern continued over the dress. The dress stopped a few inches above her knees, the lace went an inch past the underdress. A black belt went around the waist line. Henry looked at the back of the dress, it would cover up Rose's scars.

"Yeah, but... isn't it a little short. I mean it's snowing outside," Henry said.

"Oh that's a simple solution, give her your jacket," Britney said. Henry nodded in agreement. "Now the moment of truth," Britney said as she took the tag out from the back of the dress. Britney squealed as she slightly jumped up and down. "It's her size," she said excited.

"Let's get it," Henry said as he grabbed the dress and walked to the cashier. He handed her the dress, the cashier scanned it. Henry swiped his card through the machine.

"Would you like that wrapped, sir?" The cashier asked as she smiled. Henry could tell that she has to smile the entire day, her smile looked forced.

"Yes, please," Henry said as he nodded. The girl in lightning speed put the dress in the box and wrapped the box in a red and green wrapping paper. She handed the box to Henry. "Thanks," Henry said as he walked away with Britney.

Once they were out of the store Britney tightly hugged Henry. He hugged back. "Thanks for the help, Britney," Henry said as he pulled away.

"No problem, it was my pleasure," Britney said. "Now I have to go back to my job before there's a riot," there was a short pause. "Are you going to get anything for your mom?" She asked, he shook his head, no.

"She said she didn't want anything."

She nodded and walked into her store. 'Oh and Henry, do anything I would!" Britney yelled across the mall. People looked in the direction she was speaking to Henry. His cheeks turned a bright red as he speed walked out of the mall. He continued that speed until he got to his car. He hopped in and put the present in the passenger's seat.

He started to drive home, wanting to be on the couch with Rose's arms wrapped around him and her hands in his hair. He pulled out his phone again, he had more calls that he needed to make.

After what felt like an eternity he arrived home, even though his trip to the mall was short he was exhausted. He didn't want to change clothes. He laid the present on the table and sat down next to Rose. She was tightly hugging and the pillow. Henry picked Rose up and placed her in his lap. He put his hand on the bottom of the pillow and pushed it up. His arm replaced the pillow. She hugged his arm tightly and curled closer to him. She subconsciously placed her hand on his hair. He smiled as he closed his eyes, he started to rest.

He felt something poke his face. He continued to feel it. He opened his eyes to see that Rose was the one poking his face. "Yes?" He asked.

"Two things. One, why are you in going out clothes and two, why is there a present on the table?" She asked as she pointed to the present.

"Well I'm wearing clothes because I went to the mall to get you that," Henry said as he pointed to the present on the table. She glanced between the present and Henry.

"That's for me?" Rose asked as she pointed to the present. He nodded his head.

"And one thing that's sometimes done on Christmas Eve is opening one present," Henry said, within a millisecond she had grabbed the present.

"So I can open it?" She asked, clarifying. Henry lightly laughed as he nodded his head. She tore off the wrapping paper and pulled the lid off the box. She held up the dress and looked at it. She stood up as she held it up against her, she spun around once.

"Oh my gosh it's beautiful. Thank you," Rose said as she hugged Henry tightly, laying the dress on the couch next to them.

"No problem, Short Stack," Henry said as he hugged her back. "I'm glad that you like it."

"Of course I do, it's beautiful," Rose said as she pulled away. He kissed her on the lips, wrapping an arm around Rose. She kissed back, running her fingers through his hair.

"Oh what's that?" They both heard Lisa say. They pulled away from one another.

"What's what?" Henry asked as his cheeks turned a bright red again. Rose's did as well.

"The dress," Lisa said as she pointed to it.

"Oh, Rose and I are going on a date tonight so I got her a dress."

"Aw my little boy is growing up," Lisa said as she pinched his cheek with her hand. He pulled away from her hand.

"Mom, I left the house a while ago. I've been 'grown up' for a while now."

"I know, but now you're going on a date," Lisa said as she jumped up and down. Henry rolled his eyes before he looked at his watch.

"Speaking of which we should probably get ready," Henry said as he stood up. Rose stood up as well.

"Rose, can I help you get ready?" Lisa asked, her eyes pleading Rose to let her. Rose nodded her head. Lisa squealed again. "YAY! Let's go," Lisa said as she shoved Rose upstairs into her room. Henry walked into his room to get ready.

"Ok, now you can look," Lisa said excited. She had done Rose's hair and makeup.

Rose turned around to look at herself in the mirror, her eyes widened. She had loose curls in her hair. She had on makeup, the makeup was a light smokey eye. The smoky eye made her dress pop. She also had on contour, outlining her cheekbones. The dress was form fitting, showing off her curves and laying loosely around her at the bottom. She was wearing black wedges that went up to her mid shin, adding about an inch or two to her height.

Rose lightly squealed and hopped from foot to foot. She turned around and hugged Lisa tightly. "Thank you so much," Rose said excited.

"No problem, it was my pleasure sweetie," Lisa said, there was a pause. "Now Henry has been outside your door for thirty minutes, let's show him that the wait was worth it."

They both walked to the door. Rose laid her hand on the door handle and opened it. Taking a deep breath as she did so. Henry was leaning against the railing, his arms crossed over his chest. He was wearing a black coat and pants, his undershirt, belt, and tie was white. His hair was slicked back, it was the first time that Rose had seen Henry use hair products.

When Henry saw Rose his eyes widened, becoming as wide as possible. He stopped leaning against the railing and uncrossed his arms, he fixed his suit, standing up straight. His mouth slightly hung open and his eyes remained the same.

"Uh, uh...I, you, uh... you, l-look, uh-"

"Spit it out, son!" Lisa said becoming inpatient. Henry snapped out of his daze.

"You, you look *beautiful*," Henry said as he walked towards Rose.

"Thanks. You're not too shabby yourself," Rose said as she looked at his suit. Henry stared down into Rose's eyes, she stared into his. He wrapped his arms around her waist and she placed her hands on his shoulders.

"Why thank you."

"Hey, you two are going to be late if you keep standing there," Lisa said. They both snapped out of their dazes. Henry grabbed Rose's hand as they walked down the stairs. They walked to Henry's car. He opened the door for her and she hopped in. He closed the door behind her and walked to his side. He started to drive to the restaurant.

Chapter 51

They arrived at the restaurant. Three men in tuxes were outside waiting. They had their coats on, their arms were crossed. As they breathed out their breath showed in the air. Henry stopped the car in front of them, one of the men ran over to Henry. Henry got out and handed the man his keys. Henry ran to Rose's door and opened it for her. She got out and Henry closed the door behind her, the valet drove off to park the car.

Henry interlocked his arm through Rose's arm and walked inside. They walked up to the host that was stationed behind a light oak host station. "We have a reservation," Henry said. The host looked up at him. A shocked expression appeared on his face.

"Please follow me sir, ma'am," the host said as he looked at both of them. He started to walk to the table. Henry and Rose followed. The host motioned to a table. Henry walked behind Rose's chair, sliding it back so she could sit. As Rose started to sit Henry slid the chair underneath her. He sat down in his chair. "A waiter will be here in no time," he said as he handed them their menus and walked off.

Rose looked around the restaurant. The side of the table was stationed against the glass window that was the length of the wall. The view of the window was a river, an illuminated ferry slowly moved across the river, even though it was freezing outside. The tables were a mixture of light and normal oak, making it look rustic, as well as the chairs. A bare light bulb hung from the ceiling above their table. A small candle was on the table, the fire dancing as the people walked by it.

"What's wrong?" Henry asked. A small amount of concern in his face. Rose looked at him and noticed the watery glow that was clouding her vision.

"Nothing, just... I would've never thought that I would get to be in a beautiful restaurant like this, wearing a beautiful dress, and sitting across a man that would do this for me. Since I was..." she trailed off. Henry could tell she was talking about being a pet.

He reached over the table and grabbed her hand, softly caressing it with his thumb. "I promise you'll never have to live like that again," Henry said as he faintly smiled. Rose smiled back as she gave his hand a squeeze.

"Thanks," she said as their grips slowly moved away from each other's.

"No problem," Henry said as he caressed her hand one last time before he pulled away. As he did so the waitress walked to their table. It was a girl that had light brown hair that was pulled up into a tight ponytail. She had on a black uniform with a small white tie. A huge smile was on her face as she placed a cup of blood and water in front of Rose and Henry.

"Hi, I'm Holly, I'll be your waitress for tonight. Is there anything else I can get you to drink?" She asked as she held her pen to her notepad. She was badly hiding her excitement at the fact that she got to wait on a Lord.

"I'm fine with blood, thanks," Henry said to her. She nodded vigorously as she turned her attention to Rose.

"Uh... blood is fine, thanks," Rose said. Holly nodded her head again, she folded up her notepad and tucked her pen into her breast pocket.

"Ok, I'll be back shortly to take your orders," both Henry and Rose nodded. Holly walked off, away from their table. Henry and Rose started to look at their menus.

The waitress came back to their table, notepad and pen in hand. "Are you guys ready to order?" She asked. Henry and Rose nodded their heads.

"I'll have the poached salmon," Henry said as he closed his menu and handed it to the waitress.

"I'll have the filet mignon," Rose said as she closed her menu and gave it to the waitress. She nodded her head as she walked away.

Awhile later their food arrived and they started to eat.

The waitress handed Henry his credit card and walked away. Henry and Rose stood up. Henry held out his arm and Rose interlocked their arms. They walked out of the restaurant. Henry turned right, avoiding the valet place. "Hen, the valley place is that way," she said as she pointed backwards with her free hand.

"I know, but I have other things planned," he said as he continued to walk.

"Like what?" She asked as she looked up at him.

"You'll have to wait," Henry said as he smirked. Rose's face fell as she gave him a sad face. Henry looked away from her face, there was a pause. "I should've picked a different dress," Henry grumbled.

"What, why?" She asked as she looked down at her dress, trying to find something wrong with it.

"Because a lot of men are staring at you," Henry said as he gave some of the men death stares. Rose looked at some of the men that Henry was glaring at.

"Don't worry, none of them are as hot as you."

"Good," Henry said. There was a short pause before he looked down at Rose. "Even William?" Henry asked as he raised an eyebrow. She looked up at him.

"Don't push it," she said warningly.

"Ok," Henry said as he nodded his head.

"Now will you tell me what we are doing?" She asked as she gave him more puppy dog eyes. He smiled as he saw her face.

"Yes, we're doing this," Henry said. Right as he said it he pressed a button, trees lit up. The trees had white Christmas lights spiraling around them, lighting up a path leading into the forest ending at a hill. Rose's eyes widened. She squeezed Henry's arm tighter in excitement. A small, high pitched squeal came out of her. Henry and Rose turned down the path. Rose looked around the illuminated trees in awe.

"When did you have time to do this?" Rose asked amazed.

"This morning after I bought your dress," Henry said. He felt Rose's arm squeeze tighter around his. A faint smile appeared on his face as he looked at Rose's awe filled face. They continued to walk through the path until they walked into an opening. The opening led to a hill. Henry reached over and grabbed a blanket off a tree branch. They walked to the center of the hill. Henry laid down the blanket in the snow, the waterproof part was on the bottom.

Without warning Henry sat down, pulling Rose with him. She was pulled on top of his lap, she was sitting sideways. Henry's arm was wrapped around her back, supporting her.

Rose looked out at the view from the hill. The hill overlooked the same river that the restaurant did. She felt something wet hit her arm, she continued to feel it. She looked down at her arm and saw snowflakes fall on her. She slightly shivered. Henry noticed. He took off his jacket and laid it over Rose. She slid her arms through the sleeves. She pulled the sides of the jacket over her, it covered her completely.

She wrapped her arms around the back of his neck, he started to slowly rock back and forth. "You want to know something?" Rose asked. Henry glanced down at her.

"Yes, what is it?"

"I think you're hotter than William," she said. He sighed out of relief.

"It's a Christmas miracle," Henry said as he looked up into the sky. He felt Rose run her fingers through his hair. He looked down at her. She moved her hand back and forth, messing up his slicked back hair.

"But," Rose said as she continued to mess up his hair. "I like your hair better like it usually is," she continued to mess up his hair as he smiled

"Noted, I'll keep that in mind," Rose laid her head on his chest and he rested his chin on her head.

They had been sitting there for over an hour. They both decided to go home. Henry folded the blanket as Rose brought the jacket closer to her. It had started to snow harder.

They interlocked their arms and then their hands. Rose leaned into Henry as they walked. Henry held the blanket in his free hand. Once they were out of the path Henry turned off the lights.

They arrived at the valet, one of the men took off running to get Henry's car. He drove the car up to them and hopped out. He handed Henry his keys as Henry gave him his tip. Henry opened Rose's door and she hopped in, Henry shut the door behind her. He hopped in his seat and started to drive home.

"Thank you for that, it was amazing."

"No problem, there's no other person I would want to do that with," Henry said. Both of their cheeks turned a bright red.

They arrived home. Henry parked the car and opened Rose's door. She got out as he closed it behind her. They walked inside.

Joey and Lilly were sitting on the couch watching a movie. Their hands were interlocked. Henry and Rose stopped behind the couch as they saw it.

Lisa came running towards them. "Joey and Lilly are having a little date," she said as she looked at them. "Speaking of which, how did yours go?" She asked excited.

"It was amazing," Rose said as she leaned her head against Henry. Henry placed a soft kiss on her head.

"Awe!" Lisa whisper shouted. She jumped up and down. "That's adorable!" There was a short pause. "What happened to your hair?" Lisa asked as she pointed to Henry's hair.

"Rose liked it better the way it was."

"Oh thank you, I didn't want to tell you, but I agree," Lisa said. Henry's face dropped.

"I feel so loved," he placed a hand over his chest. "How did I become so lucky to get a mom like you, that never criticizes me," he paused. "I feel so lucky," he said in a crying voice. He wiped away a fake tear.

"Ok, Mr Prissy you're interrupting their movie," Lisa said as she pointed to Lilly and Joey. She started to shove Rose and Henry upstairs.

"I'm interrupting their movie?" Henry whispered to Rose. She shrugged.

"I don't know, just go with it," she said. They both walked into their rooms to change.

Henry knocked on Rose's door. She was sitting on the bed. "Come in," she said. Henry opened the door and walked in. He sat down next to Rose.

"Since Joey and Lilly have taken the couch, you want to go to the library?" He asked. She grabbed his hand and teleported them to the library. They appeared in the plush chair, they were sideways. Rose's back was in Henry's chest, his arm was wrapped around her. "Can you please grab my book?" Henry asked as he pointed to the book on his desk.

Rose teleported to his desk, grabbing his book. She teleported back to the chair. She leaned over and grabbed her book. She handed Henry his book. He took the arm that had the book and wrapped his around her again. He rested his book on her hip, he started to read. Rose rested her book on the arm of the chair and started to read as well.

Rose's book fell on the ground as her hand went limp, she was resting. Henry rubbed his eyes with his free hand. He closed his book and laid it on the ground as well. He was exhausted and by looking at Rose he could tell she was too.

He took the arm that was wrapped around her and moved her on top of him. He sat up with her, she grabbed his t-shirt and buried her head in his chest. He stood up, holding Rose bridal style.

He walked out of the library. All the lights were turned off, everyone was asleep. He walked upstairs into Rose's room. He swung the covers back and laid her down. He started to stand up but she pulled him back down, her hands grasping his shirt. "You have to let go," he said to her. She shook her head. "If you don't let me go then I can't wrap your present," Henry said as he smirked. Within a second she released his shirt and he stood up straight. He grabbed the covers and laid them over Rose. She snuggled closer to the covers.

He leaned down and placed a soft kiss on her forehead. "I love you," he whispered.

"I love you too," she said as she reached up her hand and ran her fingers through his hair. He walked out of her room, closing the door behind him.

He walked into his room. He had another busy night ahead of him.

Chapter 52

Henry walked into his room and shut the door behind him. Henry grabbed the blanket out of the bag and pulled off all the tags, throwing them away. He re folded the blanket and laid it on the ground. He grabbed wrapping paper that he had brought up a few days ago. He had bought it years ago, but still hadn't run out. He laid the wrapping paper under the blanket, trying to rap it.

Mom, there was a pause. *Mom!*
What?!
I need help.
With what?!
Wrapping a present.

A few seconds later Lisa stormed into Henry's room. Her hair was in a messy bun, loose strands hung everywhere around her face, some standing straight up. One of her eyes was half closed. She rubbed her eyes with her hands and groaned, clearly upset that she wasn't resting.

Henry was laying on the ground. Wrapping paper was everywhere, some was ripped others were crumbled up and tossed randomly around the room. Wrapping paper was laid across Henry, only his face was visible. A small thin smirk appeared on Lisa's face.

"Does the grown man need help wrapping a present?" Lisa asked in a mocking tone. Henry only nodded his head. Lisa reached down and pulled the wrapping paper off of him. He sat up as Lisa crumpled up the wrapping paper and threw it away.

Lisa grabbed the roll of wrapping paper, laying it beneath the blanket. She covered the top of the blanket, folding one end over the other. She taped the sides of the paper after she had folded it. She grabbed the present and handed it to Henry. "There," she said as she walked out of his room and back to hers.

Henry looked at the present in utter shock. *That only took her a few seconds*, Henry thought as he inspected the present. He couldn't find anything wrong with it. He grabbed a sharpie and a note card.

To: Short Stack
From: Hen

He walked downstairs to the Christmas tree, he laid it under the tree along with the other presents that Lisa had wrapped earlier on. He walked back to his room. He wrapped the covers around him and closed his eyes. He started to rest.

"Henry!" He didn't answer. He felt someone shaking him, the voice sounded like it was Lilly's. "Henry!" She continued to shake him. He groggily opened his eyes and looked at her. "It's Christmas, get Rose and come downstairs," Lilly said as she repeatedly hit his arm.

"Fine," Henry said as he sat up. Lilly ran downstairs. Henry rubbed his eyes as he stood up. He heard the vibration of his phone against the nightstand. He looked down and saw his dad's name on the screen. He watched as his phone went black. His phone started to ring again, he grabbed the phone, angrily. He pressed answer as he held the phone to his ear. He didn't want anyone to hear his dad on the phone. "What!" Henry said a little bit more harsh than intended.

"Hi, son... I just called to say that I am sorry," there was a short pause. "I don't like that you are dating her, but your mom was right. You are a grown man and can make decisions by yourself. I don't like or respect them, but it's your choice and I'm sorry I got involved."

"And?" Henry asked. He was talking about Lisa.

"And I'm sorry that I treated your mom so poorly. It's Christmas, I don't want there to be any hatred between the family."

"Ok, thanks for calling, bye," Henry said. Before Phil could protest Henry had ended the call. He rubbed his face with his hands. He needed something happy to take his mind off of his Dad.

He walked into Rose's room. She was in her cocoon like structure. He sat down on her bed. "Rose, it's time to get up."

She groaned out of annoyance. "I don't want to," she said as she snuggled closer to the covers.

"But it's Christ-" he was cut off as Rose grabbed his hand and teleported them to the Christmas tree. "-Mas," Henry finished. Rose had teleported Henry to where he was laying face first into the ground, she was sitting crisscrossed. He groggily sat up as he rubbed his face.

Lisa, Lilly, and Joey were already sitting at the tree. Henry knew that getting breakfast was out of the question. When he was a kid Lisa wouldn't allow anyone to eat until she had made Christmas dinner.

Lilly squealed as she held up a pink Polaroid camera. She hugged the camera tightly to her chest as she continued to squeal. She had always liked looking at breathtaking imagery, but could never save it.

Henry looked at Joey. He was surrounded by a few puzzle boxes and various other things. Henry looked at Lisa. *Rider and Zoey are properly buried.* He laid his hand on hers. When he pulled his hand away Lisa felt two small things in her hand. She opened her hand and looked in it. On a necklace chain was Zoey's and Rider's rings. Lisa looked up at Henry who gave her a sympathetic look. Her eyes started to water.

Thank you, she thought as she laid her hand on his and gave it a squeeze. Henry looked at her. On the outside she had a smile on her face, but in her eyes was pain and sorrow. He could tell that the first Christmas without Rider was going to be hard. There was a short pause before he remembered what his Dad had told him.

Mom, Dad called, he says he's sorry, there was a long pause. Lisa pursed her lips at the mention of Phil.

Give Rose her present, Lisa said. Changing the subject. Her lips were still pursed as she blankly stared at the Christmas tree. Henry got the message. He nodded his head as he reached over, grabbing Rose's present and handing it to her. She tore through the wrapping paper in a matter of seconds, throwing the paper this way and that. Once the paper was off it revealed a blanket, she ran her hand over the soft fabric. She noticed there was part of a word on the blanket. She couldn't tell what it was trying to say. She stood up, unfolding the blanket so she could read it. The blanket unfolded, she held her arms up all the way so she could see it.

Short Stack, will you marry me?

She dropped the blanket in utter shock of what it said. She covered her mouth with her hands and blinked several times. As the blanket fell it revealed Henry on one knee, in his hands was a small box and in the box was a wedding ring.

Chapter 53

Rose stared in shock at the ring. The ring had a dark blue gem in the middle, around the blue were many tiny diamonds. They sparkled in the light, making it look like glitter. The diamonds went down to the side, it stopped above the middle.

"Short Stack, will you marry me?" Henry asked. Lisa, Joey, and Lilly all gasped. "We have been through *everything* together and after each time I love you even more. I couldn't picture myself with anyone else, except you."

"Yes, yes, of course," Rose said. She wiped away a stray tear that had rolled down her face. Henry smiled as he stood up, very happy. He wrapped his arms around Rose's waist and pulled her closer to him. He leaned his head down and placed his lips onto hers. She wrapped her arms around the back of his neck and stood on her toes, she deepened the kiss.

They finally pulled away from each other. Both were breathing heavily. Henry took the ring out of the box and placed it on her left ring finger, next to her promise ring. She never felt right putting the ring on her ring finger. She wanted to save the ring finger for her wedding ring.

"How, when?" Rose asked. She was still breathing heavily.

"Remember when I got the pretzels and it took me ages to get them?" He asked. She nodded her head. "That's when I got the ring," She looked down at the ring again and hugged him. Thanking him repeatedly. They heard Lisa sniffle, they both looked at her. "Mom, don't cry."

"I-I'm s-sorry, but m-my baby boy is all gr-grown up," she said. She wiped away more tears and sniffled some more.

Henry motioned for Lisa to come to him. She stood up and walked to them. Henry wrapped his arm around Lisa and kept the other arm around Rose.

Lisa wrapped her arms around Henry's and tightened her grip. She continued to cry onto his chest. Henry patted her back and kissed the top of her head. "I'm s-so happy that I-I'm your mother in law," Lisa said to Rose. She wiped away more tears.

"I'm glad that I'm your daughter in law," Rose said. Her parents had always told her about this kind of thing, she didn't know a lot, but she knew enough.

"Mother in law?" Lilly asked. There was a pause. "Does that mean that you're my mom too?" She asked. Her eyes sparkled as she looked at Lisa.

"Yes, it does," Lisa said. She knew that it wasn't how it worked, but Lilly was only thirteen and needed a mom. Lilly stood up and joined the group hug. She was lightly crying. Henry glanced down at Joey. He was still sitting on the ground. He looked down at his presents and ran his finger over the puzzle. He was trying not to notice how happy they were.

"Hey, Joey, you're a part of this family too," Henry said. Joey looked up at them, shocked.

"Really?"

"Yeah, come here," Henry said. He motioned for Joey to join the group hug. He ran to them and wrapped his arms around them.

"Thank you."

"No problem." Henry said. There was a short pause. "Besides you're the only boy so I wouldn't survive without you," Henry said. All the girls looked at him, they all hit Henry in the chest and arms multiple times. "Ow," Henry said. He rubbed his arm where Lisa had punched him. All the girls gave him death glare as Joey inched his way out of the line of fire.

Henry held up his hands. "I'm sorry, ok?" He asked. There was a pause. "Hey mommy, will you please go make the dinner?" Henry asked as he engulfed Lisa in a bear hug and death grip. She struggled in his grasp, but to no avail.

"If you let me go I will," she said. She struggled more. Henry pulled away and gave her a toothy smile.

"Thank you, mommy."

"Uh huh," Lisa said as she walked to the kitchen and started to prepare dinner. Henry turned his attention back to Rose.

"Now as for you and me, let's relax," he said. He wrapped his arms around Rose's waist and leaned down he became eye level with her. "I want to spend time with my wife," he said. He quickly kissed her on the lips. Without warning her picked her up bridal style and carried her to the library. He sat down in the chair with her in his lap.

Rose wrapped her arms around the back of her neck and face into his chest. There was a long moment of silence as Henry rocked back and forth. "What was your Christmas present?" Rose asked. Realizing that he hadn't gotten anything. He looked down at her. He was still smiling.

"You saying yes," he said. The smile was still on his face, as well as Rose's. She rested her head on his chest. He leaned down his head and placed it in the crook of her neck. He quickly readjusted them. Rose faintly screamed in the shock. She grasped his shirt with both her hands.

Henry was now laying down in the chair, Rose was on top of him. His head was on the footrest and his feet were on the top of the chair. Rose's legs were on either side of his waist, she absentmindedly ran her fingers through his hair. He absentmindedly traced patterns on her back with his finger. They both closed their eyes. Rose's hand still running through his hair and Henry's still tracing patterns on her back.

"This is perfect," Rose mumbled. Breaking the silence, she didn't open her eyes.

"What is?" Henry asked. He didn't know if she was talking about the proposal, ring, relaxing, or Christmas.

"Everything," she said. She smiled into his chest. Henry felt her smile on his chest. He smiled as well. Everything was perfect.

Chapter 54

Henry and Rose were snapped out of their thoughts when they heard the door being knocked on. "Can I come in?" Lisa asked.

"Yeah," Henry said. His eyes were still closed as well as Rose's. Her hand was still running through his hair and his hand was still tracing patterns on her back. Lisa walked in and looked at them. She clasped her hands together and tilted her head to the side.

"Aw, that's so adorable," there was a short pause. "Don't move, I'm getting my phone," Lisa said. She ran out of the room and came back a few seconds later with her phone. She took the picture and sighed contently. "I'm going to make a scrapbook out of you two," Lisa said. Henry's eyes shot open.

"Please tell me you're not going to be one of those moms?" Henry begged.

"No, I think it's going to be my new hobby."

"Why?! You used to be at least somewhat cool, but now..." Henry trailed off. Lisa crossed her arms as she tapped her foot.

"If it's all the same I think you should take up scrapbooking," Rose said. Henry turned his attention to her.

"Why do you encourage my mother's crazy?" Henry asked.

"It's not crazy," Lisa said. Henry could tell she was getting a little mad at him. He needed something to change the subject.

"Why did you come in here?" Henry asked.

"Oh yeah, dinner is ready."

"You mean to tell me we've been in here fighting while the food has been getting cold?!" Henry asked in utter shock. Henry looked at Rose and she looked at him. He didn't need to say anything. Rose teleported them into the kitchen.

They both looked in awe at the Christmas dinner. There was turkey, mash potatoes, gravy, sweet potatoes, ham, and steamed vegetables. Henry rubbed his hands together as he licked his lips. Rose grabbed a plate and started to place food onto it. Henry did the same. Joey and Lilly were seated at the table, their plates full. Lisa had already made her plate, it was resting on the table.

Henry and Rose sat down at the table, their plates piled high. They all started eat. Lisa sat down in her seat and started to eat as well. *Thank you, son for waiting for me like you have done so many times before.* Lisa said sarcastically.

No problem, Henry said. He continued to stuff food into his mouth. Lisa rolled her eyes as she continued to eat.

They had all finished their dinner and placed their plates in the dishwasher. "Thank you for the dinner, it was delicious," Rose said.

"You're very welcome," Lisa said. Both Lilly, Henry, and Joey said thank you as well. Henry walked up to Rose.

"So... do you want to go outside and walk?" Henry asked. Rose looked out the window.

"The snow is pretty high. I'll be lost in it," Rose said. She could tell the snow was going to go to her knees or higher.

"I'll carry you."

"Ok, let's go," Rose said. They both walked to the coat rack. Henry slipped on a hoodie as did Rose. They both put on shoes and walked outside. Henry bent over and Rose jumped on his back. She wrapped her legs around his waist, locking her ankles. She moved her arms over his shoulders. Henry grabbed her legs, supporting her. He started to walk.

"Hey, Lilly, will you do me a favor?" Lisa asked. Lilly looked up from the puzzle that Joey was trying to piece together.

"Yeah, what do you need?" Lilly asked.

"Can you take pictures of Rose and Henry outside? I'm trying to make a scrapbook," Lisa asked. Lilly's face lit up. She grabbed her Polaroid and squealed excitedly.

"I'd love to," Lilly said as she threw on her jacket and shoes. She ran outside, with her Polaroid in hand and a huge smile on her face. Lisa looked at Joey. He was trying to find all the edge pieces.

"Can I sit?" Lisa asked. He looked up from his puzzle and nodded. She sat down on the couch next to him. He was sorting through the pieces, finding the edge ones. He was assembling it on the coffee table. "So what is the puzzle?"

Joey reached over and grabbed the box, he handed it to her. She looked at the picture. It was a picture of a galaxy. Lisa's eyes widened as she saw it was a thousand piece puzzle. She could tell that a lot of the puzzle was going to look the same. They would have to rely on the various blues, purples, greens, and whites to tell where everything is. She started to help Joey sort the edge pieces from the rest of the puzzle.

Henry and Rose had made it to the side of the house, the snow went up to Henry's knees. He knew that if Rose were to get off his back it would go to her waist.

Lilly was a good distance behind them, she was walking where Henry had walked so she wouldn't be consumed in snow. Every now and then she would take a picture, shake the photo, and see how it would turn out. If she liked it she would safely tuck it in her jacket pocket if not then she would crumple it up into her other pocket.

Henry stopped walking. "Why did you stop?" Rose asked. She furrowed her eyebrows in confusion.

"Because I'm tired of walking and holding you," Henry simply stated.

"What does that mean? You're tired of holding me?" Rose asked. Some fear seeping into her voice.

"It means-" in a split second he had pulled apart Rose's legs from each other. He threw her up off his back and quickly turned around. He caught her and held her away from him by her armpits. She was above the snow. "-that I'm not going to carry you anymore," Henry said as he smiled. "And if you teleport anywhere else outside you'll be consumed in snow and if you teleport inside my mom will be mad that you aren't spending cute, adorable time with me," Henry said making the last part sound like his mom.

Rose quickly wrapped her legs around his arm as well as her arms. She disappeared and reappeared behind him. She pushed Henry forward. He fell into the snow, she hopped on top of him and started to shove snow on his face. Henry reached behind him and grabbed Rose's hand. He quickly flipped them over, him on top of Rose.

"Why would you do that?" Rose asked.

"Because messing with you is fun."

"I hate you so much."

"No you don't. I believe that you say that, but you really love me," Henry said as he smiled. "I mean, you did say yes."

Rose raised an eyebrow. "What makes you think I love you in this moment?" Rose asked. Another smile appeared on Henry's face. He leaned down his head, stopping his lips centimeters from hers. He remained there a few seconds before Rose placed her lips onto his. He smiled into the kiss as he deepened it. Rose ran her fingers through his hair, messing it up. A few seconds passed before Henry pulled away, the smile still on his face.

"That's how I know you love me," Henry said. The smile was still evident on his face. He leaned down again and kissed her. They both closed their eyes.

Out of the corner of their eyes they saw a flash go off. They both sat up and looked in the direction of the flash. They saw Lilly holding her camera and fanning the picture. Lilly looked up, when she saw Henry and Rose staring at her, her eyes widened. She stood up and started to run back to the house.

Rose teleported in front of Lilly and grabbed a huge handful of snow. She shoved it in Lilly's face, Lilly fell over backwards. Rose teleported back to Henry.

"Little siblings always ruining the moment," Rose mumbled under her breath.

"I have a feeling that my mom did this," Henry said. A mischievous smile appeared on his face. "Can you please teleport me behind the couch?" Henry asked. Rose nodded her head as she grabbed his hand and teleported them inside.

They appeared behind the couch. Lisa and Joey were working on the puzzle intensely. Henry walked behind Lisa. "Hey mom! Do you have anything you want to tell me?!" Henry yelled. As he did so he grabbed her shoulders. She screamed as she jumped up, she relaxed as she realized it was Henry.

She turned around and faced him, an innocent expression on her face. "What do you mean?"

"Mom, we caught Lilly," Henry said. He pointed to the front door. Lilly hung up her jacket and removed snow from her hair and face. She walked to Lisa, the pictures in hand. Lilly handed Lisa the pictures. Lisa took the pictures and looked at them.

"Aw, you two are so cute," Lisa said. Henry looked at the pictures. It showed Henry giving Rose a piggyback ride, Henry holding Rose above the snow, and them laying in the snow kissing. Lisa quickly ran upstairs and went into her room, she came back and sat down on the chair next to the couch.

Henry and Rose both took off their shoes. Henry took off his hoodie while Rose kept hers on. Lilly sat down on the couch, next to Joey and started to help him with the puzzle. Henry sat down in the couch while Rose grabbed the blanket from under the Christmas tree. She came back and sat down on Henry's lap. Henry wrapped his arm around her and leaned back on the couch. Rose laid the blanket across them and leaned her head back, resting her head on Henry's shoulder and slightly leaned the side of her head on Henry's.

"Rose?" Lilly asked. Rose looked at her, awaiting a question. "Can you tell the story of mom and dad getting married?" Lilly asked. She could barely remember the story, her parents had only told it to her a few times.

"Yeah," Rose said. She paused as she remembered everything her mom and dad had told her. "One day mom was scavenging for food when she ran into dad. They were both ecstatic to at least see another person. They decided to stay together. About a year passed and dad was falling for mom and she for him. He, of course, couldn't get a ring so he tried for about a week to make one out of flowers, but couldn't. So he collected her favorite flowers, roses and lilies and made a bouquet out of them and proposed. She said yes and about a year later I was born. They decided to name me after the rose and you after the lilies," Rose said. She was unconsciously twisting her ring around her finger.

Lilly and Joey both yawned, tired. Lilly stood up and hugged Rose and thanked her for telling the story. Joey and Lilly both walked into their own rooms. Lisa stood up.

"I'm going to go to bed too, see you two love birds in the morning," Lisa said. Henry groaned out of annoyance as Lisa walked upstairs. Henry grabbed the remote and turned it onto RARVABIHY.

"I'm not going to let you look at William by the way."

"Don't worry, I'm not. I have you."

"Yay," Henry said as he golf clapped his hands in excitement. Henry readjusted them to where Rose was laying on top of him. He wrapped his arms around Rose as they both turned their attention to the TV.

Henry reached over and grabbed the remote and turned off the TV. Rose's eyes were closed and her face was on his chest. Henry readjusted them to where they were sideways. He sat up and grabbed Rose, he started to stand up. Rose grabbed the couch and pulled them down again. Henry was on top of Rose.

"Can you please stay with me? I have less nightmares when I'm with you," Rose said. Her voice was slightly shaking in fear of thinking about having to go back to her old life. Henry heard the fear in her voice.

"Yeah, I'll stay," Henry said. He readjusted them to where Rose was on the outside of the couch and he was on the inside. They were both sideways. Henry wrapped his arm around Rose and buried his face in her neck. He closed his eyes and started to rest.

Rose smiled as she looked at her ring one last time before she closed her eyes and started to rest.

Chapter 55

Lisa took the photos of Henry and Rose asleep. She slightly squealed as she looked at them. She saw Henry twitch and quickly ran upstairs to not get caught. Henry opened his eyes and looked at Rose. She was curled up into his chest and one of her hands were grasping onto his shirt and the other was in his hair. Her face was nudged into his shirt. The blanket was off of Henry and covering Rose. She was curled up in that as well. Henry slightly moved to readjust himself. Rose fluttered her eyes open and looked around.

"Sorry, I didn't mean to wake you," Henry said. He readjusted them to where Rose was on top of him. He stared into her eyes and she stared into his.

"You didn't wake me," Rose said in a quiet voice. "I was just resting," she said simply. Henry nodded his head. Rose brought her hand up and looked at her ring again. A smile appeared on her face as she continued to look at it. A low chuckle sounded from Henry. Rose looked up at him. "What?" She asked confused.

"Nothing.., you're just staring at the ring and you started to go cross eyed," he said as he slightly laughed again.

"I can see the ring better when I go cross eyed," she said in a quiet, almost embarrassed voice.

"You know you look cute when you go cross eyed... Can you do it again?" He asked. She shook her head, no as her cheeks went to a bright red. "But you look adorable, pwease?" Henry asked as he gave her puppy dog eyes and stuck out his bottom lip.

"Fine..., but only if you continue to do that face," Rose said. "Deal?" She asked. A wide smile spread across Henry's face.

"Deal," there was a short pause. "Now do the face."

Rose sighed as she went cross eyed on Henry and playfully stuck out her tongue. He laughed again. Rose went un-cross eyed.

"Now do your face," she said. Henry stuck out his bottom lip and gave her puppy dog eyes. "I'm hungry. Will you make me something?" Rose asked. Henry nodded his head, the face was still on his face. Rose got off of Henry and stood up.

She jumped up and down as she shivered, cold. She quickly grabbed the blanket and wrapped it around her. Henry got off the couch and wrapped his arm around Rose. Rose leaned her head against Henry as they walked. They made it to the kitchen. Henry grabbed Rose's waist and lifted her up onto the counter.

"So what kind of pancakes do you want this time and do you want anything else?" Henry asked. There was a short pause.

"I want regular pancakes," there was another short pause. "Can I help you cook?" Rose asked. Henry stopped dead in his tracks and looked back at Rose.

"Of course, Short Stack. Come here," he said as he motioned for Rose to jump off the counter. She jumped off the counter. "This is going to get in the way," Henry said as he grabbed Rose's blanket and placed it on the counter. Rose shivered.

Henry saw her shiver. He lifted up his arm. "Come here," he said. Rose quickly ran to him. Henry wrapped his arm around her as she snuggled closer to him. He walked to the cabinet and grabbed two bowls and laid them down on the counter. He walked to the fridge and grabbed milk, buttermilk, eggs, and butter. He laid those on the counter next to one bowl. He then walked to another cabinet and grabbed salt, flour, sugar, baking powder, and baking soda. He laid them next to the other bowl.

He grabbed a glass measuring cup and cut the butter into two tablespoons and placed the butter in the measuring cup. He handed it to Rose. "Heat this up until the butter is melted," Henry said as he pointed to the microwave. Rose nodded as she walked to the microwave and placed it in. She set the timer for twenty seconds.

The timer went off. She opened the door and grabbed the cup and looked at the butter. It was melted. She walked back to Henry and placed it on the counter. Henry had placed measuring cups on the counter. "Put two cups of flour into this bowl," Henry said as he pointed to the bigger bowl.

Rose grabbed the one cup measuring cup and put it in the flour. She filled it up and poured it into the bowl, she did this two other times. "Now put one tablespoon of sugar in there, two teaspoons of baking powder, half a cup of baking soda, and one fourth teaspoons of salt," Henry said. Rose grabbed the ingredients and added them to the bowl. Henry handed her a spoon to mix the dry ingredients together.

"Now in another bowl do three cups of buttermilk, one half cups of milk, three eggs and the melted butter, "Henry said. Rose did what she was told. Henry handed her the mixer. She placed it in the wet batter and looked for the on button. Henry laid his hand on hers and flipped the switch.

Rose slightly squealed as it hit the side of the bowl. She wasn't expecting that much power to come from that tiny machine. She looked at Henry and he moved his hand it a circular motion. She copied him.

After a few more seconds Henry slowly started to add the dry batter to it. She continued to stir as Henry continued to add the batter. Henry placed the empty bowl onto the counter and waited a few seconds. After a few seconds he laid his hand on hers and turned off the mixer.

He grabbed the bowl and walked to the stove. He looked at Rose and she grabbed the bowl and started to pour the mix on it. She started to make a giant pancake.

"That's big enough," Henry said as he grabbed the bowl from Rose.

"But I wanted a big pancake."

"Ok, I'm sorry," Henry said as he held his hands up. Henry looked at the stove and could tell he wasn't going to be able to fit his pancake on the stove. He grabbed two spatulas and walked back to the stove. He positioned the two spatula under the pancake. He grabbed one and so did Rose. "On three flip it. One... two... three," on three they flipped the pancake.

They repeated the process again and put her pancake on a plate. Henry made himself a smaller pancake. Rose sat at the island and started to eat the pancake.

They had both finished their pancakes and placed their plates in the dishwasher. They both saw a flash behind them and turned around to see Lisa holding a camera. "How long have you been standing there?" Henry asked.

"The whole time," Lisa said as she took another picture. Henry sighed.

"Short Stack, we're going to go outside," Henry said as he walked to the coatrack. They both put on their coats and shoes. They walked outside and made it to the side of the house. Henry carrying her the entire time.

Henry let Rose get off his back. Henry laid down on the snow and Rose laid on him. "Why did we come out here?" Rose asked.

"Because I wanted to talk about some things with you and I didn't want my mom to go crazy," Henry said as he pulled out his phone.

"What do you want to talk about?"

"Our wedding and honeymoon," Henry said as he went to the internet.

"Ok. What about them?"

"When do you want our wedding to be?"

"Sometime in the spring."

"What about our honeymoon?"

"Around the spring too."

"What if on our wedding day when it was over we head to our honeymoon?"

"Sounds good."

"Where do you want to go?"

"Where is there to go?"

"The beach, across country, anywhere you want to go."

"What's the beach?"

"An amazing place where there are oceans, sand, and so many other things," Henry said in a little bit of shock.

"That sounds interesting."

"So do you want to go there?" Henry asked. Rose nodded her head, yes. "Ok, sounds good," Henry said as he started to scroll through his phone. He was looking for a place to go and when to book it. "There's actually an opening in April. We could celebrate your birthday while we're there," Henry said. Rose's eyes were closed and she only nodded her head.

"When we go back inside can you teach me how to make a cake?" Rose asked. Henry nodded his head, yes.

Rose laid her head against the oven door. "You're too close to the door," Henry said as he grabbed Rose and dragged her away from the door.

"But the cake is so pretty," Rose said as she scooted closer. Henry pulled her away again. They both saw the flash. Henry banged his head against the oven door.

"Stop taking pictures," Henry begged.

"But you two are so cute together," Lisa said as she took another picture. Rose laid her head next to Henry's on the oven door.

A few seconds went by before the oven beeped. "It's done!" Rose squealed as she threw Henry back, away from the door. She put on oven mitts and grabbed the cake. She laid it on the counter. Henry closed the oven door and stood up.

He waited an hour or so before he grabbed a knife and started to frost the cake. When he was done he cut a piece for Rose. She sunk her fork into it and started to eat it. Henry did the same for himself.

They had both finished about two or three pieces of cake. Henry face planted on the couch and Rose fell beside him.

"I'm so full," Henry said as he turned on his back.

"Same," Rose said as she did the same. "Thank you for teaching me how to cook."

"My pleasure," Henry said as he smiled. There was a short pause.

"Why did you start to plan the wedding and honeymoon?" Rose asked as she glanced at Henry.

"Because those will happen before we'll know it," Henry said. "Now, let's rest."

They both closed their eyes as they started to rest. Rose curled closer to Henry as Henry wrapped his arms around her. They both started to rest.

Lisa walked by them with the blanket in hand. She smiled faintly as she saw Rose and Henry laying together. She laid the blanket on both of them. Rose curled closer to the blanket, taking most of it off Henry. Lisa smiled as she took one more picture. She was happy that Henry was finally truly happy, he had never gotten that in his childhood and even in some of his adult years. She walked upstairs.

Chapter 56

~April~

Zoey pulled the trigger, before Rose could teleport the bullet went into her chest. She coughed up blood before she fell over, dead. Henry cried and screamed at Zoey as he looked at Rose. She aimed the gun at his chest and fired.

Henry's eyes shot open. Rose was over him. One hand was cupping his face while the other ran through his hair. "It's ok, it's just a dream," Rose said as she continued to comfort him. Henry wrapped his arms around her and brought her closer to him.

"I thought I lost you," Henry said.

"I'll never leave you," Rose said. At hearing Rose's words Henry relaxed. They both closed their eyes as they started to rest.

"Oh my gosh they're still resting!" Lisa practically yelled. She went over and started to shake Rose and Henry. Britney helping. "Wake up, you need to get ready for the wedding!" Lisa said as she continued to shake them.

"The wedding isn't today," Rose mumbled.

"Yes it is, now get up!" Britney said. Both Rose's and Henry's eyes shot open.

"Shit!" Henry said as he quickly stood up from the couch.

"Language!" Lisa said through gritted teeth. Britney pushed Henry upstairs into his room. He closed the door as Britney leaned against the wall, outside the rooms. Lisa went into Rose's room with her.

About thirty minutes later Henry opened the door to his room. He was wearing a black tux with a midnight blue tie. The tie wasn't tied, it hung over both his shoulders. He knew Britney was going to fix his tux. She shoved him back in the room and started to fix his suit. She straightened it out, making sure there were no wrinkles. She tied the tie around him and straightened it out to perfection. She stood away from Henry, looking at her work. She gasped loudly as she quickly knelt down to his shoes.

"Can't even roll up your pants," she mumbled as she rolled up his pants until they were just above his shoes and perfectly even. She took the edge of her shirt and started to scrub away a small scruff he had on his shoe. When she was satisfied she stood up and looked at Henry's face.

"You need to shave," she said.

"I shaved yesterday."

"Believe me you need to shave," she said as she shoved him into the restroom and threw a towel around him. The towel was protecting his tux from the shaving cream.

"Why?" Henry asked as he reluctantly put shaving cream on his face.

"Because your face will be soft so then Rose will want to kiss you more."

At the mention of that Henry grabbed his razor and started to shave.

He took the towel and started to dry his face. Britney turned him around and looked at his face. She was looking for any cuts. When she was satisfied that he hadn't cut his face she looked at his hair.

"What are you going to do with your hair?" She asked as she pointed to it.

"Nothing," Henry said. Britney's eyes grew wide.

"Why? At least gel it back or something. This is your wedding for goodness sake!"

"I'm not going to gel it back because Rose said she likes my hair like this the best," Henry replied. Britney cupped her hands together and sighed contently.

"That's so sweet. But at least let me trim your hair?" She begged. Henry sighed, defeated.

"Fine," Henry said. Within a few seconds Britney had dragged a chair into the bathroom. She grabbed Henry's shoulders and made Henry sit down. She wrapped a towel around Henry. She ran out of the room and came back with scissors.

"Ok, I just went to Rose's room and she is so pretty!" Britney squealed. Henry started to tap his foot nervously.

"Please, I'm already nervous," Henry said as he continued to tap his foot. Britney pushed the top of his hair to one side.

"Sorry," Britney said as she continued to cut his hair. Henry was watching her every move, making sure she wasn't cutting off too much.

After about twenty minutes Britney was done. Henry ran his fingers through his hair. She had made the sides shorter and the back. The front was longer than the back. Henry stood up as Britney straightened out his tux again. They both walked downstairs. Henry took a deep breath before he opened the door.

Lisa finished cutting Rose's hair as she took a step back and looked at it. She had cut Rose's hair a few inches below her shoulder and she had layered it. Rose had on a floor length wedding dress. The dress had a v-neck and a clear layer over her upper chest. The clear part had a pattern of white diamonds. The dress was sleeveless. It hugged her upper body and waist, but then became loose around her legs. Sparkles layered the rest of the dress, making it look like glitter. Rose had white eyeshadow on mixed with glitter and winged eyeliner.

Lisa started to curl Rose's hair. Rose was nervously tapping her hand against her leg. "Don't worry you'll be fine."

"How do you know?" Rose asked.

"Because you are beautiful and Henry won't take his eyes off you and if you think Henry is cute when he doesn't try wait till he really does," Lisa said. Rose's cheeks blushed a dark red. There was a pause. "You excited to go to the beach?" Lisa asked. Rose nodded her head.

Lisa put down the curling iron and stood back and looked at Rose. "You look so pretty," Lisa said. Rose stood up as Lisa hugged her, Rose hugged back. "You're the best daughter in law I could have asked for," Lisa said as he eyes started to water.

"And you're the best mother in law I could have asked for," Rose said. Lisa handed Rose her bouquet. The bouquet was like her parents, roses and lilies, the only difference was that the flowers were dyed blue.

They stopped outside the main doors. "You'll do fine," Lisa said as she walked out of the doors. Rose took a deep breath before she opened the door.

Henry was standing in front of the fountain, to his left was Joey holding a pillow that had their rings. He was in a tux similar to Henry's. Lilly was standing across from Henry holding a basket that had blue flower petals in it. Her hair was curled as well and she had on a midnight blue dress.

There were chairs set up on either side of the aisle. The aisle had blue flower petals layered across it. A photographer was kneeling down to the side of the aisle. Britney and Lisa were sitting together while Phil sat by himself. Henry felt like he needed to invite his father even though he didn't like him and Lisa and Phil had officially gotten a divorce, Phil was still his father.

It wasn't a huge or long event, but they agreed it didn't have to be. Rose made it to the end of the aisle and stood across from Henry. Henry grabbed both her hands and looked her in the eyes.

You're beautiful, Henry said.

You're handsome, Rose said. *Even though my dad isn't here, I know he would've approved you.* Henry gave Rose's hand a squeeze.

"Now may I have the rings?" The man asked. Joey took a step forward and faced Rose and Henry. "Place the ring on your spouse's ring finger," the man said. Henry placed Rose's ring on her finger and Rose placed Henry's band on his finger. Henry's ring was black with a blue line running through the center of it

"That symbolizes the bond between the two of you. Henry do you take Rose to be your lawfully wedded wife?"

"I do."

"And Rose do you take Henry to be your lawfully wedded husband?"

"I do."

"I now pronounce you husband and wife. You may kiss the bride."

Henry pulled Rose against him and slammed his lips onto hers. She kissed back as she wrapped her arms around him. Henry wrapped his arms around the bottom of Rose's waist.

Your face is soft.

Thank you Britney!

No problem, Britney said. Rose threw the flowers. Britney jumped up and caught it. She yelled "yes" as she made everyone look at the boutique. Britney returned to Lisa who continued to cry on Britney's shoulder while holding down the camera button on her phone. Britney was recording with her phone. The photographer was moving all over the place, taking as many pictures as he could.

Henry and Rose finally pulled away from each other. Everyone started to clap and cheer. Soon everyone was talking to everyone. Henry walked up to Lisa. She wrapped her arms around him and hugged him tightly.

"Mom," there was a short pause. "Mom," he said breathless. "I can't breathe," he said. She finally pulled away and cupped Henry's face with her hands.

"My baby boy is officially married," she said. Henry wiped away a tear from her face. "I'm going to go get the photographer to send me the pictures, I'll be right back," she said as she walked away.

Henry watched as Britney lunged herself at Rose and hugged her in a death hug. Britney pulled away and started to talk a million words per minute. Henry saw something move in front of him. He turned his head to see Phil standing in front of him.

"Hi dad..." Henry trailed off.

"Hi son," there was a short pause. "Congratulations, I'm happy for you."

"Thanks dad," Henry said. Phil spread out his arms and awkwardly moved his arms forward and backward, deciding whether or not to hug Henry. He finally decided to hug Henry. He awkwardly hugged Henry as Henry awkwardly hugged Phil. They finally pulled away. There was a short pause.

"May I talk to Rose?"

"Why?" Henry immediately responded.

"I just want to talk to my... daughter in law. Then I'll head out, no trouble. I just want to talk," Phil said. Henry thought about it for a second.

"Rose," he said as he motioned for Rose to come to him. She walked over to them. "My dad wants to talk to you," Henry said. Rose hesitantly nodded. There was a moment of silence.

"Son, I just want to talk to Rose. Just me and her."

If you say anything-

I know, I know. I won't.

Henry walked away and stood next to Britney. She started to talk to him, but soon stopped when she realized Henry wasn't listening. She followed Henry's death glare to see Phil talking to Rose. She quickly stopped talking and she joined Henry in the death glare.

"Congratulations," Phil said.

"Thanks," Rose said. There was a pause.

"I know the last time we met we weren't on the best of terms, but I want to put all of that behind us," Phil said as he awkwardly held out his hand for Rose to shake. She hesitantly shook his hand. "Welcome to the family," Phil said as he walked away and hopped in his car and drove off.

Henry walked over to Rose. "He didn't say anything bad, correct?" Henry asked.

"No, he was polite," she said. Henry nodded his head. Without warning Joey hugged Henry and Lilly hugged Rose. They hugged back. They all pulled away and started to talk.

"Um, excuse me." Lisa asked as she tapped on the photographer's shoulder. He turned around and faced her and lowered his camera away from his face. He had blonde hair that was styled to the right side and a fair face with noticeable cheekbones. He looked to be around Lisa's age, though it was hard to tell.

"Yes?" He asked as he kept his eyes glued to Lisa.

"Uh... can you send me the pictures please?" Lisa asked. A smile appeared on his face.

"Yeah, give me your number and I'll send them," he said as he subtly winked. Lisa's cheeks blushed a deep red as she pulled out her phone and gave it to him. He typed in his number and handed it back to her.

Henry pulled out his phone and glanced at the clock. "Rose we should go grab our bags. We have to leave for the beach soon," Henry said. Rose nodded her head as they both walked inside and started to change.

About thirty minutes later Rose walked out of her room wearing a grey shirt with white short shorts. She had taken off her makeup, but kept the curls. Henry was leaning against the balcony, he was wearing black knee length shorts and a short sleeve burgundy shirt. His suitcase in hand. Rose was carrying a suitcase and duffle bag was swung over one shoulder. Henry grabbed Rose's suitcase as they walked downstairs. They were almost at the door before Joey lunged himself at Henry and Lilly at Rose.

Joey latched on to Henry's leg as Henry continued to walk, dragging Joey behind him. "Please don't leave Big Bro, please," Joey begged as his voice cracked. He had recently turned fourteen and with doing so had begun to hit puberty. Henry and Joey had gotten a brotherly relationship so Joey called Henry Big Bro and Henry called Joey Little Bro. Henry felt it was his chance to be the older brother that Rider never was for him.

Lilly had stopped Rose dead in her tracks, having latched onto both Rose's legs. "Do you have to go?"

"Yes I do, now please let go," Rose begged. Lilly refused to budge so Rose teleported. Rose made it to the car and soon after Henry used his super speed and hopped in the car. He locked the doors as Joey came running after him. Lisa had managed to grab Lilly. The driver started to drive.

"Wait!" Rose said. The driver slammed on the brakes. Rose teleported inside and came back holding all of Henry's hoodies. "Ok, now we can go," Rose said. The driver started to drive again.

Henry looked at all the hoodies. "Are those my hoodies?" Henry asked.

"Yes, I never go anywhere without them," Rose said. Henry simply shrugged as he pulled Rose closer to him. Rose made a pillow out of one of the hoodies and a blanket out of the other.

Rose started to tap her foot as she realized for the first time in her life she was going to the beach.

Chapter 57

By the time they arrived at the airport it was nighttime. Rose sat up.

"Are we here yet?" Rose asked as she looked around.

"No, we have to go on a jet, then we'll be there," Henry said. Rose's eyebrows furrowed in confusion.

"Jet?"

"Yeah, come on," Henry said as the driver opened the door for them. Rose grabbed all the hoodies and got out of the car. The driver was grabbing their bags and placing them onto the jet. Rose stared in awe at the jet. Rose and Henry walked up the stair to the jet. Rose looked around the in awe.

The seats of the jet were white. There were two seats facing each other on the left side of the jet as well as the right, a small table was in between the seats. A couch was stationed in the back of the jet, it went straight and then curved against the wall to the restroom, a table was in front of it and was as long as the couch. A table was on the other side of the jet, across from the end of the couch and the chairs on the other side of the jet, four chairs were stationed at the table. Surprisingly enough there was a fairly wide walkway in between all the seats and couches. There were blinds over every window.

Rose ran and jumped onto the couch. "This is so comfortable," Rose mumbled into the couch. Henry chuckled as he walked over to her. He picked her up and sat down, he placed her next to him. "So how does this thing work?" Rose asked.

"You mean the jet?" Henry asked. Rose nodded her head. "It flies us to the beach," Henry said. Rose's eyes widened at the word fly.

"Fly?" Rose asked. Henry nodded his head. "How is that possible? Things aren't meant to fly," Rose said worried. Henry slightly laughed.

"Don't worry it'll be fine. Jets and planes fly, it's perfectly safe," he said. Rose's face was one of worry and doubt. Henry laughed as he wrapped his arm around her. He kissed the temple of her head. "Don't worry, I'll protect you," Henry said. She physically relaxed at his words.

A flight attendant walked towards them. "Hi, I'm Elizabeth," she said as she excitedly waved at them. Rose and Henry slightly waved back at her. "First off we need to go over what to do if the jet were to crash,"

Crash! I thought you said it won't crash!

She said if we were to crash, Henry said as he gave her hand a little squeeze and caressed her hand. She relaxed at his touch.

"Ok, that completes the procedures. Please buckle up and we'll be out of here in no time," she said as she walked away. Henry and Rose buckled up. Rose tightened the belt as tight as it would go and grasped onto Henry's arm.

Within a few minutes the jet was moving. Rose was looking out the window and watched as the airstrip rolled by them. As the jet neared the end it started to lift off the ground. Rose grasped onto Henry's arm tightly. He lightly laughed as he looked at Rose. Her eyes were tightly shut and her face was buried into his arm.

He wrapped his other arm around her. The jet soon leveled out and they were flying smoothly. Elizabeth came back out. "Ok, you can now unbuckle and roam around the cabin. I'll be back with food and drinks later," she said as she walked off again.

Henry unbuckled his seatbelt and Rose's. Her eyes were still tightly shut and she was still grasping onto his arm tightly. Henry stood up. Rose wrapped her legs around him as he walked to a window. He sat down in the seat next to it.

"Short Stack, open your eyes," Henry said as he pushed hair out of her face. She shook her head, no. "I promise you want to see this," Henry said. Rose slowly opened her eyes and looked out the window. What she saw was amazing.

The sky had a variety of pinks, blues, purples, oranges, and yellows. The sun was setting as half of it was covered in clouds, making the clouds orange and yellow. Henry kissed her on the cheek. He sat down next to her as they both watched the sun set.

They arrived at the airport. Rose and Henry got off the jet as people loaded their luggage into a car. They hopped in the car as the driver started to drive to the beach.

Henry watched as the clock on his phone turned twelve. Henry wrapped his arm around her and kissed her on the lips. She kissed back as she ran her fingers through his hair. He smiled into the kiss before he pulled away.

"What was that for?" Rose asked as she started to play with his freshly cut hair.

"Happy birthday," Henry said. Rose's eyes slightly widened as she realized she was no longer a teenager. She was now an adult.

It was now early morning when the car arrived at the beach house. Henry was playing a game on his phone while Rose watched him play. The driver opened the door for Henry and Rose. They looked up at him.

"Sir, we are here," the driver said. Henry and Rose hopped out of the car as the driver grabbed their bags. Henry opened the door as the driver walked in. "Where do you want these sir?" The driver asked.

"There is fine," Henry said as the driver placed the suitcases onto the ground in the front hall. Henry reached in his pocket and pulled out his wallet. He handed the man what he owed him and his tip. The driver nodded as he hopped back in his car and drove off.

Henry turned around and saw Rose looking out the window that was the length of the wall. The window was tinted so the sun wouldn't affect them. Rose's face was shoved against the window as she looked at the beach. The sand was white and had no debris on it. The water was crystal blue and the waves were white as they curved and rolled across the sand. The sun was rising, half of it was covered up by the water. The sun made the water around it yellow and orange. The sky was pink, orange, and yellow. The sun was a dark shade of yellow and a light shade of orange.

Rose quickly ran up the spiral staircase to the second floor. The second floor was a loft that was as big as half the house. The floors were a light colored wood. Couches and chairs were scattered around the house. They were white while the pillows were a dark blue.

Rose was teleporting in and out of every room. Henry had carried their suitcases into the master bedroom. The bedroom had white walls, the covers were white with a print of blue seashells and the pillows were blue. Henry walked back out into the main room. He looked around, looking for Rose.

Outside he saw a wooden walkway to an octangular gazebo. The gazebo had a half curved couch on one side and two chairs across from it. A fire pit was in the middle of it.

He felt arms and legs wrap around him as Rose jumped on his back.

"It's so pretty here!" Rose said excitedly. She hopped off of his back and grabbed his hand and arm. She started to drag him to the glass sliding doors. "Let's go to the beach."

Henry pulled her into him and wrapped his arm around her. "Hold on. You don't even have a swimsuit," he said. A sad expression came across Rose's face. Henry put his hand under her chin and tilted her head upwards. He kissed her on the lips quickly and pulled away. "I said you don't have one, I never said we couldn't go get some," he said. Her expression changed to a happy one.

"Can we go now?" She asked. Henry nodded his head as he walked to the kitchen. Laying on the kitchen counter was the house key, wifi password, and the car keys. Henry grabbed the car and house keys. He walked to the garage as Rose followed. They hopped in a black old muscle car. Henry revved the engine as the sound of the rustic engine purred through the air.

Henry laughed at the sound of the old engine, his laugh was one of joy and excitement, he was used to the electric sound of the engine. Out of the corner of his eye he saw Rose buckle her seatbelt as she blankly stared in front of her. Henry backed out of the driveway as he headed to the store.

They arrived at store. There were rafts and beach chairs in the outside of the store. In the windows were towels. Rose and Henry got out of the car and took off their sunglasses once they were inside. The store looked like everything was placed at random. Shirts and shorts were on racks across the store. Swimsuits were lining the walls. There were even crabs and other animals on display. Rose looked around the store in awe.

They made their way to the swimsuit area. Henry started to search for swim trunks - wanting new ones - while Rose searched for bikinis. He had an armful of swim trunks as he walked into the changing room. Rose had an armful of bikinis as she walked into another changing room.

They both hopped in the car and started to drive to the beach house.

"Hen?" Rose asked from the bathroom. Henry opened the door and walked in. He was wearing a knee length burgundy swim trunks, there were pockets all over the trunks.

Rose was wearing a dark blue bikini. The top was a triangular top and was a clip on in the back. The straps in the front went up and around the back of her neck. The bottoms were one piece until it reached her side, it split apart in the middle of her side, making it two straps and connected at the back of her side.

"Hen?" Rose asked again. Henry snapped out of his daze and looked her in the eye.

"Yes?" He asked.

"Can you put makeup on my back? It's waterproof so it won't come off," Rose said. Henry took the makeup and makeup brush out of her hand. He put the foundation on his hand. He ran the brush through the makeup, he started to apply it to her back, covering the scars.

He only knew how to do this because when his father wouldn't give him any attention he would hang out with his mom. That meant watching her apply her makeup ninety-five percent of the time. Lisa had also showed him how to do it because she said "girls will want a man who understands what they're talking about. Especially when it comes to makeup."

"Where did you get this?" He asked as he continued to apply it.

"Your mom gave it to me before we left," Rose said. Henry nodded as he put more makeup on his hand.

When he was finally done he wrapped his arms around her waist and laid his chin on her shoulder. "You ready to go to the beach?" Henry asked. Rose's face lit up and nodded her head. They walked out of the screen doors and onto the beach. The sun no longer affected Rose like it used to, because of the fact that she was half human.

Rose looked around in complete awe and wonder. She ran ahead of Henry on the sand.

"This is amazing," Rose said as she ran back to Henry. Henry's face looked around the beach. Without looking at Rose he reached out and grabbed both her arms. He brought her into his chest. "What are you doing?" Rose asked, confused.

"There are guys looking at you.., so many guys.., too many guys," Henry said as his grip tightened around her. "I should have looked at you after you changed into each swimsuit," he paused. "So many guys," he said in a whisper.

Rose looked around. A few guys were staring at her as they walked by. Their eyes trailing up and down her body. Henry grabbed her left hand and held up the finger with the ring on it.

"Yeah, but a lot of girls are staring at you," Rose said. She looked at the girls. They were looking Henry up and down. Some moved their sunglasses lower so they could see him better.

"Guys and girls are different. Guys are stupid and will most likely act out what they are thinking. Girls will rarely act out what they think."

"You don't know what they're thinking."

"I will in about two seconds," Henry said. There was a few seconds of silence before Henry's eyes widened. "Ok we are going into the water where no one will see you," Henry said as he grabbed her hand and walked to the edge of the water.

Henry pointed to a sandbar. "Teleport us there," Henry said. Rose teleported them to the sandbar. The water went up to Henry's chest while Rose was swimming. Rose grasped onto Henry's arm so she wouldn't tire herself out.

"Get your hair wet," Rose said as she ran her fingers through his hair.

"I don't feel like it."

"Please," Rose said. She gave him puppy dog eye and stuck out her bottom lip. Henry looked away from her face. When he looked away Rose's face fell. She teleported in the air, above the water and cannonballed into the water next to Henry. Water splashed all over Henry. When Rose came out of the water she saw Henry's face. His mouth was open as water dripped from his hair into his face and some in the water. His eyes were closed and his hands were above the water, as if he had tried to block the water from hitting his face and hair.

He opened his eyes and looked at Rose. A huge toothy smile was on her face. She swam over to him and started to play with his hair.

"Was that necessary?"

"Yes, it was," Rose said. She swooped all his hair to the right side, she brought some of it into his face. It wasn't as long as she was used to. She started to style it into a side Mohawk.

Henry placed his hands on her hip so she could sit there as Henry held her.

Rose brought his hair up and twirled it in the front, making his hair look somewhat like a unicorn. Henry put his hand up and felt what she had done. He was mortified. He went underwater while still holding Rose. His hair undid what Rose had done as it floated freely. Rose's hair floated freely as well. While underwater they stared into each other's eyes. Rose went cross eyed as Henry stuck out his bottom lip and gave her puppy dog eyes. They both laughed as they surfaced.

"You want to go walk?" Rose asked.

"Anything you want," Henry said. Rose teleported them onto the sand. A slight breeze picked up and Rose slightly shivered. Henry wrapped his arm around her and moved her to where she was closer to the water so guys couldn't see her as easily.

They started to walk.

They made it back to the beach house. They had spent almost the entire day on the beach and the sun was now setting. They walked into the house and shut the door. They walked into the master bedroom. Rose grabbed her suitcase and laid it down on the ground and opened it. She started to unpack.

"You're beautiful in that swimsuit," she heard Henry's voice say. She stood up and faced him, an eyebrow raised.

"I thought you didn't like me in the swimsuit," she said a little confused.

"I like it when only I'm looking at you," Henry said. He wrapped his arms around her waist and leaned his head down.

He kissed her. She wrapped her arms around the back of his neck. She stood on her tiptoes as she deepened the kiss. Henry placed his hands on her waist and pulled her closer to him. Rose jumped up and wrapped her legs around Henry's waist. His grip on her tightened as he held her.

Rose felt her back press against the wall. She ran her fingers through his hair. They continued to kiss as both their grips tightened around each other.

In an instant they were on the bed. Henry was on top of her as each of his hands was on either side of her head. Rose's legs were still wrapped around Henry's waist. Henry continued to kiss her. Henry's hands moved to the back of her swimsuit. She wrapped her arms around his upper back and lifted herself off the bed about an inch. Henry started to un-clip the back, somehow managing to still kiss her. He felt Rose pull away from him.

"Henry?"

Henry stopped kissing her and fiddling with the strap. He looked her in the eyes. His eyes were a different kind of red than what Rose was used to. They were a light red on the outer rim of his eyes, but around his pupil it turned to a darker red. Henry looked at Rose's eyes, they were similar.

"I've never done this before," Rose said. A tiny hint of fear was in her voice. Henry leaned down and quickly placed his lips on hers.

"Neither have I," Henry said when he pulled away. Rose's eyebrows furrowed in confusion. "I was waiting for the perfect one to do it with. You're that perfect one," he said as looked her in the eyes. There was a short pause as they stared in each other's eyes. "Ready?" Henry asked.

Rose ran her fingers through his hair. A smile appeared on her face. Rose nodded her head, the smile still evident.

"Ready."

Chapter 58

Rose laid in bed with Henry. She was wearing his hoodie and spandex. Henry was wearing sweatpants. Rose was curled up in a ball as her face was nudged into his chest. Henry's arm was wrapped around her as it went through her hair. Their swimsuits laid on the floor. One of Rose's hands was in his hair as the other was holding his hand.

Henry saw the light threw his eyelids coming through the small crack in the blue curtains. He opened his eyes and looked around. Rose was hogging the blankets and covers, but Henry was hogging most of the bed. Henry never really liked all the blankets and covers on him, he liked spreading out on the bed. Rose liked snuggling with all the blankets and covers, but she liked to curl into a ball so they fit together.

Henry buried his face into Rose's neck as he closed his eyes and started to rest again.

Rose's eyes fluttered open, she felt Henry's strong arm around her and Henry's face nudged into her neck. She laid there contently until she needed to use the restroom. She started to wiggle out of his grasp but his grip only tightened around her.

Rose teleported out of his grasp and into the restroom. She closed the door as she walked to the toilet.

She washed her hands as she opened the door. Henry's arm was moving around him as he looked for Rose. He opened his eyes and looked around as he stretched. The sun was behind a cloud and made the room look dark, they could barely make each other's faces out.

Rose froze as she saw Henry stretching. Henry looked at her as he did she dropped her head.

"I-I'm sorry I d-didn't mean to wake you," she said as the familiar stutter came back. Henry recognized the stutter as his eyebrows furrowed in confusion.

"What are you talking about?" He asked as his voice came out raspy and tired.

At the sound of his voice she snapped out of her daze

"You look like your brother in the dark."

Henry's sighed as he threw his head back and ran his fingers through his hair. He motioned for Rose to get in bed. She crawled into bed with him. Henry grabbed her and pulled her closer to him. They were now face to face. He kissed her forehead.

"Do you remember what I told you at the restaurant?" Henry asked. He looked her in the eyes. She nodded her head. "I meant what I said and that's a promise," he said. Rose kissed him as she grasped his hands.

After a few seconds Henry groaned and pulled away.

"I'm going to go take a shower," Henry said. Rose nodded as she ran her fingers through his hair. Henry placed his lips onto hers again. He pulled away and stood up. "I'll be back as soon as I can," he said as he walked into the restroom. Rose sat up and teleported to the kitchen.

She looked around and tried to find something to eat or drink. She walked to the coffee maker and looked at it for a second. She saw k-cups stationed on a rack, it was left by the people that owned the house. She grabbed the one that said vanilla. She read what the coffee machine said. *Place cup into machine.*

She examined the cup and placed it into the slot in the machine. She pressed the lid down on the cup. It said to choose what size cup. Choosing a medium size she laid it in the place for the cup. She pressed the medium cup button. She watched as the hot coffee poured into the cup.

She grabbed the cup by the handle and walked to the giant window. She watched the waves roll onto the beach, boats sailing, people swimming, and so forth.

Continuing to take small sips of her coffee she looked at the beach.

She felt strong arms wrap around her waist and Henry's head rest on her shoulder.

"Is that coffee?" Henry asked. Rose nodded her head. He reached over and grabbed the cup from her hand. He took a sip of the coffee. "Ew, that's way too sweet," he said as he went back for another sip. Rose grabbed the cup from his hand.

"If it's too sweet than don't drink it again. Go get your own," she said. Henry held up his hands as he walked to the coffee machine. He started to make his own.

About a minute later he came back with his coffee. Rose noticed the bite mark on his hip that she had made as half of it showed from his low sweatpants that hung off his hips. Rose grabbed his cup and took a sip of it. Her face turned bitter.

"Is that just black coffee?" She asked. Henry nodded his head as he took back the cup. He wrapped his free arm around her. "Want to go to the gazebo and finish our coffee?" Henry asked.

Rose nodded her head as she teleported them to the couch. Henry was sitting long ways in the couch as Rose sat in between his legs and his arm still wrapped around her.

Henry leaned down his face to her shoulder and kissed her cheek. After the quick kiss they continued to drink and talk for awhile.

They both laid their empty cups of coffee on the glass table and looked at the view.

"Want to go to the beach?" Rose asked.

"Yes," Henry said. They both grabbed their cups as Rose teleported into the kitchen. They laid the cups into the dishwasher and she teleported them into the bedroom. Rose grabbed her swimsuit as she walked into the restroom.

She changed into her swimsuit. The top of her swimsuit was burgundy while the bottoms were black. The top was cut triangular, the back of it was a clip on and the top tie was a regular tie. There was no design on the top or the bottoms. She opened the door and saw Henry leaning against the wall.

He was wearing black swim trunks. It had many pockets scattered on it. The swimsuit covered his bite mark. When Henry saw Rose he turned around and started to bang his head on the wall.

"What are you doing?" Rose asked.

"There... will... be... so... many... guys... staring... at... you..," Henry said in between each bang. Rose walked over to him and grabbed his head, stopping him from doing it any more.

"Don't worry about them. If they stare at me too long you can beat them up," Rose said. Henry only nodded his head. "Now, help me put my makeup on," Rose said as she walked into the restroom. Henry repeated what he had done.

They walked out of the house and to the beach. Rose teleported them to the sandbar again. Rose swam around as

Henry just stood there. He laughed at the sight of her trying to touch the floor, but would go under water every time.

She looked at him and gave him the death glare. At the look of her face Henry went under water and came back up, his hair wet. He walked to Rose and she started to play with his hair. He wrapped his arms around her to support her.

Rose parted his hair down the middle and curled the sides of his hair. Henry shook his head and undid what she had done. His hair was now swooped to one side. She started to put his hair into a Mohawk again. Henry took a deep breath as he went underwater again. The Mohawk undid itself. Rose went underwater too and started to play with his hair. She ran her fingers through his hair and moved it out of his face only for it to float back.

Henry ran his fingers through her hair and held it out of her face so he could see her. Henry, with his free hand, pointed beside Rose. She looked over and saw a fish. The fish was blue at first glance but as it moved back and forth green, yellows, and purples showed up.

Henry and Rose resurfaced as they were both breathing heavily. Henry took his hand and pulled his hair back. Rose did the same.

"That fish was so adorable-" she was cut off as she screamed and jumped on Henry. Her legs wrapped around his chest and her arms around his head. "It just touched me!" Rose said. Henry laughed at her freak out of a small fish touching her.

"It could be worse. It could've been a shark," Henry said as a small smirk lit up his face. In a second he no longer felt Rose on him. He looked around and saw Rose on the land.

You would've left me if it was a shark?!

Depends.

One what?

Whether or not it bit you. Like if I saw it and it wasn't close to us I would take you too, but if it had bit you...

Henry's face was shocked.

I also saw you smirk so I was messing with you too.

Henry's face didn't change until he saw two guys walking towards Rose. Henry could tell by the way there shoulders were brought back and how they were walking a little bit like a chicken that they were flexing. Henry started to swim back to shore as quickly as he could.

Rose watched as Henry swam at her, she was a little confused until she heard a voice: "hey sweet cheeks," a deep voice said. She turned around and saw two guys staring at her. The one that had spoken had blonde surfer's hair and was muscular, but not as muscular as Henry. The one standing next to him had light dirty blonde hair that was wet from being in the ocean.

"What's a pretty girl like you doing at the beach all by yourself?" The other man asked.

"I'm not by myself. I'm with my husband."

"Where is this 'husband' of yours?" The surfer asked as he motioned his hands in bunny ears at the word husband.

Rose was about to open her mouth, but she stopped as she felt a strong arm wrap around her waist, Henry's arm.

"I'm here." Henry said. At the sight of him the two men slightly backed up. "What were you fine gentlemen talking to my lovely wife about?"

"Uh... we were just telling her she's lucky to have a husband like you," the man said.

"I'm sure you were... but now that you've told my wife something she already knows you can leave."

Both the men nodded as they speed walked away. Henry's eyes followed them until they were completely behind him.

"That is why you shouldn't be by yourself because a lot of guys find you attractive," Henry said as he started to walk. His arm was still around her waist. She slightly leaned against him as they walked.

"A lot of girls find you attractive."

"Yeah but have you seen any of them come up to me?"

"No."

"My point exactly." His grip tightened around Rose as they continued to walk. The sun started to set to the side of them. Rose leaned her head onto Henry's arm and he slightly leaned his head on hers.

"Hen?" Rose asked.

"Yes, Short Stack?"

"I forgive you for calling me heavy that one time." Henry's eyes slightly widened. He had forgotten that he had done that. He was shocked that Rose remembered that.

"Thank you for forgiving me." Rose nodded as they continued to walk.

By the time they arrived back at the house the sun had set. The sky was a dark blue.

They walked into the bedroom. Henry grabbed his phone and checked his notifications. He saw he had a missed FaceTime call from his mom. He recalled her and waited for her to pick up.

When she picked up he saw she was in the living room.

"Hey honey!" She said excitedly.

"Hey mommy," he said. Rose walked up to Henry and got in the camera. She squealed as she saw Lisa. She waved as Lisa waved back. In the background they saw Lilly jump up and down and started to dance behind Lisa. "Why'd you call?"

"I can't call to say hey to my baby boy?" Lisa rose an eyebrow.

"No, no, you can totally do that. I was just wondering."

"How's your honeymoon?" Lisa moved her eyebrows up and down. Henry's cheeks blushed a bright red.

"It's good." Henry squinted his eyes to the couch. He saw Joey working on another puzzle and there was a man sitting next to him. "Is that a man?"

Lisa looked behind her to the man. "Oh yeah, that's Jake."

Henry's eye twitched. "Can I talk to him..?" His eye twitched again. "Please?" His eye twitched again.

"Sure. Jake can you come here please?"

Jake got up from the couch and walked to the camera. Lisa gave him the camera. Rose stood away from Henry. She could tell that Henry needed space. Henry readjusted the camera to show off his muscles better. Henry recognized the man as the photographer.

"Aren't you the photographer?"

"Yes..." the man trailed off. His voice slightly quivered in fear.

"Why are you," Henry paused. "In my house?"

Lisa grabbed the phone from Jake. "Henry, Jake and I are... dating."

Chapter 59

"You're dating? It's only been a couple of days." Henry's muscles tightened.

"Well we're not dating, dating. We both have interest in each other, but we're not dating. We're just interested in each other," Lisa said. Henry's mouth slightly fell open by about an inch and his eye twitched again.

"Can I please speak to Jake?" Henry asked as he gave her a toothy smile. Because he was so tense it came off weird.

Lisa nodded as she called for Jake again. Jake grabbed the phone from Lisa.

"Listen to me and listen to me carefully," Henry said. Jake nodded his head. "When I come home I don't want to see a single hair out of place on my mom, Lilly, or Joey. That shouldn't be a problem though because I don't believe you're that stupid to touch my mom and when I hired you it was because you don't have a problem with humans. So no one should have a hair out of place."

Jake nodded his head.

"Now repeat back to me what I want to see when I return home."

"You don't want to see a single hair out of place. I promise that won't happen," Jake said as he tried to make his voice strong, but he failed.

"Good." Lisa grabbed the phone from Jake again.

"Ok, bye honey, love you." She blew him a kiss as she hung up. Henry didn't move as his phone went to black. Henry's arm was still in the air. Rose stood up from the bed and walked to Henry.

She jumped up and grabbed the phone from his hand and laid it on the nightstand. She walked back to Henry and snapped her fingers in front of his face. He didn't move.

"I'm going to go watch TV." Henry still didn't move. "It's going to be RARVABIHY." Henry still didn't move. Rose raised an eyebrow. "I'm going to look at William," she said as she started to walk out of the room. She felt Henry's arm wrap around her and the next thing she knew they were on the bed. Henry was hovering above Rose. Henry leaned down and placed his forehead onto hers.

"Please don't. There are already so many men staring at you," Henry said as he intertwined both his hand into hers.

"I won't, I was just trying to get you to move," she said as she smiled. Henry sighed out of relief as he dropped on Rose. His body completely encased hers. Rose tried to wiggle and push Henry off of her, but he was too heavy. She was having trouble breathing.

She teleported to the side of them. As soon as she did Henry's arm wrapped around her and pulled her into him. Henry turned on his side and pulled her closer to him. His grip tightened around Rose.

"At least let me change," Rose said into his chest. After a few seconds his grip finally loosened around her. She stood up and grabbed his hoodie. She pulled it over her swimsuit and then took off her top from the inside of the hoodie and she changed into shorts. She turned around and saw Henry sitting in bed wearing sweatpants.

Rose walked to Henry. Henry grabbed her waist and turned her around. He made her sit in his lap as he wrapped his arm around her. He laid his head on her shoulder.

"Seriously though. Do you want to watch TV?" Henry asked.

"Yes," Rose said. Henry stood up with his arms still around her. Her feet were dangling in the air. Henry threw her up in the air. As he did so she turned around facing him, he caught her. She slightly screamed as she grasped onto his shirt. Henry took his free hand and wrapped her legs around him. He wrapped one around her waist and the other grabbed her leg.

"Stop throwing me," Rose said. Henry looked up as if he were thinking.

"Nah," Henry said as he started to walk.

"I'm being serious."

"So am I. I'm not going to stop throwing you."

"Why?"

"Because your face is adorable when you're scared."

"That's the only reason you throw me?"

"Yes. Thank you for understanding." Henry said. Rose rolled her eyes.

Henry made it to the second floor on the loft. He walked to the railing and grabbed the TV that was hanging, by an arm, on the ceiling. He brought it down until the metal arm was fully extended.

Henry walked to the couch. He unwrapped Rose's legs from around him and sat down. He positioned Rose sideways on his lap. She started to play with his hair as Henry went to Netflix.

Henry switched it to RARVABIHY. They both turned their attention to the TV as Rose continued to play and mess up his hair.

"If you hurt him I will kill you!" Rose said to the TV. She stood up and pointed to it. Henry grabbed her and sat her back down on his lap.

The wife's killer and boyfriend grabbed onto Williams shirt and lifted William's beat up body into the air. William weekly grabbed at his face and neck, but he was too beat up for it to do any good. Blood was streaming out of his nose and mouth, one of his eyes was swollen shut. The killer pointed the gun to William's chest. As he did so the screen cut to black and the words 'to be continued' popped up on the screen.

"What?!" Rose screamed. Henry's eyes widened in shock as well. He couldn't believe that they would do this to them. "They can't do that!" Rose continued to scream. She ran at the TV, but Henry quickly grabbed her. He carried her downstairs as she kicked and screamed.

Henry sat down on the bed. Rose wrapped her arms around Henry as he brought her closer to him. "I know it's sad but we'll get our answers when the next season comes out."

"I know but... did you see what he did to his face?" Rose said.

Henry blinked several times. "I thought you were over him," Henry said as he switched their positions to where he was hovering over Rose. "I mean you kind of have a husband," Henry said as he motioned to himself.

Rose smiled as he leaned down and started to kiss Rose. He grabbed her waist as he continued to kiss her. Rose wrapped her arms around Henry's neck. They both smiled into the kiss as Henry's grip on her waist tightened. It was going to be another sleepless night.

Rose opened her eyes and looked around. She was snuggling with a pillow. She sat up and looked around for Henry. The bathroom door was open so he wasn't in there. She looked at the pillow and saw a note attached to it.

I know that the latest episode upset you, (aka William's face getting hurt) so I thought that you should come to the kitchen.

P.S. I know that this is late, but better late than never.

Rose stood up from the bed and walked to the kitchen. Henry was sitting on the counter and next to him was a cake. It was only one layer, but it was cut in the shape of a heart. The cake was a dark blue and a white frosted rose was in the middle of it.

Rose walked up to Henry. He handed her another note.

P.P.S you've told me that I'm hotter than William and you can't go back on your word. ;)

Rose laughed as she hugged Henry. Henry hugged her back. Henry kissed the temple of her head as he pulled away and started to cut the cake.

They had both eaten about two to three pieces of cake. They had been reading in bed for about thirty minutes, waiting for the food to settle.

"You want to go to the beach?" Rose asked as she finished the chapter. Henry didn't respond. Rose scooted closer to Henry and ran her fingers through his hair. She gave him puppy dog eyes and stuck out her bottom lip. She could tell that Henry was starting to consider it. He looked at her, she read his face. Rose sighed as she went cross eyed.

"Let's go," Henry said as he stood up and started to find his swimsuit. Rose grabbed hers and walked into the restroom. The top of her swimsuit was a dark blue. The swimsuit was outlined in black as well as the straps. The bottoms were black with silver chains hanging from the side of it and the sides were split.

She walked out and saw Henry. His swimsuit was burgundy. He looked at her. She could tell what he was thinking. She grabbed his face and brought it down, closer to her face.

"Remember you can punch them," Rose said. Henry kissed her forehead.

"This is why I love you," Henry said. They both walked into the restroom as Henry started to apply her makeup again.

They walked out to the beach and Rose teleported them to the sandbar. Rose jumped on Henry.

"It's freezing!" Rose said.

"Back to the land. Back to the land!" Henry said. Rose teleported them back to it. They both shivered and slightly ran in circles to warm themselves up. They started to speed walk down the beach to continue to warm themselves.

They made it back to the place in front of the house. Rose wrapped her arms around Henry.

"Can you please get chairs and my book so I can read out here?" Rose asked as she went cross eyed again. Henry laughed as Rose also stuck out her bottom lip.

"Of course. I'll be right back." Henry started to walk away, but stopped. "Oh if any man comes to you, tell me." Henry said as he turned back around.

A few minutes had passed and Rose looked around and saw the two guys from yesterday looking at her.

Henry?

Yes?

Those two guys are looking at me.

She heard the sound of metal on metal. She turned around and saw Henry standing there and two chairs were laying on the ground. Henry handed Rose the two books. He smashed his balled up fist into his open hand. The two men quickly turned around and speed walked away. Henry watched them leave. Once they were out of sight Henry started to set up the chairs.

They sat down and started to read.

Henry was sidetracked by hearing two girls talking too loudly. He glanced up at them. One of them waved at him, flirting. She had bleach blonde hair that was in loose curls. The other girl had light brown hair that was in natural waves. Their swimsuits were small and skimpy. Henry turned his attention back to his book. He was sidetracked again as one of the girls dropped her sunglasses in front of Henry. She bent down in front of him. Henry leaned back in his chair as he moved his face away.

The girl stood back up and turned around to face Henry. She was, however, met with Rose. Her arms were crossed over her chest and an eyebrow was raised.

"Sorry, but he's taken." Rose held up her ring finger.

She's adorable when she's mad, Henry thought.

The two girls giggled, trying to make it less awkward, and they walked away as they swayed their hips too much. Henry grabbed Rose's waist and sat her down on his lap.

Rose looked back at him as a smile appeared on her face.

"What were you saying again about how girls don't flirt?" Rose asked, the smile still evident.

"I said they rarely flirt."

"Sure," Rose said as she rolled her eyes.

"No, that's what I said. I swear."

"Sure."

Rose reached over to grab her book. Henry grabbed it and threw it backwards. "What was that for?" Rose asked. She started to stand up to grab it but Henry pulled her back down.

"That was for not believing me."

"You're unbelievable."

"I don't think I am."

"Key word there is think."

Henry laughed. Rose's face remained serious.

"Oh come on. We're on our honeymoon. Let's not 'fight'." Rose's face didn't change. Henry moved his face in front of her and gave her the puppy dog eyes and stuck out his bottom lip. A few seconds went by before Rose's face broke out into a smile. "There she is." Rose ran her fingers through his hair.

"Can I ask you something?" Rose asked.

"Of course."

"How do you know Britney?"

"She's my ex. Our parents, aka my mom, set us up together. We liked each other, but not to the existent my mom was hoping, we only liked each other as friends. So we broke up and decided to remain friends."

"I'm glad that you met her, I like her." Henry let out a breath he didn't know he was holding in. He didn't know what to expect, they were married.

"What was it like having you're powers at first?"

"It was... scary. I could hear everyone's thoughts in my head. My mom helped to teach me how to control it though. Her power is similar, she told me when she first got her power she could tell when everyone was lying or telling the truth so she had to block out the rest and focus on what she wanted. I had to do the same." Rose nodded.

There was a pause.

"Is that all your questions?" Henry asked.

Rose looked up and placed a finger on her lip, thinking.

She's adorable. A smile appeared on his face. *And she's all mine.*

"For now," Rose said as she lowered her finger. She placed her hands on Henry's. Henry nodded his head as he laid his chin on her shoulder. She leaned her head onto his.

In front of them they could see the setting sun. The sky was lit up in pinks and purples. Rose leaned her head against his chest and Henry laid his head on hers.

"I never want this vacation to end."

"Neither do I." Henry kissed her cheek as his grip around her tightened.

Chapter 60

"I don't want to go!" Rose said as Henry carried her out of the beach house. She was limply dangling over his shoulder. They had stayed at the beach house for about a month and Rose had grown attached to it. The driver was carrying the bags and loading them into the trunk.

Henry was somewhat glad to be leaving. He got tired of all the men staring at Rose, especially those two men that seemed to look at her every day. He was also tired of all the girls that would flirt with him, the only reason he liked it was because Rose was adorable when she was mad. He was also excited to go home to meet Jake. His muscles tightened at the thought.

Henry carefully placed Rose in the car. He sat down next to her, her face was pressed against the car window. The driver started to drive away. Rose pushed her face against the glass even more.

Henry was silently laughing to himself as he looked at Rose's smooshed face. Rose removed her face from the window and looked at Henry. He gave her puppy dog eyes and stuck out his bottom lip, trying to cheer her up. Rose smiled at his face as she leaned her head against him. Henry laughed.

"I can't believe that you are still scared of fish."

"Hey that fish bit me."

"Fish don't bite."

"Well that one did." Henry laughed again.

"Don't worry, we'll be home before you know it and away from the fish."

The car pulled up to the house. They got out and grabbed their bags. Rose teleported Henry into the house. They looked around, taking the house in again. That was short lived as Lilly tackled Rose to the ground. Henry laughed at Rose before he was tackled by Joey.

Joey hugged Henry as tight as he could and Lilly hugged Rose as tight as she could. When Joey was done hugging Henry they both sat up. Joey hugged Henry again.

"Thank you for coming back." Joey said. Henry could hear the voice of a man that had been 'abused' by girls.

"What did they do to you?" Henry asked. His voice was low.

"I fell asleep one night and I woke up to find they had given me a makeover." Henry shook his head, he couldn't believe they had done that to Joey. "Lipstick, eyeshadow, eyeliner, foundation, they even painted my nails." Henry hugged him tighter as he told him he was ok. Joey finally pulled away, his face was strong again. "I'm fine, it's ok," he said, trying to regain some of his dignity.

Jake walked out of the kitchen with Lisa. Henry stood up and walked to Jake. He stopped dead in his tracks as he saw the size of Henry. Lisa looked at Henry and sighed, she walked over and started to hug Rose.

Henry extended his hand to Jake. He hesitantly extended his hand to Henry. Henry gave a strong handshake as he looked at Jake, he was about an inch smaller than Henry and not as muscular.

"I'm Henry, Lisa's son."

"I'm... I'm Jake, Lisa's boyfriend," Jake said, confirming Henry's suspicion that they had started to date in the month he was gone. "I kept my promise and didn't touch Lisa, Joey, or Lilly," Jake said, nervous. Henry nodded his head.

"I'll be the judge of that," Henry said. He turned to see Rose talking to Lisa. "Mom, can you please come here?" Henry asked. Lisa said one last thing to Rose before she walked over to Henry. She hugged Henry and he hugged back.

When they pulled away Henry started to inspect Lisa. "What are you doing?" Lisa asked.

"Just... checking something out," Henry said as he moved her head side to side. He was done with his examination. He turned his attention back to Jake who was stiff as a bored. Henry extended his hand to him again. He shook it. "You did well," Henry said. Jake let out a breath that he had been holding in as he relaxed more.

"I'm going to go to the store, I'll be right back," Lisa said as she grabbed her car keys and walked to the garage. Henry grabbed his bags as did Rose as they walked to his room. They both decided that they would share Henry's room.

They walked in and Rose looked around as she realized that she had never been in here before.

The walls were painted a light grey that were almost the color of dull silver grey. A window was against the wall and with it was a window seat that had black and grey pillows on it. The dresser, nightstand, cabinet, and closet door were all black. The closet door was open and hanging in the door frame was a pull-up bar. Henry's bed was stationed next to the restroom, the bed frame was black and the covers were also a fog grey and there were black pillows. His room was bigger than Rose's room. Rose dropped her bag as she looked around in awe.

She sat down on the bed, she was however so small that she had to jump to get on the bed. She sunk into the soft bed as her legs dangled in the air. Henry laid his bags on the ground as his phone rang. It was his mom.

"Hello?"

"I totally forgot that I had put a casserole and lasagna in the oven. Can you please go check on them and then ask Jake what else to do," Lisa said.

"Ok, I will, bye mommy," Henry said. The thought of helping Jake was less of a problem for him now.

"Bye Henny bear," Lisa said as she hung up. Henry pulled the phone away from his face and sighed at his mother's new nickname for him. He looked back at Rose who was swinging her feet on the bed.

"I'm going to go make dinner so I'll be right back. Why don't you bring your stuff from your room here?" Henry asked. Rose nodded as she outstretched her arms. Henry walked to her and picked her up. She wrapped her legs around his waist. "Is the bed too high?" Rose nodded her head. "I'm not going to change it because you're so cute when you have to jump up on something."

"But it's too tall."

"Don't care, you're adorable." Rose smacked his head. "Ow," Henry said as he laid Rose down on her bed. "I'll be back," Henry said as he walked away. Rose started to rummage through her things as she grabbed what she needed.

Jake was helping Joey with yet another puzzle as Lilly sat in the chair reading. Henry tapped Jake on the shoulder who quickly turned around. "My mom said you would tell me what to do with dinner."

"Yeah, let's go." Jake stood up and walked to the kitchen with Henry behind him. Jake grabbed things and started to prepare. Henry checked on the casserole and lasagna.

"So how long have you been coming to my house?" Henry asked.

"Every day because Lisa needed help with Joey and Lilly, so I would come over to help."

"What's your power?"

"Telekinesis." Jake moved the salt that was next to Henry into his hand, he started to season what he was cooking. "You?"

"To be able to read people's thoughts, look at memories, and use telepathy," Henry said.

"That's a mouth full."

"Yeah, try learning how to block out people's thoughts and only focus on what you want when you're a kid."

"I feel you, when I was trying to learn how to control my powers every object I looked at would fly across the room. I broke so many vases," Jake said as he laughed.

"You think that's bad, I learned about the birds and the bees that way," Henry said as he slightly laughed. Jake smiled at the fact that Henry was starting to warm up to him. It was also a huge relief that he knew Henry wouldn't kill him.

Lisa walked in and upstairs to Rose's room. She handed Rose a bag and Lisa walked downstairs to the kitchen. She saw Jake and Henry cooking while talking and laughing. She sighed in relief that Henry hadn't killed Jake.

"I see you two are getting along," Lisa said as she hugged Henry. He hugged back and kissed her head.

"He's not too bad," Henry said as he looked at Jake. Jake smiled. Lisa walked up to Jake, he wrapped his arms around Lisa. Henry picked up Lisa and pulled her out of Jake's grasp, he set her down behind him. "Don't push it."

Jake nodded his head. "Sorry, my bad," Jake said as he went back to cooking. Lisa rolled her eyes at Henry's protectiveness of her. She checked the lasagna as Henry started to help Jake.

Dinner was ready.

Hen?

Yes?

Can you please come to your room really fast?

Yeah, I'll be right up. Henry started to walk upstairs and into his room. Rose was sitting on his bed crying. Henry rushed over to her. He cupped her face with his hands and wiped away her tears.

"What's wrong?" Henry asked concerned.

Rose shook her head, no. "Nothing is wrong."

"Then why are you crying?"

"I'm pregnant."

Chapter 61

"You're pregnant? Are you sure?" Henry asked. He was only asking because he couldn't believe that he was going to be a father.

"I took the test three times," Rose said. She glanced into the restroom where a box of pregnancy tests laid on the counter. Lisa had gotten the test when she went shopping.

Since they were vampires everything developed faster so the test only took about ten minutes to show up.

Henry's face lit up as his smile reached ear to ear. He hugged Rose as he picked her up and spun her around. Rose hugged back as she buried her face in the crook of his neck. She closed her eyes and breathed in his scent, she couldn't believe she was pregnant, especially since she used to be a pet.

Henry finally stopped spinning her around as she placed her feet on the ground. Henry reached down and placed his hand on her stomach. His hand was so big it covered her stomach. His other hand cupped Rose's face. He looked from her stomach to her eyes.

"I'm going to be a father," Henry said in almost a whisper. He could barely believe it. Rose nodded her head as she placed one of her hands on Henry's hand that was cupping her face and the other that was on her stomach.

"You're going to be a father," Rose said, reassuring him. Henry leaned down and kissed her, she kissed back.

They finally pulled away from each other.

"Can we go downstairs, I smell dinner?" Rose asked. She was starving. Henry nodded his head. "Can we tell them?" Rose asked.

"That's your choice," Henry said. Rose nodded her head as she teleported into the kitchen. They teleported in front of Jake. He slightly jumped back when he saw them.

"Jake, this is my lovely wife, Rose," Henry said. Jake extended his hand to her and she shook it.

"Nice to meet you," Jake said.

"Nice to meet you too," Rose said. Jake nodded as he walked to the table. Lisa had insisted that Jake stay for dinner because he helped make it and so Henry and Rose would get to know him better.

Rose and Henry both grabbed plates and started to place food onto it.

Rose placed her fork on the plate. She took in a deep breath of what she was about to say.

"Uh..." she trailed off. Everyone looked at her. "I have something to tell you..." she trailed off again. Henry placed his hand onto hers to calm her down a little bit. "I'm pregnant," she finally said.

Joey's hand stopped in mid air with his drink in hand as his eyes went wide. Lilly choked on her food as she quickly grabbed her water and started to drink it. Lisa's fork fell out of her hand and clattered onto her plate, the sound echoed throughout the house. She had known that Rose might be pregnant because she had had to go to the store to buy the test, but she still couldn't believe it. Jake just sat there as his eyes grew wide.

A few seconds passed before Rose felt arms around her. It was Lisa. "My daughter in law is pregnant!" She said excited. "I'm going to have grandchildren!" She said. She stopped hugging Rose and started to hug Henry.

She wrapped her arms around his neck as she squeezed, happy. "Mom," Henry said in an airy voice. "Mom, I can't breathe, please... let go," he said as he tapped on her arm, almost like he was tapping out. She finally pulled away as her eyes started to water.

Lilly and Joey were both hugging Rose in a death grip. Jake shook Henry and Rose's hands.

When everyone was done hugging. They all sat back down. "Now, Rose there are some things you need to know," Lisa said. Rose nodded her head. "The pregnancy will be faster than a humans. Vampires are only pregnant for about five, six, at most seven months. Your child, since you were turned, will be a vampire," Lisa said. Rose nodded her head.

Henry and Rose walked into his room. Lisa, Lilly, and Joey were already asleep, and Jake had left after dinner. Rose pulled the hoodie over her and climbed into bed. Henry pulled his sweatpants on and took off his shirt. He climbed into bed with Rose. He wrapped his arm around her, his hand resting on her stomach. Rose curled closer to him as she thought about her pregnancy. She knew that those five, six, or seven months were going to be the fastest months ever.

~six months later~

Rose teleported Henry and her into the kitchen. She was wearing one of Henry's hoodies and a pair of pajama shorts. Henry had bought extra-large hoodies so Rose could be more comfortable. He wanted Rose to be as comfortable as possible. Especially since Henry found out that Rose was having twins.

"What do you want for breakfast, Short Stack?" Henry asked. Rose placed her finger on her mouth and looked up, thinking. Henry smiled, he loved it when Rose would do her cute thinking pose.

"I want chocolate chip pancakes and blood ice cream," Rose finally answered. Because Rose was pregnant she had to drink more blood than normal, her favorite form of it was in ice cream.

"Blood ice cream? You had that for dinner and dessert last night," Henry said. Rose raised an eyebrow and stared at him. He quickly opened the freezer and grabbed the ice cream. He grabbed two spoons and laid them in the ice cream and he slid the container across the counter to Rose. Henry liked to eat the ice cream with Rose, neither of them liked putting it in a bowl so they just ate it out of the container.

Rose grabbed the spoon and placed it into the ice cream. She was about to eat it when she felt something wet run down her leg. She looked down and realized her water had broken. She felt a sharp pain in her stomach.

"Hen!" Rose said in pain. She dropped to the ground on her hands and knees, she was breathing heavily. She was in labor. He quickly rushed to her as she cried out in pain again. Henry cupped her face with his hands.

"I know it hurts but you have to teleport us to the hospital, ok?" He asked. She nodded her head as another wave of pain washed over her, she felt beads of sweat run down her face. She thought about the hospital.

She teleported them to the hospital, Henry had managed to stand her up. She was so weak that she couldn't support her weight. She fell into Henry as he picked her up and carried her to the front desk as quickly as possible. She grasped his shirt with both her hands as another wave of pain came over her

"My wife is going into labor!" He said quickly. The nurse quickly called over more doctors and Henry placed Rose into a wheelchair. The doctors started to wheel her to the labor and ICU. Henry was running beside her as he called his mom.

"Hey mom, Rose is giving birth so I need you to run over to the house and get Lilly and Joey," Henry said as he hung up. He didn't have time to speak to Lisa right now.

Lisa had gotten her own house not long after Rose and Henry came back from their honeymoon. Jake was still dating her and they had plans to talk about getting married in a few more months.

Once they wheeled Rose into the room everything seemed to happen so fast. The nurses and doctors put on their masks, gloves, hats, and a surgical gown. They changed Rose into a hospital gown and changed Henry into what the doctors and nurses were wearing.

"Ok, I need you to breathe," the doctor said to Rose. Rose started to take deep breaths as she grasped onto Henry's hand. "Push on three. One, two, three," the doctor said. Rose pushed as she screamed in pain and squeezed Henry's hand tighter.

Henry's eyes widened at what he saw. He felt light headed. He turned around and placed his face into Rose's pillow. Rose screamed again. She was grasping Henry's hand so tight she was surprised she didn't break it. All Henry could do was gently caress her hand.

"Ok, that's one," the doctor said. He handed one of the nurses one of the babies. "Push one more time," he said. Rose screamed as she pushed again. "And... that's two." The doctor handed the nurse the other baby.

The nurses had wrapped the babies up in blankets. Rose's pressure on Henry's hand lessened as the pain did. She leaned back in her bed as she felt sweat run down her face, she was still breathing heavily.

The nurses walked to Rose and handed her one baby. Rose grabbed the baby and looked at it. It was a boy, he had dull red eyes and one strand of brown hair. He started to cry.

"Kaden," Rose said in a small voice. Henry and Rose had come up with the names a long time ago once they knew she was having twins and that one was a boy and one was a girl. Henry had raised his head from the pillow and was staring lovingly at Kaden. He reached his hand over and placed his finger near Kaden. Kaden grasped his finger. Henry smiled in disbelief that he was a father.

The nurse handed Rose the other baby. Rose placed her in her other arm.

"Violet," Rose said in a small voice again. Violet's eyes were closed and she had more hair than Kaden, it was brown as well. They had wanted to continue to call their children after flowers so they could almost honor Rose's parents. They chose the violet because it was Henry's favorite flower. Rose was shocked to learn that Henry, the big muscular, tough man's, favorite flower was a purple violet.

Violet stopped crying as she felt Rose's arm around her and she grasped onto Henry's other finger. Both the nurses reached down and grabbed Kaden and Violet.

"We're sorry, but we have to make sure they're healthy," the nurse said as they grabbed them. Rose reluctantly loosened her grip around them and Henry reluctantly pulled his hands away from them. Kaden and Violet started to cry again as they were pulled away from them. The nurses walked out of room. The doctors didn't need to make sure Rose was ok because she would just heal. The doctor inserted an IV into Rose that was a bag of blood. The doctor gave Henry a blood bag too, the doctor had watched Henry almost faint and knew he needed it.

Henry took off his mask, gloves, hat, and surgical gown. He threw it into the hamper as he climbed into bed with Rose. Rose yawned, giving birth had exhausted her.

"You can go to sleep, if they come back I'll wake you," Henry said. Rose looked at him.

"Promise?" Rose asked, she didn't want to miss her children.

"I promise I'll stay awake the entire night if I have to," Henry said as he cupped her face. She moved her face into his hand more and closed her eyes, almost immediately she started to rest. Henry kissed her on the forehead as he moved closer to her. He sunk his fangs into the blood bag and started to drink it.

About thirty minutes had passed when the door opened again. Henry looked up to see who it was. It was Lisa, Jake, Joey, and Lilly. Lilly and Joey had on their collars and leashes. Lisa saw Rose resting.

Sorry I brought Jake, we were out together when you called.

It's fine. Henry said. He had started to consider Jake as almost a father figure to him. Lisa and Jake sat down in the chairs while Joey and Lilly sat on the ground in case the doctors came back into the room.

Henry had lost track of time, but he was starting to get restless. He wanted his kids back with him. He wanted to see Rose holding their kids. He wanted to feel their small hands wrapped around his finger. Everyday Henry would place his hand on her stomach so he could feel them moving, he wanted to feel them moving again. He just wanted his kids.

Lisa was working on one of her scrapbooks. She had decided to make a scrapbook before they were married, when they were married, when Rose was pregnant, and after Rose gave birth. Henry had told her that was overboard and she didn't believe him.

The door opened and in walked two nurses, each carrying one child and each rolling a crib with them. They placed the cribs next to Rose's side of the bed. Henry cupped Rose's face with his hand as he gently caressed it. She slowly opened her eyes and looked at Henry. Henry pointed to the nurses. Rose turned her head and her face immediately lit up. She reached out her arms as the nurses placed a child in each arm.

"They're healthy, you can leave the hospital in about three days or less," the nurse said. Rose and Henry nodded as they walked out of the room. Both Violet and Kaden were sound asleep. They naturally snuggled closer to Rose and wrapped their hands around Henry's finger. Henry heard Lisa blow her nose behind him. Not soon after he felt Lisa's arms around him. Lisa was overjoyed that she was finally a grandparent.

Lilly and Joey were on Rose's side of the bed, both staring at Kaden and Violet in amazement. Jake hesitantly wrapped his arm around Lisa, the last time he had done so Henry had gotten mad at him. Henry grabbed Violet from Rose and held her in his arms.

A smile appeared on his face as he looked at her.

He couldn't wait until the three days were over and he could go home with his new family. He looked at Rose who was smiling at Kaden. He could tell she was thinking the same thing.

Chapter 62

Henry and Rose were awoken as they heard crying. They had been home for a few weeks, in that time they had been awoken every few hours by Kaden and Violet.

"Go," Rose said into Henry's chest.

"I don't want to," Henry mumbled.

"Just go."

"But what if they're hungry?"

"Then you can bring them in here."

"But what if-" Henry was cut off as Rose kicked him out of bed. He fell on the floor and laid there a few seconds, the warmth of the bed left him as a cold breeze hit him hard. The crying was still echoing through the house.

"Go," Rose said, this time more sternly. Henry groaned as he reluctantly stood up and walked into Rose's old room. They had made Rose's old room the nursery. Half the room was painted a baby blue while the other half was a baby pink. On the pink side of the room was Violet's crib with an outline of black birds flying from the crib and into the corner of the wall, getting smaller and smaller with each bird. On the blue side was Kaden's crib with a black tree with an owl on the branch.

Henry walked to Violet's crib, he looked down into the crib to see Violet crying. Her blankets were scattered around the crib, her eyes were closed as she cried, it was a nightmare. Henry reached down and picked her up, holding her in one arm.

"Sshh, sshh, it's ok, daddy's here," Henry said in a soothing voice. He slightly rocked her back and forth as he held her closer to him. "I know they're scary, I get them too."

He heard Kaden start to slightly cry. Violet's crying had started to wake him up. Henry walked over to Kaden's crib. Henry reached down his hand and Kaden grabbed his finger and curled closer to it. Henry smiled as he looked at Kaden and Violet.

Kaden stopped crying as he fell back to sleep, his grip didn't loosen around Henry's finger. Henry slowly pulled his finger out of Kaden's grip, scared to wake him. Once he pulled his finger away he carefully leaned down and kissed Kaden's head.

He readjusted the blanket on Kaden and walked to Violet's crib. She had fallen back to sleep, snuggled into Henry's arm and chest. He gently laid her down in her crib. He grabbed the blankets and wrapped them around her, she snuggled closer to the blankets as she curled into a little ball. Henry smiled as it reminded him of Rose and how she slept. He leaned down and placed a kiss on her forehead.

He walked back to his room to see Rose curled up on his side of the bed, her arms were around his pillow and the covers and blanket were wrapped around her. He walked to his side of the bed and picked Rose up. He moved her back to her side as he wrapped his arm around Rose.

She snuggled closer to Henry and buried her face in his chest.

"What was it this time?" Rose mumbled into his chest.

"Just a nightmare," Henry mumbled. They both tried to rest before they would be awoken in a few hours.

"I'll swave you!" Kaden yelled. Henry and Rose's eyes opened as they heard his voice yell. They both sat up in bed, even though it had been a few years they both felt like they were recovering from being awoken every few hours.

Henry and Rose looked at each other, they read each other's faces. Rose teleported them into the kitchen. Rose sat on the counter as Henry did the same, they loved watching their kids play.

Violet and Lilly were on the top of the stairs. Violet was wearing a pink, sparkly princess dress with a pink and silver tiara, fake earrings, and a princess wand. Lilly was beside Violet, the dresses were too small for her so she just had a pink tiara.

Kaden and Joey were at the bottom of the stairs. Kaden had on plastic knight armor with a sword, shield, and helmet. Joey just had a plastic sword.

Once Joey and Lilly had turned eighteen they decided that they wanted to be changed so they would stay with Henry, Rose, Violet, and Kaden. They didn't want to leave their family.

Lisa and Jake were married and living happily together. They would occasionally visit to check up on Lisa's grandchildren and Henry. Phil would occasionally drop by to see Kaden and Violet as he slowly mended his relationship with Henry and Lisa.

"Befror you save us you must slay the monstre," Violet said in a dramatic tone. Lilly pretended to faint at the mention of the monster. Kaden got down on one knee and placed his sword across his chest, the plastic making noise with every movement. Joey mimicked him.

"Where would we find the monster, so we may rescue the fair maidens?" Joey asked as he looked up. Lilly sat up 'coming out of unconsciousness.'

"There!" Violet said dramatically as she pointed to Henry and Rose. Both their eyes widened and the smiles that were once on their faces disappeared. Lilly and Joey both smirked, containing their laughter.

Kaden directed his attention back to Violet and Lilly.

"We will slay the monstres to rescre the maidens," Kaden said as he stood up with Joey. They both clinked their swords together as they smiled.

"I bid thee farewell, when you return I shall give you a token of my gratitude," Lilly said to Joey as she blew him a kiss. Joey was now determined. Kaden and Joey started to walk to Rose and Henry who were discussing their game plan.

"Ok, so you teleport me there, which will get us away from there," Henry said as he pointed from one place to the other. Rose noticed Kaden and Joey stalking towards them.

"Every man for himself!" Rose said as Kaden and Joey ran at them. Rose teleported away from Henry as Joey swung his sword at him. Henry rolled off the counter and landed in the floor, Joey swung again. Henry rolled out of the way as stood up and ran.

Rose stood next to the couch, watching as Joey tried to kill Henry. Something flew by her and she felt something hit her back. She turned around to see Kaden, his sword in her back.

Rose fell on the ground 'dead.' Kaden started to stalk towards Joey and Henry. Henry was somehow still avoiding Joey's attacks on him.

Rose, help!

Can't, I'm dead.

How did you die? Your power is teleportation!

I was attacked by a five year old with super speed, it's next to impossible!

Henry was interrupted as he saw a flash move behind him, he turned around to see Kaden. Before Kaden could swing

Joey stabbed him. Henry fell on the floor, 'dead.' Joey and Kaden stood over Henry.

"I saw him move!" Joey said even though Henry hadn't. Both Joey and Kaden started to rain down blows on Henry.

"Ow!" Henry said as he tried to block the swords.

"It speaks!" Kaden said as they continued to hammer down their sword on Henry. Kaden raised his sword and brought it down on Henry's chest. Despite Joey still hitting him Henry stopped moving and played dead.

Both Joey and Kaden breathed out a sigh a relief. Joey wiped away a fake bead of sweat from his forehead. They both walked back to Violet and Lilly. They walked up the stairs as both Joey and Kaden took a knee.

"We've slayed the monstre," Kaden said. Lilly walked to Joey.

"I give thee a token of my gratitude," Lilly said as she placed her lips onto his. Joey smiled into the kiss, they pulled away. Violet was too busy talking to Kaden to notice.

There was a moment of silence.

"I'm bored," Kaden said as he threw down his sword and took off all his armor. He was wearing a green dinosaur shirt with blue pajama pants. His hair was styled similar to Henry's, but on a smaller scale, he also looked more like Henry.

"Same," Violet said as she took off her dress and threw her tiara and wand on the floor. She was wearing a pink shirt and pink pajama pants. Her hair was above her shoulders and she looked like Rose. Lilly took off her tiara, she was grateful because the tiara was squeezing her head. Joey threw down his sword as they all walked downstairs.

Rose and Henry stood up from the floor. Kaden ran at Henry and latched himself on his leg.

"I'm hungry," Kaden stated as Henry continued to walk. Henry swung his leg more so Kaden would get more of a ride.

"What do you want?" Henry asked.

"Mac and cheese!" Kaden said excitedly.

"You've had that four times in a row," Henry said.

"But I want it," Kaden whined.

"Ok, you can have mac and cheese," Henry said. He stopped walking as Violet stood in front of him. She reached up her arms. Henry smiled as it looked like Rose when she was too lazy to teleport on or out of his tall bed, or when she just wanted to be carried.

Henry leaned down and picked her up, he balanced Violet on his hip as he walked.

"What do you want?" Henry asked Violet. She placed her finger on her lip and looked up. Henry smiled again as she did Rose's thinking face.

"Mac and cheese!" She said excited.

"Mac and cheese you shall have," Henry said. He felt Rose hop on his back. Henry made it to the kitchen and lifted his leg onto the stool so Kaden could get off, he also pivoted his body so Violet could sit on the counter. Once Violet was off he felt Rose's legs wrap around him. He grabbed a pot and started to boil water.

The end credits rolled across the as the movie ended. Rose looked around. Lilly was sitting in the chair with Joey on the floor, Lilly's hands were running through his hair as he leaned against the chair, resting. Henry was sitting sideways on the couch, his back against the arm of the couch. Rose was sitting in between his legs, her back leaning against his chest. Henry's arms were wrapped around her and his head was nudged into her neck. Kaden was sitting in between Rose's legs as his head rested on her stomach, resting. Violet was sitting in between Kaden's legs, she was curled into a small ball, resting. One of Lisa's scrapbooks was resting on her as it was open. When Lisa had finished the scrapbooks she gave them to Rose and Henry and their kids loved to look at them.

Let's put the kids to bed, Rose said.

Ok. Afterwards you want to go outside? Henry asked.

Yes, Rose said as she grabbed Violet and Henry grabbed Kaden. They put the kids to bed and walked outside. They laid down in the grass, and stared into the sky. They looked at the star filled sky as Henry held Rose close to him and Rose snuggled into him.

"Why did you choose me, out of every pet why me?" Rose asked breaking the silence. She had had this question since he started to be nice to her, but always forgot to ask him.

"I felt like I was almost... drawn to the Pet Shop. I had no intention to get a new pet, but it had been itching at my mind for a while so I decided to go. When I saw you I felt drawn to you. I didn't see the bruises or the scars that you had, I saw beautifulness. You were perfect in every way and I couldn't imagine myself leaving the Pet Shop without you... Does that answer your question?" Henry asked.

Rose placed her lips onto his as she wrapped her arms around him. Henry was in shock for a second before he kissed back. They finally pulled away.

"What was that for?" Henry asked.

"For giving me a perfect life," Rose said as she smiled. Henry smiled as he laid back down, and Rose laid on top of him. Henry wrapped his arms around her and he stared into the sky. Rose grabbed his hands and stared into the sky as well.

Everything is perfect.

The end.

Can't get enough of Rose and Henry? Make sure you sign up for the author's blog to find out more about them!

Get these two bonus chapters and more freebies when you sign up at molly-stegall.awesomeauthors.org!

Here is a sample from another story you may enjoy:

Chapter I

Worst Birthday Ever

"Happy birthday!!!" They chorus as soon as I step into the kitchen.

Mom is beaming, carrying a stack of pancakes dripping with maple syrup to the breakfast table. A single candle is burning right on top of it. Dad is already sitting at the table, smiling wide.

"Hyaaaahhhh!!!" I hear my sister yell as she bounded down the stairs behind me.

I blow the candle out before she even reaches the bottom of the stairs.

"Genesis! Damn it!!!" she yells in frustration.

"Autumn Harmony Fairchild! Language!" Mom admonishes her.

I flash my sister a victorious grin before I turn back around and give Mom and Dad an angelic, innocent smile.

My sister Autumn is two years younger than I am. Last week was her birthday, and I blew out the candle on her special birthday pancakes. I knew she would try to get back at me. Unfortunately for her, I came downstairs early today, and just like that, I've foiled her evil plan of revenge.

Mom disappears into the living room and I give my sister another mischievous grin. She takes her seat beside me at the breakfast table, scowling at me.

Not only are our birthdays close together, Autumn and I look almost the same, from our light hazel eyes to our red hair. Sometimes people think we are twins. The only difference is that Autumn's face is a little bit rounder than mine and my red hair is a darker red, closer to auburn, while Autumn's is more of a strawberry blond. I'm also a bit taller. I'm 5'11" which is just a little over the average height of most she-wolves, and Autumn is 5'9".

"Happy Birthday, by the way," says Autumn "Are you excited yet?"

"Excited about going to school on my birthday?" I ask back, sharing my stack of pancakes with her. Mom gave me too much.

"No, silly! About possibly meeting your mate today!" she replies, looking at me as if I've lost my marbles.

"I don't know...I'd be more excited if I don't have to be stuck in school the whole day on my birthday." I am, but I'm not going to admit that to her.

Yeah, we're the regular werewolf family, and as werewolves, we get the gift of sensing out our mate as soon as we turn eighteen. That means for me, sometime during lunchtime today, if my mate is already eighteen and he's living somewhere around here.

"I had to go to school on my birthday too," she reminds me. "I can't wait to turn 18 so I can meet my mate already." She sighs. "Oh, I bet he's so hot. Hotter than your mate. The hottest guy in the whole pack."

"My baby girl might be meeting her mate today!" mom exclaims as she comes back from the living room where she hid my birthday gift. She places my gift on the table and says, "You're excited, right?"

I'm going to be asked this question over and over again today, it seems.

"No, she's not. She's not going to let any boys near her until she's at least 40," announces dad.

I resist the urge to roll my eyes at both of them as I rip open the wrapper. I already knew what's inside: a new airbrush paint set and mediums. I'd been giving obvious hints about wanting it for months.

"Thanks, Mom, Dad! I can't wait to try it out." I give them both a hug.

Actually, I am very excited about meeting my mate. I can feel my wolf, Ezra, being restless and excited the whole night.

My Ezra is excited, which makes me even more excited. That's why I'm all dressed up today. Well okay, so I'm dressed the same way I always dressed for school every day, in jeans and a t-shirt. Nothing special, but yeah, I am very excited about possibly meeting my mate today. Not that I would ever admit that to my parents. Goddess, no! That would be so embarrassing.

Autumn and I walk to school. It's just a 15-minute walk. The weather is mild and I always enjoy the short walk.

When we get to school, Autumn heads off to where her friends are waiting, while I stroll inside to where my friends usually hang out.

Penny, Reese, and River are hanging out by our lockers as usual. Reese and River are mates. Penny hasn't turned 18, so she hasn't found her mate yet.

"Happy birthday, girl!" yells Penny as soon as she spots me, drawing the attention of most other students loitering the hallway.

She pulls me into a hug and soon after, Reese and River do the same.

"You're going to have to wait until after school for your gift," says Reese excitedly.

"You're going to be 18! Finally. Are you excited?" asks Penny.

"I don't know. I think I'm a bit nervous," I admit.

"Yeah, I'd probably be nervous too, meeting our mates for the first time...but it's exciting too!" shrieks Penny, clapping her hands excitedly.

"Don't be nervous, Genesis. It'll be okay," soothes Reese.

"It's better than okay. It's the best thing that's ever happened to me," says River, wrapping his arms around Reese.

"Awww...isn't he sweet?" coos Reese with that look in her eyes as she stares up at River. "Anyway, we'll see you losers at lunch!" she says as River pulls her away.

"Later, bish!" says Penny. I just give them a little wave before I start digging my locker for my books.

"Boy, I wish we can mate with one of those hotties," she suddenly whispers as she stares dreamily over my shoulder.

I turn around to the sight of three male lycans walking down the hallway. They are so tall, about 6'5 or taller.

You see, lycans are different than us regular werewolves. For one thing, they are known to be the direct descendants of the moon goddess, so they are treated like nobility in the werewolf world. In fact, our king is a lycan.

Second, they are bigger, faster, fiercer, smarter, stronger, and more powerful than any werewolf, even alphas. They are like killing machines when provoked. You don't want to mess with them.

Third, in their human form, they are better looking and more attractive than us regular werewolves who are considered to be better looking than most humans...like way more. So, lycans are godlike smoking hot.

Fourth, they don't have to belong to a pack. They can travel anywhere alone and not be considered rogues.

And fifth, they don't have mates chosen for them by the moon goddess like us regular werewolves. They get to choose their own mates, either another lycans, regular werewolves, or even humans they're attracted to. They would form a bond, much like a werewolf's mate bond, or even stronger if they're both attracted to each other, to begin with. Once, I heard a story about a lycan who took an already mated she-wolf, leaving her mate broken since there was nothing anybody could do about it.

There are only three male and two female lycans in our school of over six hundred students. Only 10 percent out of those six hundred students are humans. All the teachers and the administration of this school are werewolves too.

The three lycans heading this way right now are Lazarus, Caspian, and Constantine. The female lycans, who are not around right now, are Serena and Milan. I haven't seen those two around for a few days now. They are, of course, drop-dead gorgeous.

I think Serena is mated to Lazarus, and Milan may or may not be mated to Caspian. There are rumors that those three boys are closely related to our ruling king, but we don't know for sure. There's not much else that we know about the lycans in our school. Not even their last names. They keep to themselves and pay no attention to us mere werewolves and humans. That makes them so mysterious and much more attractive to the female population here.

So yeah, those three godlike Adonis are drop-dead gorgeous. Jaw dropping. Panty melting. And I so would be making a fool of myself if I don't stop drooling over them—like Penny—and all the other un-mated she-wolves around us right now.

I quickly turn back and start pulling books I need from my locker. There's no way a lycan would be interested in an

Omega like me. Lycans are attracted to strength, intelligence, and beauty. Besides, I might be meeting my mate today. Flutters of excitement start in my tummy at the thought. My wolf Ezra is getting excited. We've been waiting for this for years.

I grab Penny's hand and drag her along to get to our class before the bell rings. We share English lit together.

"I can't wait to get out of this place soon. Thank goodness we only have a few months of school left." I inform Penny.

"Oh, I don't know...I don't mind school. There are lots of hot guys around like those lycans," she says. "Or like those boys...too bad they're such jerks and man-whores," whispers Penny in my ear as we pass the popular group in our school.

Logan Carrington, our future alpha is kissing or rather shoving his tongue down the throat of Mia Brown, the head cheerleader. They're together, but everybody knows they're seeing other people on the side. Zeke Walker, future delta has his arms around Elle Johnson and Marie Jacobs, while talking to Hunter Stevens, the future beta. I think Hunter isn't so bad. He doesn't seem like a player like the other two. He talked to me once or twice before and seemed pretty nice.

"I wonder if he's digging for hidden treasure down her esophagus," I whisper back and Penny starts laughing.

Hunter turns to look at us, then his eyes shift to me, looking amused. I think his lips twitch a bit like he's trying not to laugh. Cuddly bunny and fuzzy slippers! He must have heard me.

I practically push Penny into our English lit class, while trying to hide my flaming face.

Yes, I do think those boys are pretty hot. There's no way in hell I would admit it to anyone, though.

Logan and Zeke have this class with me and Penny. They enter the class ten minutes after the lecture started. Not that the teacher would say anything.

Logan slides into a seat in front of me and my wolf stirs. I stare at the back of his golden head for a bit. Logan is about 6'2", well-muscled; high cheekbones and sharp features like a model; bright blue eyes and golden blond hair. When he smiles, wow. His straight white teeth and those adorable dimples are simply to die for. Well, maybe I have a bit of a crush on him. Just a little bit. I think a lot of the girls here do.

The rest of the classes went pretty well—boring and uneventful. Art is the only subject I look forward to. Did I mention that my mom is an artist? Well, she is, and I'm very proud of her. Lavinia Fairchild is quite well known. Every werewolf household here has at least one or two of her prints or originals. My dream is to go to an art school and be as good as her.

We are sitting at our regular table during lunchtime when I suddenly smell that wonderful smell I can't describe. Whatever it is, it smells awesome! Ezra, my wolf is fighting to be let out and take control. I guess I was born during lunch time. I stand up and start following the smell. I can't help it. I have to find it. I vaguely hear my friends calling my name, but I can't seem to focus on anything else but that smell.

My nose brings me to the popular group's table. Oh no, I can't seem to bring my feet to stop. Ezra's taking control. Everybody stops talking. *Logan Carrington? My mate is Logan Carrington? No, no, no, no.*

His beautiful blue eyes widen as he looks up at me. His eyes soften as they roam my face. I can see lust and hunger flitting across his face briefly as his eyes move up and down my body. But then he looks away quickly. His breathing turns ragged. My wolf howls with joy and my first instinct is to jump on him and stake my claim.

"Follow me," he says gruffly, and swiftly walks out the cafeteria through the back door.

I follow him across the lawn to an oak tree. The tree provides a bit of privacy from prying eyes.

"What's your name?" he finally asks. His beautiful eyes are not even looking at me. I can't seem to tear my eyes away from his perfect face. The sun is glinting in his golden hair. The shadows fall across the planes of his sharp features.

"Genesis...Genesis Fairchild," I finally answer.

"Fairchild? You're an Omega, aren't you?" he says. "I can't have an Omega as my mate. My pack needs a stronger luna, not someone weak like you. Besides, I love someone else. Mia makes a better Luna than you ever will." Each word is like a knife slicing through my chest. Ezra whimpers.

Oh no, suddenly I know what's going to happen. My heart starts to race, my breath comes out short and shallow. I don't know what's happening to me. All I know is that my heart is breaking.

"I, Logan Carrington, future alpha of Shadow Geirolf pack, reject you, Genesis Fairchild, as my mate and future luna of my pack," he utters coldly, not looking at me once.

My wolf cries and howls in pain. She doesn't understand. Why is our mate hurting us so?

"Hey baby, what's going on?" says Mia, wrapping her arms around him. *Where did she come from?*

"Nothing to worry about, sweetheart," he answers.

She looks me over with disdain. She pointedly pulls Logan's head down and plants her lips on his for a claiming kiss. He wraps his arm around her waist, and then they turn and leave. I watch her whisper something in his ear and they both laugh.

I watch them laugh as I fall to the ground, clutching at my chest. Oh, goddess, it feels like he just plunged a knife deep into my chest and twisted it. Then he just keeps yanking the knife up and down, left and right over and over again until there's nothing left of my heart but a bloody, twisted ugly gash in my chest. Ezra curls up in pain then goes silent.

* * *

I'm lying on my bed now. Everything was a blur after I fell. I remember seeing my friends Penny, Reese, and River running to me, calling my name in panic. They were asking me what was wrong. River carried me to his car. I don't remember anything else. The three of them must've brought me home.

"Talk to me, honey. Tell me what happened," says mom gently, pushing my hair from my forehead.

"He rejected me, mom. My mate rejected me." My eyes start tearing up again. I still find it hard to believe that this is really happening to me. I wish this was just a horrible nightmare.

A thousand different emotions chase across mom's face: disbelief, anger, pain, sadness....

All the pain comes back. I start twisting in my bed and mom wraps her arms around me. Even mom's comforting loving arms can't stop or ease the pain away.

"It hurts so bad. Make it stop...make it stop. Mom, please make it go away." I sob, clawing at my chest. "I'd do anything...just make it stop." *Goddess, it hurts so much. I want to die.*

"My baby. My poor baby girl," cries Mom. Tears run down her face as she hugs me close, willing my pain to go away.

After what feels like hours, I calm down, or maybe I'm just too exhausted to even shed a tear. Only my chest is moving up and down. Sleep doesn't come easily. In the middle of the night, all alone in the darkness, tears leak out again, falling down my face silently. My wolf, Ezra, is completely silent now, but I can feel her crushing pain, as well as my own.

I had been looking forward to meeting my mate since I was four. Mom told me about it like it's the best thing to ever happen to a werewolf. I had been waiting for someone who would love me and protect me and be by my side no matter what.

All werewolves look forward to meeting their mates. It's very rare that a mate gets rejected, but it happened to me. What is wrong with me?

All werewolves know you only got one chance at having a mate. What now? Will I ever be loved and have a family? Will my wolf, Ezra, ever come out and be the same again? A werewolf without his or her wolf is only an empty shell. Most would eventually die or go crazy after they lost their mates. Their wolves decide to disappear when the pain gets unbearable. Now I understand how very painful it is, and we're not even mated yet. Will I die or go crazy too? I hope Ezra is strong enough to stay.

How could the moon goddess do this to me? What did I do to deserve this? I didn't ask for an alpha. She could've matched me to another lowly omega and I'd still be happy. As long as I am loved, I'll be happy.

How did this day turn out so bad? Worst. Birthday. Ever.

If you enjoyed this sample then look for
Catching Genesis
On Amazon!

Other books you might enjoy:

Fangs vs Claws
Rua Hasan
Available on Amazon!

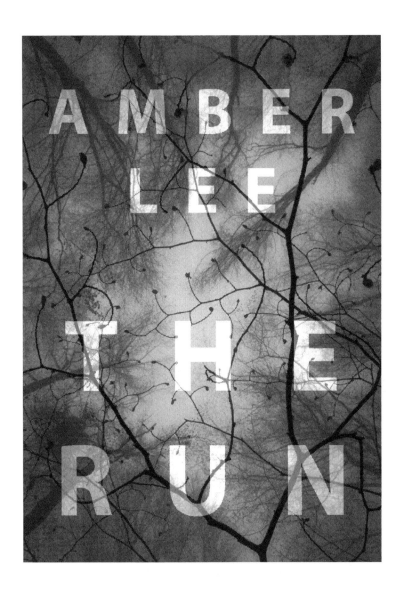

The Run
Amber Lee
Available on Amazon!

Introducing the Characters Magazine App

Download the app to get the free issues of interviews from famous fiction characters and find your next favorite book!

iTunes: bit.ly/CharactersApple
Google Play: bit.ly/CharactersAndroid

Acknowledgements

I would, first of all, like to thank all my fans. Without them, none of this would have been possible. They are honestly the reason why I have been blessed with so many opportunities. Secondly, I would like to thank my editor, Winnie Rose. She made my book come to life, as well as making it look amazing. Lastly, and certainly not least, I would like to thank God. He gifted me with this talent to be able to write, and without Him, this dream of mine wouldn't be a reality.

Author's Note

Hey there!

Thank you so much for reading The Vampire's Pet! I can't express how grateful I am for reading something that was once just a thought inside my head.

I'd love to hear from you! Please feel free to email me at molly_stegall@awesomeauthors.org and sign up at molly-stegall.awesomeauthors.org for freebies!

One last thing: I'd love to hear your thoughts on the book. Please leave a review on Amazon or Goodreads because I just love reading your comments and getting to know YOU!

Whether that review is good or bad, I'd still love to hear it!

Can't wait to hear from you!

Molly Stegall

About the Author

Molly Stegall, most famous on Wattpad for her book: The Vampire's Pet, resides in Chattanooga, Tennessee. Molly found her voice and power in writing, where she was able to create the books that all her fans love. When she's not writing you can find her playing soccer for her school, acting, drawing, and spending time with her friends. Molly hopes that in the future her books will be turned into movies.

Made in the USA
San Bernardino, CA
23 April 2018